The Gambler's Apprentice

West Word Fiction

The Gambler's Apprentice

H. LEE BARNES

UNIVERSITY OF NEVADA PRESS   RENO | LAS VEGAS

West Word Fiction

University of Nevada Press, Reno, Nevada 89557 USA
www.unpress.nevada.edu
Copyright © 2016 by H. Lee Barnes
Manufactured in the United States of America

LIBRARY OF CONGRESS CATALOGING-IN-PUBLICATION DATA
Barnes, H. Lee, 1944-
The gambler's apprentice / H. Lee Barnes.
pages ; cm
ISBN 978-0-87417-998-9 (hardcover : acid-free paper)
ISBN 978-1-943859-05-4 (ebook)
1. Fathers and sons—Fiction. 2. Cardsharping—Fiction. I. Title.
PS3552.A673854G36 2016
813'.54—dc23
2015033800

∞ The paper used in this book meets the requirements of
ANSI/NISO Z39.48-1992 (R2002) Permanence of Paper.
Binding materials were selected for strength and durability.

FIRST PRINTING

This book is dedicated to Stephen Jones
who knew the history of one famous maverick gambler
and shared the stories with me.

The Gambler's Apprentice

Part I

||||||||||||||||||||||||||||||||||||||||||||||||||||||||

Dead Men Don't Pay Debts

Texas, June 1917

Men leaned on fence rails, watched the sky, and sniffed the air. For the better part of six years, clouds, heavy and black, had floated in from the south, bringing hope, but season after season they vanished on the horizon. Cattle grew thin; crops wilted. Farmers plowed stubble into the ground and prayed that the next season's crops might flourish. They recalled times when water coursed along feeder streams, cotton boles produced long fibers, and steers fatted themselves on rangeland lit emerald in sunlight. Some lost homes to banks, others farms and ranches that two generations of their fathers had worked. Adding to their burden, Wilson's war had stolen away their sons. Some saw the hand of God in matters, others the hand of the Devil. Even the most Christian among them eventually turned their rage to the heavens, cursing nature and God himself.

1 It was another spring without bloom. Dust hung over the horizon where rolling hills met the midmorning sky. His eyes shaded under his hat, Clay Bobbins gazed at the distant Balcones, where an amber haze lay still as a stalking cat. He shook his head and turned his attention to the door to Old Lopez's hovel. In a field nearby, the Mexican's donkey brayed and struggled fitfully against a rope that bound its neck to a pole. Finally, as if in despair, it scraped the ground with its hooves, lifted its honker skyward, and released an unearthly sound that sent Lopez's hens to the top rail of the fence.

Clay took a pinch of snuff from a canister, pressed it between his lip and gum, then glanced in the direction of the burro and spat. He cut an eye toward Beau, who squatted a few feet away, shaving the end of a twig with a jackknife, his face fixed in concentration.

Clay spat again. "He don't come out soon, I'm fixin to go!" His words boomed across the ground.

Willy and Beau exchanged looks. Arguing was the one thing Willy's pa seemed to enjoy more than complaining, but if confronted with silence and left to rant, he often spent his anger. Willy gripped the handle to the well pump, cranked the handle up and down, and watched water spill out of the spigot into the trough.

"He entertainin royalty in there?"

"Can't say what he's doin!"

"Weren't a real question, Willy. And don't shout at me. I ain't deef, just don't hear good, not since them bastards near killed me."

Willy cranked the handle harder. He'd heard Clay's account of the battle of Las Guasiman so often he could mouth each word verbatim as his pa recounted how a mortar blast lifted him from the ground and landed him some fifteen feet away. After a few swigs from a bottle, Clay offered up the tale of the war with Spain to anyone with an ear—his traveling over seas so rough men vomited up their intestines. One heaved himself overboard. The versions varied depending on Clay's audience. Some took him into jungle brush so dense a man could barely see his hand. In others he waded into a cane brake as the field burst into flame or lay on a slope, his ear bleeding as he crawled toward his rifle. Two decades later Clay clung to his hatred for all who spoke the Spanish tongue.

The brindle mongrel guarding Old Lopez's door locked eyes with Clay. It rose from its haunches and showed his teeth. Like his master, the dog's capacities had diminished, and the guttural warning that came from his throat was the ghost of a growl.

"Damn thing's half blind. Was mine, I'd put it out of its misery," Clay said. He turned his attention to Beau. "What you gonna do with that stick?"

Beau shrugged and held up the twig, one end now sharpened to a point.

"Crazy," Clay said. "Ain't enough you got a club foot. You had to be crazy too."

Willy squinted at the horizon, where a dust devil pitched manically across the sunbaked ground. He imagined escaping the clutch of his family and leaving Bedloe. He'd never seen a city, but had been seduced by stories told over a cracker barrel—the streets of San Antonio teeming with people, baskets of fruit and baked bread sold by women wearing checkered aprons, a carnival of sorts. He longed to see the rest of Texas and places beyond. He'd tried joining the army, but the recruiter in Corcoran City had laughed when Willy told him that he was eighteen. The sergeant said, "You ain't a day over fifteen and probably ignorant to boot," and had sent Willy packing with a warning not to waste the government's time.

Dream as he may, Willy was bound to an iron yoke. His ma needed him. His sisters. Beau. Even his pa. He tied the bandanna around his neck, freed Lucy's reins from the hitching post, and walked her to the trough, where he stroked her withers. The filly brought him a sense of selfhood. His pa couldn't ride her. She'd bucked Beau off more than once. Willy's sisters wouldn't go near her.

"When you finish with that wild thing, water up mine," Clay said. "I'd ask Beau, but he's plenty busy doin nothin. Not a thought in that head."

Willy looked at his pa and thought, deaf in one ear, blind to hearing in the other. "He ain't hurtin nothin, Pa."

Beau rarely spoke, and when he did, words backed up in his mouth. He just kept scratching at the ground with the pointed end of the twig.

"Did I say he was? Just talkin, boy. Like to see him put as much concentration into shovelin horse shit outta the stalls. And what the hell was he thinkin goin and makin friends with 'at old fool in there. 'At's part of why I'm wastin time here."

Beau, his expression flat, looked up and stared at Clay.

Clay spat a blot of snuff on the ground, stuffed his hands in his trouser pockets, and walked over to Beau. He studied the sketch. "Ears is too long. Looks like a damn mule. Willy, is 'at Lopez ever gonna come out?"

"He didn't expect no company."

"Well, he's got some. Beau, stop whatever it be you're doing and tell the old fool I ain't of a mind to wait much longer."

Beau snapped his eyes at Clay and dropped the twig, then stood and erased the drawing with the toe of his boot. "Huh, huh, he's cah, comin."

"Boy, do as I . . ."

The cowhide door to the mud warren cracked open. An arm emerged. Then Old Lopez stepped into the sunlight and saluted them, two fingers to his brow. "*Un momento más, por favor.*" Leaving the door ajar, he stepped back inside the shadowed interior.

Clay shook his head. "He ain't out soon, we're goin. Don't matter none what your ma says. Confounds me how a woman can believe in a Christian God and at the same time put stock in some old Mexican's witchcraft. You could of told her we was goin to Corcoran City. She wouldn't of knowed no different. No, you had to up and say we was goin to Mexico. You hear me, Willy?"

Willy removed his hat, wiped sweat from his forehead on his sleeve, and stared at the thinly leafed branches swaying in the treetops. He kept a safe distance in case Clay decided to strike him and straightened his back. "Didn't say nothin to her about Mexico. Was you said it."

Clay glanced at the door. "Ain't like every idea she ever had was a good one. Havin you was one."

"Maybe she's worried 'cause of Ernesto."

"I told you not to mention that name."

They stared at each other for a time, neither of them inclined to look away.

Old Lopez appeared at the threshold, in his hand a leather pouch that he held up for them to see. He turned sideways, squeezed through the narrow opening, and stepped into the sunlight. The dog stood and wagged its tail. The old man spoke softly to the animal. It grunted, then eased its belly on the ground, where it lay flat, its head propped on its paws. The *viejo* took a deep breath as if to inhale the day in a single gasp, and then he gathered his aging frame and began to walk.

"*Hace calor. Vámanos por la sombra,*" he said and lumbered past them, scratching at the tufts of wiry gray hair that hung down the back of his neck like a cobweb.

"*Aquí.*" He motioned for them to join him in the sparse shade under the chestnut tree.

Clay stood his ground and gazed disdainfully at the old man. "Damn woman should stick to lightin candles for saints. 'At's superstition enough for any damned soul."

"He aims for us to follow," Willy said.

"I know what he aims for us to do." Clay stepped in the direction of the tree. "Let's be done with this nonsense."

They walked to where Old Lopez waited, Willy in the lead, Beau, dragging his left foot, behind Clay. The Mexican smiled, bent forward at the knees, and held himself in a position that required he balance himself by shifting his weight knee to knee. The others gathered about, kneeling on the ground as the *viejo* placed the pouch to his ear. In a raspy voice he went about the esoteric particulars of his art, humming and uttering incantations, alternately alliterative and dissonant.

Clay nudged Willy. "What the hell's the crazy old coot sayin?"

"He understands English, Pa." Willy said.

"Then he ought to talk it," Clay said. "'Sides, what we're doin here don't make no sense in any goddamn language, boy. What's he sayin, Beau?"

"Ah, ah, askin a ca, crow to speak," Beau said. "Said *cuervo*. 'At mu, means ca, ca, crow. *Llamame*."

Willy gazed at Beau in near astonishment. He found no rationale for Beau's odd gift except that it was a miracle. When speaking Spanish, the language Beau had acquired working in the cotton fields, words often came from his lips without his faltering.

Old Lopez went on with the ritual, and when finished with his musings, he shook the bag twice and handed it to Clay, motioning for to him to shake it.

"Plain crazy," Clay said accepting the pouch. Then as told, he rattled the contents several times and waited.

Old Lopez shut his eyes. When he opened them, he said in English that no future was guaranteed, that today's wisdom can be voided by tomorrow's foolishness. Then, addressing Clay, he said, "*Tiras las piedras*."

Clay merely stared at the old man.

Beau pointed to the pouch. "He sa, says for you to ta, ta—"

"Never mind. I know what the hell he wants."

Clay loosened the leather string at the throat of the pouch and dumped the contents on the ground. Three amethysts, two turquoise, a bloodstone, and a flint arrowhead lay spread out. Old Lopez moved about in a crouch, studying the lay of the stones at angles. After squinting at the pattern and mumbling under his breath, he looked at Clay and shook his head.

"What the hell you shakin your head at?"

The *viejo* aimed a finger at the flint arrowhead pointing southward and rattled off a string of Spanish words. In the midst of Beau's struggle to translate the words, a huge raven swooped down from a high branch. It squawked shrilly as it passed over their heads. Old Lopez went to his knees and raised his hands as if the future were revealed in the lacquered calluses.

"*No se va a Mexico,*" he said softly.

Clay didn't ask for interpretation. The old man's expression conveyed all that need be expressed. Clay reached into his trouser pocket and retrieved a half-dollar. He held the silver coin up for the old man to see, then tossed it on the ground near the stones.

Clay looked at Willy. "Lopez here said everything is just fine and 'at's what you'll tell your ma. Let's go."

His voice now calm as a priest delivering mass, Old Lopez stood and spoke. "*Las piedras dicen que solo El Viento manda a Mexico.*"

Clay, already heading toward the horses, turned and faced the *viejo*. "Now what's the old fool saying?"

The boys stood between the two men, who were staring at one another, their expressions filling the gap that language couldn't.

"Well? What'd he say?"

Beau said with no hint of a stammer, "Says the wind alone rules Mexico."

The *viejo* gathered up the stones. Without looking back, Clay took the reins in hand and mounted his gelding. Beside him Willy took hold of the pommel, placed his boot in the stirrup, and swung atop the filly. The old man rose and walked to his shack. He stood in the shaded threshold, the dog at his side, tail wagging, jowls drooling. He held the coin in a fist and gripped the cowhide door with his free hand. "*Señor necesita usted una bendición,*" he said.

"What'd that fool say now?" Clay asked.

Beau shrugged, as he was given to when not interested in replying. Willy reached down with his free hand and took hold of Beau, who swung up behind him. As they rode by, the tethered burro still struggled to free itself of the rope that bound him, but neither the rope nor the stake gave any measure to his struggle. The donkey released a high-pitched cry that seemed eerily human and forsaken. Willy leaned forward in the saddle and prepared himself to lie to his ma.

2 Far to the south clouds sheeting the distant peaks drifted slowly northward. Willy sat outside a livery on a ten-pound bag of feed and gazed at the blue dome of a sky. He looked to the south and wondered if rain would fall, or if the clouds would pass on. The horses, tied to a nearby hitching rail, drank from the trough. Since sunrise Willy had divided his

attention between the road to Villa Acuña and his doubts about what had happened to Ernesto.

Why, he wondered, would a good man abandon a wife and daughters? He'd spent a year building them a home.

Willy had been witness to events when Ernesto's wife, Clarita, came to see Clay, demanding to know the whereabouts of her husband. Clay had dismissed her fears, offering that Ernesto was off being a man and would come back whenever it suited him. After a month had passed, Clarita returned in tears, asking again where her husband was. Though the question lingered, Willy figured part of the riddle was that whatever had happened to Ernesto happened here in Mexico.

That was one matter. Willy now considered his own dubious circumstances. Rain had fallen the day after they'd been to Old Lopez's. Beau uncovered a hen's nest in a bramble with a half-dozen chicks and brought them home. They seemed signs that the drought was ending and the land would again yield crops. Cattle would thrive. Work would be had, and there'd be no need in going to Mexico. He'd told Clay as much, but Clay was no more inclined to be persuaded by words than by stones. Two days later they'd crossed the border, as Clay had put it to Willy, "to do bidness."

Willy pondered what Old Lopez would call such business. Maybe foolishness. Yes, *that*. He glanced up the narrow rode that led to the town and caught sight of his pa, a shadowy silhouette stirring up dust as he came in Willy's direction. In one hand he held a bottle of tequila. Willy bit down on a strand of shuck and watched Clay trudge up the dusty track. He noted that Clay's gun belt and pistol were missing from his waist.

A few strides away from where Willy sat, Clay spat out a wad of snuff and in a raspy voice said, "Here." He unbuttoned his shirt above his belt and withdrew a flat bindle of waxed paper that he tossed to Willy.

"'At's some tortillas I brung you. Thought you might be hungry." He turned his back to Willy, stroked the withers of his gelding, tucked the bottle of tequila away in his saddlebags, and mounted. "Time's come. Let's get ourselves on these nags."

"Thought we was goin yesterday," Willy said.

Clay walked the horse over to Willy and looked down. "I said we's goin. Get on that filly."

Willy didn't meet his gaze, staring instead at his pa's shadow in the dirt. "Got me question."

"'At's a damn surprise."

"Why didn't you have that Bobby Grimes come with you, 'stead of me?"

Clay adjusted his hat and looked off. "Seems a couple a beeves here and there didn't make it to Corcoran City when him and his boys was pushin into the stockyard for me. 'Side, I ain't sure him or his fool friends got the belly to be here. Mexico ain't no place to come if ain't no stones in your sack. One thing you got, boy, is a fool's pair hangin between your legs. If nothin else, you got that much from your pa."

For the next few seconds both were silent, then Clay turned his horse about and put the animal to a trot heading west.

Willy unraveled the paper package and took a bite from a stale tortilla. Although tempted to mount Lucy and ride to Bedloe instead of following his pa, Willy didn't move to do either. Instead, he chewed and watched his pa's horse raising dust as it plodded west.

Some two minutes passed before Clay bridled his animal about and returned at a lope. He reined the horse to a halt next to Lucy. "Finish that tortilla and get on your saddle, boy. And none of your lip, hear?"

"Got nothin to say."

"Panther Jack's awaitin us. Six days. A quartermaster be waitin too. With money."

Willy pointed to Clay's right hip. "Where's the Colt?"

Clay didn't answer, just reined his horse about and spurred it in the same direction from where he'd come.

"Prob'ly lost it playin cards or on some whore," Willy muttered. He wrapped the bindle and stuffed it in the bib of his overalls, then stroked Lucy's neck, took up the reins, and mounted.

THE RAIN HELD OFF for the length of the day. They rode southward several miles, then turned west and entered a stretch of barren land. In the distant West lay a course of flattop bluffs, and beyond them a mountain range rose high above the plain. Tales he'd heard hadn't prepared Willy for the land, alkaline and nearly lifeless, its harshness a metaphor for the unpredictability of Mexico.

As evening came, the sky broke loose. With no place to shelter themselves, they donned slickers and rode on. In the early hours of morning, the clouds thinned and the rain subsided. At midmorning they watered the horses in a runoff at the base of a bluff and set down in the shade side, where they slept until noon. When Clay awoke, he looked at the mountains, toed Willy with his boot, and told him to mount up. They followed a cart trail south and west.

The sun stood hot and relentless above the arid span that lay ahead. The night's moisture rose in shimmering tendrils from the earth's surface. Soon vagrant thunder heads rolled in, high and white, and passed to the north, phantom ships seeking harbor, their dark shadows casting momentary but blessed relief upon the travelers. His hat pulled down, Clay rode bowed over his saddle horn as if in prayer. Willy followed two lengths behind.

They entered a floodplain where dampened sand pillowed the earthen crust. The animals labored over the soft track. The surface of a marsh pool glistened in the midday sun. Birds broke out of the reeds and took flight. Gathering en masse, they circled and rose and dived like a vibrant wave, only to again land in the same reeds. Sometime later Clay and Willy came upon a shallow creek. They paused to water their horses and fill canteens. Soon after a farming village appeared to the west. Those working in the fields stood from their tasks to watch the riders pass on.

They followed a trail dug by cart tracks until it split north and south in a valley closed in by two low ridges. Clay took the trail north. An hour later it ended. Ahead lay a vast dry bed of hot sand, sharp rock, and stunted shrubs, no landmark in sight, save for the distant peaks to the west and south. Clay halted and they sat their saddles as he scanned the horizon. He removed his hat and rubbed his fingers through his thinning scalp.

"We lost?" Willy said.

"Ain't no one lost. Stay here."

Clay rode south about a quarter mile, where he turned and beckoned Willy forward. Willy spurred Lucy to a gallop, then slowed her to a walk as he neared Clay. He circled his pa once and came up beside him. Clay pointed to foothills on the eastern slope of the range. "That way."

Willy gazed at the angular peaks on the far horizon. "'At's a far way."

"You wanna quit?"

"Didn't say nothin about quittin."

"Good enough." Clay kneed his horse forward.

They descended into the empty land. In the heat of the late afternoon vaporous spires rose from the desert floor. They rode until they came upon a wall of volcanic rock, its jagged edges jutting out like spearheads. Clay dismounted and told Willy to do the same. "God ain't showed much mercy here," he said.

They led the animals on foot around the malpaís, the only evidence of life a few skittering lizards and the occasional colony of cactus wedged between boulders. Some three hours later they came to a ravine. The damp bed was hoof beaten and flat. They mounted and rode loose rein on their animals until the path curved right and rose steeply. They spurred their weary mounts up and out of the ravine to a stretch of steppe land spreading north and south and to the foothills in the west. Here chaparral thrived along with yucca, tall cactus, and islands of wild grass that bent northward. Though Willy only imagined it, the air seemed lighter. Here Clay signaled him forward and pointed out a deep cleft between two distant cimas, then to a trail a mile distant that snaked south and west.

"Them foothills, 'at's where we'll put up for the night. By mornin we'll be up there where the mountains catch the rain."

Clay snapped his reins. Willy again fell into the rhythm of the ride, the only sounds on the silent land, the horses' hooves striking ground, and an occasional screech of a hunting hawk. Once, in the distance, they spotted a scattering of rangy longhorn grazing on the grass and sage. Willy asked if they were going after them. Clay said no right person would concern himself with such animals, too wild to herd, nothing but half-leather, good only for shooting and taking hides.

As they came out of the llano and into the foothills, the trail curved and sloped gently for time, then steeply again as they neared the mouth of a narrow gorge. A few yards into the meandering defile of striated rock, Clay's gelding shied. It scraped the ground with a hoof, then turned and bucked. Clay stood his weight on the stirrups until the animal gradually steadied. Lucy too became agitated. Willy halted a few yards behind Clay, leaned forward over the filly's neck, and spoke soothingly to her.

"Smell 'at?" Clay said.

"Yep. Skunk?"

Clay said, "Or some dead meat."

Willy tied a bandanna over his mouth and nose, touched Lucy's flank with his spurs, and rode on. The wind that had come from the south throughout much of the day shifted from the southwest, the stench coming with it. At each turn in the winding arroyo, the stench grew stronger. The horses spread their nostrils and nickered. Squawking what seemed insults, some vultures flew to the boulders and gazed down from atop their perch.

Beyond a colony of dead plants encircled by frenzied flies at the base of a boulder, four bodies lay entwined in a manner that made it nearly impossible to determine where one corpse ended and another began. Their cotton pantaloons and bolsas had been shredded. The horses stood patiently, as if some unfathomable instinct allowed them to reconcile death in ways that man could not. A solo bird kept at its task, ripping off a ribbon of blackened flesh that it held in its beak briefly before lifting its head and swallowing it.

Until now, Willy had seen the dead only in repose at a wake. Fascinated and repulsed, he watched a set of antennae quiver in a hollow eye socket. Slowly, a beetle wiggled free from the cavity and came into the light. It spread its mandibles, snapped them closed, and submerged again.

Willy shooed flies away with his hat.

"What the hell you doin, boy?"

Without answering, Willy dismounted, then picked up a fist-size rock, and heaved it at the vulture. The bird released a chilling screech and flew off, its rickety wings stirring the air.

"'At's enough, Willy. Let's get."

Willy mounted and they rode on. "What you think happened?" he asked.

"They was shot."

"Yes sir, but why?"

"Politics, boy. Same as sent me and Panther Jack to San Antone to join up with the Rough Riders. They's enough agitation here'bouts since them soldiers cross't to fight Carrizal last year. It's a revolution down here. Who knows? Maybe federales did it. Maybe Carranzitas. Maybe they's bandits. Maybe they's federales theirselves. Hell, don't matter. Dead men ain't got no debt. Least not to the livin. 'At's all you need know, Willy."

When the shadows from the sinking sun enveloped the land, they made camp in a spot where water from the previous night's rain had pooled in a limestone hueco. Willy hobbled the horses so they could graze on the thin tufts of clump grass that sprouted in the damp earth. Clay built a fire from branches of a dead paloverde. They sat and ate beans. The sky clouded, but they were spared rain. In the morning they ate hardtack and mounted. No more than a dozen words had passed between them.

Before sunrise they reached a valley beneath the eastern slope of the mountains. Here they sighted a second scattering of Mexican longhorns. When Willy suggested rounding them up, Clay dismissed the idea with a laugh. "They'd likely kill our horses if we tried. No, 'at Mexican's got hisself some beeves worth the work. You'll see."

They rested in the shade of a patch of stump oak where the horses grazed on puffgrass and chaparral. They ate salt biscuits and jerky, and then Willy slept off and on for the remainder of the day and into the night. A short while after midnight, Clay shook Willy awake and told him to mount up, that they were going to the top.

BY DAWN THEY PASSED out of rangeland blanketed in hip-high chaparral and newly sprouted puffgrass and into lava-blackened foothills. The trail disappeared for a time, and they rode over stone-hardened terrain, winding their way upward between colonies of cactus and yucca and patches of loose rock. Lucy was a cutting horse and not meant for the trail. The climb took a toll on her. Willy didn't want to push her, but Clay didn't slow. A hundred yards ahead, he rode as if obsessed, hat back and bent over his saddle as he crisscrossed the slope, searching the ground for a sign, sometimes circling back over the same spot to study it again. From time to time he stopped to signal Willy forward or turned in the saddle and chastened him for lagging behind.

By midmorning he found the trail, and they left the rocky slope, headed in the direction of a steep canyon between two high peaks. Clay waited for Willy, then telling him to stay close behind, spurred his mount in the direction of the mountain. Willy fell in behind by two lengths. A woodland of fir and aspen lay an hour ahead, but first they had to cross a stretch of scrub oak and juniper. Halfway through the shoulder-high brush they disturbed a small herd of deer that took flight and startled the horses.

They passed out of the deep scrub. Juniper gave way to fir and aspen, and the temperature dropped. Ribbons of sunlight splintered down though the high boughs to the shadowed earth.

Clay sat his horse and waited for Willy. "Up there." He pointed high up at the rocky peak, then at where the trail led through the woods.

They rode the trail for a half hour, until they reached the base of the cliffs. Clay halted his horse at the mouth of a narrow ravine. Willy pulled Lucy up beside his pa and gazed into the shadowed chasm. A winding trail on the north side of the slot canyon rose steeply upward and disappeared a few hundred feet ahead. There, on either side of the trail, sheer limestone cliffs rose hundreds of feet, forming walls that blocked sunlight. A myriad of boulders, remnants landslides, lay in mass on either side of the trail.

"'At's it," Clay said, pointing high up to where the trail vanished and reappeared and vanished again as it meandered back and forth in a series of cutbacks. Appearing as no more than a thin line etched into the face of the north wall, it seemed insurmountable. Willy was tempted to say as much, but he held his tongue.

Clay said, "Ain't no one gonna see us here. Me and Jack made it once. Brought back some fine beeves 'at time. Not them mangy range cows we saw. You'll see."

"Happy to hear it, pa. You intend for us to push 'em back down 'at trail?"

Clay narrowed his eyes on Willy. "Hush that mouth, boy. Let's go."

A short distance into the arroyo, they caught sight of a brown bear whose smell spooked the horses. Clay drew the carbine from its scabbard and rode on with it resting across his saddle. When they reached the foot of the ascent, he glanced back at Willy. "Ain't no room on it for turnin around."

"I ain't turned around yet," Willy said.

"Just sayin is all."

The trail narrowed and hugged the edge of the cliff. Willy looked down in the middle of the second cutback and realized immediately he had to keep his eyes on the trail. Loose rock on the trail floor worked hard on the horses.

Farther along, they rounded a sharp turn and encountered a heap of stone and scrub and broken limbs that blocked passage. Willy looked down at the shadowed maw that held a graveyard of toppled boulders. A man, he thought, could vanish here trying to turn about, a man like Ernesto.

"What now?" he asked.

"Ain't but one choice, boy." Clay dismounted, bent over, and grappled with a huge rock that he rolled to the edge and dropped down the precipice. Willy watched it tumble down and bound off a jagged overhang, break apart, and complete its journey in pieces.

"Get on down and give me a hand."

Willy swung down from his saddle and walked forward cautiously. In time he took an unexpected pleasure in watching stones pummel into the chasm where they clacked and rebounded off the limestone facade before hitting bottom with a detonative thud. When they'd cleared enough detritus for them to pass on, Clay mounted and maneuvered his gelding around what was left of the rocks. The trail elbowed sharply and faded into the shadows of the cliffs. Willy walked Lucy around the rubble.

On the opposing cliff, a bighorn stood as still as the rock itself and stared down from his purchase. Then, as if broken from a trance, it bounded up the steep incline, seemingly without effort. Wondering how long it had been observing them and what else might be, Willy watched it climb the face of the cliff to the top. Then he placed his boot in the stirrup and swung his leg over the saddle.

AT MIDDAY they emerged out of the shadows of the gorge on a shelf just short of the mountain's crest. The horses, lungs heaving from the climb, stood wet and shivering. The flat mantel of iridescent limestone was ringed by walls of conical and egg-shaped boulders, stacked slapdash as if nature had left the task of arranging them unfinished. Willy dismounted and stomped his heels to get circulation in his feet.

"They ain't much to look at, Pa."

"Didn't promise no paradise."

Willy dropped the reins and walked toward the edge of the escarpment. Wind came hard from the southeast and rushed up the near-vertical drop. It pressed so hard against him, it seemed he could lean his weight into it and the air would hold him from falling. Still, he stood a safe measure from the edge. He'd never been so high, and the sight seemed to rush at him along with the wind. The plain sprawled eastward from the foothills, seemingly all the way to the ocean Panther Jack spoke of, a body of water his pa's friend described as so immense it was "painful for the eye to behold." Before this, Willy figured such a sea existed in Panther Jack's imagination, but as he gazed out, he saw that it must be as his pa's partner had described.

"We come the long way so's not be seen," Clay said. "Plenty flat down there. We'll pass on 'tween them two bluffs to the north. Day and a half in the crossin."

Clay had said that once they had the cattle on the move, they'd follow a road north to the river, but the only sign of passage Willy saw was an uneven burro track tracing northward from the foothills to the flattopp bluffs where it vanished as if something imagined.

Clay dismounted and gestured with a thumb to a cluster of boulders behind him. "They's a hueco over there 'neath that crack in the rocks. Over there's where I'll be. Water up the horses, boy."

Willy made no effort to move.

"Hear me? Horses need water."

Willy gazed down a moment longer, then gathered up Lucy's reins and led her to where Clay waited. "You said it was a road."

"What's 'at?"

Willy raised his voice. "I said it ain't no road!"

"Ain't here for the pleasure of arguin with you." Clay spat a stream of snuff juice on the rock and narrowed his eyes on Willy. "Can't run no steers to the river. We'll walk 'em like it was Sunday and all 'at was ahead was churchgoin with your ma. You need to learn being thankful."

Willy took in their surroundings and mumbled, "Yep, plenty to be thankful for."

Clay led his gelding to the boulders, dropped the reins, and removed the saddle. He laid that at the foot of a boulder and turned to Willy. "You gonna water them anytime today?"

"I'm lookin," Willy said.

Clay untied his load and tossed his saddlebags, bedroll, and saddle blanket beside the saddle. "Day you was born I should'a put you in a sack and drowned you in a pond."

"Wouldn't need no sack. Can't swim."

"Proves you ain't a fish is all."

Willy grabbed his canteen from the pommel, dropped Lucy's reins and stomped his boots until he felt blood circulating in his toes, then gathered the reins of both animals and led them past Clay. He stared for a moment at his reflection in the shallow pool, filled his canteen, let the animals drink, and hobbled them in the shade of the tallest boulder.

Clay sat on the ground, shoulders propped against a boulder, hat tilted back. "I said they'd be water."

"Yep."

Clay pointed where the boulders canted upward gently. "Go on up, but don't get seen."

Willy removed his hat, lay belly down, and inched his way to the edge of a shelf that overlooked the land, a vega of grazing land bristling with tall grama and wildflowers in fresh bloom. Willy edged forward and looked straight down.

Below, fir and juniper grew dense on the mountainside where an arroyo plunged nearly straight down and terminated at a thicket of scrub and reeds. Felled trees lay crosswise on the banks of the wash. At the center of the sodden thicket, a glimmering pond fed water to a narrow channel that meandered through the vega. A mile beyond, water from the pond irrigated a field of maize. To the west of the field atop the crown of a foothill, facing the vega below, sat a hacienda, its lime-washed walls spangling in the sun and its tiled roof glistening like polished copper. At the foot of the hacienda's walls, nestled inside a tall ring of Santa Rita cactus, sat a *colonia*, where a dozen low, flat-roofed adobe lodges encircled a *capilla* with a tall bell tower. A thin shaft of smoke swirled up from one of the lodges.

Farther away, scattered herds of cattle roamed freely. Visible mostly because of their horses' deft movements, vaqueros wove their way in and out of what Willy figured to be the main herd. From what he'd heard of vaqueros, he assumed all to be armed. He withdrew from the edge and sat digesting what he'd seen, an Eden of sorts, not the lost Eden of God's Genesis that the priest described from behind a pulpit, but one carved out of the wilderness by men. He looked out again. The clouds that had been sitting atop the distant peaks had slid down the foothills into the far edge of the valley. A storm brewing.

Two days' food between them and nothing but risk for them and stubble and sage for the horses to eat, he and Clay couldn't hold up much longer. It seemed best to rustle the cattle and move them to the border sooner than later. Willy stared at his boots for a time and considered what plan his pa might have in mind if a storm broke loose.

Clay hollered, "I'm comin up!" Scrabbling up the rock, he slipped and muttered, "Hell." Once on top, Clay sat beside Willy, rolled up his sleeve, exposing his bleeding elbow. "Maybe this here scrape's what that old Mexican was warnin about. Come."

Clay crawled to the edge of the overhang. Willy hesitated a moment before following. What was left to see? "They's a storm comin, Pa."

"Never mind that. Get over here, Willy."

They lay on their bellies, Clay taking in the lay of the land below. He didn't speak for a time, then elbowed Willy and said, "Shame one man got so much. Losin a few beeves ain't gonna hurt 'im none."

Willy chose not to speak.

Clay said, "Ain't like stealing. 'At's the world, boy. One takes from another and another takes from him. Look." Clay pointed to a saddleback where a trail led to the lower plateau, then to the thicket. "Come dark, I'll take that trail down. Bring the horses along. See where them woods is?"

"Yep."

Clay looked at Willy. "You'll be goin down near dusk."

Willy felt bile rise in his throat. He swallowed it down. "What about them vaqueros?"

"Won't know you're there if you use your brain. Let's get back 'fore someone sees us."

"Pa, it looks like another storm."

"I got eyes. Them clouds is plenty far off."

Clay slid down the boulder. Willy followed. Once down, he sat in the shade of a boulder, unstrapped his spurs, slipped his arms through the overall straps, and pulled down the bib.

Clay uncorked the tequila bottle, held it by the neck, and nodded as if in agreement with himself, then took a swallow. "Here's what we'll do." He stared off for a moment, then said, "You go down, run the cows into them woods. You listenin?"

"Yep."

"Keep 'em there. Come an hour or so past dusk, I'll be along with the horses. It'll be plenty dark. They's a trail runs from that pool a water down. We push 'em into the flats and run 'em straight north to the river. A day. Then we move 'em to the border and cross at the bridge. I got papers waiting and all. Little silver takes care a most anything down here. They's a federale turns his back. Now you know the how-ises."

Willy gazed at his pa, but didn't speak.

"I'll assume you understand," Clay said. He set the bottle of tequila aside and moved his bedroll beneath the overhang, then returned for the bottle and lay down. He tilted his hat over his eyes and said as if continuing some conversation they'd been having, "Lopez got no bidness teachin Beau Mexican. If he was intended to speak it, Beau'd be brown. My dead brother would be ashamed. Lost my hearin 'cause of 'em." He closed his eyes. "Don't worry yourself none. Ain't no one gonna be watchin for you."

Willy considered the plan a moment. "Why don't you go down and I'll bring the horses?"

"'Cause you're goin. Now, I'm gettin some sleep. Best do likewise. Night'll be a long one, so will tomorrow." Clay pulled the brim of his hat down and rested his head on the saddle.

Willy snatched a fly out of the air and slowly opened his fingers. The fly rubbed its front legs together and flew off. He glanced back at Clay, who lay on his back snoring, mouth open and contorted as if in pain. Then he climbed atop the boulder again.

The clouds were closer now. Willy saw no reason to wait. Waiting didn't seem practical. No one would see him. He thought about himself and Beau, how they'd done men's work since their adolescence and this was just more of the same, but dangerous. He considered his ma, now with a son, a baby still sucking on her breasts. This rustling was about things that mattered, his ma, his sisters, food on the table, taxes owed.

Willy scrabbled down to the boulder and shook Clay out of his sleep.

Clay bolted up. "Goddamnit, boy."

"Pa, I got an idea."

Clay twisted a finger in his ear. "Me too. Mine is sleepin."

"I'll go on down now. Come sundown, you bring the horses. 'Fore dawn we can run 'em to the river. Go north like you said and—"

"Ain't gonna be, Willy. Get to sleep or at least let me."

"But I can do it. See the—"

"Boy, go on now and leave me be."

Willy did as told, stretched out on the ground, and closed his eyes, but he didn't sleep. A few minutes passed before he felt the first raindrop. The long shadow of a cloud darkened the crest. Thunder boomed in the distance. The temperature began to plunge. Willy shook Clay. His pa sat erect, doubled his fists, and appeared about to strike, but before doing so he grasped the situation.

They gathered their gear and secured it under a boulder. Willy pulled on his slicker and hunkered down in a small grotto. The rain fell hard and cold on the limestone floor. Water pooled beneath them. For the rest of the afternoon and much of the evening, Willy sat wet and cramped beside his pa in the narrow cleft. He listened to the endless staccato of falling rain and the intermittent crescendos of thunder that shook the ground and wondered if the day would come when he could see luck from the good side of it. He'd seen enough of it from the bad side.

3 Willy spent the dark hours drifting in and out of a light slumber. Sometime in the predawn the clouds moved on. Clay and Willy sat on separate rocks and warmed themselves in the sunlight. They ate jerky and biscuits. Neither looked at the other or offered a word. Bobbin's stubborn, Ruth Bobbins called it, "worse than mule headed." Willy washed down the last of his hardtack with water and went to the horses. The storm left Lucy skittish. She reared up as he neared. He spoke gently to her until she calmed. Then he led the animals to a cluster of chaparral, left them to feed on the sparse leaves, and returned to his previous perch.

The midmorning sunlight shimmered on the rain-glazed flats, but that appeared temporary. Far to the south a bank of white thunderheads masked the peaks of the Sierra Madre Orientals, and southerly winds whined across wide llano below. Willy rested his back against a boulder, closed his eyes, and took in the warming rays. The silence between them lasted until Clay drew himself up and paced back and forth in front of Willy, who didn't open his eyes.

Clay kicked Willy's boot. "Okay, boy, it's time. Go down."

Willy opened one eye. "What you talkin about? The cold done froze my memory. Last I heard, I was goin down at dark." He closed his eyes.

Clay again kicked Willy's boot. "Damn you, boy. I'm your pa. Do as I say."

"I'm fond of it here."

Clay pursed his lips and gazed at the far clouds. He shook his head and slapped at the air with his hat. "Fine, then, I was wrong to go to a whore. 'At's the best you'll get from me."

"I figured as much. 'At why you got no pistol?"

"Woke up she was gone. Took it with her." Clay offered a hand to Willy, who waved it off and stood on his own.

"I'll be down in them woods." Willy walked past Clay without ceremony. "If it rains hard, don't be waitin 'til after dark."

"Don't do nothin too crazy."

"I could use a gun, Pa."

"Ain't got one to spare. Best don't let nothin happen. Come dark, I'll be there."

Willy retrieved a pair of moccasins from his saddlebags, rolled up his slicker, and stuffed it in the bib of his overalls. He stroked Lucy's muzzle and promised her he'd feed her oats first chance he could.

"Take your rope."

Willy shook his head. "Got no desire to be hanged by my own rope, Pa."

A MIST HUNG in the shadows. The loose ground was tricky to navigate where runoff from the night's rain left a film of water on boulders. There was no trail to follow, just a downward flume obstructed by boulders and fallen trees. At places the gorge dropped vertically six feet or more. Willy moved cautiously over the obstacles and an hour later reached bottomland. Save for a scattering of cattle, he was alone on the vega. The hacienda lay on the far side of a rise, far enough that he figured he'd be safe from the eyes of guards walking the walls.

He entered the thicket and pushed his way through the shadowed scrub. Near a beaver dam, he stumbled upon cattle lying beside the marshy shallows. A dozen in number, they were neither longhorns nor heifer, but some kind of cross-bred stock that were shorter in the leg and carried more weight than longhorn. In that his pa had been right. The cattle being there, the uneventful journey down the ravine, everything else that morning seemed just luck.

Willy cut a branch from a tall bush, tore the leaves off it, and used it to prod the animals farther into the underbrush. Once the cattle seemed settled, he walked to the tree line, kneeled, and spread the branches of a bush to look out. Cattle, a hundred or more, mostly steer and a few calfless cows, grazed higher on the grass slope. He saw that fresh clouds sat over the southern peaks. He waited in the cover of the woods for a time, deliberating his circumstances. Finally, he slapped his thigh, stepped out, and shouted, "Okay, sumbitches, shoot me now," but except for the cattle, he was alone.

The first steers submitted easily to the sting of his branch. He hazed them into the woods, where they seemed content to lie among the others. In four more trips he managed to fret a dozen more into the thicket. He counted them, twenty-two steers and four cows, enough that they could lose two or three along the trail and make the trip worth it. So far, luck was with him, but he reminded himself that it came in good and bad and that luck was a fickle master. There was no middle ground to luck, and that seemed the only truth in the world.

He took cover in underbrush, positioning himself to keep watch over the cattle and still keep an eye on the woodline. The ground smelled of dead bark and leaf mold and fungus. He hooded himself under the slicker, hunkered down, and began the wait.

Around midafternoon a stiff wind blew down from the peaks. The sky darkened. The nearby marsh came to life with insects. Tree limbs swayed. Birds took flight. The cattle pressed themselves together and lowed, their ears laid back and their tails flicking. Gradually, the clouds dropped. As the day extended into the late afternoon, shadows closed over the llano. When the cattle reared, he rose and stood himself between them and the open land. Gradually, they settled as before. Old Lopez had told Beau and him that the wisdom of the world lived in silent things. The *viejo* maintained that a man must listen to trees and grass as well as beasts. Willy huddled down again and keened his ears to the cattle, but the animals merely stared at him as if he were one of them.

A fresh gale swept through the trees. The boughs danced wildly, then just as quickly as it came, the wind diminished. A short time later, a half-dozen vaqueros rode up from the vega. They shouted and snapped whips as they circled the grazing cattle. One and two at a time they chased down strays before the animals made the woodline. Others worked at rucking the herd into an ever-tighter circle. At each pass vaqueros rode nearer, gathering strays, but seemed content not to enter the thicket in search of more.

Daylight drained from the sky. Willy watched from his blind, praying that the sky lift, that the vaqueros leave, that his pa be right in saying the journey back to the border would be, if not easy, at least less grueling than the one in. The weather and the persistence of vaqueros discouraged him. Soon the constant thip of the rain became hypnotic, and his thoughts turned away from his present circumstances.

Someday he'd free himself and his family from poverty. Like Panther Jack, whom the people of Bedloe called "that sneaky horse trader," by which they meant thief and profiteer. Willy imagined profiting from risks taken by others. He daydreamed, picturing himself with a pocket watch in hand, gold like Panther Jack's, who, when pondering a proposition, cupped the timepiece in his fingers and gazed off as he divided the risk involved in a scheme into the likely profit at the other end. He imaged himself looking out over a spread as big as all of the county surrounding Bedloe as a meal cooked, steaks dripping fat on a grill, his pa sitting nearby on a chair, chiding him.

Willy realized that the storm had broken and snapped his eyes in the direction of the cattle. Two burly steers stood swaying, as if ready to run. Willy sprang to his feet and threatened them with the branch, but the animals broke past him and headed for open ground. He watched them flee the woods and vanish into the open vega.

Rain came hard. Following the brief downpour, the clouds lifted and the sky gradually lightened. His wait stretched out another hour without incident. He became concerned about what might come with the next rainfall. That concern was replaced with another as the vaqueros rode past the trees and shouted, their whips cracking the air. He saw their fleeting silhouettes as they turned their agile ponies. One entered the tree line, ducked under a limb, and sat his horse a moment before he advanced into the shadows. He reined his mount back and forth. Twigs and leaves snapped under his horse's hooves. Willy worried that the sounds might spook the steers.

Some thirty feet from where Willy hid, the rider stopped his mount and removed his sombrero. He was young, had a thin square face, and packed a pearl-handled H&R .32 in a high-rise holster. Willy huddled down. Bile rose up in his throat. If a steer stood or broke out, his effort was for naught. Luck interceded. The cattle didn't stir, and the Mexican wheeled his horse a half circle and headed back for the vega.

Then after advancing a few strides, the vaquero halted the animal and sat it. He looked back in Willy's direction and scanned the brush.

A second rider ducked into the edge of the thicket. "Joaquin, *Oiga, venga!*"

The horseman called again. The young one slapped water off the brim of his sombrero, returned it to his head, and slowly urged his horse out of the thicket. When the vaquero passed into the open, Willy spread the branches and listened as the sound of hoofbeats gradually diminished. He pulled the collar of his slicker over his head and wrapped his arms around his knees.

Soon, the monotonous thip of the rain returned. An hour before dusk, lightning flashed in the nearby sky, followed by a pealing of thunder that made the ground tremble. The storm arrived in full measure. The cattle stirred. Some stood and lowed. Switch in hand, Willy rose, ready to cut off their charge, but the cattle merely swayed before him, as if trying to make some decision that was beyond them. Gradually, the animals sank back onto the ground. Willy returned to his blind and gazed up at the sheets of rain slanting down through the boughs. He muttered a string of curses at the fickleness of the world.

A half hour passed before the rain diminished to a slow drizzle. He kept an eye to the woodline for any sign of Clay. What if his pa had been captured on his way down? Willy dismissed that idea. Based on what he knew of his pa's history, Willy figured it more likely that Clay would pass out from drink and fall off his horse, the very fate Willy's grandfather had suffered when he tumbled from his mount and drowned in the murky shallows of a cow pond.

A steer lowed and then stood and rocked back and forth. Willy clutched his switch and stood, but was distracted from going after the steer by a crunching sound. He wheeled around and scanned the tree line north to south, but saw nothing beyond the trees and the silvery beads of rain dripping down through the branches. He relaxed, thinking his imagination had gone wild from all the waiting. He looked at the cattle again, and a vagrant thought tramped its way through his skull like a headache that hadn't yet formed. Then it hit him like a bump in the shins that he was not alone. When he looked back, he found himself facing a mounted vaquero.

The Mexican leaned forward over a saddle pommel and smiled. "*¿Qué paso, muchacho?*" He spurred the horse forward, stopped a stride away, and drew a whip from his pommel. He unraveled it and shifted it from hand to hand.

Willy stood and, in hopes of buying time to get away, said, "*Buenos tardes.*"

The vaquero urged the horse closer. "*¿Niño, estas solo?*"

"Ain't never felt more alone," Willy said and backpedaled.

They stared at one another until the vaquero dropped his smile and flicked the whip twice.

"*No tu tienes suerte.*"

Willy thought, 'At's the damned truth.

"*Bueno. Andes!*" the vaquero said, motioning for Willy to march in the direction of the vega. The cowboy touched his spurs to the horse's flanks and circled behind Willy.

Willy did as indicated, but slowly. Over a short distance he figured he could outrun the horse. His best chance for success lay in turning back and running for the brush at the edge of the arroyo, then climbing to the far side bank. It was too rocky for the vaquero to cross there. But that course of action required his somehow getting past horse and rider. Then too, the vaquero was armed.

The man spurred the horse forward until it bumped Willy in the back. "*Niño, ándale.*"

"I ain't in no hurry to get hung," Willy said.

The whip snapped on his thigh. The pain nearly dropped him. He stumbled forward, caught his balance, and picked up the pace. Willy slowed again, anticipating the inevitable bump from the horse and the sting of the whip. When the contact came, he dropped to the ground, grabbed a knee, and moaned. The Mexican halted his horse. Willy rose slowly to one knee, then stood and limped about in a circle, pointing to his knee.

"*Ándale.*" The vaquero circled his horse behind Willy and cracked his whip.

The whip sounded like pistol shot as it snapped over Willy's head. On the second thrust the whip bit his shoulder. Willy winced, but otherwise gave no indication of pain. He stepped again in the direction of the vega, the rider following close behind. Willy waited, stalling, and when he felt the horse's breath on the back of his neck, he wheeled around, veered past the horse, and made for the arroyo.

For a moment it seemed he would succeed, but he tripped over a tree root and fell to his knees. He scrambled to his feet and took off again, this time nearly reaching the bank, but the rider cornered him. Willy raised his hands. The whip cut into his side. He took off running again, but again the rider came alongside him, leaned in his saddle, and thrust the whip. The tongue of the whip raveled around Willy's ankle. The vaquero reined his mount to a stop, and Willy plunged forward.

"*Muy bueno, joven.*" The Mexican, his teeth white and even, smiled down.

Willy tried to free his ankle.

"*No, no, muchacho.*"

The rider backed the horse, dragging Willy to the edge of the woods, where he halted his mount. He loosed his whip from the pommel, dropped it at Willy's feet, and drew the pistol slowly out of his holster. Willy hastened to free his ankle. He determined that his one chance was to spook the horse and unseat the rider. He kicked the whip aside, stood, and held up his hands.

The Mexican cocked the hammer of the pistol and circled slowly, edging closer on each cycle, and speaking under his breath as if uttering a novena. Willy matched the Mexican's stare and turned in sequence with the horse, waiting for the instant when he, the horse's head, and that of the rider aligned.

A bolt of lightning lit the treetops. The rider glanced up. A second flash of lighting followed almost immediately and framed the rider against the backdrop of trees. Willy charged. It seemed easy, seemed as if the reins found his hand instead of him finding them. The horse reared. The next instant all went black.

Willy, stunned and lying at the foot of the horse, winced when he touched his chin. He felt a trickle of blood. The horse stood above him. The gun dangled from the rider's index finger. His jaw appeared unhinged. The Mexican listed left, then righted himself, his eyes open as if startled from a nap. He tilted his head to the left and tried to speak.

Another bolt lit the sky. The Mexican leaned forward. His body trembled; the revolver fired once and slipped from his hand. He leaned sideways and surrendered to gravity. Willy rolled out of the way to avoid the Mexican as he tumbled from the saddle. Inches separating them, they lay facing one another. The vaquero extended his hand toward Willy. His lips moved; his fingers twitched.

Willy clawed his way to his feet. Blood dripped from the cut on his chin. He was bruised from being dragged by the horse. Welts from the whip rose on his shoulder and side. For all of his injuries, he felt little pain. He was alive. That was enough for the moment. He had to get away without delay. He reached for the horse's reins, but the animal shied away. As it turned to run, Clay cut off its path and held it.

"Told you to stay out of trouble, boy." Rifle butt resting on his thigh, Clay led the Mexican's horse to where the man lay bleeding.

Willy looked up at Clay. "He dead?"

Clay shrugged. He handed the horse's reins to Willy and dismounted. "Get yourself away, boy, and hold that animal still."

Clay gazed up through the boughs of the trees and studied the sky. Willy led the horse away and watched his pa lever a fresh round. Clay shouldered the carbine and looked down at the Mexican. The man's lips moved in an effort to speak. When the next clap of thundered pealed, Clay pulled the trigger. He ejected the casing, levered in a fresh round, and thumbed the hammer down.

He looked at Willy. "You gonna thank me?"

"You killed him."

"He ain't got no miseries now. 'Less you got somethin better in mind," Clay said pointing to the steers, "let's get ourselves gone!"

His thoughts fixed on the dead Mexican, Willy hesitated.

"Boy, move." Clay motioned with his thumb. "Your filly's back a ways. Use his to get yours."

When Willy returned, Clay was removing the vaquero's boots. His sombrero dangled from Clay's saddle. Slung over Clay's shoulder was his gun belt. He tossed the Marlin to Willy, strapped on the gun belt, and holstered the revolver.

"Let's drag him into the bushes. Longer it takes 'em to find 'im, longer we got."

After they concealed the dead man, Willy pulled on his boots, buckled his spurs, and wrapped the Marlin and moccasins in his bedroll. He strapped the blanket to the saddle. It occurred to him that it might be him lying dead if Clay's aim had been off a fraction or if he'd arrived a second late. What he knew with certainty was what fate he'd have met at the hands of the vaquero's master. He gathered up the whip, looped it onto his pommel, and swung onto the saddle.

Clay tethered the Mexican's horse to his and sidled up beside Willy's mare. "They get on us, leave the beeves and make straight for the river. Any shootin, don't look back. I ain't answerin to your ma 'cause you got curious and got yourself kilt."

Willy looked back to get a last glimpse of the brush where the dead vaquero lay, and then he rode into the steers.

UNDER THE DARK SKY, they pushed the cattle northward through the narrow stretch between the bluffs. At dawn they descended the trail and stopped at the rim of a llano where the land sprawled for miles like an enormous plate and, as Clay had claimed, the trail widened. The clouds had moved westward, and the sky bloomed blue all the way to the Texas side of the Rio Bravo.

Ahead the track was saturated with mud, and pools of rainwater shimmered black and silver. The wet earth sprouted wildflowers, grama, needle grass, and bunchgrass. On the descent they'd have to cross three deep arroyos. Willy looked at the miles of sprawling mud that lay ahead and figured the clear sky and having all the cattle were the sole measurements of their luck.

"Get down for a spell," Clay said.

"Why?"

"Them cows need a rest and to feed a bit 'fore we push 'em cross't."

"What about us being followed?"

"Hell, boy. Them Mexicans is just wakin up. Don't unsaddle that filly."

They ate the last of the hardtack, then, spelling each other, slept for an hour apiece. At midmorning they mounted and drove the cattle in toward the border crossing at Del Rio, some thirty miles away. The sun beat down on them, hot and relentless. Patches of bunchgrass dotted the trail sides, and the cattle dawdled and stubbornly grazed. It took both Willy's and Clay's full effort to keep the small herd together and moving. Willy divided his attention between the animals and the approach to their rear. But he saw no riders. Clay seemed unconcerned, insisting that once they reached the river, their trek north would go easier.

At times an animal or two buried its hacks in the soft earth. One steer fell to its knees, sinking to its chest in mud. Willy and Clay dismounted and pushed the animal from both flanks until it was free. Their faces mud smeared, they saddled up and headed the herd north. Another steer strayed off. Willy took chase. It ran to a bramble. He found it on the far side, mired in quicksand, and tried to rope it out, but to no avail.

"Maybe you'll figure it out," he said, dropping his rope. He left it lowing and struggling to free itself.

The horses too struggled along a trail of sucking mud and near-vertical slopes where the earth crumbled beneath their hooves.

At a flooded wash, another steer tumbled backward down the bank and landed, legs up, in three feet of water. It foundered a moment and then rolled over and stood up shoulder deep in water. Willy tried to drive it up the bank, but it wouldn't budge, just stood bawling.

"More trouble 'an it's worth," Clay said.

Shortly after noon Willy and Clay drove the cattle onto the floor of the valley, where they saw a man and burro in the distance walking their way west. He removed his sombrero and waved it overhead as he watched them pass on. Other than the lone man, they saw only birds and a coyote with pups, until a short while later a herd of longhorn appeared on the western slope of the foothills. Willy estimated forty to fifty, all left to range. It seemed senseless, he and his pa traveling so far to steal a few head, and at so much risk.

They crossed the floodplain, losing three more steers. By that afternoon, they were within a mile of the valley of the Rio Bravo Del Norte and in less than the day and half Clay had predicted. To the north the waters streamed downriver toward Via Acuña. All that was left them was moving the animals a few miles, bribing the customs man, and crossing the bridge into Del Rio. Clay told Willy that if all went well, they'd reach the crossing shortly after dusk.

Willy flanked the animals on the river side, hazing strays back into the herd. Though not visible, the roaring river stalked them. At times his lack of sleep took hold, and he fell into a dazed state. Clay hollered to get his attention or rode up behind him and slapped him with his hat. Other times, Willy dwelled on the vaquero lying dead on the ground, his eyes dull as an unlit lamp. He wondered if the body had been discovered and if they were being trailed.

By midday they reached a thicket so dense that the cattle in the lead disappeared from view as they wound their way into and through the underbrush. Not one but three, as if they'd conspired to do so, abandoned the herd at once. Willy tracked them down, chased them out into the open, and badgered them back in with the herd with the Mexican's whip.

Clay rode up beside Willy. "We's too close to the river. Move 'em away from the bushes so's they won't be so much trouble. We get to Del Rio, we'll eat."

Before dusk Clay halted the herd near a bend in the river. Willy rode to the river's edge and got his first glimpse of the thundering currents. He eased Lucy up to the bank where churning water gushed white. An uprooted tree shot up out of the center, thrust up with such force that for an instant all of it but its roots was visible. Willy muttered a curse.

Clay rode up and uncorked his bottle, took the last swallow of tequila, and tossed the bottle in the river. Willy watched it disappear under the foaming surface. Deep water was his singular fear. It often haunted his sleep. At age six, he'd nearly drowned when the Braithwaite boys had tossed him into the Nueces, insisting it was as natural to swim as it was to walk. Willy went under several times before Ted, the oldest brother, realized he couldn't swim, dived in, and pulled him out. By then Willy was turning blue. Though reckless in other ways, Willy never again chanced water over his head.

"Ain't nothing we need there, Willy. Let's go ahead and move 'em." Clay pointed downstream. "We'll get there about nightfall."

THEY WERE TWO HOURS from the crossing when a fusillade of rifle fire broke loose, not from behind them as anticipated, but from the front. The bullets felled two steers. Clay reined his horse alongside Willy's and pointed north.

"They'll be on us soon enough. We gotta cross. Let's push 'em."

A second volley of gunfire came their way. "Let's leave 'em and run to the bridge!" Willy shouted.

Clay leaned over his horse's neck and took the reins from Willy hands. "Hand over that whip and do as I say, boy."

Willy held the whip out of reach.

"Give it on over!" Clay thrust out his palm.

Willy surrendered the whip.

Clay unlaced the scabbard holding the rifle and handed it to Willy. "Take it. I'll circle around and run 'em."

Willy secured the scabbard and wheeled to the left. Clay drove the cattle in the direction of the river. A third flurry of shots popped in the distance. Another steer fell. By then Clay had the herd stampeding.

They reached the bank minutes ahead of the shooters. The lead cattle tumbled down the bank and came up afloat in the current. Their snouts straining to stay above, the panicked animals treaded water and tried to turn back to shore, only to be met by another wave of white-eyed steers. The river quickly swept some downstream. Those that managed to turn back struggled to climb the bank. Two succeeded. The rest floated off to the same fate as the others. Those that balked and didn't reach the river milled about on the bank in the reeds.

Clay rode back to Willy, who sat his saddle and waited atop the bank. He'd seen what happened to the animals and had no intention of joining them.

"Get goin, boy."

Willy shook his head. The growl of the river was more frightening than the sound of bullets pelting the ground nearby. Clay circled behind Lucy, raised the whip, and brought it full force on her haunches. The filly reared up, and before Willy could hold her back, she bolted down the steep riverbank and into roiling flood. Horse and rider went under, the filly plowing water with her hooves, Willy holding his breath and gripping the pommel. He lost the stirrups, but by some miracle kept the saddle under him. Water swirled violently around him. Seconds later the river belched them up. Nostrils steaming, the filly began swimming toward the Texas side.

Willy breathed in the dank and fetid air and desperately clutched the pommel as he struggled to regain the stirrups. At midpoint, an eddy trapped the filly. Her chest heaved from her great effort to escape the torrent, but she made no headway. A flotilla of tree limbs and branches swirled around them. To the right a steer surfaced, its eyes white-rimmed saucers. The animal spun into Lucy's flank, then vanished under the water. A limb struck the filly's withers. Willy lost a stirrup. Before he could recover, the filly took a second blow. Willy felt her go out from under him. Unseated, he entered the moil, and the current sucked him under.

He struggled against the pull of the river, until finally he quit the battle. His muscles went limp, and he held his breath as he waited for the inevitable, feeling neither anger nor anguish, and turned his destiny over to the river. Wherever it spilled out, he would spill out, alive or dead.

Then, when it seemed the murk had claimed him, air beads bubbled above his head, and just as suddenly as it had yanked him under, the current catapulted him up as it had the uprooted tree. He rose to the surface and filled his lungs with sweet air.

4 It rained through the night, then in the hour preceding dawn the rain petered out and the terrain gradually took form as the clouds thinned. Stars appeared, and to the west the half-moon sat atop the horizon. Willy wrapped his arms around his knees and sat shivering on damp earth in a thicket above the riverbank. He was alive and on Texas soil, and the feel of solid ground under him was plenty to be grateful for.

His journey down the river, a perpetual process of surfacing long enough to breathe, then being towed under again, had seemed endless, as he lost his slicker, sense of time, and eventually hope of surviving. Finally, after he'd quit the fight and surrendered his fate to the river for the last time, the current slammed him against a muddy bank, where he managed to hold onto an exposed tree root until he regained strength enough to climb onto land. Wet and tired and hungry, he'd waited out the darkness, wondering from time to time about his pa. Clay wasn't likely to risk himself for a handful of steers. Willy figured he'd probably lit out for the crossing at Del Rio.

What mattered now was feeding himself, then finding his way home.

The sun hung on the horizon as if debating whether to start the day. Willy touched his chin. It was tender and the scab soft, but the wound had ceased bleeding. He considered his options. With no idea where he was, he figured it best to pick a direction and walk until he found a trail or a road north. But if he went north toward the plain, he might not come across water for some time. Drinking from the murky waters of the Rio Grande was preferable to dying of thirst. On the other hand, the don's vaqueros could well be looking for him, and he'd run a risk in exposing himself on the riverbank. Seeing no other option, he slipped on his boots, and then, famished and exhausted, he crawled out of the brush and stretched out in the sunlight for a time. When his body warmed sufficiently and his shivering subsided, he stood and began walking downstream.

He followed the bank, as much as possible avoiding open shoreline. His boots, still wet, served poorly. Occasionally, he stumbled over a rock or a limb and twice fell. His heels began to blister. Hours passed before he came upon some water pooled in a hueco beneath a rocky cleft. He drank, then rested his back on a warm boulder.

The day promised to be South Texas hot, humid, miserable, and he was hatless. By midday he'd be forced to find shade. Until then he'd move on. He slipped off his boots, tucked them inside the bib of his overalls, and stepped out barefoot. Rocks jutted up occasionally tripping him. Combating the undergrowth began sapping what little strength he had. He fell into a trance and on occasion lost his bearings and strayed inland too far. Whenever the sound of the river faded, he shook himself out of his fog and turned back to the bank.

Though receded, the river still flowed rapidly. The shoreline was level, and he settled into a steady walk, after a time gaining confidence that no one was searching for him. His hunger gnawed at him. He scanned the bushes for berries, but there was nothing. Later, the shoreline ended abruptly at a rocky embankment. The shelf rose about a hundred feet. He found a narrow path that ran upward and began climbing. As he labored to the top of the embankment, three horsemen appeared on the Mexican side. One pointed toward him. The others seemed uninterested.

A little farther, at the approach to a bend in the river, the embankment canted downward. He descended to level ground. The walk alongside the bank was easy, and he relaxed his guard. As he came out of the turn in the bend, he sighted the riders again, on foot on the opposite bank. One raised a rifle to his shoulder. As the muzzle flashed, Willy spun about, dived into a nearby thicket, and hit the ground crawling. As he inched his way into the shadows, a volley of rifle fire chipped at the leaves and branches overhead, then stopped as abruptly as it had begun. Old Lopez's warning pounding in his head, he hunkered behind a rock and waited.

A minute or two passed before the Mexicans fired again. The rounds slapped harmlessly into the dirt several feet away. He waited a while for more rounds, and then he crawled to the edge of the bramble and peered out. He saw no one. He wondered if they'd forded the river to come after him. To be cautious, he lay in the cover several more minutes, then rose and brushed himself off. He saw blood coming from sole of his foot and wondered if he'd been shot, but it just skin worn raw. He tore a sleeve from his shirt and wrapped the foot, then started out again.

THE GROUND STEAMED. The sun bore down on him, further sapping his strength. He spotted a kettle of buzzards circling downstream as he walked in that direction. He stumbled on a trail near a cove. Rust-colored water spilled into the river from a steep arroyo. The fetid odor of dead flesh drifted his way, the smell emanating from a clump of salt cedar on the far side of the cove. He headed in that direction.

Three dead steers lay rotting in the shallows, one on its back, its stiff legs aimed skyward. Undaunted by Willy's presence, the vultures busied themselves, savagely pecking strips of flesh from the dead animals while others perched nearby waited to scavenge a bite. Willy circled past them. A short distance later, he came upon Lucy. The filly lay on her side, partially buried in mud, a raven pecking at her eye. He paused at the sight of her, no more than meal for birds and larvae. He recalled the morning his pa and Panther Jack arrived at the spread with Lucy in tow. Willy had marveled at her wild spirit as she fought against the lead.

He stumbled toward her over the soft ground and halfway there fell. He managed to rise to his haunches, but collapsed when attempting to stand. After a brief rest, he pulled himself to his knees, but his arms gave way. He lay on his belly, and as the land blurred he sank into a dream, his pa shouting to him to find Beau, that the filly was coming, and then she appeared, struggling against the rope that tethered her to Panther Jack's pinto.

Gradually, the land came back into focus, and he became aware of it and of lying in the sand, frit flies and bluebottles flitting about his head. He sat up and swatted at them and listened to the river, lapping gently against the shore. He gathered himself and slowly stood. He considered what was best to do about the horse. Her tongue, black and partially eaten, spilled out of the side of mouth. "Nothin but death around me," he muttered, feeling for the first time the full measure of what he'd seen in so few days. She was reduced now to a carcass, and he was too spent to even feel sad for her because most of his sadness was over his own condition, and he wondered if his pa, too, had fallen victim to his folly.

The saddlebags had been lost to the river. Left were the saddle and blanket. He kneeled down to uncinch the saddle. He worked at loosening the cinch. He pulled with all his might, but lost his grip and fell on his back. He took hold as best he could and kept at the task for a time, stopping only to catch his breath or swat flies. In time he realized any efforts were futile. She was bloated with gas and the leather dug into her flesh so deeply that the cinch was unyielding. He walked the shore searching until he found a broken tree branch sharp enough to puncture her hide. He closed his eyes and plunged it into Lucy's side. The gas escaped her, the smell causing him to turn away and retch, but all that came up from his stomach was bile and water.

He stepped away, took several deep breaths, and looked at his hand, red and chafed from the effort. "About as sad as it can get," he said.

He went to work on the cinch, unbuckling it, then propping his feet against her back and pulling on the saddle. It broke free and revealed the rifle trapped beneath her. The bedroll was soaked and caked in mud. He sat with his feet spread apart, and using her for leverage, he tugged on the stock. He fell backward when it came loose. Then he went about digging mud away to free the bedroll. Inside, he found his moccasins, a treasure to his thinking, enough to renew his spirits.

He set the rifle and saddle aside, then stripped and placed his boots and the moccasins atop a boulder to dry. Blanket, overalls, and shirt in hand, he walked to the river. The receding water flowed languorously. It seemed another river entirely now. It was hard for him to imagine the boiling currents that had swept him downstream. He waded into the water, scrubbed mud off his garb and went back to the bank. He hung the shirt and overalls on a branch and noticed for the first time how fine the land here was. On the upside of the bank nearby, bluebonnets bloomed. A bee darted about his head. A butterfly sat atop a leaf on a scrub oak, folding and unfolding its wings.

He had only a single silver dollar in his pocket. It seemed unlikely he could buy food enough for the journey even if, by chance, he came upon someone willing to sell some grub. Neither could he rent a horse with one coin and a promise to return the animal. Still, if he found an untended horse he could borrow without getting hanged, the saddle would come in handy. He secured the bedroll to the saddle and hefted the load, including the carbine, and walked to the shade beneath a cottonwood a hundred yards or so away from the smell of death.

Neither the breach nor the barrel showed signs of corrosion. He removed the cleaning kit from the butt of the stock and disassembled the Marlin. The bore patches for the rifle were wet. He tore off a strip from the tail of his shirt and divided that into four parts. One he ran down the barrel. The others he used to dry off the workings and the cartridges. Once he was satisfied the action worked, he loaded the magazine again. He considered the Mexicans who'd shot at him and decided that after he rested, he'd head inland.

Vultures had gathered atop Lucy. Willy chambered a round, shouldered the carbine, and laid the sights down on the largest among them. The recoil felt as good as the sight of the birds abandoning the carcass in a flurry of squawking. He lumbered over to the bird he'd killed, drew out his knife, intent on feeding his hunger. Instead, the sight of its guts changed his mind. There'd be rabbits aplenty or sage hen on the journey home. In the meantime, he'd find berries and honey. After all, he'd seen bees. He returned to the cottonwood where he sat with his back against the trunk. He set the carbine aside, laid his head on the saddle, and gave himself over to the fatigue.

Sometime later he awoke to the sound of high-pitched laughter. Uncertain if the sounds were part of a dream or real, he reached for the carbine and looked about. The angle of the sun indicated it was early afternoon. His stomach felt knotted. He stood, gathered up the bedroll and saddle. The giggling came again, clear now. He glanced up where the ground rose above the shore and saw two young boys and a girl standing and looking back at him.

Suddenly aware of nakedness, Willy turned away. The children laughed and ran off. He covered himself as best he could with the saddle and scanned the ridgeline where he'd seen them. The only sounds were the thrum of the swarming flies and the murmur of the river.

If children lived nearby, food couldn't be far away. Willy dressed in his damp clothes, shouldered the saddle, and, toting the carbine in hand, followed the direction of the children. He saw a narrow footpath that wound to the high ground and began climbing it. Halfway up he became lightheaded and leaned against a sapling, waiting for the spell to pass. When the dizziness faded, he took to the trail. It hit him again, harder this time. He dropped the saddle, slumped to the ground as his vision began to blur, and, holding on to the barrel of the rifle, balanced himself.

Appearing seemingly from nowhere, a young Mexican boy stood before him in front of a line of scrub oak. He studied Willy for a fleeting moment, then vanished back into the brush.

"Come on back," Willy said, his voice little more than a whisper. "I don't mean no harm."

He couldn't summon strength to stand any longer, so he slumped down and sat with the rifle held between his knees for what seemed an hour. Somewhere in that time he pulled out the silver dollar and held it so that it would catch sunlight and the boy would see it if he returned. He thought of Panther Jack and the way the horse trader studied his watch when bargaining, a technique he employed as he calculated how to empty all the coin from another man's pocket. Finally, he returned the coin to his pocket and looked up at the sun through a spiderweb. The web and the branches it occupied gradually became the background, and the sky became the foreground. The sun seemed not to have moved. He looked at his hand, wiggled his fingers, and stared at them.

His body railed against his every effort to move, but ultimately he decided that if he was to die, he'd rather do it trying to save himself. He hoisted the saddle to his shoulder. As he did, he was greeted by wide smiles from the three brown-skinned children, two boys and a girl.

"*Tengo hambre,*" he said and motioned with his hand as if eating.

"No, no," the girl said. She pointed to her stomach. "*Tiene hambre aquí.*" Then pointing to her mouth, she said, "*Aquí es por la comida.*"

The children laughed as one. At what, Willy had no idea. The bigger boy stepped forward. He gripped the saddle pommel and said, "*Por favor permítame ayudarlo.*"

Willy saw he meant to help and let the saddle slide from his shoulder. The youngster placed it atop his head and balanced the load by holding onto the skirts on either side. The girl motioned for Willy to follow. Without the burden of the saddle, he managed to keep pace as the children scrambled up to level ground. An exhausting five minutes later for Willy, they stepped out of the woods into a clearing, where an adobe house sat shaded under the boughs of two cottonwoods.

The Indian-featured mother was dark and squat and, like Old Lopez, a descendant of the Tarascan, a farming people largely annihilated by Comanche in the previous century. She stood blocking the door of the adobe hovel and without speaking motioned him to a bench under a cottonwood. Balancing a two-year-old on her hip, she brought a jug of water and a bowl of beans and fried cornmeal. Willy shoveled food in his mouth greedily with a wooden spoon. The toddler, its black eyes wide as if inspired, studied him. Willy devoured the beans, then placed the bowl to his lips, tilted his head back, and drank the juices. He wiped his mouth on the back of his sleeve and looked into the placid eyes of the mother. He pointed at the saddle, then in the direction of the Rio Grande.

"*Gracias,* ma'am. Lost my horse to the river." Seeing she didn't comprehend him, he said in his limited Spanish, "*Mi caballo,* uh, *en el rio.*"

She responded with a disinterested nod and pointed to the bowl. "*¿Más?*"

"*Si.*" Willy held the bowl up. "*Por favor.*"

The elder girl came closer. "*Mis hermanos,* they wonder why you shoot birds naked."

"You speak 'Merican."

She nodded. "*Más o menos.*"

Willy had forgotten about killing the vulture. He looked at the almond-eyed children, their round cheeks formed in incessant smiles, punctuated by dimples. It seemed that no matter where he went, children always appeared happier than he'd been.

"Well, *señor?*"

Willy took a gulp from the jug and looked west, where the sun was sliding away. "Tell 'em wearin no clothes makes my aim better."

When the girl repeated this in Spanish to the children, their smiles faded. He smiled and nodded. Their smiles returned. He raised his eyebrows. They did the same.

He asked, "How far is it to Bedloe from here?"

The girl shrugged. "I do not know Bedloe, *señor.*"

The mother arrived with another bowl of beans topped with cornmeal. The children continued watching Willy's every move. They laughed as he scraped the bottom of the bowl. He closed his eyes as he devoured the last small bite, then thanked the mother and handed over his silver dollar. She held it in her thumb and index finger, spat on it, then rubbed it on her skirt and examined it.

"It's a lucky dollar. I'd shore give more, but I ain't got it," he said and turned his pockets inside out. "*Es todo.*"

She nodded as if to say it was fair payment and clutched it in her palm.

"Tell your ma them's 'bout the best beans I ever tasted. I ever get some money and come this way, I'll pay what they's worth."

The girl relayed this to her mother, who stood expressionless.

His strength having returned, he stood and studied the surrounding land, all brush except for a bean field in bloom. The sky was smoky gray. He shouldered his gear and turned to leave.

The mother said, "*Mucha esperanza, joven,*" and motioned for him to stay.

She left for a moment and returned with a cotton cloth folded into a bindle. She spread the white cloth for him to view the tortillas inside and handed it over.

"*Gracias, señora.*" He tucked the cloth in his bib and again shouldered the saddle.

The children followed for a while before turning back. He wondered where the man of the house was, if there was one, and if not, how the woman survived with no livestock and only a small bean field.

WILLY TRAVELED NORTHEAST in moonlight. It was cool and the ground damp and the night silent save for crickets and the occasional flapping of wings. Once he heard the buzz of a rattler. Late in the night he came across an abandoned derrick where a wildcatter had brought in a duster. Marking the supply route into the camp was a set of wagon tracks worn hard and barely covered by stubble weed and desiccated flowers. He followed the tracks until they intersected a road that curved north and east. To the west were the shadows of the Anacacho Mountains, pale and yellow on the horizon.

Wearing moccasins eased the walk somewhat, but blisters formed on his heels, and when those broke he felt every stone and twig underfoot. His shoulders stiffened under the burden of the saddle and carbine. When the blisters became unbearable, he spread the bedroll on a mound of earth away from the brush and lay down. He listened for a time to a bawling coyote. Eventually, exhaustion overtook him, and despite the pain he drifted into heavy slumber and slept through a short sprinkle. He awoke long before dawn to a trumpeting inside his head. He bolted upright and looked about. The only sound was the persistent chatter of a mockingbird. It was still dark. He looked at the land for something that would renew him, a sign of a cow or even a goat. But he was alone, and all he saw were vague outlines of slate-colored hills on the horizon.

He stretched and then urinated while trying to remember what had startled him awake. Dreams often deviled him. Those he couldn't remember troubled him most. He took out a tortilla and chewed it slowly, wondering why dreams never seemed to resolve themselves. Was it possible to conjure one that had an ending? Was it possible to go to sleep and be comforted by a dream instead of being disturbed by it? Part of him wanted to sleep again and see if it was possible. Part of him wanted to sleep because he didn't want to face what awaited him. But he had to stay awake. He pictured the dead vaquero, left on the wet ground, the suddenness of his fatal wound, his last words choking in his throat. As with a dream, Willy felt a human ending should have a meaning beyond that.

When finished with the tortilla, he gathered his gear and set out.

A while later he stopped and removed his moccasins. He looked at his heels, each swollen and blistered. He tore strips from the bedroll, replaced the moccasins, and wrapped them with the strips. He had no good guess as to how far he was from Bedloe, but hoped for no more than a two-day trek. Scant as it was, he'd have to ration his food. Sore and spent, he aimed his anger at his pa. It was enough to drive him to his feet. The night was tolerably cool. He looked at the far horizon, its edges polished by a half-moon and a billion stars, then lifted the saddle to his shoulder, took the carbine in hand, and walked into the dark, empty land.

WILLY AWOKE to the sound of a vehicle chugging nearby. He sat up and looked in the direction of the sound as what appeared to be a Model T runabout neared. He looked around. With no place to hide and no point in trying to run, he eased the rifle out and covered it with a blanket he'd pilfered the previous night from a clothesline beside a nearby farmhouse. A minute passed and it appeared the vehicle would go on, but it made a sharp turn and came straight in his direction.

The engine sputtered and died. Seemingly in no hurry to do much else, the man kept his seat and gazed at Willy. Finally, he spoke, saying good morning.

"Mornin to you," Willy said.

"Saw your fire last night, but was too tarred to drive out," the man said.

The man didn't sound like a Texan, and he didn't seem a threat. He guessed the man to be in his sixties. He wore a sweat-stained straw hat pulled down so that his eyebrows were barely visible under the brim. His dark beard was recently trimmed and graying at the chin. Willy eased the blanket off as best he could without revealing the rifle and stood.

"Whatcha got inside my blanket?" the man said.

"Nothin of interest."

"I see. You intend on keepin my blanket?"

"I was cold from the damp."

"Had us some rain, more 'an I seen in a long while. I got hopes'a bringin in some alfalfa. Yessir."

"It's a saddle gun," Willy said.

"I knowed what it were."

"Didn't mean to steal your blanket, mister."

The man looked at the saddle and the saddlebags and studied Willy's ragged condition. Willy's eyes followed the man's.

"Lost my horse."

The man smiled. "I judged that to be the case." He stepped out of the runabout and stood stoop shouldered.

"Don't want no trouble," Willy said. "I'll just move on."

"Son, you look cat scratched and half dead. Bet you ain't et much for a couple of days."

"About that."

"You totin half your weight there. Where you headed anyhow?"

"Home."

"Where'd you come from?"

Willy pointed southward. The man looked over his shoulder and turned back to Willy. His entire face seemed to wrinkle into a grin.

"There's a whole lotta where in that direction. Don't guess you wanna be any kind of specific."

"Mexico."

"'At says a lot. What say I cook you some eggs? You like eggs?"

"Got nothin to pay you with."

"Throw your saddle and gear onto the back and get in."

"You won't take me to the sheriff?"

"Pro'bly what I should do."

Willy gathered up the blanket and gun, then reached down for the saddle. The man stepped forward and eased the saddle from Willy's grip. Then he picked up the scabbard and saddlebags. They laid Willy's belongings in the back, and the man went to the driver's seat, reached under it, and retrieved a crank. He went to the front of the vehicle, ran the socket end of the crank in the socket, then signaled Willy over to join him.

"You know how to turn one of these?"

Willy and Beau had once watched a wildcatter start a Model T. They'd later crept out to the drilling sight, where the car sat parked beside the derrick. Though it took some effort, they got it started and drove away just as a crew of roughnecks came charging out of their tent. A half day later, Beau stalled the vehicle beside a farmer's fence, where it sat until the farmer appeared, and the boys sold it to him for twelve dollars silver, then told him it was stolen.

"I got some experience, yes."

"Good. You crank it, but be careful. It can whip back on you pretty hard."

It took three tries before the engine came to life. Willy handed the crank to the man and climbed into the seat beside him.

"Name's Jessip," the man said, offering Willy his hand. "Walter Jessip."

"Willy. Willy Bobbins."

"Odd name."

"Ain't nothin odd about Willy."

"No, no. Bobbins. Ain't never met one before."

"Guess now you have."

Walter fried Willy bacon and four eggs and served them to him with coffee. He set a loaf of bread on the table, laid a knife beside it, and poured himself a cup of coffee.

"Already et myself," he said. "Bread's the best I can do. My wife, she did bake some. Her bread, well, it could'a won prizes. Never did. She wasn't that kind."

Willy nodded and cut off a slice of bread, which he devoured with a bite of egg and chased that down with coffee. Then he repeated the whole process a few more times as Walter sipped coffee and made talk.

"Been alone since my boy went off and joined Mr. Wilson's army. 'Bout your age, give a year or two. Started shavin at thirteen, so he always looked older. My wife used to say he wasn't boy long enough."

Willy nodded. "Bread's just fine."

"'At's 'cause you're near starved, Bobbins."

"'At's the truth."

"If you wasn't in no hurry to get home, I could use help here. I'm getting old and didn't expect no second or third cuttin of hay, but looks like the rain fixed that idea. I'd pay."

"I got family."

"Yep, I figured as much. How'd you come to get yourself in this fix, no horse and all?"

Willy swallowed a bite and considered how to answer the question. He wiped his mouth with the back of his hand. "She drowned."

"Got to be more to that story, son."

Willy shook his head.

"Get's lonely here. Boy gone. Wife dead five years now. Good woman, best ever, I'd say. We come here from Georgia the year before she died. Left ever'thing we owned behind, what didn't burn in the fire, I mean. Come in that vehicle. Had me a feed and dry-goods store. Say, you feelin any better?"

Willy nodded, sensing the man wanted to talk, and listening to him seemed poor payment for the kindness Walter was showing. "So you had a bidness?"

"Yep. Family lived there three generations. My pa started the store. His pa and uncle come back from the war, you know, North–South. Pa died young. So'd his pa. Outlived them both and my mother too."

"Why'd you leave?"

"The fire, son."

Willy gazed at Walter, who seemed lost in a sad history of his own. Willy looked about the kitchen, everything neat and clean, curtains freshly washed and ironed, the walls wallpapered, the hardwood floor swept, the chrome handle on the coal stove's oven polished. It seemed a woman's kitchen, one his ma might keep, only nicer.

"You got someone takes care of the house?"

Walter looked up from his reverie. "You're lookin at 'im."

"I'll clean up after myself," Willy said.

Walter nodded twice and looked away. "You can keep the blanket." He pushed his seat back and stood. "I can drive you up to town if you're goin north. That'll save some walkin."

"I appreciate that. Appreciate everythin you done."

"You can leave the dishes. You've been a good guest."

Walter put what remained of the bread in a seed sack, along with some smoked jerky, and handed the sack to Willy. "It'll provision you some on your way."

They drove a dirt rode north, neither talking for a time. They came to a turn in the road where a few shorthorn were lying. Walter honked at them, but the steers didn't budge. Willy climbed out, removed his hat, and flailed the air with it as he advanced on the animals. Within seconds he hazed the last one to the roadside and climbed back in beside Walter. Walter put the car in gear and engaged the clutch. The runabout jerked forward and settled the next instant. Willy looked back at the cattle. They'd returned to the road, lying in the middle as before.

"Klan burned us out." Walter looked at Willy. "Know what they are?"

Willy nodded.

Walter shifted into second, then third, and set his back against the seat. He sighed.

"Come in the night the day I hid Jimmers. Bunch showed up at the store dressed in them sheets head to toe. May's well come in naked. Hell, I knowed 'em. Asked where Jimmers was. Said I didn't know. He was a good boy, worked his tail off. And he was more Christian 'an any a them.

"Deputy sheriff was one of 'em. Matthew Lowe said Jimmers had been with a white woman and they intended it not happen again. That's what they allus said. I'd got word they was lookin for 'im, so I done locked him in the storage room and I wouldn't give up the key. They was ready to lynch him and me to the same tree, but three farmers came in and . . ."

Walter removed his hat and ran his fingers through his thinning hair. "They found Jimmers later that night. Sad end. Two nights later, my wife shook me awake and said someone was outside. I heard a man, knew the voice belonged to Matthew, shout, 'Nigger lover.' We smelled coal oil smoke and saw flames runnin across the porch my granddaddy built with his own two hands."

Willy considered his own worries, not knowing what had happened to his own pa, his ma at home with a baby she was breast-feeding, no horse and no work. He sought something to say, some expression of his own recent understanding of the world, but he had no words to fit his thoughts or his feelings, much less to offer his condolence for this kind stranger.

"It was meanness," Walter said. "We got my son and ran out the back way, then I had to hold my wife from goin back in for her family Bible, names of six generation writ in it. She never got over that. Even when she come down with the consumption and was ready to pass on, it was that Bible in her thoughts.

"You know why I'm tellin you this?"

"No sir."

"Well, neither do I. Guess it was just in me for too long."

Walter drove another fifteen miles beyond the town and let Willy out beside the road. Willy gathered his gear and set it on the ground. He shook the man's hand and said that if he could, he would have stayed and worked for him.

SIX DAYS LATER Willy appeared on the crest that sloped toward the Bobbins' house. Nell, feeding chickens, saw him approach, bent under the weight of his load. She ran to meet him, but as she came close, she slowed to a stop and watched him shuffle past. His lips were cracked and white. His eyes looked right through her, but didn't speak. When she reached to help with the saddle, he stepped away, the weight of his load nearly pulling him over. He staggered several steps before gaining his balance.

"Willy, what happened?" She placed her hands on her hips and watched. "Where's Pa? Where's Lucy? Willy . . ."

He walked on. By then Beau was running to help, Hazel and Anne not far behind. They shouted, their voices shrill and emphatic. But Willy heard only a hum in his head telling him to keep moving. Beau yanked the saddle away. Willy grinned mindlessly and threw a feeble punch in Beau's direction, then fell to the ground.

Nell looked at his bare feet. "You're bleedin."

He squinted up at her. His mouth moved, but he couldn't talk.

"Got hisself a fever," Nell said.

Willy's eyes rolled upward. He didn't know any longer who he was or where he'd been, didn't remember a moment of it, not even walking through the center of Bedloe during a windstorm with a pack of dogs nipping at his bare heels.

5   They heard a horse approach. Beau said it might be their pa. Willy said, "I doubt it," and went to the window to peek through the curtains.

"It's the sheriff."

Beau looked at Willy, then at Ruth. "I-I, uh, ain't da-did nuh-nothin."

"'At's an amazin thing in itself," Ruth said.

Glen Fellows knocked at the door. Ruth glanced at Willy, then at the door. Willy signaled to Beau, who walked slowly to the door. Ruth pulled baby Sean from her nipple, quickly dried herself, and buttoned her dress. A second knock came. Beau waited until Ruth nodded to him, then opened the door and stepped aside.

The sheriff stood at the threshold and filled much of the door frame. He touched the brim of his hat and removed it. "Mornin, Ruth. Willy, Beau."

Willy nodded and let his mother do the talking.

"Come in and set yourself down, Glen."

"Thank you."

Ruth held the infant on her shoulder and patted his back. The sheriff bent under the crown of the door and entered. The planks creaked under his weight as he crossed the room to the table. Slack jawed, generally amiable, Glen Fellows was the tallest man in the county by half a head, and if not for Tim Hoover, who weighed more than the scales at Furrow's Dry Goods could measure, he would have been the heaviest. He turned the chair around and sat facing her.

"Ain't got nothin much to offer, Glen, 'cept water."

"I'm fine, but I'd like to water my horse 'fore I leave."

"If you want, one of the boys'll do it."

"'At's fine, Ruth. I hear tell your man's missin."

"Seems so, Glen. Been missin more 'an a few times." Ruth held Sean up for the sheriff to admire. "Baby looks more like him 'an he does me."

"Gettin big."

"Yep. Clay went away on bidness and ain't returned. He'll make it home awright."

"Maybe. How old's he?" The sheriff aimed a finger at the baby and wiggled it.

"Gittin teeth. Gonna be needin a goat or milk cow soon, 'fore he tears me up. That's what Willy did. Ruint me for near a year."

Willy glanced at his mother. She paid him no mind. Willy knew she'd long since accepted the hard ways of her life, had endured the downside of Clay's reckless ventures and gambling, and over a span of twenty years she'd borne three daughters and two sons who'd lived and five others who'd died at birth or within days of it. She relied on prayer to carry her through her days.

His mother's Catholic God didn't seem much concerned about storms or drought or the whimsy of nature or the plight of men. It appeared to Willy that to be a Texan meant also to be godly in some way. Though he'd tried to believe otherwise, he considered church a place where the pious went to demonstrate their piety, where women traded gossip and recipes, men arranged business matters, boys and girls mingled with the approval of parents, Catholics mixed with Catholics, and Methodists and Baptist did likewise. For him, attending had been about kneeling until his knees ached and feeling saddened when the tray was passed because every coin that went into it could have gone to putting food on a table or clothes on a child. Despite his ma's pleadings, he'd stopped attending services because he came to believe that the god of luck and not the God of a church was the final arbiter of outcomes.

Fellows set his hat on the table. "I was talkin to Panther Jack. Says it might take some money to straighten up Clay's bidness."

Ruth stared at the floor. "Got no money, Glen. Weren't for the lazy hens givin up an egg or two and Willy and Beau doin chores for Josh Lake, we wouldn't have food on the table."

Fellows looked at Willy and winked. "You got Willy. Enterprisin as any 'round here."

Willy leaned on the window ledge and stared at the ceiling, his arms crossed as if to shut out the conversation.

"'At's a fact, Glen. Him and Beau both. Two wildfires." She held the baby to her and looked in the direction of the door where Beau stood, whistling off-key. "Willy lost his horse somehow. Got no way to be enterprisin."

Fellows looked at Willy. "'S'at true?"

Willy pictured Lucy bloated, bluebottles swarming her. "True enough."

The sheriff turned his attention back to Ruth. "'Spose somethin could be arranged to get a horse under him for a while."

"We need two," Willy said. As Willy had long suspected, the sheriff's interest indicated that he was involved in some measure with Panther Jack and the Mexican beeves. Willy and Beau exchanged knowing looks.

"You know Clay and Panther Jack served in Cuba. Jack's got a fondness for him and his family, 'specially the boys here." Fellows glanced over his shoulder. "Maybe two horses, Willy. Not the best, mind you."

"How much money we be needin?" Ruth said.

He clicked his tongue. "Depends on who the money goes to. Some say Clay's bidness involved a revolver what belong to another fella. And they's politics ever'where. Gotta be a crazy sumbitch to do bidness in Mexico. Pardon the language." Fellows paused, his dark eyes blinking as he looked first at Willy, then at Beau. He scratched his cheek, then said, "Best if you let me talk to Willy 'bout matters. Man to man."

Ruth nodded. Sean began crying. She touched the baby's diaper and smiled. "Prob'ly best. 'Sides, Sean here forgot his manners."

Fellows excused himself and stood. At the door, he motioned for the boys to follow. Willy, still moving gingerly six days after his long journey on foot, stepped out, Beau shuffling along a step behind, his bad foot scraping half-moons in the ground. Chickens scattered indignantly and scratched at the ground. The boys trailed the sheriff to what was once a cotton field but the family now called Clay's weed field.

The sheriff stopped near the gate and propped a foot up on a fence rail. The field, cleared and planted by Willy's grandfather, served as a holding pen for cattle before Clay drove them to the Corcoran stockyard. Fellows lit his pipe and puffed furiously. He looked out over the field.

"Where's the sisters, Willy?"

"Workin over to the Sparks place. Got hisself a crop of early melon. Guess the rain comin saved him. Says he'll pay 'em when he's sold the crop."

"That Nell's a looker. How old is she now?"

"Nineteen. Be twenty by Christmas." Willy eyed the field where butterfly weed and corn cockle grew fence high. In spots an obstinate cotton plant still sprouted, its stem brittle and fiberless. He wondered how the track would look planted.

"She walked all the way to Bedloe to tell me 'bout you and Clay goin missin. I told her folks saw you and spoke to you, but you just kept awalkin. I figure Ruth sent Nell in." Fellows lifted his foot off the rung. "That's a long walk into Bedloe."

"Went on her own. Went to see you, Sheriff," Willy said, lying. He thought about his own journey, eighty miles over dirt and rock with the saddle on his shoulder and the Marlin in hand. He'd been turned away twice when he'd asked for food at farmhouses and had moved on, his feet bleeding, but he'd found goodness in two strangers and for that he was grateful.

"How'd you get that?" Fellows pointed at the nearly healed injury on Willy's chin.

"Fell maybe. Maybe a horse did it. What's it you want to talk about?"

"I'll get to it. Your pa and me got us a deal," Fellows began, then altered his tone. "Ain't the kind to be askin what happened down there, but seems you owe it to your kin to go get him. 'Course if you wanna tell what happened, I'll listen."

Willy had rustled cattle and witnessed a man die, had seen what remained of those who'd been executed. Death seemed to him a shameful end, at least what he'd seen of it. Leery of saying too much, he regarded the sheriff a moment. Better, he thought, to ask a question than answer one. "What kind'a deal, sheriff?"

The sheriff puffed his pipe and gazed off. "Well, we should talk plain. What 'bout Beau? Should he be listenin?"

"Bobbins don't talk on Bobbins, and it's hard to get a word out of him anyhow. Ain't that true?" Willy looked at Beau, who nodded.

Fellows turned around, rested an arm on the fence, and leaned on it. Willy was about to tell him not to do that, but the fence collapsed first. The sheriff landed on his back, lost his hat, and spat his pipe into the air. He rolled over onto his hands and knees, cursing as he stood. He slapped at his shirt where a pipe cinder singed the fabric. After he'd extinguished the smolders, he gathered up his hat. "Gawdamn, you people could get someone kilt!"

Willy motioned to Beau. "Pa kept sayin he was gonna fix that fence. That right, Beau?"

Beau nodded.

Fellows looked at the singed hole in his shirt, then bent over and picked up his pipe. "Clay owes me a new shirt." He brushed himself off. "Your pa brings stock through." He looked at Willy as he reloaded tobacco in the pipe bowl and pressed it down. "What I'm sayin is I know Clay's bidness. Them steers would just go on ships outta Veracruz to feed the kaiser's army. Your pa and Jack, they's helping the country. It's war over there in France."

Willy knew the sole reason for stealing livestock from south of the border was both the shortage of Texas cattle brought on by the drought and a high demand for beef by the government. "Don't know nothin about France. It's just a word."

"Gettin them beeves to the stockyard is money in your pocket. That plain talk enough?"

"Plain enough."

"Hell, Willy, we got a dozen boys from around here in uniform, and they gotta be fed. Maybe some of them Mexican beeves'll feed a few."

"I guess some might say 'at's reason enough to do what Pa done. Got hisself caught or worse, though, goin after them cows. 'At's a bit crazy. Way I see it anyhow."

"These times a man's gotta be crazy," Fellows struck a match on his dungarees, fired his pipe, and blew smoke in the air, "to go borrowin Mexican beeves."

"You got a stake in this, Sheriff?"

"Your pa says you're too smart for your own good, Willy. Which ain't somethin said about him too often." Fellows paused, as if to determine whether his flattery had an effect.

Willy showed little reaction to the remark. He stared up at the towering sheriff, scuffed the ground up with the toe of his boot, and said, "Funny to hear that 'cause he's been tellin me for years how dumb I am. Might be some folks here don't want Pa back."

"Might be you don't, but your ma does." Fellows put on his hat and looked Willy up and down. "Get ahold'a Panther Jack and work it out. He's willin to accommodate you 'til you get your pa back. Say, don't your cousin ever talk?"

"Not much. And he's the same as a brother." Willy looked at Beau, who shrugged and picked up a rock that he heaved into the field. "Sheriff, what you get from this?"

Fellows held the pipe between his teeth and narrowed his eyes on Willy. When he spoke, he seemed to squeeze the words out of his clenched teeth. "I get one dollar every head. Call it a commission."

Beau picked up another stone, but held it. "Wuh, wuh, what you duh, do for this duh, dollar?" He chucked the rock into the field.

"How old are you, boy?"

Beau spit and scratched a circle in the dirt with the toe of his boot. "Fuh, fuh, fourteen."

"No you ain't. You're thirteen." The sheriff's pipe had gone out. He struck a match on his trousers, relit it, and waited until the smoke brewed. "Here's what I do. I make sure you don't see things through bars." He puffed on the pipe. "Willy, that Nell, she sweet on anyone?"

"'Bout that commission, Sheriff. I heard of someone gettin commission off Panther Jack and Pa sellin horses," Willy said. "Is that sort of how yours is, Sheriff? You sellin 'em?"

"Might say I'm sort'a involved. You know, I was kind'a thinkin I'd come out an see if I could help your ma out an maybe Nell. Could I maybe swing an invite to dinner?"

Beau picked up another stone.

Willy grinned. "Beau, don't be throwin rocks in Pa's field. You know how particular he is about it. Hell, he's gonna plant it in some future hunert years."

Beau chucked the rock into the field and said, "Suh-same ta-time as he fuh-fixes the fuh-fence, wuh-wah-which'll buh-be nuh-never."

Fellows smiled at Willy. "Most I ever heard the boy talk. Well, Willy, what about that invite?"

Willy picked up a rock and tossed it in the field, then looked the sheriff in the eye. "Come out on a Sunday. Bring a chicken with you."

"Okay, then, we got us a deal?" Fellows said, offering his hand to shake.

Willy shook the sheriff's hand. "I pay for Pa only if Ma says she wants 'im back."

"Fair enough."

"Got me another question," Willy said.

"Go ahead."

"Why didn't you take this bidness to Bobby Grimes?"

"Same reason I'd rather have a dog than a polecat. 'Sides, that boy and his fool friends ain't got the steel in them to cross that border. My horse needs a drink, and I'll be off 'til Sunday. I be here, chicken in hand."

After Fellows watered his horse, he told Willy to see Panther Jack about the loan of two horses. He mounted and circled once. "And get that fence fixed or put a sign up 'til the thing's safe."

"Can't write," Willy said. "'Sides, who comes 'round here what can read, but you, Panther Jack, and the tax man?"

Fellows shook his head and spurred his horse to a canter.

Willy watched him ride off. "Damn sure wouldn't wanna be that horse," he said, then motioned for Beau to follow.

Ruth sat at the table, cleaning the baby. "You get some bidness done, Willy?"

"Ma, do you want him back?"

Her eyes narrowed on him. "He's your pa."

"Yes'm, but do you *want* him?"

She bowed her head in thought or prayer, closed her eyes, and nodded.

"Well," Willy said to Beau, "guess we're goin in bidness."

Willy motioned Beau outside, where they sat on the step. He plucked a stem from a clump of grass and sucked on the sweet tip, then held the stem in his teeth.

"Boy," he said, "look at the mess we got us. Someday it'll be different. You and me'll turn this into the kind'a spread our grandpa intended. Hunert, no, two hunert head, cotton, and a few acres of alfalfa, some corn, and sweet potatoes."

Willy felt he'd be content riding his own herd beside Beau and providing for his ma, his sisters, and Sean. It was a dream easy to embrace, mostly because it seemed possible.

"Would you like that?" he asked.

Beau plucked himself a stem of grass and said, "I luh, luh, like suh sweet potatoes." He fell silent as he chewed on the stem.

PANTHER JACK called himself a horse trader, though that was a small portion of his activity. He'd been a fixture in the community since five years after his service in Cuba during the war with Spain, where he and Clay had met. Since the recession of '11 and '12 when banks tightfisted their loan policies, he'd been considered a sort of public necessity. Though they begrudged doing so, when farmers could no longer take out loans from a bank, they turned to Panther Jack. An outsider to Bedloe, he was nonetheless astute in the ways of the inhabitants, living in humble circumstances so as not to draw attention to his success. His sole concession to his wealth, rumored to be considerable, was his gold watch. Farmers and ranchers and thieves respected him for not flaunting his money, but their respect ended there. A hard man when it came to collecting debts, he'd foreclosed on at least six families who'd lost some or all of their land to him, and since the six-year drought he'd come to hold several more deeds.

He sat under a walnut tree, drinking cider and tequila out of a tin cup. A gaunt, bearded man who looked more like a Hindu ascetic than a hard businessman, he carried a leather-bound ledger in his saddlebags that contained the record of every debt owed him, the book a duplicate of another ledger he was rumored to keep hidden. He was forty and hadn't cut his hair since leaving Cuba at age twenty. All that stopped his braids from touching the ground when he stood were the two-inch heels of his boots. He motioned for Willy and Beau to join him the shade.

They sat cross-legged on the cool earth. A few dozen squawking chickens bobbed about, pecking tidbits from the ground. Panther Jack remained silent, occasionally throwing down a swallow from his cup. Willy and Beau waited for Panther Jack to initiate the conversation. Panther Jack drank the last of his liquor and looked at the boys. "Long walk, huh?"

"Long enough," Willy said.

"Hot too."

"Yep, hot," Willy agreed.

"Been 'spectin you. Guess we should talk about your pa."

Assuring Willy and Beau that Clay was safe in jail in Coahuila, Panther Jack pointed out that timeliness would be essential to freeing him because if he went before a judge, the price would end up being far more than a man such as Clay was worth. "I'd pay it up, but your pa has a obligation, which is forever in arrears, but I guess you knew that."

Willy glanced at Beau. "Can't say as I did."

"Well, I got books on him. Seein as we go back, Rough Riders and all, served under Roosevelt and Pershing, well, I don't push it. Wouldn't be right tossin your ma out, her with a baby. Nope, I ain't that kind."

Willy stared at Panther Jack until the older man looked away.

Panther Jack cleared his throat. "I can show you in the book. Clay trusts my numbers."

As Panther Jack talked, Lisette, his woman, emerged from the door of the cottage. Willy had seen her sporadically at a distance, never close. She wore a black shift that molded itself to her smooth hips, and as she walked to the water pump, she seemed to glide over the ground without touching a foot to it. When she bent over to pump the handle, she gazed back at Willy, who stared at her backside. When he saw that she was looking at him, Willy's cheeks flushed and his throat went dry, but she held his gaze.

A coffee-skinned girl of ten when Panther Jack had brought her back from one of his wanderings in the Caribbean, she was the talk of the county gossips. She had large magnetic eyes and high cheekbones. On the rare occasions she spoke, she did so with a King's English accent, which, along with her regal posture, offended the ladies of Bedloe, women who didn't approve of dark skin, but especially on a woman who slept with a white man too many of their husbands were in debt to.

She pumped the well handle and watched the conversation with the wariness of a feral cat. To Willy's mind, she seemed curious about him. Maybe, he thought, she got lonely living with an old man, a peculiar one at that. Panther Jack noticed Willy's eyes stray and looked over his shoulder. He took out his gold watch, snapped open the face, and held the timepiece at arm's length. Willy nailed his gaze on the gold watch. He envied not the watch, but what it symbolized—money, attention, and now the dusky-skinned woman.

Panther Jack squinted, closed the face, and cleared his throat. "You boys can eat with me. We'll discuss what needs doin then."

The two-room cottage was cramped and the air so rank with the smell of burning lignite and fried tortillas it made Willy's eyes water. Lisette set a pot of beans in the center of the table. Panther Jack stuffed the next load of tortillas and beans in his mouth before finishing the previous mouthful. The only thing that slowed him was his considerable belching. It was hard for Willy to imagine, with an appetite like the one Panther Jack displayed, how he remained so gaunt. The woman lingered nearby, refilling bowls when they were empty and lingering longer than necessary as she ladled fresh beans on Willy's plate. When her breath grazed his neck, he felt a shiver run down his back. Several times he looked in her direction and found her looking back. Panther Jack seemed too intent on his food to notice anything but his bowl.

After his last spoonful, Panther Jack belched and downed a tall glass of water without stopping. He wiped his mouth on his sleeve, looked at Willy, and said, "Fine-lookin woman, Willy. Don't get no ideas," then immediately began to talk business. He explained that he knew a certain Mexican colonel in Piedras Negras who might provide assistance at the right price.

Lisette leaned over the coal stove as she ate. She had yet to speak a word. Now Willy tried not to notice, but his eyes seemed willed to look at her.

"They gettin funny with the war an all. Whoever's runnin things one day is in a grave the next. They's a word for it, *instability*. Thing is, Mexican cows get a good dollar from German buyers, so them *patronos* is gettin impatient. On my own, I wouldn't give two dollar for one on my table. 'At's why you see heifers ever'where and less and less longhorns in Texas." He held up his hand, then opened his mouth and removed his Sears & Roebuck dentures. "Can't eat much beef with these." He grinned at the boys, tossed the dentures on the stove next to Lisette, and told her to give them a good scrub. She pushed the dentures away with her long fingernails and wiped the back of her hand down her dress. Panther Jack merely chuckled.

"We come 'cause the sheriff said you'd put us on horses," Willy said.

Panther Jack looked the two boys over. "So, you and your cousin partnered up?"

Willy glanced at Beau, still spooning beans. Although Beau was the son of Clay's dead brother, the boys had been reared as brothers. "Me and my brother," Willy said.

"Brother then. What I meant is, are you gonna work together?"

Willy meant more than relatives and more than partners, maybe even more than brothers. Clay brought Beau home after Emit Bobbins and his wife were killed during a storm when their wagon went over a bridge railing. Ruth reared Beau as if a son, but Clay often treated him as an intruder. Although Willy and Beau had fought regularly from the time Beau turned three until he turned twelve, they'd otherwise shown a unified face to Clay and outsiders. Beau took bruises stoically. One particularly bloody scrape occurred when some men who'd come to see cockfights said they'd prefer to bet on the boys. Clay had ordered them to strip to the waist and go at each other. An audience of thirty screamed for one favorite or the other, but as the fight wore on, even the more calloused among them asked Clay to put a stop to it.

In a dispute over a bone-handled jackknife they'd purloined from Ebbin's Livery and Dry Goods, Willy had held Beau's face in the dirt and ordered him to cry, but Beau refused. Eventually, Willy released him. Spitting blood and dirt, Beau had stood with clenched fists and demanded the knife. Willy knew it was futile to go on fighting, that it wasn't about the knife, but about something too important to be stated. He handed him the knife. The next time Clay ordered them to fight, Willy refused and took a whipping, and Beau insisted on being whipped as well.

"How you intend to make it worth my while to give you the loan of two horses?"

"Same as Pa," Willy said and suddenly realized he was speaking to get Lisette's attention as much as he was to address Panther Jack.

"You're a mite young for this bidness," Panther Jack said. "But I believe you can do it, so I'll loan you two geldings. Lose 'em, you pay. Keep 'em, you pay. I won't put it on my books otherwise. 'S'at fair enough?" He belched. "Say, Willy, does Beau ever talk?"

"When he's hungry." Willy snatched a peek at Lisette, who stood in profile by the window. Otherwise occupied, she seemed to pay no attention. "How much to get Pa home?"

"More 'an a hunert, boy," Panther Jack said.

"How much more?"

"Hunert an twenty-five, maybe thirty-five."

Willy whistled at the figure and shook his head. "Seems a mite much for Pa. Ain't no one 'sides Ma wants him back." He looked at Beau, who affirmed the remark with a nod. "So, how much you get?"

"Can't take time away from other stuff for nothin."

Beau's face turned red and seemed to wrinkle into a ball of yarn. "Huh, huh, how many puh, puh, people 'round here's guh, gettin a cuh, cuh, commission?"

"I'll be dogged. He does talk. Sort of." A ball of saliva drooled down his chin as Panther Jack laughed at his own remark. He wiped away the spittle with his sleeve, then leaned back and looked at Beau. "You pay for help, boy. 'At's the way of the world."

Beau grunted his disapproval.

Panther Jack turned back to Willy. "Now, Mexican steers is bringin seven or eight dollar a head at the stockyard. Three dollars to you for each head, half-dollar more if you drive 'em to the pens south of Corcoran for me. You don't wanna do it, Bobby Grimes an his fellas'll pick 'em up at your place and move 'em. I'll make out a bill a sale, and I got a fella what'll certify 'em. More you can bring acrosst at once, faster we can get your pa free."

Willy didn't like the figures. "How come me and Beau pay Glen Fellows a dollar a cow?"

"Fellows is the law, Willy. You want the law on your side. As for the rest, ain't like you got a crop waitin to harvest or a bunch of brahma studs. Now, when you hard bidnessmen decide to do bidness with me, go down to Harvey's livery, where I got six horses. Leave the roan. Take two on loan, or they's yours for thirty dollar apiece, which I'll put in the book at five percent."

"Seems like they's too much percent to you already." Willy addressed Panther Jack, but his eye was on Lisette. Some stories had her being eighteen, others as old as twenty-five or as young as fifteen. Willy wasn't sure old she was and couldn't judge, except that she was too young for Panther Jack.

"Well, what you gonna do?" Panther Jack asked.

Willy looked at Beau, who nodded. "Okay, me an Beau'll do it, but I pay the Mexicans for Pa, not you."

Panther Jack laughed. When he stopped, he brandished one of his five-foot-long braids and stared at it. "A woman betrayed Sampson. She cut his hair, causin him to lose his strength. For money. My advice, boy? Keep your hair, don't trust no woman, and be a seller, not a buyer. Those Mexicans own your pa. You pay for him, who owns him then?"

Willy nodded. Panther Jack said their business was finished and it was time for the boys to leave because he and his woman needed a siesta. As he stepped into the light, Willy took a last look at Lisette, at the firm roundness of her buttocks and dusky smooth skin of her strong arms and wondered if she'd sever the braids from Panther Jack's head. She wiped her hands down the back of her dress and offered him not a smile exactly, but something similar.

OLD LOPEZ'S SHACK sat two miles south of Bedloe on the fringes of a community the Anglos called Adobe Town. He emerged from inside, sat on the rocker beside the potbellied stove on his porch, and waited as the boys reined their horses on the narrow path between his corn and bean fields. He waved when they turned the corner of the corn field. Willy dismounted and tied his mount to the hitching post.

Beau sat his mount and spurred his horse closer to Willy. "Uh, uh, I'll tuh, talk out here, but I ain't goin in. I know wuh, wuh, what's in there."

"You scared of an ol man?"

"I'm suh-scared a havin muh-my suh-soul buh-be ruh-removed."

"You been listenin to foolishness."

"Ain't nuh-neither. Huh-heard Muh-Ma tuh-tell Buh-Beth he sus-sucked the sps-sps-spirit ruh-right out of a wuh-woman once."

Old Lopez stood and hollered, "*Hola*, Willito *y* Beau Boy. *Bienvenidos.*"

"*Cómo está*, Mago?" Willy walked over and shook the old man's hand.

"*Bien, bien, gracias.* The boy, he don't get down?"

Willy said. "Beau, say somethin to Mr. Lopez."

"Cuh-corn's high," Beau said.

"He's being Beau strange. 'At's 'bout all you'll get from him today," Willy said. "I come 'cause a Pa. Well . . ."

"He not believe."

"Maybe now he does. Them stones you read, what else did they tell you?"

The old man stood from his rocker. "*Ven,* Willito. Come inside."

Willy followed the old man into the one-room shack. Light pierced the cracks in the walls. Half-burned logs left from the last spring's frost lay in the stone fireplace. The smell of herbs and charred wood and old-man sweat pervaded the air. Save for the shelves that held jars of medicinal herbs, a cot in the corner, and a table with one chair, there was no furniture. Lopez sat on the floor near the center of the room and crossed his legs. He signaled for Willy to take a seat with his back to the door and facing him.

Willy sank to the floor and crossed his ankles. "Can you tell me where Pa is?"

The old man looked up at the ceiling. "No, *pero él vive.*"

"Alive? You're sure."

Old Lopez nodded. "Waiting. Alive. It happen as I tol him, no?"

"Yes." Willy said, then got to the point of his visit. "I been thinkin. Can you roll the stones for me?"

The old man shook his head.

"I got money comin. I can pay later. Hell, me and Beau'll help with the fields if you want."

Again the *mago* shook his head.

"Why not? Hell, I'm offerin more 'an Pa paid."

"I cannot, Willito. No more because I rolled them for you when you were born."

"You did?"

He nodded. "Your grandmother, bless the good woman, brought you, laid you where you sit. I rolled them. *Los huesos revelan toda la futura de los bebés. ¿Entiendes?*"

"Kind'a understand. What'd you see?"

"Not so good to know. Is better to live."

Willy glanced over his shoulder at where the light came from. The sky was clear, and he could see the tree line on a hill a mile to the east where the Dixons raised a modest-size herd of Herefords. He wanted to know if someday he'd have his own ranch. He looked at the old man.

"How old are you?" he asked.

He told them he was a boy when the Alamo fell and when Antonio López de Santa Anna was captured. He said that he knew their grandfathers, one a good man, the other one who drank too much.

"Wisht I'd a known 'em. Go ahead and tell me what them stones said."

"Yuh, yuh, you okay in th-there, Willy?" Beau hollered.

"Hell, I'm fine!" Willy shouted. He looked imploringly at Old Lopez. "I'm ready."

Old Lopez closed his eyes and muttered in Spanish, words that came so fast, all but a very few were incomprehensible to Willy. The old man lifted his eyelids and blinked. "You will have money and *muchos amigos* around you. You'll live to be old. *Si, muy viejo.* Children who you will love. You will be restless and ambitious."

Willy smiled. 'At don't sound so bad."

Old Lopez nodded. "*Estás joven*, Willy. Is good to be young."

Willy hesitated. "They's somethin else, ain't there?"

"No."

"Yes. You ain't no poker player, Mago."

"You no want to know."

"I do. You saw it, you're obliged to tell me."

"*¿Estoy obligodo*, eh?" The old man shook his head. "*Bueno* . . . You will love in pain and be unfulfilled. You will die in sadness."

The *mago* rose and motioned for Willy to do likewise. "*Por favor.*"

Willy stood, still facing the seer. "What sadness?"

Old Lopez laid a hand gently on Willy's shoulder, looked him in the eye, and said slowly in Spanish, so that Willy would grasp the whole meaning, that happiness is a bed the young lie in comfortably, but one day they wake up and leave it reluctantly.

Willy thought about this for a moment, then said, "You're old. Are you unhappy?"

"An old man's fate is not happiness." He shook Willy's hand. "*Vaya con Dios*, Willy."

"*Y usted tambien, Señor. Muchas gracias.*"

He walked Willy to the door and followed him out. He patted Willy's shoulder and let his hand rest there a moment. He assured him once again that Clay was waiting. His hand slid from Willy's shoulder.

Willy mounted his horse and waved back at Old Lopez as he and Beau turned toward the trail home.

"What'd he say, Willy?"

"Nothin much. Just said Pa's alive. I got us an idea."

"Whu-whu-what idea?"

"We ain't goin for beeves the way Pa tried. Near's I see, he done it all wrong. They's plenty a longhorn in the low ranges in small herds. No one to watch over 'em. We can round us up some. One day in. One out. I saw a slew comin back. *Vámanos.*"

Willy spurred his horse at the turn, leaned forward in the saddle, and slapped the horse with his hat.

6 Under the rising September moon, the dry flats below the bluffs appeared as barren as the hopes of a discarded lover. Willy stood on the side of the trail beneath a Chinese elm where he'd tethered his horse. He measured the sound of the hoof beats approaching from down the trail. When the riders rounded the last curve, he retreated into the brush and held the Marlin at the ready. The riders slowed their mounts to a walk. Willy, assured of their identity, stepped out of the shadows and called to them.

Beau dismounted first. Panther Jack hesitated, then climbed down from his mount and said, "Goddamn, Willy, this here's not our arrangement. You and I agreed you was to bring them to where your pa did and we'd count and pay then."

Although the arrangement had been laid out clearly, it seemed strapped together in Panther Jack's favor, and Willy didn't like the way it buckled up. "I ain't my pa. Walk on over."

Beau and Panther Jack led their horses the last few feet.

"We won't need the horses. Beau'll stay with 'em."

Beau took the reins from Panther Jack and hobbled the animals beside Willy's horse. Willy handed him the Marlin.

"Anyone comes, use it to scare 'em off. Or shoot 'em if need be."

Beau nodded.

Panther Jack spat out a plug of snuff and surveyed his surroundings. "This ain't how it's done, Willy. Clay kept the cows in his field where I could see 'em. Don't see none here. How many you bring?"

"How many, Beau?"

Beau sneezed before answering. "Muh-more 'an Clay ever did."

"I don't pay 'til I see the numbers." Panther Jack looked from one brother to the next. Neither showed any indication of speaking. "Fine, then. Where are they?"

"Over there. Half a mile maybe." Willy pointed to a divide separating the two nearest bluffs, where the limestone caps glowed pale white in the moonlight.

"Didn't come prepared to hike. Maybe I'll just ride on home. You can bring the steers where we agreed."

"Never agreed to that, Jack. Was just how you said it was gonna be. Tried it that way twice now, so here we are."

Panther Jack looked at his horse, then at Beau, who stood, arms crossed over the rifle he held to his chest. He nodded and said, "Okay. Tonight, but from now on we do it my way. That fair enough?"

Willy pointed west and let that stand as his answer. "Over the other side."

They followed a coarse trail that wove up the wide gulch, neither talking. Night sounds, crickets or a bird taking wing or the occasional slithering lizard, accompanied them.

As the trek lengthened and the incline sharpened, Panther Jack said, "It ain't necessary me walkin all this way. And why don't you trust me?"

Willy didn't answer.

"Could slow down some," Panther Jack said.

Willy kept the same pace.

On the downside, the odor of manure and urine wafted up from below, and the trail steepened. At trail's end the land flattened into a wide box-end gorge. A herd of longhorns, forty-three in all, milled about.

"'At's them," Willy said. "Go on about countin."

Panther Jack surveyed the stock, his lips moving. He counted once, then again, then a third time.

"How much?" Willy asked.

"How much?" Panther Jack repeated. His licked his lips and pulled out his gold pocket watch. His fingers danced back and forth on the face of the watch, then stopped suddenly. He smiled. "You boys done a fine job. Why that comes to pretty near . . . ninety dollar. Remember they's longhorn. Won't bring as much."

"That countin the half dollar for takin 'em to the stockyard?" Willy said.

Panther Jack pocketed his watch and, clearing his throat, renewed his calculating. A few seconds passed before he looked at Willy and said, "Closer to a hunert, I'd say. Let's make it an even hunert. Hell, with what you took in with the other steers, you got more 'an enough to buy your pa back."

"Might just be a waste of money."

Panther Jack started to speak, but the sound of shuffling footsteps distracted him. He looked toward the trail and Beau. "Thought he was watchin the horses."

"Was. Now he's here."

"I don't like this Willy. I'm tellin you I don't do bidness this way."

"You will if you're doin it with me. Beau, you ready?"

Beau cocked the lever of the Marlin and aimed the barrel at one of the steers.

"What you doin, boy?" Panther Jack asked.

Beau pulled the trigger. The blast reported through the narrow wash and across the flats. The steer seemed confused for an instant. Then it bellowed and collapsed under its own dead weight. Panther Jack looked on, stunned.

Willy calmly said, "Pay's ten at three dollars. That's thirty, an they's four'a 'em at thirty. Three steers left over. Now two. 'At comes to one hunert twenty-six. If you try and cheat us a nickel, we'll shoot 'em all. Now, how much for takin 'em to Corcoran?"

"Willy, your figures're off a bunch."

Willy rose up on his toes and stood nose to nose with Panther Jack, who couldn't back away with Beau holding the hot muzzle of the rifle against his ear.

Willy looked Panther Jack in the eyes and said, "Beau, shoot another cow."

Beau lifted the muzzle off Panther Jack's ear and aimed at a second cow.

"That's crazy, boy. Stop. Let's us talk."

Beau shouldered the rifle and waited, his breathing slow.

Panther Jack raised his hands and stepped away. "Awright, a hunert forty-eight dollars at Corcoran stockyards."

"Put the rifle away, Beau," Willy said. "I don't think Panther Jack's got cheatin us in mind. Probably just a mistake he made before. You'll make that right by us now, won't you?"

"Might'a been off. Say fifteen dollars?"

"More like twenty-four."

"Okay, twenty."

"Twenty-four. Can barely read a lick, but I know numbers and I seen you cheat Pa outta his share when you and him was horse tradin. Don't play me or Beau as fools."

Panther Jack looked at the felled steer. "What 'bout the dead one? I ain't payin for no dead cow."

Willy looked over his shoulder at Beau. The two of them chuckled.

"This ain't funny," Panther Jack said.

"Think it's funny stringin us along? No, I'm guessin you don't. That cow, you're givin it to Ma, 'cause she needs to feed a family. You're a charitable man, Panther Jack, and generous with your friends. Ain't that right, Beau?"

Beau grinned.

"Anyhow," Willy said, "Ma'll be glad to hear you thought to give her a steer outta friendship for Pa."

Panther Jack cut an eye at Willy. "You're pretty hard for a boy wet behind the ears."

"I don't know what that means, wet behind the ears, Jack. But I been plenty wet all over, enough so's I know you ain't cheatin me outta one copper Lincoln."

Panther Jack shrugged, took out his bankroll, and began peeling off bills.

Beau slowly released the cocked hammer on the Marlin, then rested the butt of the stock on his hip. "*Al final, todo es nada y nada es todo,*" he said, repeating an expression Old Lopez sometimes used. In the end, everything is nothing and nothing is everything.

7 Willy and Panther Jack reined their mounts to a walk near the end of the dusty road north of where a trellis bridge spanned a deep crevice in one of the more forsaken spots in northern Coahuila. It was mostly rock and sand, not a sign of creosote or even milkweed anywhere. Concerned that the affair might be a trap waiting to be sprung, Willy circled his horse and took in his surroundings, paying careful attention to the ridgeline on the far side of the bridge. Save for a uniformed man standing a few yards away, the area seemed deserted. A southern breeze swirled dust up and blew it across the gap.

Willy knew the risk involved. Nothing in Mexico was certain. And Coahuila, with a history of resistance to federal authority and revolutionaries alike, had its own ways beyond even Mexican custom. He studied the bridge, once built for a narrow-gauge railroad intended to transport silver to the border. Other than claim jumpers, smugglers, and corrupt federales, few knew the bridge existed. The American company that had constructed it had deserted the mine and left Mexico when Zapatistas swarmed into the camp and took the crew hostage. Lacking only the laying of the rails, the bridge was complete, but in disrepair.

A Mexican officer, a young captain and not the colonel Panther Jack had foretold they'd meet, stood stiffly and saluted Willy as he and Panther Jack neared. The officer was sunbaked dark and stout and wore a white starched uniform that gleamed in the midday sun, and above his left breast pocket was a row of bright-colored ribbons. His black boots were polished. Willy thought the officer's appearance a bit foolish, but this was Mexico and the man intended himself to be taken serious.

"I'll go," Willy said to Panther Jack. He dismounted and, holding the Marlin in his left hand, approached the officer and shook his offered hand.

"*Habla usted español?*" the captain asked.

"*Poquito. Habla inlgés?*"

"*Más o menos.*" The officer pointed to the far bank. "Thee matters are feexed. Jou haff thee *dinero?*" He held his hand up and rubbed his fingers against his thumb.

Willy nodded. "I got the money."

Panther Jack dismounted and waited nearby.

Having but one choice, Willy knew he had no choice at all. He had to trust the arrangements Panther Jack had made and that the officer and his men would comply. Though wary, he acted as if this were a routine transaction. As insurance, in case matters soured, Beau lay atop a ridge behind them, armed with an '06 Springfield with a scope, a weapon Panther Jack had recently bought on the black market from an army quartermaster in San Antonio.

The officer blew a whistle. A moment passed, and then, on the opposite side of the defile, two soldiers dressed in khaki uniforms stepped out from behind a partially collapsed storage shed and pushed Clay forward. Blindfolded and manacled, arms behind him, Clay tried to sit, but they lifted him to his feet. His shirt was torn and his jaw bearded. Saliva rolled down from his lips as he cussed and struggled to free himself of their grip. One soldier shoved him onto the bridge and held him steady. A second soldier removed Clay's blindfold and gripped his chin firmly until he looked straight ahead across the bridge. The soldier let go of his chin and wiped his hands as if to rid himself of Clay's foulness.

"'Bout time!" Clay hollered.

The captain removed his hat and wiped sweat from his forehead with a handkerchief. He squinted into the brilliant autumn sky, then replaced the hat and held out his open hand.

Willy loosened the drawstring on a leather pouch containing six ten-dollar and twelve five-dollar gold pieces. He counted the coins as he laid them in the officer's waiting palm. Willy paused at seventy dollars. The captain shook his head. When Willy reached eight-five dollars, he drew the string on the pouch and nodded to the captain, who nodded in return.

The final price, thirty-five less than initially quoted by Panther Jack, satisfied the officer. He signaled for the soldiers to release Clay.

As he slipped the coins in his pocket, the Mexican raised his eyebrows. "No vale la pena, él. Es loco."

"Crazy, but my ma wants him home." Willy's tone sounded more like resignation to the fact than a justification for liberating him.

The soldiers unlocked Clay's manacles. The chain clattered as it slipped to the ground. The taller of the two aimed Clay in the direction where Willy waited and shoved him forward. Both laughed as he stumbled out onto the wooden footing of the span. Unloading a steam of profanities at the soldiers, he grabbed the right-hand rail, stood erect, and glared back at them. They merely laughed at him. One reached down, gathered a stone, and tossed it at him. The stone missed and clattered down the deep chasm.

Clay let fly another string of profanities, then, mustering what dignity he had left, he began his journey across, using the side rail of the trellis for support. The farther he advanced, the more apparent it became that he was limping.

Willy looked at Panther Jack and asked, "You hear what the man here said? He ain't worth it."

Panther Jack spat a stream of tobacco juice on the ground. "Maybe, but it's done."

"Yep, and you'd a had me believin he was worth more. If I'd let you pay, you'd of took the extra money."

"Hard life, Willy. Man's gotta try."

Though the bridge spanned only a hundred feet, Clay stopped several times to muster strength enough to go on.

When his pa reached the middle of the bridge, Willy nodded to the captain and said, "Our bidness is done. Gracias."

Patting the pocket that contained the coins, the officer thanked Willy and walked to the bridge. Clay held onto the guard rail, advancing hand over hand, one slow step at a time. He paused and spat at the Mexican officer as they passed, but missed. The officer laughed and continued on, never looking back.

Clay shook a fist in the air. "I'll be back! Then you'll see."

Willy shouted, "Come on, Pa, 'fore they change their minds!" He looked at Panther Jack. "I should of left 'im."

Clay advanced, his eyes now on Willy. Near the end of his walk, he stopped, stood tall, and flared his nostrils. By then the officer had reached the far side and stood at the abutment with his soldiers. He waved to Willy. As Clay walked the last few paces, Willy saw that he'd not only lost weight, but some teeth.

"Gimme the rifle, boy. Gonna kill me a greaser or two." His breath was rank.

"It was bidness, Pa."

Clay snorted. "Bidness, boy? Don't you see what they did to me?"

Willy just stared at him.

Clay grabbed for the rifle. Willy held it out of his reach and shook his head.

Clay snarled and turned to Panther Jack. "Jack, toss me your rifle."

Willy swung the muzzle of the Marlin in Panther Jack's direction. "Don't dare it."

"Willy's right, Clay," Panther Jack said. "Don't matter none. They's gone anyhow."

Clay looked back at the point of the bridge where the soldiers had stood. Willy asked if he was ready to go, but Clay didn't answer. He'd receded into his mind somewhere as he kept staring across the bridge. Finally, Panther Jack broke Clay's trance. He took a bottle of sour mash out of his saddle-bags, uncapped it, and after taking a swallow offered the bottle to Clay, saying it would cut some bad taste off the day. He handed the bottle to Clay. Clay, at first, didn't seem to know what to do with it.

Willy felt a wave of compassion overtake him. He'd never seen his pa look so forlorn. Clay had always seemed beyond such emotions. Gradually, Clay came to his senses. He took the bottle and drank, then took a second swallow and began coughing. He offered the bottle back, but Panther Jack told him to keep it.

Clay turned to Willy. "What's the matter with you? Ain't nothin wrong with shootin a spic soldier or two, not when they done me this way."

"You're here. 'At's the only concern for now."

Willy slid the Marlin into the scabbard, hooked his boot in a stirrup, and swung a leg over the saddle. Once seated, he looked down at Clay. "Me and Panther Jack got bidness ahead."

Panther Jack mounted his mare.

Clay looked around. Baffled, he squinted up at Willy and pointed a finger at nothing in particular. "Where's my horse?"

"Prob'ly somewhere in Mexico, where you lost it." Willy tossed a canteen, a five-dollar coin, and two silver dollars in the dirt at Clay's feet. "A donkey'll be awaitin for you at the livery in Agonia."

"A donkey."

"All I could afford."

"'At's five miles."

"Just three."

"I'm still your pa, boy."

"Comfortless as it is, 'at's a fact."

"Can't hardly walk, boy."

"Can't talk all day, Pa. I got bidness."

"I saved your worthless life."

"I'd say we's even, 'cept for the money you owe me now, and a filly."

"You part of this, Jack?" Clay asked.

Panther Jack frowned. "It's bidness."

"What kind of son leaves his pa like this, on foot?" Clay said, appealing again to Panther Jack.

Panther Jack shook his head. "He bought you back. Leave it be, Clay."

"Thought you was my friend."

Willy turned his horse north. Panther Jack did the same. They spurred their horses, raising a plume of ocher dust. Clay shouted in a raspy voice that Willy was no son of his, something Willy had decided on his own before crossing the border.

8 It promised to be an ideal autumn day. The morning sky was cloudless, a gentle breeze blew from the east, and the warm sunlight slanted through the hickory trees that lined the roadside like sentries. Barely aware of the weather and the wagon tracks he was following, Willy rode south. His main sense of the world was the gentle rocking motion of the horse under him. He'd left Beau to tend to the herd until they could drive the animals into Corcoran City. Though he'd not yet told Panther Jack that their arrangement was about to change, he was determined to change it now that Bobby Grimes and his crew were no longer part of the arrangement. Willy and Beau would take the animals straight to the pens.

He'd been on horseback for most of sixteen hours following a full week on the trail, two days going to and in Mexico and three more herding stolen steers over dusty roads to the bluffs south of Bedloe. His vision blurred as the image of the fallen *vaquero* reaching out for him stalked his thoughts.

Jarred from his daze, he blinked, and, looking up, saw the homestead straight ahead less than a quarter mile. It seemed he'd just a minute before left the bluffs and entered the farmlands. His failure to account for the time in between troubled him. He realized how vulnerable he'd been and how easily he could have been taken by surprise. Mexico wasn't the only land that was dangerous.

Except for chickens scattering out of the horse's path, he found the homestead deserted. That could only mean today was a Sunday. His ma, Nell, Anne, and Hazel would be at church, having ridden there on the bed of Tor Sorenson's Studebaker wagon. Willy thought of the last time he'd seen Tor's team, two old swayback draft animals struggling along under the burden of the bulky wagon. He'd joked to Mr. Sorenson that it was time to retire them.

Willy was rank and famished. He dismounted. Hunger could wait. What he needed first was water, and then he'd lie down for a few hours. He went to the spigot and pumped water on his face, then drank. He unsaddled the horse and led it to the watering trough. After the animal slaked its thirst, he tethered it to the hitching post outside the barn.

Sunday morning, he thought, feeling a gentle nudge of nostalgia. Sunday was the sole day of the week he and Beau were left to their own devices. The girls and Ruth went off to church in starched clothes. After finishing the morning chores, they played horseshoes or gathered up their poles and fished trout out of Redmond's Creek or stole off to the general store in Bedloe and listened to Arlo Murphy and Archie Hill, two of Bedloe's oldest citizens, recount their days as soldiers in the Confederate army.

For his sisters, church was an opportunity to meet others like them—and boys. He figured that right about now, Nell would be lecturing her sisters how to behave so they could draw the attention of boys, while pretending to ignore them. Girls baffled him. On little more than a whim, they might be carefree and assured or suspicious and shy. When teased they became angry, but they did their own share of teasing. They laughed when nothing was funny and sometimes didn't when something was. They were serious about things that didn't seem at all serious. He wasn't sure why this was. Maybe they weren't really touched by life until they became women. The proof of this he saw in his ma, who rarely laughed. She'd been touched often by the hard hand of life, and maybe that was why she was so ready to make bank on an afterlife. Right now, he imagined she was kneeling in a pew, baby Sean at her lap, whipping herself into a frenzy over one sin or another she hadn't committed in the first place. If it was like past Sundays, the girls would stay for dinner at the Sorensons and wouldn't return until past dark. Though Mr. Sorenson often exchanged heated words with Clay, Ruth Bobbins remained in his good graces. Willy didn't understand any of it. He accepted that was just the way people behaved.

He walked to the barn to fetch some hay. An empty whiskey bottle lay beside the door, evidence that Clay had come home. Willy had seen no burro. He assumed his pa had sold the animal. He opened the door and breathed in the smell of hay and something else, something decaying. A narrow ray of sunlight pierced a slit in the roof. He let his eyes adjust to the dim light before entering. A chicken left its perch atop a rail and made a clumsy attempt at flight. The sudden flutter of wings startled him. He waited until his pulse settled, then looked around. The barn was in its usual bad condition. Rails on the stalls had collapsed. The barn had been kept in impeccable condition by Willy's grandfather, who'd be mortified to see it in such disrepair.

Bloodstains on the ground, a scattering of feathers inside a makeshift ring, and two more empty whiskey bottles were further evidence Clay had returned. Willy spotted the source of the odor—the rotting remains of four roosters tossed aside near some hay bales. Willy needed sleep. First, he had to feed the horse, then he'd bury the birds. He gathered up an armload of hay and carried it to the waiting animal, then returned to the barn and grabbed a shovel and gunny sack from the wall beside the door. He held his breath and scooped the dead roosters into the bag, hauled the sack to the middle of Clay's rock field, and dumped the remains of the birds on the ground. He buried them in a hole two feet deep.

He closed the barn door, replaced the shovel, and climbed to the loft that was once a place of magic. That was when his grandpa had kept the loft five feet deep in hay and Beau and Willy had used it as a hiding place. Now the hay smelled of mildew, and there was barely enough to make a sleeping pad. Willy scooped up what he could, separating the mildewed from the dry, piling it in a corner near the loft door. He remembered his grandpa well enough to know the condition of the barn, the barn he'd built as a young man, would have left him crestfallen.

As exhausted as he was, sleep didn't come easily, on his mind Clay and the face of the dying *vaquero,* the cloying smell of the riverbank, the unrelenting current holding him in its grasp. Willy wondered how matters would change with Clay home again. He'd seen the spread fall into neglect under his pa's watch. Clay inherited the farm after his older brother, Emit, and Emit's wife died. Then Clay's younger brother, Rubin, met his end at the hand of an angry husband with a Colt revolver.

Willy pictured his grandpa mostly as a stark bearded man staring out from a tintype on the mantle of the fireplace, but he recalled how hard the old man labored in the cotton field beside the hired hands, how in late fall and winter he loaded the wagon to drive out to the range where cattle lazed in winter coat, Willy and Beau, ages four and two, lying behind him on a tall bed of hay. The spread was nearly five square miles then, taxes paid in a timely manner, the family well fed. Waist-tall cotton grew in the prime soil. Forty acres set aside for alfalfa went to plow in spring and produced four cuttings before the first week of October. Sharecroppers worked on Bobbins acreage that had long since gone to pay Clay's tax debt, and they got a fair deal from Willy's grandfather.

The smell of the rotted roosters lingered. Willy lay on his back, staring at the ceiling, thinking of Lisette. Even in his state of exhaustion, he couldn't put thoughts of her aside. Since seeing her up close, he'd thought of little else. He despaired when he imagined her with Panther Jack, and a stinging jealousy rose up in him.

In time his eyelids fluttered, and drowsiness overcame him. His sleep was troubled by images of water surrounding him and sucking him under. He heard a constant pounding. Within the hour the recurrent banging of the loft door against the wall awakened him. He wiped the sleep out of his eyes and realized it was dusk. He was thirsty and hungry, and he had to water and feed the horse again. Reluctantly, he sat up, crawled to the ladder, and climbed down.

A kerosene lamp glowed in the window of the house. Willy assumed Clay was inside. He watered the horse and led it into the barn, where he curried and fed the animal. At the trough he drank, wiped his face, and slicked his hair. Now, prepared to face his father, he stepped loudly onto the porch and opened the door. Legs sprawled out, a bottle of whiskey within reach, Clay sat sideways at the table, his eyes on the door. His face nearly skeletal, he was even thinner than when Willy had last seen him.

"Smells in here," Willy said.

Clay sniffed the air as an animal might. "Smells like a boy don't 'preciate what all's been done for him. Smells like a boy left his pa at the border with no horse and hunert-mile walk. That what I'm smellin?"

"What'd you do with the jackass?" Willy walked to the stove and dumped some lignite atop kindling inside the burner, then struck two sulfur tips and set the oil aflame.

"Me, a leg festerin, half ate by maggots. Didn't ask 'bout that, did you, boy?"

Willy fanned the flames until the coal began to spark, then walked to the cupboard and opened the bread box. "Maggots eatin the dead flesh probably saved you. Arlo Murphy says 'at's how doctors treated gangrene in the Civil War."

"I don't give a damn what that ol man says. You left me standin near cripple with two dollars to my name. That ain't forgivable."

"Don't remember you bein much for forgivin anyone for anything much."

Willy took a knife to the loaf of sourdough and sliced off a piece, which he stuffed in his mouth. Chewing slowly, he gazed at the father he'd once feared. Clay's skin was splotched red, his deep-set eyes dull as carbon, his booming voice reduced to a wheeze.

"I should of whupped you more, boy. Maybe that was it."

Willy finished his bite and swallowed. "Hello, Clay."

Clay glared at him.

Willy matched his father's hard stare. "Guess hello don't mean nothin. I'm puttin on beans. Want some?"

"Put you 'crossed that river. Could'a got myself shot. All you say is you're puttin on beans."

"That's right. I'm puttin on beans soon as the water boils. Where's Ma?"

"Don't want no beans fixed by you, boy."

"I'll fix beans just the same. Take some out to Beau."

"Your cousin ain't no better 'an you. I told you both not to be messin with your old . . ."

"Guess Ma's in the bedroom."

Willy walked to the bedroom door and knocked. Ruth said that she'd heard him and would be right out. Willy returned to the stove and placed a pot of water on top of the burner. He paced the kitchen, stopping often to look out the window. Clay studied his every move. When steam rose in the pan, Willy lidded the pot, set it on the edge of the burner, and faced Clay. "Say what's on your mind."

"I should shoot you, boy, rather 'an have you treat me this way."

"Beau an me's pushin thirty more head into Corcoran tomorrow."

"Should of done it long ago."

"By the way, I buried them roosters. How much you lose on them?"

"Nobody said I lost."

"It's a good guess you did." Willy turned away and opened a cupboard. He took down a jar and set it beside the stove. "Beau and me got us a fresh deal with . . . Never mind. It don't include you. I'll give Ma 'nough from it to keep the house."

"Jack done gone behind my back?"

"He's been goin behind it a long time. Likely fixed the books on you too."

"No. He wouldn't."

Willy smiled. Panther Jack was as wily as Clay was hardheaded.

"You owe me, boy."

"Yep, 'at's the truth of it."

Ruth opened the door. A scarf shrouded the left side of her face. She took a seat at the far end of the table near the wall. She, Clay, and Willy exchanged glances. Willy broke off a piece of bread, popped it in his mouth, and watched his mother and father as he chewed.

"Your boy's got no respect," Clay said.

Willy swallowed. "Ma, I'm fixin to make beans and wonderin how much Clay took of the money I gave to you."

"Shouldn't call him Clay, Willy. He's your pa," Ruth said.

Willy took two steps toward his mother. Clay, his leg buckling as he stood, tried to block Willy's path. "Ain't your house, boy. Ain't your woman."

Willy shrugged and stepped around him. Clay took a step toward Willy, who raised his palms and stepped back. Clay advanced. Willy stood his ground.

"I don't wanna do it," Willy said. "But don't come no closer."

Clay stood, fists clenched at his side. "May have to, boy."

Willy shook his head. "No, I won't fight you."

His nostrils flaring as if smelling the air for fear, Clay looked Willy up and down. There was no fear to sniff out. All that was behind Willy. He cut an eye in the direction of his mother, and as he did Clay fired off a round-house that clipped Willy on the cheek. Clay cocked his fist back and threw a second blow. Willy sidestepped it. Clay lost his balance and reached for Willy with one hand and the table with other. Willy watched him crumble to the floor.

Clay lay, looking up. He clutched his knee. Willy stepped over him, walked to his mother, and removed the scarf. Her cheek was bruised. "How much?" he asked.

"He's your pa."

"How much you give 'im?"

She looked at Clay, who held his knee in both hands. The smell of steaming beans filled the room. Willy repeated the question.

"The whole bit."

Willy walked back and stood over Clay. Without speaking, he kneeled down. He helped his father up and walked him to the chair. Then he went to the stove, where he lifted the lid on the pot of beans and stirred them.

Ruth came to Clay's side and laid her hand on his shoulder. "Willy, your pa's hurt."

Willy stirred the beans. "It'll be needin peppers." He began searching the cupboard for dried peppers.

Willy filled his stomach, then went out and saddled his horse.

Beau would be hungry, and the cattle needed to be moved. Willy returned inside. Ruth was in the bedroom, but Clay remained at the table, a glass of whiskey nestled in his fingers. Willy ladled beans into a jar.

"You ain't talkin?" Clay said. He rubbed his knee and took a jolt from the bottle.

Willy shook his head. He found another jar, filled and capped it, and walked to the bedroom. He knocked softly. His mother sat on the edge of the bed, the baby pressed to her as she rocked back and forth.

"Won't be back while he's here," Willy said.

She nodded. "What about the family?"

"Don't worry. Beau and me'll take care'a y'all."

"Willy, he's your pa. What you did was wrong."

"Doin wrong is what I know." He touched her bruise. "Don't let him do you that way."

"They's biscuits in a sack in the pantry," she said. "Make sure no harm comes to Beau. I'll talk to the Lord for you two."

"Can't imagine him listenin about the likes of us. Never has." Willy nodded. "Beau won't be comin back neither."

Ruth's eyes seemed to recede in their sockets. "That boy does whatever you tell him, so you tell Beau to come see me first. I ain't his blood, but I'm his ma same as if I gave him birth. Never treated him like it was any different. I won't have him bein contrary like you."

"I'm leavin now." Willy laid seven silver dollars on the bed. "Don't give it to him. I'll get more to you later. Tell Nell to marry Glen Fellows if he asks."

Willy looked over his shoulder.

Clay stood in the threshold as if to block Willy's exit. "I ain't the kind to hang over a fence, lookin at a field of dyin stems while waitin for clouds to bring rain, boy. And you ain't no different."

Willy walked to the bedroom door and stared at Clay until he stepped aside. "My house," Clay said, "and you ain't welcome here no more."

Willy looked around at the slat-board room, bare except for the bed, a chair, three daguerreotypes of Willy's grandfather, and a wooden crucifix Clay stole from a church in Mexico and gave to Ruth as a gift. Willy nodded and brushed past him. Outside, Sorenson's wagon, filled with the Sorenson girls and Willy's sisters, rounded the gate. As Willy neared the road, Nell shouted to him. He answered her with a wave, pointed the horse south, and leaned into the saddle, on his mind the woman and Panther Jack, both of whom he had to deal with, but in different ways and for different reasons, but first, he and Beau had to drive the cattle to the pens in Corcoran City and meet the man who arranged the final sale.

9 The air was dry and the sun high overhead. Corcoran City's main streets were teeming with people who'd come for the county fair. Mule teams and draft horses plugged their way up Sam Houston to Central Avenue, pulling wagons that swayed and groaned over the rutted road. Dust rose up and drifted on an idle breeze. Belching smoke, an automobile nearly struck a wagon. The driver honked at a teamster hauling grain. The wagon driver turned the wagon and stopped his team diagonally, blocking the roadway of Central in both directions. He set the brake.

The car's driver stood up and waved a clenched fist at the wagon driver, who spat a stream of tobacco juice on the road. "You hog's ass," the car driver shouted.

"You gonna eat the slop outta my hog's ass now, boy," the wagon driver said.

"Best move on or get down," the car driver said.

The man on the wagon spat again and swung down from his bench, which prompted the car driver to climb out of his car. They drew to the middle of the road, where they circled and glared at one another. One and two at a time, people forsook other matters and formed a ring around the antagonists as they exchanged spittle-laced profanities.

Willy and Beau joined the spectators. Unconcerned, Panther Jack hopped up the step to stand under the canopy-covered sidewalk. He held one of his ropelike braids and twirled it slowly, while commenting to no one in particular how he was seeing more and more of "them contraptions," and how they smelled worse and made more noise than any team of mules, and the only good thing he saw in them was that they didn't leave shit on the road. He said he'd ridden in one and kept flying out of the seat with every bounce, landing on his braids until he thought he'd yank his own head off. "Gaw-damn contraptions."

Egged on by the crowd, the adversaries took turns pushing one another. The argument ended suddenly when the teamster, a burly bearded man in overalls, knocked the driver down, lifted him from the ground, hit him twice again, then, wiping sweat from his own head, left his adversary sitting cross-legged in the dust. On the way to his wagon, he paused long enough to kick the door of the automobile.

Willy and Beau joined Panther Jack under the overhang and ambled down the planked sidewalk of Center to the corner of Stephen F. Austin. They turned into an alley and stopped at the white door under the sign "Phylo Baker, Livestock Broker." Panther Jack opened the door, and the three of them stepped inside. A cowbell clanged against the doorjamb, announcing their entry. At a desk near a pine counter, a heavy-jowled man, engrossed in a ledger, glanced up. His face seemed an exaggeration. His brown eyes, set wide apart, bulged from their sockets. His eyebrows grew weed-like from his forehead. His purplish lips stood in stark contrast to his pale skin. He greeted them with a wave, closed the ledger, and stepped from behind the desk.

He extended a hand to Panther Jack and tightened his grip as he pumped the other's hand up and down, then let go abruptly. "Be them?"

"Be 'em," Panther Jack said. He looked at his hand as if examining it for damage.

"Boys, name's Baker, Phylo Baker." He offered his hand to Willy and shook it with the same kind of enthusiasm he'd shown Panther Jack. "You boys be the ones Jack was talkin up. Willy and . . ." He searched his memory. "Matt?"

Beau moved his rifle from his right to his left hand, shook the man's hand, and announced himself in a flat tone. "Buh-Beau Buh-Bobbins."

Phylo's smile was unrelenting. "Well, I knew it was one'a them Bible names. I ain't much for formalities, so how many can you boys bring up at a time?"

Willy shrugged. "Three or four dozen, maybe more."

As if molded, Phylo's smile remained fixed. "How often, boy?"

"Depends on the river. If she stays low or if the rain comes."

"I buy by the head, not weight. No Texas beef mixed in. Sure as someone steals a dyin calf off the King Ranch, we'll all be in the shade of too many too tall Rangers explainin matters in our underwear. Brand inspectors don't care enough to check Mexican cows."

"Don't wear underwear," Willy said.

"Then you'd be naked, I guess." Phylo looked at Panther Jack. "He always so literal?"

Panther Jack shrugged.

"What's *literal* mean?" Willy asked.

Panther Jack exchanged a smile with Phylo. "Means no imagination."

"I ain't got no imagination for people makin fun of me." Willy looked around the store, stocked with farm and ranch supplies and feed. He figured that Phylo used some of that feed to fatten the cattle before he sold them. "And I ain't for formalities neither. What you gonna pay?"

"Same as I pay Panther Jack here."

"Which is?" Willy noted the look Phylo gave Panther Jack.

"Eight dollar," Panther Jack said.

"That's right. Eight dollar."

Willy shook his head and turned to Panther Jack. "Told you I didn't like it when you said it was a coonass we'd be dealin with. Figure we can cut a deal in San Antonio. Me and Beau'll find us someone there to sell to. Don't every cow in Texas go the army."

Taking nothing but longhorns from the flatlands just south of the border, he and Beau had managed to bring six small herds north in shorter time and at far less risk than Clay had. Because the river had remained low, they'd managed crossing back and forth with little difficulty. It was true that longhorn could be stubborn and even dangerous and didn't fetch as much money, but their long legs covered ground faster than the stocky shorthorn. Willy figured he was in a good bargaining position, especially since he'd convinced Panther Jack to let him and Beau bring the cattle to the pens in Corcoran City.

"I've got twelve dollar a head in mind," Willy said. "Plenty of stomachs to feed and not enough beeves to feed 'em. I'd say with the war and all goin on, they's worth more now than they was durin the drought."

Phylo Baker whistled through clenched teeth. "Twelve? It's a mite more 'an those longhorns're worth, boy."

"We'll just take them cattle back to Bedloe and find where they's worth more." Willy motioned toward the door with a nod, and Beau turned to leave.

Before they reached the door, Phylo Baker said, "I gotta deal with phony paper, take risks. Nine dollar, and that means for the mangy ones too, and some of them is mighty poor stock." Phylo's smile didn't diminish.

"We be takin the risks. They's a war goin on. Gov'ment buyin Texas steers 'til they's none available. I know what's fair with cows. That right, Jack?" He waited for an answer, but Panther Jack wasn't forthcoming. "We want twelve."

"They's all bone and tough to sell. I gotta bear the expense of shippin 'em to Lawrence or Galveston." Phylo's smile tapered at the corners. "Can't do it."

"I hear differ'nt. Hear they go to Fort Worth, half the rail time. What can you do?"

The shopkeeper thought a moment and shook his head. Willy motioned to Beau again and turned toward the door. Before they took a third step, Phylo said, "'Leven."

Willy took a Liberty dollar from his pocket. "Heard at the same time the price of Texas beeves is up to sixteen a head or more wholesale, and they ain't much'a them. Let's toss for it. Ten if you win, twelve if not." He sent the coin in the air and told the buyer it was his call.

"Heads," Phylo said.

The coin hit the floor rolling and circled around the desk leg, ending up beneath the chair. Except for Beau, who seemed either to know the outcome or not care, they surrounded the desk and bent down on hands and knees. Willy looked back at Beau and winked, then at Phylo, who'd relinquished his smile. Willy pocketed the dollar.

Outside, Panther Jack congratulated Willy for pushing a tough bargain. "He thought a youngster like you would be easy. Guess we split the extra dollar," he said.

"Weren't you made the deal."

"Ain't a fair way'a doin bidness, Willy. We're partners."

"Here's somethin to know 'bout bidness with Beau an me," Willy said. "What's 'at?"

"Him and me is partners. Beau, put the gun to Panther Jack's neck." Beau complied.

"Not again, Willy." Panther Jack closed his eyes and leaned away from the cold barrel. "It ain't funny."

"Ain't intended to be, Jack."

Panther Jack looked toward the bend in the alley. "Folks'll hear any shootin. They'll be lookin in the alley."

"Maybe. You got one chambered, Beau?" Willy said.

Beau grinned. "Yuh-yep."

"Cock the hammer."

Beau did as told.

"If I told you right now to pull that trigger, would you, Beau?"

"I wuh, would, Wuh, Willy," Beau said, his blue eyes open wide.

"Hear that? You been takin 'vantage of Pa for a long while, Jack, and now me and Beau. Told you once, I ain't lettin you cheat us. Family like us got needs. How much commission that Baker fella payin you?"

"Commission?" Panther Jack started to turn his neck to get a view of Willy, but Beau pressed the barrel harder.

"Yep, commission."

"I sell to him straight. Make two dollar a head."

Willy jabbed a finger in Panther Jack's ribs. "How much?"

"Two dollar a head, Willy."

"No, you makin five or more a head, and Pa payin the sheriff a dollar? I'm stuck takin care of Pa's debt, which don't appear to shrink. Seems you should be payin the sheriff."

"It was your pa's deal."

"Nope. Fellows is sweet on Nell, but you only sweet on that pocketbook of yours and those books you keep. Partners 'sposed to be fair with each other."

Panther Jack said, "Willy, you keep this up, I'm feared I'll go in my pants."

"You better be afraid of dyin, not pissin your pants. Beau, ready to pull that trigger?"

Beau smiled. "Yuh, yep."

"Willy, I been thinkin it over. Maybe I should take care'a Glen." Panther Jack's face was flushed and wet with sweat. "Now, if you boys don't mind, I sure need a drink."

Willy pushed the barrel aside and patted Panther Jack on the shoulder. "It's a fair bargain. You keep your five the way it is, and we'll give up half a dollar a head to you. That way we'll be even when it comes to bribin the law. The rest is comin to me and Beau."

"Ain't a bargain if you use a gun."

"You continue cheatin us, I won't be so understandin." Willy smiled. "You been a lucky fella a long time. But me, I'm the luckiest fella you ever seen.

Don't forget they's two of us. One don't get things straight, the other will."
Willy handed Panther Jack the Liberty dollar he'd used to win the bet. "I'll
buy you that first drink."

Panther Jack slipped between two buildings to relieve himself. When he
stepped out of the shadows, he said, "What makes you so crazy, Willy?"

Willy grinned at Beau, then Panther Jack. "The heat. It makes all us crazy."

AFTER A DINNER of strip steak and chili, they stayed the night at Furr's
Hotel. They were too tired for the thirty-mile trip to Bedloe, and, anyway,
Willy insisted it was a hard ride to attempt in the dark. Panther Jack stationed himself at the bar, where he ordered a bottle of tequila and a gallon
of cider. Muttering, he tipped the bottle to his lips. Willy told Beau to make
sure Panther Jack made it to the hotel room and no farther.

"And don't be in no hurry tomorrow. I'll be awhile," he added.

"Where you off to, Willy?" Beau asked.

"I got bidness."

IT WAS CLOUDLESS, and a quarter-moon lit the trail in. Leaves shimmered
white and the earth smelled damp. Lathered from the ride, chest heaving,
the horse balked at the trailhead. Willy reined it into the tree line, then dismounted and led the animal. When Panther Jack's shack came into view,
Willy walked the horse to a patch of bluestem grass and hobbled it. He
paused long enough to study the lay of the place, then posted himself in
the shadows beneath a hickory tree, where the approach and the shack were
in view.

The boughs swayed, and the moon dappled the ground with patches of
white light. He stared at the window. A burning for what was behind those
walls ached in his groin. He'd once seen the Sorenson bull crash through
the side of a barn, jump a fence, and sprint across a field to mount a cow.
The urge he now felt was akin to that. Still, he lingered in the shadows, trying to build up the courage to cross that final distance to the door.

Several more minutes passed before he finally stepped out, passed over
the clearing, and mounted the front step. His hands trembled. He tightened
one into a fist and started to knock. But again doubt clouded his actions.
He imagined how he must appear, young and foolish, dusted up and sweat-
ing from a hard ride. He tried to remind himself he'd survived the swollen
river, walked for days on bleeding feet with a hunger-shrunken stomach,
smuggled some two hundred head of cattle across the border, and bribed a

Mexican officer to free Clay. But he'd never been with a woman, and passing all those tests wasn't enough to prop up his confidence. He began to wrestle with the conflicting feelings.

He'd seen her three times, never a word passing between them, and she belonged with another man, his business partner. Though the man had cheated him and his pa, those actions didn't justify another kind of cheating. And there were differences to consider. She was black and older and an outcast in the community, the object of gossip. On the other hand, he and his family were in ways outcasts.

The idea of his coming here seemed crazy.

Still, he'd sensed a loneliness in her, an isolation, that he himself sometimes felt. And the way she'd looked at him, appraising him as one might if she too were curious, perhaps aroused. He raised a fist again to knock, but didn't. He'd weighed the idea of his coming here long enough to feel foolish for having done so. Finally, he stepped back from the porch, turned, and walked away.

As he neared the trees, he recalled her standing over the stove, cutting an eye at him. He pictured her bent over and walking gracefully out of the door, then imagined her beneath him, eyes looking deep into him. He took another step, then wheeled about and walked full stride to the door. He knocked twice and listened for any sign of her. He heard nothing and knocked again. This time he barely heard the whisper of her bare feet crossing the room. The latch turned, but the door didn't open.

"Excuse me," she said. "Mr. Jack is not home."

The accent in her voice stirred his desire even more, but he hesitated. The hesitation drew out long enough to squelch his resolve. "I'll go," he said and turned to leave.

The door cracked open, revealing a slash of white muslin that flowed to the floor, a sliver of shining brown skin, and a bewildered eye looking out. "Please?" she said.

Willy stepped closer. "Remember me? Willy Bobbins."

She motioned with a single nod and said, "Yes, again, Mr. Jack's not at home."

"I know. He's in Corcoran sleepin off a drunk."

She looked him over with that one eye. "It's late, Mr. Bobbins. Tell me the nature of your calling. I will pass it on to Mr. Jack."

"Callin, huh? Well, sure. I ain't good at this sort of . . . Truth is, miss, I never before . . . My bidness, I guess you'd say, is with you. I saw you, and ever since, my thoughts ain't been all mine, and I got this ache." He pointed to his chest.

The door opened wider. He saw her in full, lovelier now than he recalled.

"You think because you're white you can come in the night without invitation, with my man gone? You think you can take me like some white man took my mother?"

Her words, the way she formed them, her voice, they all knifed into him. What she said mattered in a way he couldn't fully yet fathom. "Sorry, ma'am. I mean, about your mother."

For a time she stared at her feet, then said, "You're young. Do you know what you're doing? What goes on here?" She tapped her temple softly.

Willy noticed how long and slender her fingers were, how the knuckles bent nicely so that her hand looked like a wing. He swallowed and spoke. "Truth is, I don't know what I think, 'cept I been thinkin 'bout you ever since I saw you in the doorway. Thinkin so much, I rode straight through to beat the sun here. Maybe just comin and seein and hearin you talk's enough. Maybe I should say, sorry to wake you and get back on that horse and ride. Soon as I do, though, 'at ache's gonna be right in the middle of my chest again, and I don't know as I can rid myself of it."

She opened the door and gripped the doorjamb. She craned her neck, peered out in both directions, then looked him in the face. "You're a wild thing, Mr. Bobbins. You take chances. You make assumptions."

Her accent made the words sing. He knew he couldn't match her speech in any way and was ashamed of his own, which prior to this moment he'd never considered. All he could do was speak his mind. "I come 'cause somethin in me is burnin for you. I ain't sayin it's right, but it *is*."

Using the backs of his fingers, he tenderly touched her hand. She didn't resist. That emboldened him. He brushed her cheek and told her she was beautiful.

She bit her lower lip and stepped back. "This is . . . wrong."

"Yes, ma'am. But what I seen of things, it's as right as anything I know. Hell's bells, if you was to say take me away, why, I'd put you on the back of that horse and ride us to heaven if I knew the way, or right into hell if you was to say that was where you wanted to go."

He knew these weren't words he'd speak in sunlight or perhaps ever again. He saw both his passion and his inability to control it as failings every bit as severe as his not being able to swim. He wondered if a man could drown in his want of a woman. Was this what Old Lopez had implied?

She swallowed and looked at him. "You should go, I think."

Beguiled as he was by the way the nightshirt was held aloft by her breasts, he made one last appeal. He gazed into her face and said, "I ain't good at none of this. I never been with a woman. I just wanna be with you. I ain't talkin about no thousands of years. But I figure you been lonely awhile yourself, livin out here, no one but . . ."

She placed a trembling hand to her mouth.

"Didn't mean to scare you none. I'll leave." He turned and stepped away from the door.

She cleared her throat. He stopped and looked back over his shoulder.

"Tie your horse behind the tack house."

"My horse?"

She nodded. "Yes, then come back."

When he returned, Willy found the door ajar and the interior dark. His pulse raced as he closed the door. He called out to her. She didn't answer. The bedroom door was cracked open. He walked to it. The dim glow of the quarter-moon filtered through the windowpane. He saw her outlined by the pale light. She waited on the bed, stretched out, feet and ankles bare, and his mouth went dry.

He crossed the floor and took a seat beside her. The air was thick with her smell, and he felt the warm nearness of her flesh. He laid his hand on hers. She let it rest there. "I ain't kissed but one girl," he said.

She cupped his chin with her free hand and guided his lips to hers. They were as soft as her skin was hot. His heart beat violently as if he were again submerged in deep water. She pulled her mouth away and looked at him. She nodded, but didn't speak. Beside the bed were a bucket of water and a cloth. She pointed to them and said, "Take off your shirt."

His fingers seemed like sticks as he fumbled with his buttons. She shook her head and told him to sit. She unbuttoned his shirt and helped him shed it. She turned him away from her, gathered up the cloth, dipped it in the water, and ran it over his neck, across his shoulders, and down his back. She told him to turn around so that she could do the same to his chest. The dampness of the cloth soothed him, and the hard ride to the dwelling and any lingering apprehension he felt vanished. He wanted the feeling to last and at the same time wanted her to finish because the ache in his groin was overpowering. She laid the cloth aside and picked up a dry cloth.

"There, Mr. Bobbins," she said as she dried him off.

"Willy."

She gazed at him. "Fine. Willy it is."

"Was I right?"

"About what, Willy?"

"You bein lonely and all."

"If you talk too much, you'll ruin the spell. Yes, I have been lonely. Turn your back." She slid her nightshirt over her head and freed her breasts. "Now look."

She took his hand in hers and lifted it to her breast. He cupped it, measuring its weight and firmness. It seemed to change shape to fit his hand. She touched her lips to his, barely a touch, and her breath rushed over his face as she pulled away. Beneath his trousers, he was rigid. She ran her hand down his belly over his pale skin. Then her mouth clamped on his, her tongue prying his lips apart.

When the two of them separated, he was breathless. She watched, her eyes expectant, as he fumbled with first his buckle, then his buttons. He managed to push his trousers to his knees, but no more than that.

Pressing her gently to the mattress, he lay beside her. "Call me Willy again."

She laughed, called him Willy, and eased him on top of her.

10 As arranged, they rendezvoused at the First Methodist Church a half mile from Panther Jack's on a hill on the outskirts of Bedloe. Unlike the girls who circled together outside church and talked feverishly as if an entire life span were too short to say all that needed saying, Lisette spoke slowly and seemed to value words as she parceled them out. She called him her young man and didn't bother with preliminaries of any kind, just shed her dress and helped him strip. He was amazed at how pliant her body was. Afterward, she moved to the far end of the pew and cried. He saw no reason for her to cry and found her mood baffling.

"Why you cryin?"

"I don't know."

"You don't? They's gotta be some reason."

She cupped his cheeks in her hands. "I'm crying because I'm happy."

"That don't make sense."

"Fine. I'm crying then because I'm sad."

Tears shimmered on her cheeks. He moved nearer her, took her hand, but she pulled free and left him to sit in another pew. After several minutes went by in complete silence, she came to him, kissed his forehead, said she'd see him the next night, and left. He called to her as the door slammed shut, but she was gone.

BECAUSE OF HER TEARFUL DEPARTURE, Willy didn't expect to find her the next night, but he rode to the church anyhow, recalling as he did the mysterious earthy smell, the wetness of her, the warm pull of her hands on the small of his back, and the thrill of entering her. If not for his ma and the family, he'd ride to Panther Jack's and lift Lisette onto the back of the horse, then find Beau, and the three of them could ride off to where life offered more. To his joy and surprise, she was waiting in a pew.

As they had the night before, they undressed, this time undressing each other, and made love. Afterward, they sat with their heads pressed together, looking out the window at a swaying branch, her calm, him confused. He wondered about the mystery of her, how she came to be with Panther Jack, who her family was, what her dreams were, but mostly what drove her moodiness the night before.

"I didn't think you'd come."

"I didn't think I would either, but if I left you waiting here, I would be sorry." She pulled away and studied his face. "You're young."

She said it with such gloom, Willy wondered if it was bad to be young or bad to be old, or both.

"You're young too," he said.

She sighed. "That's not true."

The melancholy in her voice troubled him. He wanted her to be happy. He was, at least when with her. Though she was black and from an exotic place where they spoke highbrow, he suspected she was much more like him than not, and that she too wanted to be happy. He wrapped his arms around her and held her gently.

"I'm happy," he said.

Holding her, naked, their passion exhausted, Willy felt the need to talk. His only friend was Beau, and conversation with him was nearly impossible. He told her about how rich the hacendado was and tried to explain how his pa hated the man, but at the same time envied and wanted to be like him.

"Guess he hates 'im 'cause life ain't like that for him. Hell, I'd like to live like that too. If I did, well, you'd be with me, and anyone said anything, I'd . . ."

"You would what?"

"I don't know. Just wouldn't tolerate it."

She laid her forearm over his. "I'll never be white for you."

"Don't matter. Damn the world."

He talked about his ma and his sisters, and she listened. He could tell she was truly listening. He liked that about her. Willy began to see why she'd cried and began also to see that intimacy was about not only being unclothed and entwined, but also wanting to know about the secret world of the other. He finished the account of his first visit to Mexico, leaving out the part about the *vaquero*. "Now, tell me somethin, somethin you ain't told people."

"I don't talk to people. What would you like to hear, Willy?"

"I don't know. When you talk, it's like I have a hunger I didn't know about."

"You may not want to hear it."

"I would."

She described St. Croix, the long curving beach, the sea as blue as Willy's eyes. She spoke of exotic food, fried plantains and boiled fish, the rare meal of chicken cooked with rice, and her mother's house, built on stilts to keep mosquitoes from feeding on them at night. She saw fights between her mother, called Eva Girl by everyone, and her mother's lover, Charles. He was a fisherman, her mother a seamstress. Their arguments often took them outside, where they'd beat on each other until exhausted. Neighbors stepped out of their huts to witness the battles.

The fights, Lisette said, always concerned the accusation that Eva had gone with another man. Charles tossed in that Lisette's father was a white man. Eva spat back that "rape was not love." After the fights, he left for days and returned full of more accusations, and the fight resumed.

"My father, the man who raped her, was a Spanish sailor who'd deserted his ship."

Now that she'd begun, she seemed possessed by the telling of it, as if words were the experience itself. Each piece of her story came with greater urgency, and Willy, feeling equally compelled to listen, sat in silence, his eyes fixed on her lips as they shaped her history.

Her mother and Charles reconciled with a passion equal to that of their fights, but Lisette said it was merely Charles restaking his claim. Their sex took place behind a sheer sheet used as a screen, and on moonlit nights Lisette could witness it. It seemed to her just another act of violence.

"I was fourteen the day Charles came home unexpectedly one morning after filling his boat with fish early. He seemed anxious to brag about the catch." She suddenly fell silent. Her leg touching his trembled. She squeezed

Willy's hand in both of hers and said that was enough for a night, that whatever else he heard would bring him sadness or anger or both.

"It'll make me sad not to hear."

"It's horrible." She stared at the window, her face shining in the pale light. "He found my mother with a man, and he . . ." She paused for a time, then began again, her words gaining momentum as she moved her hands back and forth as if to orchestrate her story. "His name was Phillip, a coconut harvester who sold coconut juice and meat to sailors in port. Charles hacked both my mother and Phillip to death. I discovered the bodies, naked at opposite ends of the room, Phillip with half a face, Mother bent and twisted, arms over her head as if hiding her shame."

She covered her mouth and looked away. He waited. There was more, he was sure of it. He laid an arm over her bare shoulder and with his other hand softly ran the back of his fingers over her throat. She took his hand and kissed his fingers, then looked at him.

"Charles severed off her breasts and cut off Phillip's penis. But he'd undressed and posed them to justify the murders. Phillip had come only to have her sew his britches. He hadn't been with her." Lisette leaned her head into Willy's shoulder. Her voice lowered to a whisper, she said, "The machete was soaked in blood. I picked it up. I thought to use it on myself. My mother was my life."

Willy took her cheeks in his palms and kissed her forehead. "'At's worse 'an anythin I imagined."

She covered his mouth with her hand. "There's more, Willy. I moved to my uncle's house. When I was nine, he sold me to a man for forty American dollars."

Willy pulled away and studied her face. "Sold?"

"Into prostitution." She bowed her head momentarily, then looked up and again stared at the window. "I've been with many men. That's who I am." Her tone had taken on an anger that wasn't apparent before. "Want me to stop, Willy?"

He didn't want to hear whatever was to follow, but neither did he want her to stop. "If you want."

"First, say something to make me laugh."

He searched for some story light enough to take the darkness out of the moment. He recalled the incident in church.

"You know old Mr. Sorenson. Well, he can't hear good. So he kinda figures ever'one's like him and can't hear. He farts, all the time. Don't matter if women're around or if he's standin next to a priest. He let one go in High Mass when I was six or seven. Stopped Father Blankenship in the middle of benediction. Whole congregation looked his way, but old Sorenson just looks around to see what they was lookin at. He goes up to the priest after church and says how good the service was that day. Priest says to him, 'Thank you, Samuel. I forgive your earlier comment, though it seemed far more sincere.'"

She smiled and seemed lighter for a moment, then cast her gaze on the window. "One night a Portuguese sailor smuggled me aboard his ship. When it landed in Galveston, he sold me to Mr. Jack."

Willy turned her face toward his. He gazed into her eyes. Because he understood anger, he wanted her to be angry and to show it, but her sadness seemed to have transported her beyond anger. That bewildered him. She stood and walked to the window. He admired her long elegant legs and curved back as she stood looking outside, her face, bronzed and glowing in the wan light, innocent for one who'd experienced life as she had, a woman-girl reconciled to serving a man like Panther Jack. He wondered if it was wise to love someone when any future seemed hopeless, but he couldn't help it—that was what he felt for her now.

"Willy, the reason I'm with you is that you looked at me the way no man ever did. Your eyes did not prey on what they saw. Even Mr. Jack, when he wants me, looks at me that way."

"I don't want to know how he looks at you."

"I'm older by three years, but . . ." She closed her eyes. "Hold me now."

They didn't make love again that night. Instead, he held her in his arms until the gray sky announced dawn. They parted with an embrace, but without kissing.

11 The moonless sky made the night ideal for moving cattle across the flats and safely to the Corcoran stockyards. A steady wind blew over the rolling land. Willy rode toward the bluffs at a lope. He was saddle sore, his horse nearly played out, and he needed time to sort through matters. He'd considered riding by Panther Jack's, but he hadn't, for good reason. He didn't care to see Lisette and Panther Jack together, and he needed to get the cattle moving. The sooner they could get the steers penned and paid for, the better. He and Beau were followed on their previous

journey. This trip, Willy had made it a point to circle back and check their rear, the Marlin at the ready in case.

He'd been concerned about going into Bedloe and leaving Beau alone with the cattle, but he had to hand over Glen Fellows's share from the last cattle sale and give him money for his ma. Willy's intention had been to leave right away, but Glen kept delaying him, spinning stories and updating him on local and family news. Gilmartin, the oldest Sorenson boy, had been repairing Clay's fence as a ploy to see Anne, Willy's youngest sister. Hazel came down with a cold and gave it to baby Sean. Clay got drunk, limped out into the chicken coop to get himself an egg, and passed out. Ruth found him on the ground with a broken egg in his hand, rubbed his hand on his face, and left him there the entire night.

Glen had held off telling Willy what had really been on his mind until Willy was mounted and ready to leave—that he'd be taking Nell to the autumn barn dance at Jed Riley's. He'd asked if Willy approved. It seemed strange to Willy that a man Fellows's age, a lawman at that, would concern himself about their going to a barn dance together, but he'd said that it was a fine idea. That had satisfied the sheriff.

Willy slowed the horse as he neared the bluffs. He waited for Beau to step out of the scrub and challenge him. When Beau failed to show himself, Willy reined the horse in a slow circle, listening for some sign of him. He heard only the chirping of crickets and the gobbling of a wild turkey somewhere up range. He dismounted, walked into the brush on the side of the trail, and whispered Beau's name. He got no answer. He studied the shadowed box canyon where they'd settled the herd, but saw nothing of note.

Beau had to be somewhere nearby. He wouldn't leave his post at the trail side without good reason. He had the rifle, their sole weapon. Unarmed now, Willy regretted that he'd not bought a weapon from the several that Phylo had claimed "walked away from an armory at Camp Wilson." Willy stared at the walls of the arroyo for a time. The only objects clear enough to see were the ridges of the bluffs and the silhouettes squat junipers cast against a purple sky.

He called out, "Beau! Where the hell are you?"

His voice weak and distant, Beau answered, "Wuh-Willy."

Beau said something more, but his voice faded. Willy shouted, "Damn you, boy! Where are you?" His neck stiffened as he listened for an answer, but heard not even the sound of cattle. He dropped the horse's reins and advanced on foot, calling out and waiting and moving another few feet toward where he thought Beau might be. Beau's breathy responses guided him.

"I'm close. Once more, Beau."

"Uh-up huh-here," he answered. "Huh-huh-hurt. Thuh-thuh-they huh-hurt muh-me."

Willy glimpsed motion in the bushes and plunged into the thick brush, where he stumbled over a rock and fell. "Hell's bells," he muttered and scrambled to his feet. He found Beau behind a boulder next to a holly thicket.

"You okay, boy?"

Beau smiled up. "Juh-just uh-a luh-little huh-hurt."

Willy dropped to the ground beside him. "What happened here?"

"Thuh-they's guh-gone."

"Thought you was shot or somethin."

Beau pointed to his right leg. "Whuh, was."

Willy leaned closer, but it was too dark to clearly see the damage. He touched Beau's trouser leg, sticky with blood. Beau moaned.

"Can you stand?"

"Thuh, they ta, took muh, my horse and thuh, the cuh, cows."

"Know who it was?"

Beau shook his head. Willy helped him to his feet and circled an arm around his waist to support his weight. As they descended the slope, Beau, between gasps and grimaces, explained that he'd heard a noise in the arroyo and left the trail side to check on the cattle. Two men hidden in the brush jumped him. One wrestled the Marlin from him before he could use it. The other held him while the first tried to tie him up, but he'd broken free and tried to run for the bushes, but he didn't get away because of his foot.

"You recognize 'em?"

"Nuh-nope. S-suh-strangers."

When they reached the trail, Willy picked him up and carried him to a boulder. "Here, let's get you up on a rock." Willy seated him and patted his shoulder. "We'll get you to a doctor."

But Beau wasn't finished with his story. "Wuh, wuh, one of 'em shuh, shot fuh, five, suh, six times. I guh, got hit buh, but didn't let on. He wuh, wuh, wasn't muh, much of a shuh, shot. Guh, guh, got muh, me in muh, my leg." He smiled through his clenched teeth.

To Willy's recollection, this was the most Beau had ever talked in English. "Wait here. I'll bring up the horse."

"Wuh-Willy?"

"What, boy?"

"Huh-he sha-shot mu-me in mu-my guh-good leg." Beau pointed to the leg with the club foot and said with barely a stammer, "Ain't ruh, right he did that. Now I'll have two luh, limps."

Willy boosted Beau onto the saddle. When Beau was straddled, he climbed behind him and told him to hold on. Beau leaned his weight against Willy, and they began the seven-mile ride to Corcoran City.

THOUGH BLOOD KEPT DRIPPING down the horse's flank, Willy assured Beau that he'd be fine, but that belied Willy's worry that it was true. He felt responsible for what had happened to his cousin. At times he spurred his mount, hoping the animal would respond, but although the gelding had plenty of heart, it was trail worn from its earlier efforts and strained under the weight of the two of them. When Willy goaded the animal, it loped a few strides, but then gradually slowed again to a walk.

Beau, pale and barely strong enough to hold on to the pommel, rode without complaining. Beau had never been a quitter. Now Willy prayed that he'd arrived in time to save him and that Beau's stubbornness, if nothing else, would serve to keep him alive.

"We'll get a doctor, Beau. You hold on."

Two miles outside of Corcoran City, the horse began to falter. Willy dismounted and led the animal. As he walked, he recalled how he and Beau took turns breaking Lucy, one on top riding bareback as the other held a rope looped around her neck. Neither had ever broken a horse, and she proved a bad one to start on. He closed his eyes and pictured the filly bucking and kicking the air as Beau crawled away from her hooves, gathering himself. Willy had grabbed her hackamore before she'd done Beau damage. Beau had dusted himself off, dragged his lame foot across the dusty corral, and mounted her. They'd broken her by outlasting her stubbornness.

It was the darkest part of the night when Willy tied the horse at the back of the store and hollered Phylo's name. Getting no response, he pounded on the door. Phylo Baker still didn't answer. Willy beat on the door again and again. Finally, the storekeeper called through the door, asking who was there.

"Goddamn, you know who it is. It's Willy. We need us some help." Willy turned and looked at Beau, struggling to stay on the saddle. Willy rushed to help him down.

The door flew open. Phylo met them with a cocked shotgun. He looked at Willy, then Beau, and set the weapon aside. "What happened, boy?"

Willy said, "This ain't no part of our bidness dealins, but I got nowheres else to go."

The merchant waved them inside, asking repeatedly what had happened.

Willy waited until he set Beau on a cracker barrel by the counter before he spoke. "He's been shot. I figure bullet's still in him. It ain't good. You okay, Beau?"

Beau nodded and looked at the wound. Now that they were in light, they could see the bleeding had slowed. Beau touched the wound gently and winced.

"Mr. Baker, I'll be needin the loan of a gun."

The merchant paused to take everything in, then said, "We don't need trouble."

"No one wanted it, but we got it." Willy stared at him, his gaze unblinking. "I'll need a rifle and a pistol if you got both. I'll bring 'em back when I'm done. I'll leave Panther Jack's horse here. Borrow one of yours if it'll be okay. Can you get Beau a doctor? I'll figure out how to pay for it."

The merchant said that except for his own, he kept the guns locked upstairs. He lumbered across the floor and labored up half a flight of stairs and paused. He leaned over the rail. "Do you know who did it?"

"I aim to find out."

"What happened to the cattle?"

"Gone, rustled. Pleased to hear you ask."

"Why's 'at, Willy?"

"If you didn't, I'd be thinkin you already knew."

The merchant nodded.

"You got any idea who'd take 'em?"

"Nope. But my guess would be they ain't bringin 'em into Corcoran City. He needs that doctor." Phylo continued up the stairs.

Willy put an arm around Beau, who was now shivering. "Bring a blanket, too!" he shouted, then said, "It's gonna be okay, Beau."

Phylo descended the stairs, in one hand a Winchester carbine and in the other an army Colt .45 automatic. He descended slowly, as if in thought. At the bottom he sat down on the stairs and motioned Willy over. Willy patted Beau on the shoulder and crossed the floor.

Phylo looked up and handed Willy the Winchester. "This here," he said and held up the pistol, "is a army issue. If you have to, you can leave it behind. Rifle too."

Willy nodded and took the pistol. "I thank you." He looked at the auto-matic. He'd never seen one before. "Show me how this works. I ain't never used one."

Phylo demonstrated how to load the magazine, unlatch the safety, pull the slide to chamber a round, and grip the full handle so it would fire. Willy unloaded the weapon and operated the mechanism until familiar with it to a degree that satisfied him.

"Remember, you gotta grip it real good to fire it," Phylo said.

Willy looked at Beau, his face now starched and expressionless. "I'll fig-ure out how to pay you for Beau."

"Don't fret on it. Gotta have the two'a you in good health. I'm fond of our arrangement. I best get that blanket. Boy's shiverin plenty hard." The mer-chant added that he had two well-rested horses in the livery. "Take either, Willy. Or both."

"How about them spyglasses? Might need 'em."

Phylo hurried to his desk, retrieved the binoculars out of a drawer, and offered them to Willy. "Be careful. Don't worry about Beau. I'm gettin that blanket, then goin for the doc. Hope he's sober." The merchant charged up the steps, moving lightly for a man of his bulk.

Willy took a last look at Beau, who, resigned, it seemed, to the pain, sat stoically on the cracker barrel. He appeared almost serene as he raised his open hand and gave a feeble wave. Willy thought, *So trustin he'd throw hisself on flames for me.*

"I'll see you in few days, hear?" Full of resolve, he walked through the door.

WILLY'S PURSUIT extended into a week. He twice lost the trail, then picked it up the next day as the herd moved north and west, destined for where, he had no idea. Though he was on the trail, he'd not yet sighted the cattle or even their dust. The land he'd crossed, much of it grazed out, was nearly as dry as Bedloe. The rolling upper plateau, habitat to pronghorn and mule deer, was a monotonous track to ride, up one grass-covered hill and down another, only to reach the next so similar to the others, he sometimes felt as if he were climbing or descending the same hill over and over.

Once an antelope broke the horizon, scurried over a field of bluestem, and disappeared into a cedar break. Besides tall grass, mostly what remained here of wild Texas were scattered stands of white oak and islands of milkweed. Much of the rest had long been tamed by farmers descended from German immigrants. Their business dairy and farming, vegetables and cabbage and corn and wheat. Irrigation had saved their farms and pastures from the same suffering that nature had inflicted on the rest of Texas during the drought. Seen from a distance, the houses they'd built resembled the quaint pictures Willy had seen painted on calendars.

Nearly a week had passed, and he was still riding the rolling hillscape of green meadows and fenced-in farms. He had four bits in his pocket and a stick of jerky left to him. On the side of the trail he came upon some walnut trees growing near an irrigation ditch. He stopped to fill a saddlebag with fallen dry nuts and graze the horse. He cracked a few nuts open to eat on the trail, then proceeded up the wagon road to the next hill.

A mile later he passed a white farmhouse with a slate roof. The house was surrounded by pine trees, and the grass on the pasture was thick and deep green. He followed the track for another mile when he encountered a truck coming from the opposite direction. The driver slowed and came to a stop a few feet ahead of Willy. He was middle-aged and wore bib overalls washed spotless. He waved for Willy to stop.

"Where're you headed, son?"

Willy pointed northwest. "Up there a ways."

"But where? That's a lot of country ahead."

"Can't say for sure," Willy said. "You know where I can buy some hardtack?"

"Where'd you come from?"

"Around Corcoran City. Bedloe. Down where the Balcones kinda start."

The farmer sized him up for minute. "You look hungry, son. Follow me."

An hour later, Willy was inside the white farmhouse he'd passed, sitting at the farmer's table as the man's wife, a stout woman wearing a brown dress and well-starched white apron, filled his plate a second time. The two of them seemed hungry for conversation, the wife talking mostly about their own son a year older than Willy who'd joined up as a doughboy to fight the kaiser and show that he and his family weren't Germans, but Americans.

After she filled Willy with scrambled eggs, ham, and pumpkin bread, she placed a cup of coffee and a plate with a pastry in front of him. She said that strudel was her son's favorite food and asked if he'd honor her by eating some with her. Before he left, she gave him a loaf of rye bread and a few sticks of jerky wrapped in a cloth. The farmer had left them alone to fetch Willy's mount from where it grazed in the meadow with a few Holstein.

"All I got to pay you with is this." Willy took the half-dollar out of his pocket.

"We don't take money in exchange for kindness," the woman said. "Where're you off to, son?"

"I got bidness."

"Stay with us and rest. You can pay us with your company, and maybe you could use some work. We can pay you, and my husband could use the help now that our boy's gone."

Willy thanked her and said that under other circumstances, he'd take up her offer. But he couldn't for now. Too many people in Bedloe depended on him. She asked if he minded if she said a prayer for him.

"Ma'am, that's an offer I'll kindly take."

She kneeled down before a cross in her living room and prayed out loud, appealing to St. Christopher to watch over Willy and guide him safely, then to St. Jude to guard Willy's soul, because, as she explained to the saint, his purpose seemed somehow dark and lost before it began. The farmer walked Willy's horse to the porch and waited outside. When Willy stepped down from the porch, the farmer handed him the reins, said the horse was fed and watered.

"I thank you for ever'thing," Willy said. "You're fine people."

"I got crops coming in. Could use help. Son left me shorthanded, and you could use a few more days at my missus's table."

"Yes sir, I could. I explained to the missus that I like it here and would stay, but, well . . ."

The man looked at Willy kindly and nodded. "Haven't seen cattle bein drove through here in years. Cattlemen here mostly ship 'em by rail to feed pens somewhere before they go to market. Your business with three men and a small herd?"

"Might be."

"Then God go with you."

"I hope 'at's the case." Willy mounted and turned away.

"The wife lights votive candles for our boy. I suspect she'll light some for you as well."

EARLY THE FOLLOWING MORNING, after passing out of farmlands in the hill country, Willy sighted them in the bowl of valley rimmed by juniper and oak. Three in all, two miles ahead, they pushed the herd north on a wagon trail. Willy dismounted and lay atop a rise. He watched them through binoculars as they worked the cattle. From the look of them, they appeared experienced drovers. He needed to be certain he recognized the horse they'd taken from Beau, a quarter-horse Appaloosa mix, and the steers. What he saw confirmed all.

He hung back and trailed them all day from a distance. That night he set down on high ground and ate bread and chewed on jerky as he watched their campfire from a half mile away. He parsed out one plan based on the chance of success, then another and another. They held the advantage in numbers. Surprise and weapons were his sole allies. He considered riding down on them that night as they camped, but figured they might post a guard who'd hear him approach on horseback. Next, he thought about approaching their camp on foot. That seemed even more likely to fail. Finally, he decided to take them unaware when they were occupied with the herding. They'd have no reason to believe they were being hounded down. He'd ride up to them smiling and tip his hat like any pilgrim on the road, another hand looking for some work.

Satisfied, he wrapped the saddle blanket over his shoulders. He had to steel himself to make it through the night without turning back. Working the cotton fields, he'd witnessed a man stab another in a fight over a woman. He'd seen decayed bodies of executed men, and the look of confused resignation on the face of the dying Mexican as he stretched out his hand, was seared into Willy's memory. But Willy had never considered shooting a man. He wondered if he had the will to do it.

He weighed the risks he'd taken in rustling cattle against what he'd gained from it and thought of how his life had shifted in so few months. How many? Two? No, three. He wondered if it was worth it after what happened with Beau, and he pictured Beau as he sat at Phylo's, his face pale, leg badly wounded, no sign of anger in his eyes, nothing in them but trust. He could doubt Lisette, but not Beau. He owed him. Nothing was truer. Realizing that gave him the resolve he needed for the day to come.

He dozed off from time to time and was startled awake late in the night by a dream that he seemed doomed to always endure—the dead Mexican's hand reaching for him, fingers moving as if motioning for Willy to follow him. He knew he'd be forever joined to that dying man, and he understood what Old Lopez had actually seen in the stones, and it wasn't just loss. The stones had predicted he would be bound for life to images of death.

THE DROVERS MOVED the cattle out at dawn. Overtaking them would be easy. He watched from cover and waited an hour before saddling his mount.

To be certain of its operation, he emptied the pistol of its magazine and drew back the slide, then replaced the magazine and chambered a round. He left the safety off and concealed the pistol inside his shirt. He felt the cold steel against his skin where it was tucked into his waist. Even as he mounted, he still had reservations. Those rode with him alongside his resolve as he spurred the horse down to the wagon trail.

He thought of Lisette, trying to imagine a happy future with her some-where. Anywhere. He wanted to think she was hoping for that day as well, but he couldn't be certain. He needed to think the impossible because he needed the impossible to counteract what was about to happen, needed to hold on to hope to escape the sense of obligation that drove him forward. Yet he was determined not to let thoughts of happiness bend his resolve. He had to do what he was obliged to do. That notion steeled him.

A little while later, he overtook the drovers. Riding around them might arouse suspicion. He wanted to get their attention, but not put them on guard. Two worked the flanks as one heeled from behind. Dust roiled up. His best choice was to approach on the next isolated stretch and greet them in an unconcerned manner, just another drifter cowhand passing by. He closed on them gradually. When roughly a hundred yards to the rear of the herd, he cov-ered his nose and mouth with his bandanna and brought the horse to a lope, ready to pass their right flank.

The drover bringing up the rear rode Panther Jack's horse and led another on a loose tether. Willy approached, surprised at being unnoticed until beside him. The man carried a single-action revolver with walnut stocks in a shoulder holster. When he looked over, Willy touched the brim of his hat and rode on. As he gained on the others, he saw that they were armed only with rifles, and those were in scabbards. The nearest carried his pa's old Mar-lin saddle gun, taken from Beau. The drovers, obviously aware and seem-ingly wary of his presence, were nonetheless too occupied with the cattle to pay him close attention. Instead of touching the brim, Willy removed and waved his hat. He wanted them to see the face of a pink-skinned youngster, a boy unthreatening and on the trail by himself. As he came parallel to the main herd, they shifted their eyes between him and the herd. He reined his mount farther right and settled into a canter until even with the one who rode the right flank. The farther one looked over, waved to him, and went about his business. Willy replaced his hat and spurred his horse, as if hurry-ing to get in front of the dust.

He decided to take on the drover with the Marlin first. In passing, he waved to get the attention of the closer one and shouted, "Don't see many longhorns these days!"

The man cupped an ear. Willy reined the horse left to close some of the distance between them. Again, he shouted what he'd said the first time, but barely loud enough to be heard. The rider touched a finger to his ear. Willy nodded and rode even closer, repeating what he'd said, loud enough now to be heard clearly.

The drover smiled and shouted back. "'At's a damn fact!"

Now ten yards away from, Willy pointed ahead and hollered, "Figure I'll get past your dust! Been eatin it for a few miles now!"

The rider nodded. The ploy had worked. Soon the nearest was occupied with a stubborn steer and too busy to pay any mind to Willy. His gut burning, Willy rode forward a few paces and reached inside his shirt. In one fluid motion, he wheeled his horse to the right, circled, and swept down on the near rider. The pistol recoiled before Willy fully realized he'd pulled the trigger, and he nearly lost his grip. The rider grabbed his side, lurched forward, and fell from his saddle.

There was no time to shoot a second round. Willy reined his mount and headed for the next man, who was pushing a few head back into the herd. Thinking his best chance was to charge at the man, Willy leaned forward and drove his spurs into the horse's flanks. The drover looked up. Realizing his situation, he pulled his rifle from its scabbard, but by then Willy was an arm's reach away. Willy grabbed the barrel of the man's rifle with his free hand and fired the .45 twice, hitting him in the hip and the belly. He jerked on the rifle and unsaddled the rider. The horse, freed of its rider, took off at a gallop. Willy heaved the rifle aside and turned his horse.

The third thief had cut loose the horse he was leading. He drew his rifle and levered in a round. Willy cut around the herd, riding low in the saddle. As he charged the last man, he fired three shots, all missing their target. But his shooting so panicked the rustler that he turned his horse and galloped off.

Willy pulled his mount to stop, stuck the .45 in his waist, and dismounted. He calmly withdrew the saddle rifle Phylo had loaned him, stepped around the horse, kneeled down on one knee, and chambered a round. He tucked the butt of the stock into the pocket of his shoulder and pressed his cheek to the wood. He took a deep breath, released it, aligned the sights on the rider's back, then squeezed the trigger.

Willy took the recoil, chambered a fresh round, and again looked over the sights. He adjusted his aim to the left and fired. The cowboy slumped forward. Willy fired again. The rustler snapped backward and tumbled off his horse. He rolled to his hands and knees, then struggled to his feet. Limping, he circled about as if dazed, his hands raised above his head as if to surrender. Too far left, Willy thought. He centered the sight blade on the man's breastbone, shifted aim slightly right, and squeezed off a fourth shot. The man looked at his chest, then dropped to his knees and collapsed facedown.

Willy, certain the last man he shot was dead, was unsure about the others. He hoped one had lived so he could question him about how they'd come to steal the cattle. He mounted his horse, looked around, and rode to the nearest one. The cattle spread apart to make passage for him. He looked down at the drover. His head, split open in the back, lay atop a rock. He lay faceup, his glazed eyes open. The bullet hadn't killed him, but the fall had. Bad luck, Willy thought.

He spotted the third about thirty yards away, dismounted, and walked to where he lay on his back, in pain, but alive. His horse had pulled up nearby and stood waiting. The man watched his every move as Willy shifted the rifle from hand to hand.

"What you doin?"

Willy smiled and lowered the weapon. He propped it on a nearby boulder and held up his empty hands for the man to see. He said, "My pa sent me into the Rio Grande, where I near died. But I'm guessin you ain't interested in hearin my history. I'm guessin what's on your mind is your future."

"Why'd you do this?"

Without answering, Willy walked to the man, stood over him, and looked at the wound. The hole in the rustler's side was a few inches above the pelvis. "Must hurt."

The man grimaced. "What's it to you?"

"Well, I'll tell you." Willy ground a heel in the man's side. The man screamed. Willy lifted his boot. "Me, I'm a pleasant type, who just wanted to meet the fellas what took my cows, shot my brother, and stole Panther Jack's horse and my pa's Marlin. Name's Willy Bobbins. What's yours?"

"Gabe." He winced and took several deep breaths. "Gabe Audrey."

"Where you from, Gabe?"

"Up to San Angelo way."

"Never seen it. Heard'a it. Fine country, they say. That where you headed?"

The wounded man grimaced and held his breath a moment, then said, "Abilene to sell the cows. Planned on headin on to New Mexico, where they's no oil rigs or fences."

"Kind of a talker when you get the feel for it. You're doin fine so far. Just want the name. Who told you about our cattle bidness?"

"I need a doctor."

"Yep. That's the damn truth. Now, figure on how bad you'll need one after I step on that wound a few more times and put some cow shit in it and sit beside you and watch it fester for a day or so." Willy looked at the country. "I see where we can hole up a few days, 'less you want to give me a name."

The man shook his head. Willy walked over to a pile of fresh droppings, picked up a large turd, and returned to the man. He kneeled down and pulled the man's shirt open, exposing the bullet hole. The man looked at his wound, then at Willy's hand. "Don't. I'll tell you."

But Gabe lied, giving a name Willy had never heard of. Still, he heard the man out, then stood and shot him once in the head with the .45.

Despite all he'd gone through to get them, Willy had to leave the cattle. If a sheriff or some good citizen came upon the dead men and cattle tracks, he'd have more explaining than he cared to do.

He went through the drovers' saddlebags and bedrolls. They had only dried beans and coffee. Willy would need those for his return trip. He emptied their pockets of a total of five dollars and twenty-four cents in coins and, using a rope and horse, dragged them one at a time several hundred feet to a dry wash. He unsaddled their horses and tossed their saddles and belongings over the cut bank alongside the bodies. He lacked the time, the tools, and the inclination to bury them, but figured they might have something in their belongings to identify them to a stranger. Maybe, if the stranger was a Christian sort, he might locate their kin and they could bury them. Otherwise, Willy thought, the buzzards could have them.

He saw that Panther Jack's horse had thrown a shoe. He slapped his hat on the flanks of the men's horses and shooed them off. After securing the men's weapons in the saddle blanket of Panther Jack's horse, he tethered it to the one Phylo Baker had provided and mounted. As he rode off, Willy thought of a better purpose. He pictured Lisette waiting for him in a pew in the Methodist church, her eyes anxious. Despite the risks he'd taken and the deaths he'd inflicted, he had nothing. Panther Jack had a house, sad as it was, and a small spread and money and books on people who owed him. Willy stole Mexican longhorns and, as it seemed, to no good purpose, now that the last of them were left to wander the range of central Texas until some fortunate soul claimed them.

Unlike his pa, he felt no gratification in taking cattle from a rich Mexican. Willy didn't hate a man for having a good life. It's what he himself wanted. He'd taken no satisfaction in killing the men either, three dumb drovers, one who just wanted to go where there were no fences. If there was such a place, it didn't seem a bad ambition. Now he had three dead men's weapons, two small bags of dried beans, enough in coin to pay a farrier to change the shoes on Panther Jack's horse, and a festering and unwelcome sense of remorse. That was what he had left to show for risking Beau's and his own lives.

He rode the wagon track east, the gruesome idea of death riding with him. He tried not to think of Old Lopez and his stones, dwelling instead on the kind farmer and his wife. He believed in their goodness and thought of how virtue like theirs existed in world of evil. He weighed it against the motive of their son, who'd gone off to fight for some notion or other and left them worrying about him. He pictured that kind lady kneeling before a rail, her votive candles alight, praying to the saints for her son and for him as well. "Hell!" he shouted in a voice that boomed back to him as he passed between two cliffs, "I ain't worth your prayers and 'im gettin hisself kilt ain't gonna make him no more American than he was born to. Just make him not alive is all."

He thought he should pass that thought on to the boy's parents, but he could never face them again, not after today. She'd prayed for his soul, and now he wasn't worthy of it. As he rode on, he dwelled on the consequences of his deed, not just his, but his pa's, his grandpa's, and his dead uncle's deeds, three generations of Bobbins men, some good and some bad in each and in him as well. But he didn't make those drovers steal the cattle or shoot Beau. They did that on their own. Maybe his pa was right. The way of the world was one man taking from another and then another taking from that one, and only killing ends the cycle. The idea of him blaming himself for every act seemed flawed, just as he saw holes in the idea of blaming others for what he did. He could've let the last one live. But, then, could he let a witness survive? When it came down to it, it was just business, the same as Panther Jack bleeding money from those who had little enough of it.

He understood that he had to get smarter, learn how to shed his feelings. He saw meanness as the only strength his pa understood and wondered if that was his legacy and his own strength. If so, what kind of a man did that make him?

At the first railroad bridge he came to, he led his mount onto the tracks and rode down the center of the rails for ten miles. When he reached a stretch of hardpan, he departed the railroad bed and headed south. He'd left eight days before with enough jerky for a four-day ride, and the journey had taken more than a week and he'd come through it alive and the beans would keep him alive and he would find a life, maybe, if lucky, like that the farmer and his wife had. And his son would not go off to war, and he'd never have to kill again. At the moment he was resolved to all that. He was now certain that, at sixteen, he'd become a man, just not a good one.

12   They sat their horses, taking in the land. Willy wondered if they'd been detected and was someone watching. He looked at Beau, who, though he appeared much as he always had since recovering from his wound, was noticeably changed in other ways. He'd given up drawing animals in the dirt, often sat staring at his hands, and slept sitting up when they were on the range. That one incident aside, their fortunes had gone well. On the last three journeys they'd rounded up enough beeves to depart Mexico after a day and push the cattle to Corcoran City without incident.

"You awright, boy?" Willy asked.

"Fuh-fuh-fine. Yep."

Willy lifted the binoculars and scanned the horizon. He saw no signs of cattle or man anywhere for miles. Small herds of longhorn left to range the hundred square miles of the grassy slopes north of the bluffs had been common two weeks before, but the only cattle they'd encountered this crossing were two carcasses of steers that had fallen prey to black bear or mountain lion. Certainly, other Mexicans and Yaqui, and even some federales, stole cattle, but their stealing a few head here and there wouldn't account for entire herds vanishing, especially in such a short span of time.

The most logical explanations, as he saw them, were that the don's *vaqueros* had rounded up the vagrant herds and moved them to high ground to join the main herd or to stockyards at the railhead in Piedras Negras. That left but one choice to Beau and him—the hacienda. It was a risky choice, but with some luck they could still manage to steal a few head and get safely away.

"Ain't nothin out there, boy." Willy lowered the glasses. Already he was devising a plan. "Guess we'll head that way." He pointed toward the peaks that guarded the don's hacienda.

"Wuh-wuh-where?"

"Where they's plenty of beeves. You ain't never seen nothin to match what you'll see tomorrow."

Beau uncorked his canteen and took a drink, then touched his boot heels to his horse's flanks. Willy spurred his horse and pulled up beside him. He was always amazed at how game his cousin was, a boy with a club foot and a stutter.

THEY ARRIVED at noon the next day, ate hardtack from their provisions, and set down atop a crest overlooking the hacienda. Their plan was to ride down long after dark, skirt the *colonia,* and cut twenty head out of the herd. It seemed a wild idea but one, that in his convincing Beau, Willy had come to believe would succeed.

He looked through the army binoculars. On his single journey here, Willy had seen the don's residence from too great a distance to appreciate its full grandeur. Cobble walkways wound throughout the grounds and connected the seven buildings that constituted the estate. Two orchards flanked the main house.

What most impressed Willy was the riding arena to the south, where he spotted the man he presumed to be the don about to mount a horse. It wasn't the don that impressed him, but the mare. Two young men and four girls stood nearby a hurdle, where the don held the mare's bridle. As they watched, the don, outfitted in jodhpurs, knee-high boots, and a white fedora, mounted the palomino. Saddled, the don sat the horse and turned toward the stables, where a groom led a tall roan stallion with a flowing mane out from its stall. The handler crossed the arena, and upon reaching the gathering he offered the reins to one of the young men. Without hesitation, he saddled himself. The horse bucked and sidestepped as it fought the reins. For an instant, it seemed ready to bolt, but the rider rose in the stirrups and steadied the animal. The lean, long-necked horses were the finest Willy had ever seen.

The don spurred the palomino mare and rode it alongside the corral fence. The young man on the stallion followed, and the two circled the arena in tandem, gathering speed. As they circled, it was apparent in the straight-back way they rode and the manner in which they reined their mounts that both were skilled horsemen. On the fifth lap, the don leaned forward in the saddle and turned the mare away from the fence. Using a quirt, he urged the animal in the direction of the hurdle. The horse vaulted the obstacle effortlessly and landed on the far side of a muddy pit. The don halted the palomino and waited as the other rider circled his mount once more before he reined the horse toward the barrier. Though the horse cleared the crossbar with similar ease, it splashed mud as came down. The don shook the young man's hand, and then both rode to the nearby stables, where two grooms waited to take the reins.

Willy handed the glasses to Beau. "'At's what we want someday."

Beau looked down. A smile formed. "*Es verdad,*" he said.

"If we could steal us them horses," Willy said, "we'd make more 'an we would bringin back a hunert head of beeves." He nudged Beau. "Best get back 'fore someone sees us. They's a man on that tower looking up."

Beau scanned the walls of the hacienda again. "Thuh, they's muh, more 'an one."

"Don't matter if they's a thousand. Let's get." Willy took the binoculars from Beau, and they scrabbled down the rocks to where the horses waited.

AS DUSK DREW NEAR, they could hear the faint sound of music. Willy signaled for Beau to follow. They scaled the rock to the crest. Willy looked down at the *colonia* through the field glasses. What seemed the entire population was gathered in the square, where several cooking fires glowed amber. Activity appeared just as vibrant in the hacienda. Torches illuminated the walls, and in the center of a tiled patio beside the main house, a large gathering was seated around a table. Willy saw this as fortuitous.

"Whatever the goins-on, they gonna be damned tired when it's all done," he said. "Let's get us some sleep."

Beau went to his horse and unsaddled it. He lifted it and his saddle blanket onto his shoulder and labored over to where Willy waited. He tossed his saddle down on the flat ground beside Willy's and lay down. His wound had taken a month to heal, a month spent in a loft above the livery where Phylo boarded horses. In the interim, Willy rejected Panther Jack's suggestion that he take Bobby Grimes or one of his crew with him into Mexico. "Easier to trust a rattlesnake," Willy had said.

Instead, while waiting for Beau to get better, Willy had dug postholes and wired fences for old man Sorenson, earning a few dollars, most of which went to helping his ma. Though Beau's leg seemed healed and he didn't complain, Willy suspected the leg was still game and figured Beau rightly should be in Corcoran City recovering. But he had plans that required money, and this venture was the most profitable way to it. Besides, he couldn't do their business alone, and he couldn't trust anyone else.

"Wuh-wuh-Willy?"

Willy rolled on his side and looked at Beau. "What?"

"Nuh-nothin."

"You okay?"

"Yuh-yep, fuh-fine."

"Then let me sleep." Willy lay on back and closed his eyes.

"Wuh-Willy?"

"I'm tryin to sleep."

"Uh-I suh-saw Puh-Pa tuh-tuh talkin wuh-with Buh-B-Buh-Bobby."

"Grimes?"

Beau nodded.

"Don't mean nothin. Get some sleep."

The distant sound of trumpets hitting high notes floated up to them, the melody muted and sad. The earth beneath him was like flint, and sleep didn't come right away. Willy thought about his prior venture here and began to question the wisdom of coming again. His hope was that this time he and Beau would experience better luck.

THE TOE OF A BOOT striking his calf aroused Willy out of his sleep. It took an instant for him to realize where he was. He looked up at the shadowy figure of a man wearing a sombrero and then saw a revolver in his hand. He felt a chill run down his back as he realized what the man's purpose was. Another Mexican stood a step from Willy's head, holding a shotgun, its barrels aimed down at him. The first man motioned for Willy to stand. He rose slowly and saw that two other *vaqueros* held guns on Beau, who was having difficulty standing. One jerked him to his feet, while the other rammed a rifle butt into his side, knocking the wind out of him. It took Beau a moment to recover. "I duh-duh-didn't huh-hear 'em," he said.

"Me neither," Willy said.

The man on Beau's other side struck him in the chest with a fist and said, "*Silencio!*"

They bound Willy's and Beau's hands with rope, then looped the running ends of ropes around their necks. The *vaqueros* shoved them to get them walking and marched them down a trail. A fifth Mexican followed behind, leading the horses.

The sound of distant music floated over the crest. They reached a stand of fir, where the Mexicans' horses waited. They uncoiled the ropes from around Willy's and Beau's necks and lifted them atop their horses, then tethered the horses to their own.

MEN ON EITHER SIDE of them, they stood in the don's orchard, the air lush with the smell of roses, lime and orange trees and roasting meat. A few yards away an artesian well fed a gurgling stone fountain. A cobbled path lined with shrubbery and blooming roses led out of the garden to the courtyard wall. The man who seemed to be the *capitaz* took Willy's arm and directed him to a wider cobblestone walkway.

Willy sniffed the air. "Somethin around here has to smell like horse shit."

The man behind him pressed the butt of his shotgun into Willy's back and nudged him along. They walked through a rose garden to a stone wall that curved toward the main house. Ahead inside the walled courtyard, mariachis played a lively *ranchero* as an audience clapped and struck their heels on the tile floor in time to the music. The *capitaz* led the way up a series of steps that ended at the courtyard gate. There he stepped aside and, with a sweeping motion of the hand, presented Willy and Beau to a dozen men in formal attire and women in flowing gowns. They were gathered around a table near an open-pit fire. The fire and a row of flambeaux cast shifting shadows on the white walls.

The music didn't stop. The men and women gazed at the interlopers with curiosity for a moment, then continued as before, smiling and tapping their heels on the floor. A series of white linen clothes stretched across the tabletop. Within arm's reach laid out in decorative fashion were an array of fruit and salads in bowls and plates with tortillas and pastries, food enough to feed the two dozen celebrants.

The revelers' eyes, illuminated by the fire, glistened. Their faces carried a singular expression of shared delight and amusement at the sight of two Americans standing bound before them.

"Thu-this is puh-plum cuh-crazy," Beau whispered.

"Hush, boy."

The host sat at the head of the table. A man of indistinguishable age with salt-and-pepper hair and olive complexion, the don had a double chin and jowls that jiggled when he laughed. He looked in the direction of Willy and Beau, nodded, then continued his conversation, talking over the music as a servant poured wine. He seemed, like the others, in good spirits. Two *cholos* manning fans woven from palm leaves stood nearby and fanned insects away. Another served wine from a *garrafón*.

The don stood. He raised a hand and the music stopped. All eyes followed his progress as he walked slowly toward Willy and Beau. When he was face-to-face with them, he made a flourished bow and smiled back to those seated at the table. The guests seemed amused by this display of formal manners. Seen in the binoculars, the hacendado had appeared harmless and Lilliputian. Now, standing before him, Willy saw in his calm manner a quite different man—gentlemanly, confident, dangerous.

The *capitaz* handed the binoculars over to the don, who smiled and hung the strap around Willy's neck. To the delight of the *vaqueros* and those at the table, he tugged on the field glasses.

"*Es mejor que una cuerda.*" he said, garnering an outburst of laughter from the table.

"*No comprendo,*" Willy said.

"Better a rope maybe?" the don said, his accent thick. "Jou come here why?"

Willy said, "Travelin by."

The don chuckled. The gathering followed his lead, some among them murmuring their approval.

"*De dónde son ustedes, joven?*"

"*De Tejas,*" Beau said, speaking so boldly that Willy snapped an eye in his direction.

The don turned his gaze on Beau. "*Pues, son ustedes banditos? Que es tu intención? Para robar ganados?*"

Beau looked at Willy as if to assure him, then said, "*Nuestra intención no es mal. Es ver la tierra y no más.*"

The don took hold of the binoculars and held them up for Beau to see. "Why jou espy?"

Beau shrugged and told him that the hacienda was too beautiful not to stop and see, but they were afraid to come down and look. When they saw the horses, they were saddened that they could not see them closer. "*Señor, sus caballos son magníficos.*"

The don seemed impressed as he weighed the answer.

"Ain't never heard you talk so much," Willy whispered. "Keep goin."

The don motioned the *capitaz* aside and carried on a whispered conversation. The men nodded in agreement, and the leader came beside Beau and untied the bindings. Another man did likewise with Willy. They rubbed their wrists and waited.

"Jou hab hungry? *Tienen hambre?*" the don asked.

"*Si, señor. Tenemos mucha hambre,*" Beau said.

"*Bueno.* Come." The don turned toward the table.

The men stepped back, and the hacendado motioned for the boys to follow. He stopped short of the table, turned to Willy and Beau, and asked their names. He had no difficulty pronouncing Beau's name, but Willy's came out as "Wheely" and offered some problem as he introduced them around the table, paying particular attention to his wife and eldest son, the rider of the stallion. He left them standing and picked up a plate, then walked over to the spit, where he sliced off a cut of beef that he carried back to the table and placed before an empty seat. He then took another plate and repeated the performance. The audience watched all this in amused silence. He came back to the table and said something to the gathering that brought a round of laughter from them, and then he motioned for the boys to take the chairs where the plates waited.

"What'd he say?" Willy asked Beau.

"Tuh, too fuh, fast."

"I think he's makin fun of us."

The don scooped up his wineglass and lifted it head high. "*Salud y cien años a todos.*"

Those at the table echoed his words. Two servants hurried to either side of Willy and Beau and began filling their plates with roasted potatoes, pinto beans, and squash. Willy imagined meals at home, hands grabbing wildly, no laughter, anxiety hanging over the table, the family concerned Clay might at any time erupt. If the world was right, he thought, all this would be his, his and Lisette's. He struggled to find a word to describe it. Joy, he thought. Joy.

Then, in his periphery, he noticed a shadow swaying back and forth on the stone path that led toward the stables. Willy looked up high and saw the origin of the shadow. On a rope tied to a beam secured between two stone columns, the body of a man, his face swollen, his tongue black and protruding like a chunk of coal, swayed as if marking the seconds of the night. Each swing seemed to further stretch his grotesquely elongated neck. Beneath the hanged man, a boy, no older than ten, used a pole to swing the human pendulum.

Willy leaned into Beau's shoulder. "Look, but don't stare."

The others at the table seemed unperturbed by the hanged man. None looked in that direction. They drank and ate and talked in lighthearted tones.

THAT NIGHT, Willy and Beau slept on beds in quarters near the main house. In the morning just after daybreak, a woman entered and led them to a room where two bowls of water and washcloths sat on a table. She also pointed out a slop pan. Later, the same woman returned and guided them to a patio in the center of a garden where a stone-top table was set with breakfast for them. She asked if they wanted "*copitas de café*." They ate *migas* and tortillas and drank coffee beside the garden. Shortly after they ate, the *capitaz* arrived. He told Beau that they were to accompany him.

They passed the don's courtyard. Willy glanced toward where the man had been hanging the night before. The body was gone. The *capitaz* didn't speak, just motioned them along the stone path until they arrived at the arena. He opened the gate, then crossed the arena to the stables on the far side and slipped into a stall.

"Wuh-wuh-what ya-ya thu-think, Wuh-Willy?"

"I ain't got thought one, 'cept I hope we ain't the next guest hanging from a rope."

The *vaquero* led the stallion out of the stall, walked it unsaddled in their direction, and stood it before the boys. He asked Beau if either wanted to ride it, cautioning them that only the don's son had ever stayed on the animal successfully. Beau translated what was said.

Willy shrugged. "I'll ride it I if can keep it, which ain't likely."

"Uh-uh-I cuh-can ruh-ride it."

The *capitaz* looked at Beau's club foot and chuckled.

"Suit yourself. Tell 'im to saddle it up."

The *vaquero* shook his head and spoke English for the first time. "No esaddle. Jou ride, jou live."

It seemed at first an odd if not misstated remark, but Willy saw in the *capitaz*'s eyes that he'd made no mistake. Willy stepped between Beau and the Mexican. "I'll ride that stud. Tell 'im what I said, Beau. And don't do nothin else."

"*Comprendo*," the man said.

Beau aimed his thumb in the direction of the path. Willy turned and saw the don and his son heading toward them. Following behind were the family and two of the male guests from the previous night's feast. The don greeted them with a wave. His son, a boy about Willy's age, stood aloof and watched from a few feet away.

They shook hands with the boys and said in English, "Jou unerstan thee *proposición*."

Dumbfounded, Willy looked at him. "You speak—"

"Jes. *Inglés*. I do not speak it in front of my company who do not speak it. My family all speak." He turned to his son. "*Es verdad?*"

His son affirmed what he'd said with a curt nod.

"We hab a wager, he and I. He say nobody ever ride thee horse. I bet jou can. Jou or Beau."

Willy nodded. "Me then."

"*Bueno. Vamos a ver.*" The don signaled to the *capitaz*.

Willy climbed over the fence and dropped to the ground. The *capitaz* handed him the reins. The horse tensed and shied back. Willy held the reins in his right hand and stroked the horse's neck with his left. He gradually worked his hand up the horse's neck, whispering in childlike tones, swearing he intended no harm. When he felt the animal relax, he cupped his palm around the ear and fondled it with his fingers. Then he slid his fingers down the animal's face to its nose and let his hand linger near the nostrils. He felt the horse's hot breath on the back of hand and figured it was time. He led the horse in a quarter circle so that it faced away from the watchers. He ran his hand over its left flank and up its back, measuring its reaction. The hard muscles trembled under his touch, but the horse didn't otherwise respond.

"I'm gettin on now," he said and swiftly thrust himself atop the animal, sliding belly down across the horse's back. He made no effort to complete the mount, just relaxed in that position to reassure the animal. The stallion took two steps, shivered, and gazed back at Willy with one eye. Willy sensed no fear in the horse. He gradually eased his right leg over and sat. Still he waited. The horse huffed and stepped sideways, as if impatient with the wait.

Willy stroked its shoulder and said, "Let's show 'em."

He brushed his heels on the stallion's flanks. It took a few seconds to bring the reluctant animal to a trot. Willy, who'd ridden for years without a saddle, quickly found his old skills at balancing himself and applying the precise amount of pressure with his knees and knowing when to let a horse run. He brought the stallion to a gradual gallop and circled the arena twice before he stopped at the fence, where the don waited. The son stood at a distance and glared, but the don was smiling.

"Jou are a *vaquero*, no?"

"Fine horse." Willy smiled and dismounted.

"My men hab fed and watered jour horses," the don said. "We hab *pan dulces* for jou. I would hate to hang such guests."

AFTER DARK they lay atop a bluff on saddle blankets under the open sky. Willy contented himself to look at the stars and think about Lisette. He imagined her riding behind him on one of the fine horses and for a time fantasized about stealing the stallion. Selling it would earn more than a hundred steers, enough for him to take Lisette to someplace like New Orleans or even north into Yankee land, where she'd be accepted and they could build a life. Ultimately, he dismissed the whole idea. Stealing the horse might offer all that, but attempting it would lead to a bad end.

For once, Willy was thankful for Beau's silence. He didn't want to talk about what they'd seen or the danger he'd placed them in. He had the responsibility of the family on him, and that was his guiding star for now. Still, he imagined hearing the beautiful horses whinny. Though he'd seen them and had ridden one, they now seemed nothing but fancy. What wasn't fancy was the body dangling at the end of a rope, impelled to swing by a servant boy. Willy understood in full the real power of authority. It was something ruthless, to be respected and feared. A man had to keep others from taking what he had, no matter how little or how much. He looked at the sky. The stars seemed bolder and more imposing than he could recall.

IN THE MORNING they ate jerky and biscuits and rode north and east in search of enough strays to make up a herd, sad in size as it might be.

13

She was seated in the front pew and turned when the door creaked open. It was a moonless night, and he couldn't make out her expression. She'd come. That was encouragement enough. He walked to the pew, said hello, and slid into the seat beside her. The church had been her idea. It was within walking distance of Panther Jack's and deserted at night.

"He was drunk when I left." Her hand moved toward his. She brushed her fingers over his knuckles, then slid her hand under his and squeezed.

"I been thinkin about you," he said.

"I know."

"I ain't got nothin. No money, no house."

"I know."

"But I got ideas," he said, not certain exactly what those ideas were, just vague notions of changing his situation. He also didn't know the words of love, and those few he thought to say embarrassed him.

"We don't have much time, Willy Bobbins."

"I know," he said, echoing her earlier words.

"What do you know?"

"That we don't have much time."

She raised his hand to her lips and kissed it. "Now you."

He kissed her hand and let go. "I'll be goin away awhile."

She didn't say anything to that. He fell silent as well. He listened to her breath, feeling the heat of her body near his without touching her. He wanted something better for them than furtive meetings and hurried love-making in a Methodist church. What, he wondered, would it be like to own a fine buggy and a fancy horse to pull it? To extend his arm for her like a gentleman and help her step down from her carriage? To have a bed to share instead of a hard bench?

"Maybe I should go," she said.

"No."

"Then kiss me and don't be a boy about it. I'm a woman."

He wanted her, but hesitated. A bead of sweat dripped from his armpit and rolled down his arm. She cupped her eyes with her hands and let out a deep sigh. Then she stood as if to leave. He reached over and grabbed her hips. "Don't go."

She bent down, lifted the hem of her dress, then took his hand and guided it up under the fabric. She was moist. His fingers moved as if of their own will, touching the folds of her tissue and playing with her as he'd imagined, but never had before. She was new again to him and at the same time familiar. His blood pulsed.

She left him exhausted and confused, telling him that she'd come again whenever he desired, but if he ever lied to her even once, she'd never again come. He didn't understand what she meant. He had no reason to lie to her. He pulled up his overalls and hurried outside to ask what she'd meant, but she was already somewhere between the church and Panther Jack's.

14 They'd pushed forty head to the border this trip, and Willy intended to get every one of them to Corcoran City. When it was dark enough, he left Beau and rode to the river. This trip and one more, then he'd have enough money to leave stealing cattle behind him, maybe buy his own seed pair, build a life. He had those dreams and the

ambition to pursue them now. The market for stolen Mexican beef would dry up.

Word had it that the war was going well for the Allies and Americans were largely responsible for turning the tide. As he rode to the riverbank, it wasn't the big events of the world that concerned him, but some more immediate. He was hungry and needed sleep.

Willy approached the Rio Grande, its surface rippling like a carpet of wet snakes in the dim light of a quarter-moon. The air was rank with the smell of earth and fecund plants. More than a quarter mile away sat the Texas side, a blur of vegetation and shadow. The span was a long one to traverse, but the river ran slow and shallow. The southern bank slanted gently to the water's edge, and near the middle a narrow island of sand and reeds separated the current into two.

They'd crossed here three times now. Willy figured it wasn't wise to establish that kind of pattern, but he wasn't about to risk deep water and swift current. He held a profound respect for the river and a grudge against it. Besides crossing, he had other concerns, not so much with Rangers or Mexican authorities or the don's *vaqueros* as with opportunists. He was still undecided if the drovers he'd killed had been sent or were just a band of scofflaws who'd stumbled on an opportunity. In any case, he figured it wise to be cautious and assume someone had betrayed them. At the top of the list were Panther Jack and his own pa.

He scouted the Mexican shoreline for federales or Comancheros, a few who still ranged along the border, then crossed to Texas, at its deepest point the river barely reaching his horse's flanks. The bank on the northern side was steeper, and here the enterprise was most vulnerable. Willy spurred the horse up the bank and turned south. The vegetation impeded him and the horse balked at entering. Willy pressed his spurs into the horse's flanks and pushed it through a thicket with branches that slapped at his legs whiplike. Mosquitoes swarmed around him. He decided that even a desperate thief wouldn't hide here and turned north.

He followed the trail upriver, where he came upon an idle campsite. He dismounted and checked the coals. They were cold. Then he rode inland until satisfied it was safe to bring the cattle across, then he returned to where he'd forded the river, thinking as he did that in three days' time Lisette would be waiting in a pew.

As he crossed the river back to Mexico, he contented himself thinking of her. These days he tended to link his thoughts of her with him to his memory of the kind farmer and his wife and to a simpler life than he'd imagined before. He wanted to be good, in a sense that goodness served a better purpose for those he cared for. He'd tell her what he intended, convince her, if possible, that they could leave and go west, far west, maybe New Mexico or Arizona or Nevada, where he'd heard there was room for a new life and land was cheap. A seed pair of Hereford and land, those were what he needed—they needed.

He reached the far side, pulled down the brim of his hat, and turned upriver. He brought the gelding to a trot and didn't slow until he arrived at the marsh reeds where he'd left Beau. He couldn't find him.

"Damn. What now?" he muttered.

He urged the reluctant horse into the chest-high mire. The animal struggled forward, its hooves sinking into the wet ground. Relying on his ears to guide him, Willy paused and listened for cattle. He swatted insects away from his face, but mosquitoes in Mexico were no less unrelenting than those in Texas. He was tired of insect bites, of long nights with no sleep, of eating hardtack, and mostly of the rustling business.

He entered a thicket. As he did, the branches moved in front of him, and a steer lurched out.

"Willy, that you?"

"Yeah."

Beau, mounted on his horse, emerged from dense shadows of the thicket. "Hell, thought the Muh, Mexicans done cuh, caught you."

"Mexicans?"

"Su, some come along. Heard 'em after you left."

Willy swatted at a cloud of buzzing insects. "Let's get outta here before we ain't got no blood left. Where's the herd?"

"Moved 'em buh, back a ways. Cuh, come after th, this one," Beau said, meaning the steer that now had plopped itself down in the mud.

"You left a whole bunch for one? Sometimes you show no sense, boy. 'Specially since you was shot. Get that one on his feet, and let's go."

Willy pulled up his bandanna. Ropes in hand, they fell to the rear and goaded the animals to a trot, while ready to turn back any that broke away. Hearing over all the commotion was difficult. They kept each other in sight and let the action of one guide the other. An hour later, the river came into sight. Willy circled to the front and came up beside Beau to tell him it was time to run the herd.

Just then Beau motioned for him to look back. Some distance away, a muzzle flash lit the night, then another. Then more. A round cracked the air. Whoever was shooting, they were doing so from horseback as they rode in the direction of the river. Willy figured he and Beau could make it across easily if they abandoned the steers, but leaving the cattle wasn't yet an option. The river was a short run, and the stringy longhorns were half wild, nearly as tall as a horse and almost as fast.

"We can make it! Let's run the damn things!" Willy shouted.

Both rode to the rear and routed the animals. Willy fired a shot into the air, then dug his spurs into the horse's flanks and fired again. The herd, as if a single mindless beast, headed to the river. The lead steer stumbled and was quickly trampled by the others. The water separated for an instant as the first of the herd plunged in.

Willy and Beau lashed out with their ropes, hooting and whooping and driving them to the middle of the river before their pursuers gained the southern bank.

Willy pulled his horse to a stop at the sandy island and said, "Keep 'em goin, Beau."

Beau turned to join him.

"I said, get on now!" Willy shouted.

He hoped a shot or two would force the riders off their mounts. He reined his horse up onto the island and, rifle in hand, dismounted and slapped his horse on the hindquarters. He crawled into some reeds, hugged the ground close to him, and crawled through the reeds to the water's edge, where he peered out over the river. The moon cast light on the far bank. He counted six. Two waded their horses into the shallows and stopped. He sighted over the barrel and fired, chambered another round, and fired again. His horse skittered and rode off. Willy fired a third shot. One of the riders cried out and splashed into the river. Riderless now, the horse turned back and rode up the bank.

Lucky, Willy thought.

The others fired as one rode to the aid of the fallen man. Willy laid the barrel in the rescuer's direction and squeezed off a shot. The man retreated, leaving the other to float downstream. The others dismounted and scattered, some firing wildly in Willy's direction. Bullets splattered the water far short of him. He figured one could squeeze off a lucky shot just as well. He had to move position. Assuming that Beau had herded the animals up and away from the bank, he began crawling. He reached a dense growth of reeds and wriggled inside. He settled behind a large rock to take aim, fired twice, then retreated from the reeds and scrambled up the slope.

He came to his horse and found it standing in a mud hole. A fusillade came just as he reached his mount, but the bullets pelted the reeds below. He gripped the pommel and swung himself onto the saddle. The horse reared. He grabbed its ear and twisted it until the horse settled down, then reined it north. It struggled out of the mud. Willy figured his best chance was in keeping the island between him and the assailants.

The men continued to fire blindly in his direction. A bullet careened off the river nearby. Another slapped into the riverbank beyond. Another cracked overhead. He made the shore, drove the horse up the bank, dismounted, and dived behind the trunk of a cottonwood.

He thrashed his way forward into the bushes until he could view the far bank. With the cattle gone now, he wondered if the Mexicans would still have any incentive to cross. He could barely make out the figure of a man's half-surfaced body caught in an eddy. The others were no longer in sight, but he figured they might try to pull their confederate out. He retreated from the bank and crawled to his horse, where he gathered up two tobacco pouches filled with ammunition from the saddlebags. He returned to the bushes and lay quietly.

The men called to one another, but he couldn't locate them. He heard horses moving, then the next instant caught sight of three riders following the bank west. He fired twice in their direction and then waited a few minutes before mounting. A mile north of the river, he overtook Beau.

"Wuh-we luh-lost fuh, four," Beau said. "Wuh-we oughta guh-go buh-back and guh-get 'em."

"Don't know if you mean cows or the shooters. Either case it's loco. Let's get." Willy sheathed his rifle, gathered his rope, and reined his horse into the herd.

A NORTHERN WIND arose. The farther they advanced, the colder the night became. The wind blew all the next day and into the next night. They kept watch. Except to let the cattle graze, they didn't sleep or rest. As night fell on the second day, they drove the animals into the sheltered canyon inside the bluffs. The rocky walls provided some shelter from the wind. They roped in a barrier to hold the cattle and lit a fire, but Beau had lost their beans and coffee during the run, so they settled for eating biscuits and jerky. They spread their saddle blankets, rolled up their trousers, removed their boots, and warmed themselves on the flames.

Willy, content to be dry, warm, and free of mosquitoes, rested his head on his saddle and scratched at the bites. The thought came to him that their assailants might not have been the don's *vaqueros*, might not even have been Mexicans. The drovers he'd killed may have acted on happenstance, but these men seemed to have had a plan.

"Beau, when you heard them riders, did they come up to you from the south?"

Beau said he didn't know where they came from.

"But they was lookin around, right?"

"I guh-guess."

"Okay."

"Wuh-why?"

"Get some sleep. We got us a ride. I'll watch for awhile."

Beau soon sank into deep slumber.

Willy was at crossroads, rethinking his plans. It seemed now that stealing beeves was too risky and wouldn't likely get him or anyone a better life, nor was driving stolen cattle up from Mexico going to last if the old-timers who hung around the dry-goods store were correct. They said that the Allies were winning and the war was ending. That would curtail the need for Willy's services. Phylo Baker and Panther Jack would move on to other shady business, and he and Beau would be left out.

He thought of all they endured, the slowness of the journey, constantly breathing fine dust that rose to the height of a rider's nose and settled there. Beau was lucky to be alive. What if he'd been killed? Willy would've suffered under the weight of his being responsible for it. Hell, he thought, I already am. He looked at his cousin, his best friend, his brother, the boy he'd battled with who'd learned Spanish effortlessly though he couldn't speak his own tongue without twisting words, loyal as an old hound. A boy at peace for the moment.

Willy considered the half-dozen times he and Beau had brazenly crossed the Rio without incident, herding cattle into Texas as if contracted by the don to steal his own beeves. They'd put some skill into it, but it was mostly just luck that brought them home each time, nothing more. What had happened to Beau was proof of that. All Willy wanted now was what the cowhand he'd killed had wanted—a slice of good land somewhere, a piece of the world to share with his woman, his ma and brothers and sisters. And peace. He figured he was just dreaming as he had as a boy hiding in the barn loft. Dreams belonged to fools and created fools, and he was no fool, except perhaps when it came to Lisette. His eyelids fluttered and closed.

Willy awoke with a rifle barrel tickling his cheek and the shadowy figures of two men standing over him. One put the toe of his boot to Willy's ribs and forced him onto his belly, but the bandannas they wore didn't fool him. They tied him up in silence. They didn't speak and it appeared intentional. But had they spoken, it wouldn't have mattered. He knew who they were, and they weren't from Mexico and they had no claim to the cattle.

Once Willy and Beau were bound, the men removed the hobbles from their horses and shooed them off. Then they led their own mounts in, saddled up, circled the herd, and drove the cattle past the campfire. Willy and Beau had to roll out of the way of the steers hooves as they passed by. A final insult.

Willy lay sideways on the bare ground, straining to sit. As the last of the steers departed, he called to the rider heeling them, "Bobby Grimes! I know it's you and Juan Cortez and Lonnie Banks and Freddy Lopez. Me and Beau here's gonna wait for you in Bedloe! You don't bring us our money in two days, I'm gonna shoot your foot off. Bet on it, boy!"

He had no intention of killing them, not over cattle. He just wanted the money that he and Beau had coming, and dead men don't pay debts.

When the thieves were gone, Willy said, "Get over here and let's get us untied, Beau."

"Yuh, you fuh-fell asleep."

"Never mind. Start working your fingers."

As they lay squirming and fumbling to free themselves, Willy blamed himself. The cattle had been taken without a fight. As soon as he'd recognized Bobby Grimes's snakeskin boots, he recognized Bobby's three companions. But who was the fifth man? And the one he'd shot? Why did they leave Beau and him alive? The longer he and Beau struggled to untie each other and the more he thought on it—the route of water holes, fording the river where they did at night, holing up at the base of the plateau the day before—the more certain he was that he could never kill the man who he figured set them up.

After a prolonged effort, Willy slipped off his bindings and freed Beau. They rubbed their limbs back to life and walked the road north, Willy slowing occasionally to help Beau along. He'd ciphered through everything that offered a clue as to who'd betrayed them, and he knew why he and Beau weren't killed by the thieves.

"Know who did this to us, Beau?"

"Buh, Bobby Grimes. Yuh, you fuh-figured it ruh-right."

"Him awright and the rest of his fool friends. And I'd say Panther Jack," Willy said.

Part II

||||||||||||||||||||||||||||||||||||||||||||||||||||||||||

The One Sure Losing Bet

There were two kinds—the prophets and the profiteers. Sentiments and the politics were on the side of the prophets, who, even before the law was proposed and any votes tallied, held their Bibles head high and exalted legal abstinence the salvation of mankind. They stood in town squares and railed against the evils of liquor, the sin that must be outlawed. Audiences hollered Amen to whatever shouted phrases the Bible holders proclaimed in the name of the Exalted. This movement would change the nation, change it so men went home to their wives and children. In the hazier seams of communities, others, less vocal, also saw the change as inevitable. Instead of wringing their hands, the profiteers prepared. The law would not be a salvation for them as it was for the morally degenerate and weak-minded. For them it was opportunity, potential for profits. Vice, after all, is also worshiped.

15

On the morning of the fourth day, Willy woke up determined to fulfill his promise to Bobby Grimes. He slung his saddlebags over one shoulder, his and Beau's canteens over the other, and walked to the livery. Glen Fellows stepped out of the jailhouse and followed him inside, but didn't say anything. Standing near the door and staring out the window, the sheriff puffed on his pipe and hummed a ballad as Willy talked the merchant into two horses for five days at a dollar and ten cents a day.

"In advance," Mr. Ebbin insisted, his open hand extended.

Willy counted out the money. "I'll be wantin jerky and salt crackers. And bridles. Got saddles is all's left me." Willy added another two dollars to the count.

Ebbin said he'd bring the horses around the front and tie them to the rail.

The sheriff neither moved nor spoke until the supplies were delivered and Willy had them packed inside the saddlebags. Then he intercepted Willy at the door. Fellows tapped the tobacco out of his pipe bowl and placed the pipe in his shirt pocket. "Outside." He motioned with his head toward the door.

Willy nodded and passed through as Glen Fellows held the door open.

The sheriff leaned on the hitching rail. "Heard you was interested in Bobby Grimes."

"Just rentin horses, Sheriff."

Fellows gave Willy an agreeable smile. "Ain't gotta be so stiff, Willy, you and me bein partners and all. Not to mention I have a fondness for your family."

"What family would that be? Nell, I'm guessin."

"Anyhow, what I hear is Bobby came across some stock."

"Cattle are damn hard to find lately. That's why I ain't paid no commission."

"I understand."

Mr. Ebbin brought the horses around and tied them as he said he would.

Willy squinted at the dusty road that led out of town. He didn't know where Bobby was, but he did know it was time to find him. Money didn't stay with a man like Bobby for long. "I gotta be findin Beau. If you'll excuse me."

Willy went to the water pump. As he filled the two canteens, Fellows reached across and stroked the withers of the horse closer to Willy. "Not much, these nags. Barn sour and in a hurry to quit bein a horse after a few miles. I'm thinkin you got a long ride, Willy." He retrieved his pipe and pressed the bowl into a tobacco pouch. "I understan Bobby's gone south and east to have a high time on someone's money. Maybe to a border town."

Willy smiled. "Tell you somethin, Sheriff. I think Nell's sweet on you. Maybe you should go around and see after her more often."

"Think so?"

"Yep. You can bank on her appreciatin you more, 'cause you helped Clay, which it might'a been best to leave him rot in Mexico, seein as how he's so fond'a Mexican soldiers."

"Couldn't let no harm come to 'im, Willy. Could we?"

"No, sir, couldn't. I don't think Bobby would like it much."

The sheriff set the stem in his teeth, struck a match on his trouser leg, held it to his pipe, and puffed. "You can't be sure about what you're sayin."

Willy shrugged and walked to the horses. He tossed the saddlebags over the back of one and untied them.

"Maybe I'll ride out and see her today," the sheriff said.

"Tell ma I said hello."

"I'll just do that, Willy."

Willy mounted one of the horses bareback. He held the reins of the second horse across his lap.

Pointing the stem of his pipe at Willy, Glen said, "They's one more small thing, Willy. I wouldn't want you meetin up with Bobby in my county. Some might see it as a conflict'a interest. I mean by that if I'm obliged to Nell." He stepped to the side and motioned for Willy to pass.

"I got a lotta respect for a man in your position, Sheriff, but a promise is a promise wherever it's fulfilled."

IT TOOK THREE DAYS to track Booby Grimes to Eagle Pass, where after asking around about a redheaded cowboy with buckteeth, Willy was directed by a citizen to a tavern a little outside of the town named Hole in the Boot. Except for the strangely appropriate name, it was indistinguishable from a hundred other saloons in Texas. Willy had only a vague plan as he dismounted about a hundred yards away from the building and tied the rented horse to the hitching rail beside his own chestnut gelding. Beau tied his horse beside Willy's.

Willy said, "You stay with the horses."

"Buh-but I-I—"

"Boy, I ain't got time for you to spit your way to a thought. Do as I say." Beau glared at him.

"Okay, I'll be sorry about that later. You wait, okay?"

Willy didn't know who or how many were with Billy, but any one of them could walk through the bar doors any second. His best chance for success lay in catching them by surprise.

Leaving Beau with the horses east of the saloon, Willy walked to the side of the building. To get a look without being seen, he'd have to duck under the window and crack open the swinging doors just enough to see where Bobby was. He was about to mount the steps when the doors swung open and a black porter stepped out with a spittoon in hand. Willy backed around the corner. The porter turned the corner and saw Willy, looked Willy over, and said, "I don't want no trouble."

"I don't wanna bring you none."

The man started to pass around Willy, who laid a hand on his arm.

"I'm guessin you could use a half-dollar."

"'At's what they pay me."

"For a day, I'd guess." Willy held a half-dollar out for him to see. "For some information."

The man shook his head. "I see trouble."

"Ain't yours, but the money is. All you gotta do is tell me where inside the man who rode that chestnut gelding is sitting."

"Don't know no one who rides that horse."

"He's a redheaded fool. Big front teeth what stick out. That one, see?"

"Yeah, I know 'im. Spat on me instead this here." He held up the spittoon and grimaced. "Did it yesterday, too."

"'At'd be him. No respect. Want this half-dollar?"

The man considered the proposition a moment. "He won't know it was me did it?"

"Not from me, no sir. Deal?"

"I got no use for him. Ain't no better than what goes in here." The porter held the spittoon even higher, then set it down and extended his hand. Willy dropped the half-dollar in the man's palm. The porter closed his fingers around the coin and locked it in his fist. "He's sittin in the second table left when you walk in. He's facin the door."

"Who's with him?"

"They's three at the table, but I can't say who's with who and who ain't."

"Fair enough. Anyone asks me, I ain't seen you. So you got no worry from this."

The porter nodded, dropped the coin in his pocket, and left to finish what he'd come outside to do.

Willy returned to where Beau waited, unsheathed the 30-06, and told Beau to bring the horse up after he went through the doors. Then he walked up the street until he was directly in front of the doors. He took the steps in one stride and on his second pushed through using the butt of the rifle and stood in the open doors. It was lighter inside than he'd anticipated, and his eyes quickly adjusted. Standing in the threshold with the sunlight at his back, he'd figured it'd take Bobby a second longer to recognize him. He was right.

He spotted Bobby, shouldered the Springfield, and aimed the barrel at his ankle. Chairs and tables skidded across the planked floor as the other men scrambled for cover. Bobby, his face bleached of all expression, shouted, "No, Willy!"

Willy fired and after taking the recoil pulled back the bolt and chambered another round. The second shot ripped off both boot and foot. The smell of smoke and nitrate overpowered the stench of beer and tobacco smoke. Bobby whimpered as he tried to draw his revolver, but Willy held the rifle on him as he crossed the room. He snatched the revolver from Bobby. "Was it worth it, boy, losing a foot for stealin my beeves?"

Bobby shivered and looked at his mangled ankle. He had no appropriate answer.

Willy swept the barrel of the rifle around the room. The others in the saloon lay still on the floor or stood against the wall stiffly as if they themselves were a part of the wall.

"This man stole my cattle and my horse, which is tied up out front. Anyone have an argument with that?"

No one answered.

Willy backed out of the saloon, dropped Bobby's revolver in the water trough, and went to the stolen horses. Beau was waiting. Willy handed the rifle to Beau, untied the two horses, and gave him the reins.

"You got no reason to get messed up in this business. Go home, sell that chestnut, and give the money to Ma."

Beau asked what Willy was going to do next.

"I'll be okay. It ain't your problem."

He watched Beau loop a lead around each horse's neck, helped him secure the last, and said, "Go on now. Take the way north same as we came. I'll be fine."

Beau was nearly to the town limits before Willy started walking in that direction. It was a mild day and the walk pleasant enough. Twenty minutes later, he entered the door of the Eagle Pass sheriff's office and confessed to shooting the foot off a cattle- and horse-rustling son-of-a-bitch.

16

The dry-goods store, a one-story adobe building with a wooden floor and sod roof, served as the justice court. The sheriff behind him, Willy sat manacled, facing the justice of the peace. The magistrate, a dark-haired man with the face of a ceramic figurine, sat below a four-pane window. The sun blazing through the glass cast a glow around the man's head and a shadow the shape of crucifix on the floor. The magistrate eyed the room and signaled for the bailiff to call the court to order. He started to speak, but before a word came, he fell to coughing violently and turned his back to the gallery. He uncorked a bottle, took a long swallow, then slipped the bottle into a vest pocket and cleared his throat.

"We're starting now," he said, his voice raspy but strong. "State of Texas versus Willy Bobbins. How old are you, boy?"

"I ain't done nothin to the state of Texas," Willy said. "Hell, I appreciate it more 'an most folks. Someone was to ask me if I was a Texan, I'd stand proud on it."

"Right. But no speeches, son. That's my job. What's your age?"

"Seventeen and some."

"Makes you an adult in Texas. You be straight with us, hear?"

"Yes, sir."

"So's you'll know, in Texas, sixteen's the law. Now, this is only a preliminary hearing to see if you should stand trial. You understand that?"

"You sound like a educated fella, Judge. If you say so, that's the way it is."

The gallery snickered. The judge gave the audience a hard look and ordered Willy to take his seat. He advised him anything he said might be used as evidence. Willy sat.

The judge read the complaint against Willy and told the sheriff to remove the handcuffs, that Willy looked harmless enough. Then he read the law as it applied to attempted murder.

"Murder?" Willy blurted. "Ain't no attempt at murder, Judge. I told that cattle-thievin sumbitch I'd shoot his foot off. That's all I did. If I meant to kill 'im, he'd be dead sure as rats eat cheese."

"Watch your language, son."

"Can't call a thief a thief?"

"Can't call a sumbitch a sumbitch in my court. Even though he might be."

The gallery laughed.

"Callin him a thief okay?"

"Never mind that. Boy, how do you plead?"

"Plead to what?"

"Attempted murder."

"Didn't do that."

"That's a not guilty?"

"Guess so, sir."

"I about said my say. Let's start. Mr. Prosecutor?"

The attorney representing the state's case confirmed that he was ready to proceed.

"Your Honor, I'll call Mr. Robert Grimes to the stand."

With the help of two others, Grimes entered the room. The prosecutor called him to the stand, a chair placed next to the justice of the peace's table. As Grimes headed to the table, he wobbled, obviously not yet comfortable with his new life on crutches. The audience turned to watch him. When he faced the gallery to take the oath, he glanced at Willy and immediately looked away. He swore on a Bible and lowered himself tenderly into the seat, a high-backed chair with chipped varnish.

The judge looked him over and said, "Be truthful, best someone like you can."

The county attorney asked if he recognized Willy.

"Yes, sir."

The lawyer stood beside Willy and struck a posture as he aimed a finger at Willy. "If he's the boy who shot you, point to him."

"Yes, sir." Bobby pointed to Willy. "That's him sittin right there. Willy Bobbins."

"Did he have any reason to do so?"

"Beg pardon?"

"Did you take cattle and two horses from Willy Bobbins?"

The justice of the peace raised his hand to stop Grimes from answering. "Mr. Holder," he said, "whose case you tryin to make?"

"Your Honor, I want to get to it before anyone else does. Crippling a man isn't right, no matter what he did."

"All right then. Go on ahead."

The attorney instructed Grimes to answer.

"Yep." Grimes looked at the gallery. "Weren't his in the first place. He stole 'em from some Mexican. Can't see how no one can steal what's already stole."

Willy fidgeted in his seat. He had his own questions to ask Bobby, such as who put him up to rustling the cattle.

"Are you saying he brought cattle over from Mexico, which were stolen?"

"That's what happened as I figure it."

"And what did you do with the cattle?" the lawyer asked.

"I didn't take 'em back to Mexico."

The spectators chuckled. Willy smiled. The lawyer repeated the question.

"Sold 'em."

"Who to?"

"Some fat cracker in Corcoran City."

The answer wasn't lost on Willy.

"For how much?" the attorney asked.

"Ten dollar a head."

Willy stood. "Stupid clodbuster. They's goin for twelve."

Again the gallery laughed, as did the prosecutor. When the magistrate regained his own composure, he told Willy to resume his seat, not to interrupt any questions or answers, and, if possible, to keep his mouth shut.

"Fine," Willy said, "but you can see for yourself this boy's a fool."

Grimes looked at the judge. "Me bein a fool don't give 'im no right to go and shoot my foot off."

Again the gallery chuckled. The attorney switched the line of questioning to address the shooting itself. Grimes described it, emphasizing how he was unarmed and helpless. Willy quickly mentioned how he'd been unarmed and helpless when Bobby stole the steers. The judge asked Willy if he wanted to be tied and gagged.

"Don't think so."

"Well, put your hands to your mouth and keep 'em there."

"Yes, sir."

Nine witnesses followed, each saying Willy came into the Hole in the Boot, aimed and fired, chambered a second round, and fired again.

When the prosecutor said the state's case was concluded, the judge asked Willy if he had anything to say. "You don't have to talk, boy. 'Course, it's gonna look bad if you don't, though the law says it won't."

"Judge, you seem like a fair-enough fella. I'll talk."

The judge told Willy to take the stand and swore him in. "It's your say now, and keep it short and no swearin.'"

"What them fellas said about me shootin him was perdy much the truth. See, I come from up around Bedloe. Nothin much there 'cept dusty roads and hot summers. And the sheriff's a nice-enough fella, and the judge and him kind'a let folks settle up problems."

"This ain't Bedloe, Willy. Could you sort'a make it short? People here want to get on with bidness," the magistrate said. "Some of 'em, anyhow."

"Oh, sure. My point being Bobby here stole my cattle. Now, where they originated from don't matter. Some Mexican cattle is stole; some's bought. And some's headed out to feed the army of that fella they call the kaiser, who happens to be the enemy of any good American. So I'm told. And if them cows happen to wander acrosst the Rio, well, who's to say who they belong to but the man who's got possession of them? I heard possession is nine-tenths of the law."

The judge leaned over and looked at Willy. "Are you any closer to gettin to the point?"

"Yes, sir. See, them steers was in my possession and on their way to market, and my cousin Beau has papers that make them cows mine, legal-like. 'Sides, legal cows or no don't have nothin to do with the horses what I bought fair and square from Panther Jack, if anything that man ever did was fair and square, which it ain't. But I got papers on the horses, too. That's what's important as I see it. Now, if Bobby had stayed around Bedloe, the matter'd be settled up. Hell, it's perdy clear I could'a kilt his ass. I only took his foot off. Someone has to let 'im and others like him know right's right and wrong's wrong." Willy sat back and folded his arms. "In a way, I was on the same side you're on, Judge. Justice."

The judge grinned. "That's all you got to say?"

The door opened, and Beau entered with Panther Jack. "No, sir. I got more to say."

"Get to it 'fore you wear out my patience."

"Well, sir, I didn't run. I waited for the law, 'cause I figured what I'd done was right. He's a horse thief."

"A horse thief?"

"Yes, sir." Willy pointed to the back of the room, where Beau and Panther Jack leaned against the wall. "Those two can tell you."

The justice of the peace asked what they could contribute to the case. Beau pointed to Panther Jack.

"Huh-he suh-sold th-the huh-horse outside tuh-to Willy."

"Who're you, son?"

"Buh-Buh-Beau Buh-Buh—"

"Never mind, boy. The day ain't long enough for what you might say. You," the magistrate said pointing to Panther Jack, "can you swear to it? Sellin the horse to him?"

Panther Jack hesitated. Beau nudged him with an elbow, and he nodded.

"Willy done been messin with my woman," Panther Jack said.

Everyone turned around and looked in Panther Jack's direction.

"Well, he ain't on trial for that," the justice of the peace said. "And you bein a cuckold ain't no business of this court. We're interested in a horse. You understand?"

"Yes, sir."

"Good. Ain't no point in you takin the stand." The judge handed the Bible to the sheriff, who went to the back of the room and held the book out for Panther Jack. "Raise your hand," the magistrate said and swore Panther Jack to the oath. He told him to speak clearly and loudly.

Panther Jack gave his full name—Andrew Jackson Jackson.

"You got two last names."

"Jackson's my middle name and my last. People call me Panther Jack."

"Why's 'at?"

"Well, it was 'cause as a boy I got knocked off a horse by one."

"Okay, Jackson Jackson. What you got to say?"

"Horses out there is mine all right. Well, not mine. I sold them to Willy up there. Paid 'em off, he did. And timely."

"You got anything to say about the cows in question?"

"No, sir. Nothin I'd share willingly."

"'At's what I thought. Mr. Holder, seems what we got is a passel of fools doin fool's bidness. Willy Bobbins, you got anything further for us to hear?"

"Yes, sir. Just this. I know the motorcars is around, but we're not surrendered to them yet. We ride in Texas, and a horse is to a cowboy same as a foot is to a walkin man. Anyone who'd take a horse right out from under a man would take food from that man's family. Any Texas man, and this room's full of 'em, understands that ain't tolerated. That's the sum'a it."

"Ain't that so!" a man in the audience exclaimed.

The judge called the prosecutor to the stand. They held a whispered council for several minutes, during which the lawyer nodded several times. When the judge dismissed the attorney, he turned to Willy.

"The court drops the charge of attempted murder, but we can't have such goins-on around here as cripplin up a man. Could be mayhem, but that's another matter. Would you be willing to change your plea from not guilty of attempted murder to endangerin public safety and dischargin a weapon in a public place? Otherwise, the district attorney will file on you for mayhem."

"Don't know what mayhem is, Your Honor, but weren't no public in danger. I been shootin long enough to hit what I intend to."

"Fine, how about dischargin a weapon?"

"Sounds fair. 'At's what I did."

The magistrate smiled. "You ready to be sentenced?"

"Guess so."

"Well, this is your first offense and you're young, and we are talking about shootin a horse thief. Ninety days in the county lockup. And next time you shoot some thieving sumbitch, don't do it in my county."

Willy thanked the JP and offered his wrists to the sheriff, who promptly manacled him. As he walked by Bobby Grimes, Willy suggested Oklahoma was a fine place to move to, if a fella had a mind to move. The sheriff's deputy took charge of Willy, marched him across the street to the jail, and locked him up. A newcomer in the next cell sat up on his cot and looked him over.

"Well, well, what do we have here?"

Willy heard another voice whispering his name. He walked to the window, held on to the bars, and stood on his tiptoes to look out. Beau was outside, mounted on a horse, a second one at the ready. "Cuh-come tuh-to guh-get ya," he said.

Willy shook his head. "Go on home and look out for ma. I'll be out down the way. See you in ninety days."

Beau didn't appear to like the idea, but he nodded.

"I ain't told you before," Willy said, "but me and Panther Jack's woman, well, he was right. Tell 'er I'm comin and she's to wait. She'll know where to be."

Beau appeared disappointed, but he nodded. Willy watched him wheel the horses around, then sat down, resigned to his fate.

"Name's Sonny," the man in the next cell said, "Sonny Archer."

Willy turned to him.

"Whatcha in for?" Sonny Archer asked.

"Ninety days."

"No. Your offense. What'd you do?"

"Shot a fool's foot off. Took no pleasure in it. Was bidness. What you in for?"

"Not showin the sheriff the respect I should of. Come to Maverick County and didn't make a gentleman's introduction."

"'At don't sound like no crime."

Sonny smiled. He had a broad open smile, the kind that set people at ease. He walked over to the bars and extended a hand. "Didn't catch your name."

"Didn't throw it."

"Hell, we're gonna get along real fine."

"We'll see."

17 Under Sonny Archer's studied gaze, Willy shuffled the deck and stripped it. He dealt the cards, five starter blackjack hands. Sonny shook his head.

"Better, but you got lobster claws for hands."

"Don't know what a lobster is." Willy scooped up the cards, shuffled, and dealt them out again.

"No, boy."

Willy gathered up the cards and handed the deck to Sonny. "I quit. You're too lucky."

"Quit? Wanna spend your life cuttin tough leather with a dull knife? You're a believer in luck, Willy. What I'm tryin to teach you is smart luck. Now watch."

Sonny shuffled twice, stripped the cards, and shuffled two more times. "Let's switch to poker."

He held the deck out for Willy to cut. Willy placed the top half to the side, leaned his back against the inside wall of the cell, and watched as Sonny slapped the deck back together and dealt. He was as fascinated as he was frustrated by Sonny's card tricks. Dealing not only to Willy, but also three imaginary players, Sonny pitched the cards, his eyes never leaving Willy's. The cards spiraled out into the air and landed one on top of the other on the blanket as though he'd laid each down and aligned them. One by one, Willy picked up five cards and shuffled them facedown.

He looked at his hand, slowly fanned the cards out, and arranged them in order.

"I'll take two," he said, tossing two aside.

Sonny dealt the cards facedown. Willy picked them up and held the hand close to his chest to set it—two pairs, nines over threes. He discarded two and placed the cards flat on the cot.

"Dealer takes two," Sonny said. He laid his cards aside and arranged the other three hands, ensuring they weren't exposed.

"What'll you bet, Willy?"

"You mean, if I had money?"

"Told you I'd accept credit."

"I ain't one for debt, my own or those who owe me and don't pay. And I know you ain't given no one a straight deal."

"Okay then. If you had money."

Willy pondered strategies Sonny had coached him on—raise on a pair and see who stays, determine who stays just to stay or who plays a tight hand, who's given to bluffing. High pair, tens or better, deserve a bump. Nines over threes, two pair, worth a five-dollar raise.

"Five dollars." He figured it was a reasonable bet.

"Too much, boy, too much. See here." Sonny spread the cards. "It's all about distribution."

Willy looked at the cards—three tens, a jack, and a four.

"If you've got a hand worth playin, chances are someone else will. You say your pa was a poker player."

Since old enough to recall, Willy had watched stone-eyed men with stiff backs and calloused hands sit on wooden barrels gathered around a wooden table in the Bobbins' barn. With a kerosene lantern providing light, they slapped coins and bills on the table and held cards close to their vests, but none, according to his pa, could play worth a damn. Most sat out their hands, playing on hope against fools who were no better. They played and downed gulps of whiskey until all were drunk and skinned out of their bankrolls by Clay and Panther Jack. Sonny's poker was a whole new game.

Willy peeked again at his hand. "Said he sat at the game and played. Didn't say he was a player."

"Well, he didn't teach you much."

"Taught me not to sit and lose."

"Willy boy, by the time I was fifteen, I could calculate odds. A man can beat 'em with a good bluff sometimes, but if you're ridin a thin bankroll, you can't rely on a bluff. Use this instead." Sonny pointed to his temple. "You figure five hands, and you got two pair, nines high, they's bound to be someone else what got a higher pair, maybe three of a kind. More players playin, the better a chance'a evenin out the distribution, see."

"Distribution, what's 'at?" Willy said. "And how'd you know I had nines?"

"Frequency of occurrence, boy."

"Frequency of occurrence? You know any English, Sonny?"

"Watch." Sonny gathered up the cards and slapped them together for another shuffle.

Fast-talking Sonny, who said he was forty, had become a cardsharp at age fourteen, traveling the South with his father, playing poker and later dealing blackjack and faro at Elks Clubs or in back tents at county fairs or back rooms in bars. When gold was discovered in the Yukon, Sonny went north. Rather than kneeling in snowmelt and swishing a pan, he'd used a deck of cards to pluck treasure from the pockets of hundreds of men who'd frozen their fingers panning out nuggets.

"You gotta know your own game, even if it's cookin or stealin. I come back from the gold rush with a hard-come-by fortune, Willy. Enough to live out my life on. But I played another man's game. Stocks. Investin, some call it. The crash in oh-nine wiped me out. So it was back to cards, a gentleman's game, I assure you. Now pay attention here."

Sonny demonstrated a false shuffle, not once, but three times. To Willy's consternation, each looked perfectly normal. Sonny showed the move again, slow this time, pressing the cards together in an even weave and pulling them apart smoothly.

"You gotta doubt about a man's shuffle, make 'im to bring the halves together with the tips of his index fingers, like this." Sonny displayed the way to shuffle, using only pressure from the outside tips of his index fingers. "See?"

"Do it again."

Sonny shuffled, dealt out another hand, and turned his cards over.

"Look at yours, boy. They's one hand better 'an mine. Thing is . . . bet it up slow, see how a man plays a good hand and how he plays a bad hand. Maybe let 'im think he can win a bad hand, too. You didn't shoot that horse-stealin fool's head off, 'cause you didn't know if they'd hang your ass. You shot his foot off. Same here. Go for the foot if you ain't sure about the head shot and a hangin."

"You ever talk slow?"

"How much longer you got, boy?"

"Enough time that you could slow up some." Willy looked at the bars, the yawning deputy beyond, and the adobe wall with the window full of daylight. "Just checked my marks. Sixty-four days, I figure."

"That's enough for now." Sonny Archer spread the deck and lay back, fingers entwined behind his head. "It's time for some shut-eye. And a lobster's a fish that ain't a fish. Like a crawdad. You got crawdads where you come from?"

"In Redman's Crick. Have a few walkin around Bedloe on two legs as well."

"'At's same as ever'place I been to."

Sonny closed his eyes and began snoring almost at once. Willy picked up the deck and shuffled it three times, then dealt out blackjack hands. Spreading cards faceup, he hit each until reaching seventeen or breaking the hand, with the dealer showing a nine. The next hand he dealt, the dealer showed a six. He played each hand for the dealer to break, staying on a fourteen, a twelve, and doubling down on a ten. The dealer's hand broke. With nothing to serve as coins or chips, Willy calculated imagined bets. In all, Willy played twenty-one hands before he set the deck aside. Twenty-one was a good number to stop on.

Sonny had introduced Willy to a new set of possibilities, all of them connected in some way—time, money, odds. Anything that could be computed fascinated him now—ounces, pounds, inches, miles, coins and bills, and card hands, numbers reduced to a value, like time itself. He looked at the clock on the wall by the sheriff's desk. The pendulum swung back and forth as the contraption tirelessly ticked off time. It was 3:22. Willy wanted to calculate minutes for the very reason that motivated Panther Jack to do so—to make money. Sonny was right. Pay time. Pay attention.

Besides teaching Willy the tricks of the cardsharp's craft, Sonny passed on the itinerant gambler's peculiar brand of wisdom. "Willy, remember, they's all good ol boys even if they's cops." Sonny wasn't angry at being in jail, said that he had it coming because he'd set up shop without getting to know the sheriff first. "Got to understand, Willy, it's bidness to ever'one. They's enough in it to share." He detailed his many adventures running backroom games from Mississippi to Texas. He laid down rules to follow: Best to let a sheriff or a deputy win more hands than he lost; always know where the nearest exit is; keep one gun in plain sight and another hidden; if possible, have a trusted hand nearby with a third gun; don't draw a weapon in a fistfight; don't take everything a man has, especially leave him his pride; make a man feel good about himself even as you sweep his money into your pile.

And always, he insisted, *always* remember, the sun never shines at night. Willy hadn't yet figured out what the last of Sonny's tropes meant.

"Patience, boy," Sonny had said. "One thing at a time. You learn your two-by's through nine-by's, and you'll know the percent to a dime. It's all the same wherever you go. Just make sure *your* percent is the high side of ever'thing."

They played cards with the deputies. Sonny was especially fond of Pitch, a game of bidding and playing tricks wherein trump was the most powerful suit, and capturing the high card, the jack, the low card, and pulling in the most game points was called "Shooting the Moon," and it paid double from everybody else in the game. He bragged that he was the best in the world at this game and never had to cheat to win. As soon as the sheriff left for the night, his deputy, Miles Oberlee, pulled up a chair to the bars and told Sonny to deal. Willy sat in because the game was dull without a third hand. Oberlee never laid out cash, but paid Sonny in fresh tobacco and Mexican brandy. Once a week, the deputy snuck a whore from Piedras Negras into the shower with Sonny.

Willy looked over at Sonny as he slept. The sun shone through the bars and lit the floor. He could hear people on the street outside. Some, he thought, pan for gold, and once they have it, they can't wait to spend it. No more rustling, he vowed. Cards, calculations, and a careful eye offered better possibilities. He picked up the deck, shuffled four times, stripped, shuffled again, and dealt out four hands of blackjack. So much to learn, he thought. He wished Lisette could come and visit, but wishing, like dreaming, was a fool's game. Sonny didn't have to teach him that.

18

The day before he was to be released, Sonny invited Willy to sit for a few last hands. He shuffled as Willy watched for signs of a gypsy move, the term Sonny applied to his tricks. Certain Sonny had given the deck a clean shuffle, Willy cut it. Then Sonny, his little finger dangling like a worm on a fishing line, dealt out five poker hands and told Willy to pick up the third one. "Left the joker in, Willy."

Willy spread the cards so that only he could see—three aces, a ten, and a four.

"What'll you take, boy?"

Willy knew the play was to try to improve three of a kind to four unless it was stud poker and he saw the fourth somewhere on the board. If that was the case, hold jacks or better. He discarded the ten and four. "Two."

Sonny dealt him two cards and smiled as Willy picked them up.

"You don't gotta look, Willy. You got five aces. Five. Best hand a man could have."

Willy looked anyhow. The first card was the joker, the second the ace of diamonds. He thought he'd seen all of Sonny's tricks. "How?" was all he could say.

"You sat to the right and was the last hand. The aces and joker was all on the bottom. I high-sided the deck, riffled up twenty cards on each half, kept your hand on the bottom for three shuffles, and brought 'em to the top on the last shuffle so's you'd cut to the bottom."

Willy shook his head. "I'll be . . ."

"Yep. Then I dealt all the other hands from the top and two of yours from the top, givin you the last three on the bottom. Kept your eyes distracted by anglin my pinkie here out." He held the finger up in crooked fashion to make his point. "Remember how I said I was doin time for not makin a gentleman's introduction?"

"I kinder recall it."

"Well, I come here 'cause who wouldn't to a place named Maverick County. They was soldiers trainin up the way at Fort Duncan, and they's the coal miners and never mind the cowhands. Easy pickins, once I set up shop. Problem was the good sheriff's in charge of the county, and I forgot that little matter of payin him a visit first. You might want to remember that."

"Why's 'at?"

Sonny gathered up the deck and handed it to Willy. "It's yours, a parting gift. This was your final lesson in here. Want more, I'll be down Brownsville way. Come by when you get out."

"'At's all you got to say?"

"No. One more thing. The only bet you're sure to lose is another man's woman."

Willy stiffened. "Why's 'at?"

"Even if you win her, you're sure to lose 'er or she'll end up costin you more 'an she's worth 'cause she'll remind you always what she gave up to be with you. Wise advice, Willy. Heed it."

SONNY WAS RELEASED in the afternoon, but returned that night when Miles Oberlee came on duty. Two whores escorted Sonny into the cell. He brought along a bottle of whiskey that he set on Willy's bunk. He handed Miles a twenty-dollar gold piece and said the money was to buy steak dinners for five, and whatever was left over belonged to the deputy. Miles opened the door to the adjacent cell that had been home to Sonny for sixty days.

"Deputy, we'd sure 'preciate you takin your time," Sonny said.

"You ain't gonna wear them women out 'fore I come back is you?"

Sonny chuckled. "Can't speak for Willy here, but I aim to try."

The deputy sized up the women. "Well, don't seem likely anyhow. How about rare?"

Sonny looked at Willy, who nodded. "Bring 'em rare, but slow now, hear?"

Miles Oberlee nodded. "You boys take care'a that fella down there."

They looked at the far cell, where a man lay sleeping off a fierce drunk.

"Be sure and keep what money's left over," Sonny said.

The deputy nodded as the door to the office closed.

Willy and Sonny strung a blanket over the bars that divided the cells, and Sonny took his pick of the two women. He uncorked the bottle, toasted to freedom, and led his pick to his former cell. Willy turned to the woman in his cell. She was squat and plump. She smiled widely. He wanted her, only because since his last rendezvous with Lisette, he hadn't tasted the pleasures of a woman. In his mind she didn't hold a candle to Lisette. The memory of his last encounter with his love made him feel shame for even considering sex with another.

The woman unbuttoned her blouse and spread it open. She stepped out of her skirt, shed her slip and undergarment. She lay back on the cot, spread her legs, and bent her knees. Looking at her this way, Willy wondered if this was what passion was reduced to—a woman laying herself open. It didn't matter, he thought, if he took her or didn't, because she didn't matter. She was another gift from Sonny, nothing more. He unbuttoned his britches and mounted her.

When Miles Oberlee returned, they sat around the deal table that served as the sheriff's desk and ate a meal of rib eye, baked potato, and corn on the cob. Afterward, Sonny invited Miles into Willy's cell as their honored guest. He brought with him a table and a chair. Oberlee eyed the two whores as he sat down.

"Well, boys, guess this'll be our last game," Sonny said, "We'll make it two-and-four-dollar Pitch."

The women joined Willy and Sonny. The one that had been with Willy moved over to the deputy and wound herself about his shoulders.

"Cards first," Miles Oberlee said and took a hefty swallow off the whiskey bottle.

The cards came one at a time, five each, so fast from Sonny's fingers that two more were gliding in the air as the first landed. Miles bid to shoot the moon and led out with the ace of diamonds. Willy played the three, Sonny the queen. The next trick was a nine, followed by Willy laying down a two of clubs because he'd run out of diamonds. Sonny captured with a nine. Miles led an eight of diamonds, which drew a seven of hearts from Willy and a four of spades from Sonny. The deputy plunked down the jack and deuce of diamonds and jumped to his feet, shouting.

He pranced about the cell, celebrating. The women joined him, arms interlocked with his, their gold-capped teeth glistening in the light of the gas lantern. They sang "La Cucaracha" and tapped their heels on the floor. In a far cell, the drunk woke up and joined in the singing. Sonny shuffled the next hand.

The game went on and on. Toward the end, Oberlee shot the moon again and won, which prompted an even bigger celebration. By that time, Sonny had gone to his saddlebags and produced a bottle of tequila. The prostitutes, perched on the back edge of the cots, watched like crows awaiting a scrap. After winning the pot, the deputy took one of the women by the hand and led her to the office.

When Miles Oberlee returned, Sonny tore up the last of the jailer's markers. The prostitutes were sacked out and snoring in a cell next to where the drunk lay twitching in an alcoholic slumber.

The deputy placed his arms around Sonny. "I'm gonna miss your sissified ass," Oberlee said. "You're a good ol boy."

Sonny pulled away and looked up at the broad bearded face smiling down at him. "You ain't about to kiss me, are you?"

Miles dropped his arms to his side and stood stiffly. "Best call it a night. My relief's comin."

"You take care'a my boy here, Deputy." Sonny took a look back at Willy, staggered to his bunk, and passed out.

IN THE MORNING Sonny's singing awakened Willy. His mouth was dry and his stomach churned. He opened his eyes and squinted at the blazing sun shining through the bars. He turned his head and blinked. Slowly, the ceiling and the walls came into focus.

Willy looked into the next cell, where Sonny sat holding a hand mirror with one hand and combing his hair with the other. "Why the hell you singin?"

"Could be 'cause I'm free."

Head throbbing, Willy sat and placed his feet on the floor. "Well, go on and let me be."

"Willy, what's six percent commission on twenty-five steers at twelve dollar a head?"

Willy blinked. "Nothin if you ain't got steers."

"How much?"

"Eighteen dollars."

"What's nine percent of eight hundred fifty dollars?"

Willy rubbed his face with his palms and thought. "Seventy-six-fifty."

"Seven-card stud. You got two pair, eights over four. Eights is showin. Six players, one showin tens, one queens. Whatta you do?"

"Shoot me a gawdamn Mississippi cracker named Sonny Archer."

"Whatta you do?"

"Any eights in the open 'sides mine?"

"None."

"My bet?"

"Yep."

"Stick for two bumps if I know they ain't players and stare at 'em until their balls shrink."

"What's the name of the place in Brownsville?"

"Don't know. You never said."

Sonny stood and walked to the bars. "The Fallin Star."

Willy nodded. "Can I bring my brother, Beau?"

"Bring 'im."

The office door opened, and the sheriff walked in. He saw Sonny sitting inside the cell, the door unlocked and open, and Sonny holding a mirror, all violations of jail rules. The deputy that had relieved Miles Oberlee lay on a cot in a cell with one of the snoring prostitutes. Between the two of them, they'd finished the bottle of tequila. The sheriff crossed the room and kicked the cot. The startled deputy sprang to his feet only to have his legs buckle under him.

"Have yourself a time?" the sheriff said. He left the deputy and approached Sonny's cell. "You like it here that much, Archer, that you wanna stay a while?"

"We started off on the wrong foot, Sheriff, but you can see I mean no harm." Sonny set the mirror aside, then stood walked out of the cell. "I'll just be goin on my way." He walked to the door, opened it, waved his hat, and abruptly left.

Willy looked at the clock. It was 7:18. The sheriff checked to see if the door to Willy's cell was secured. He looked Willy up and down and motioned him to the bars. Willy legs didn't want to cooperate, but he stood all the same and approached the sheriff, where he wobbled an arm's length from the bars. His stomach turned sour, his head throbbed, and the room began to be swirl. He pitched forward and grabbed the bars in time to prevent himself from falling.

The sheriff got a whiff of Willy's breath and stepped back. "I can see he's made no good outta you," he said. "Maybe someday, you'll be as practiced at debauchery as Sonny Archer."

"Don't know debauchery." Willy tried to keep eye contact. "I don't feel so good."

"Then you feel the way you look."

Willy clutched the bars, desperately trying to keep his feet.

"Go sleep it off."

Willy wanted to do just that, but his hands seemed welded to the bars. He was sure he'd fall if he let loose. He let go with one hand, but stood swaying back and forth as he tried to bring the sheriff's face into focus.

"Well, go on."

He felt his dinner rise up and started to turn away, but too late. He bent over and disgorged the undigested steak and corn on the sheriff's freshly shined boots.

19 It was April, a dry, pleasant morning when Willy stepped down from the planked walk in front of the jail and stood at the hitching post. Thinking it would be good to be on a saddle again, he paced back and forth, looking anxiously for Beau. Finally, he saw him turn the corner a hundred feet away and ride slowly toward the jail. In tow was Willy's chestnut gelding. From the opposite direction, a Model T came chugging by, its narrow tires slicing up dust from the roadbed. Willy watched the machine pass. When the chatter of the engine faded, he looked again in Beau's direction and waved, but rather than waving back, Beau gestured frantically for Willy to look straight ahead.

"It's me what got him all excited!" a voice called out from the middle of the road.

Willy cut an eye in the direction of the voice. Bobby Grimes, a shotgun clasped in his hands, stood on the other side of the withering dust bank, squinting at Willy. A peg, strapped to his leg, extended from his knee to the ground.

"That's some fancy footwear you got yourself," Willy said.

"Sumbitch," Bobby said, "I ain't aimin for no foot."

Willy rested his elbows on the hitching rail and grinned. "Hell, boy, you'd probably miss anyways."

"Well, I damn sure won't." Bobby took two steps in Willy's direction. As he did, the barrel of the shotgun wobbled. For an instant, he seemed untethered and reeled backward a step, but he quickly regained his balance and stood with his legs spread apart. He turned his head slightly, gazed at Willy, and spat out a wad of chew. "You ain't so smart, Willy."

Across the street Miles Oberlee stepped out of the barbershop and took in the scene. He drew his revolver and winked at Willy, who raised his arms and faced Grimes. "Make it a good one, fool," he said.

"Think I'll just take a knee off first."

Grimes cradled the butt of the shotgun in his shoulder, leveled the barrel on Willy, and steadied himself.

"Hey, boy," Miles Oberlee said. "Might wanna put that scattergun down." He calmly ratcheted back the hammer of his pistol and raised the weapon.

Bobby's eyes strayed, and he hesitated for an instant. The deputy didn't. The shotgun discharged into the air. Bobby's eyes widened. He dropped the weapon, and the next instant collapsed onto the road, groaning and holding his buttocks. The dust thinned out and spread to both sides of the street.

Oberlee walked over and gathered up the shotgun. "Guess I weren't the only one come to say good-bye to you, Willy."

"I 'preciate the gesture," Willy said.

People spilled out of nearby buildings and formed an audience on the walkways. Then the jailhouse door opened and the sheriff stepped out.

Beau brought the horses to a halt halfway between where Willy stood and Bobby Grimes lay writhing in pain.

Willy smiled up at Beau.

"Damn dust," the sheriff said and took off his hat. He brushed off his sleeves as he sized up the situation. He clucked his tongue against his cheek in disgust. "It's one mess or 'nother, ain't it? Well, I'm half glad to see you ain't killed, Willy, but sorry to see you're still here."

Beau circled the horses and brought them closer. "Hey, Willy."

Oberlee held the shotgun overhead and said to the sheriff, "Boy here was about to shoot Willy."

"I ain't stupid," the sheriff said. "Arrest 'im and get 'im to the doctor. We had us spectacle enough for one day."

The deputy tossed the shotgun to the sheriff, who glanced at Willy. "Willy, don't bother hangin around for no trial," he said and went into his office.

Willy said to Oberlee, "I'll do you a good turn someday."

Willy stepped down and into the street. Beau handed him the rope that tethered the chestnut gelding to his horse. Willy stroked the animal's throat and removed the rope. "Thought I told you to sell it," Willy said.

"Did." Beau explained that he'd sold it back to Panther Jack and gave the money to Ruth.

Just then two men carried Bobby Grimes past Willy and up the steps to the jail, Miles Oberlee following. The climb up the steps jarred Bobby. He moaned and cursed the men. Willy looped the rope around his arm and tied it to the saddle.

"You didn't steal it back, did you?" Willy asked, finding something satisfying in the idea.

"Nuh, no." Beau told him that when Panther Jack heard he was going to Eagle Pass to meet Willy, he offered him the horse for one dollar, provided the horse would take Willy as far away from Bedloe as possible. He asked Willy where it was they were going.

"Brownsville." Willy pointed east. "That direction."

"Huh-how fuh-far?"

Willy mounted the chestnut. "Don't know. We'll find it. I might have to just name this horse now. How's Dollar sound to you?"

20   The men coughed often, and their voices rasped when they talked. Conversation was brief, usually a player saying he'd stay or raise. They drank whiskey and sat under a mist of cigar and cigarette smoke. Between puffs and swallows, they peeked at cards, studied another man's face or the movements of his hands, or measured their stacks against the last wager. Some were slow, some nervous, some quick, some calm— depicting, in a sense, all men and all situations. The warm night was humid, and it added to the tension. Those who folded their hands did so in disgust or resignation, sometimes muttering profanities.

In addition to the tightening tension in the room, the air harbored the smell of the delta and the men in the parlor, their clothing, their habits, their vocations—leather and sweat, cigar and pipe smoke, beer and whiskey, and the dirt-and-oil odor that lingers on those who do hard labor. The walls, papered in burgundy brocade, were faded and stained mustard-yellow from tobacco smoke.

"Cards comin," Sonny said smiling, as was his habit.

The smile and chatter served as his mask. Sonny bragged that he considered himself a student of human behavior and spoke tirelessly of the green-felt table as "the ether of human existence," each hand bringing hope or despair, reward or rejection, failure or triumph. He sometimes added to those joy and depravity. While Sonny viewed the game as a commentary on the human condition, Willy saw it as business, nothing more, the best hand or bluff winning the pot. Money was the proof of his opinion. Take that away, and cards were a waste of time. A man could better spend his earned money in some other enterprise.

Brownsville, a bustling semitropical port town that exported trade goods and raw material to Mexico and Central America, seemed somehow less Texas to Willy. It was home to smugglers, gunrunners, and other scofflaws, and the primary tongue spoken here was Spanish. Corruption permeated most layers of government and business. Money, legitimately earned or otherwise, came in a ceaseless flow.

Even after six weeks, Willy hadn't adjusted to Brownsville's climate. Days were hot and humid and nights, if a breeze didn't rise from the Gulf, oppressively warm and damp. Sonny claimed Brownsville had all of New Orleans's bad weather but little of its good weather and none of its comforts. Willy said that everything bad about Texas and Mexico floated down the Rio Grande and came to a halt in Brownsville.

Beau, however, who disappeared in the daylight hours, seemed taken by the town, or, if not the town, the area. Or, as Willy suspected, Beau disappeared to avoid Sonny. Though Beau never openly expressed it, Willy sensed that he didn't care for Sonny. He saw it in the way Beau pretended not to understand something Sonny had said or asked. On the other hand, Beau's silent ways spooked Sonny, who never held back on his opinions. He tagged Beau as "an odd sort" or "in concert with the unordained," an expression he never explained to Willy's liking.

Beau's behavior worried Willy because it seemed as if a spell had overcome him. He'd awaken at dawn after a long night of watching over the card game and drift off early in the morning, visiting docks or, in his slow foot-dragging pace, walking the riverbank where the sluggish waters formed the delta. Afternoons, he occasionally rented a boat and rowed across the tidal waters to lushly vegetated islands inhabited by exotic birds and alligators. Some days he spent sitting alongside the marshy banks, watching tugboats ferry barges, loaded down with steel or cotton or rice, through the wide channels. Come evening, with no explanation of where he'd gone, he arrived in the back room of the hotel ready to stand watch on the night's game. Asked where he'd been, he simply shrugged.

At first, Sonny speculated that Beau had found a girl, but then told Willy that was impossible because Beau was "simply too strange to interest a girl with half a brain."

Willy, knowing Beau as he did, understood he wasn't the kind to stay indoors when there was sunlight outside, so for weeks he never pried. Sonny, on the other hand, poked at Beau, constantly trying to peel words out of him. Their third week in Brownsville, Beau took to walking barefoot. He stuck feathers in his hatband from egret, goshawk, osprey, parrot, and a variety of seabirds, no two alike. Beau's hat garnered a lot of attention and a good amount of commentary at the Falling Star and became, like Beau's extended silences, a point of contention for Sonny, who claimed the sight of the hat disturbed the players. Arguments between Willy and Sonny most often centered around Beau, who'd never been a part of Sonny's original plan. Willy took Beau as he was, stating flatly that the two of them were the same as one, and if Willy was to stay working with Sonny, so was Beau. Besides, he paid Beau from his end, always a dollar or more than Beau needed to feed himself.

And now, their seventh Saturday working the back room of the Falling Star, Beau sat, as he was accustomed, in a far corner and watched over the game as calls and raises moved clockwise.

"Eight dollars to the sailor," Sonny said.

The merchant marine, red-eyed and angry, peeked at his cards again, then glared at Sonny who'd dealt them, then at the player who'd bumped the pot to eight, a stevedore who'd made it a point to distinguish himself as a foreman as opposed to a common longshoreman.

Willy, to the right of Sonny, sat unconcerned and waited for the sailor to call the bet. His thoughts had strayed to Lisette and the land he'd ranch someday. He tapped his fingers unconsciously on the arm of his chair.

After eyeing Willy for several seconds, the sailor laid down his cards and said, "You in a hurry, kid?"

"It look like I am?" Willy said. "Your call."

"The rest of us want to move on here," the lone Yankee at the table said.

"That's right, sailor boy. We're all in a hurry," said the cowboy, the odd sit-in at the table.

The sailor counted out eight Liberty heads and flipped them one at a time into the pot. Willy followed, dropping in a ten-dollar gold piece and taking back two silver coins. In one quick motion, Sonny shuffled two stacks of silver dollars into one and pushed them into the pot.

"Pot's right," Sonny said. "Cards?"

The cowboy took two. The Yankee, who called himself Jason Abel, and used both names every time, eyed the others and asked for one card. The foreman raised two fingers. The stevedore took one. The sailor, eyebrows raised, stared at his hand, set the cards down, and turned to his left. He spat a stream of tobacco juice in the direction of the spittoon and missed the target by nearly a foot, much as he had the entire evening.

"Got no aim," the cowboy said.

The sailor glared at him. The cowboy glared back. Finally, the sailor asked for one card, which he slid to the bottom of his hand.

Willy tossed aside three cards. "Guess I need three."

The sailor looked at the others at the table in disgust. "Gawdamn, kid. What the hell you doin raisin and stayin in here for if you need three cards?"

"He's payin 'is way," the foreman said. "Leave 'im be."

Willy cut an eye at Sonny as three new cards came from the deck. Willy examined the cards and slowly set his hand.

"Dealer don't want none," Sonny said.

"That boy sitting in the corner staring at his feet, he ever talk?" the sailor asked.

"Ask 'im," Willy said.

The sailor looked over his shoulder. "You ever talk, boy?"

Beau shook his head.

"That good enough?" Willy asked.

The sailor nodded. "Why all the feathers in his hat? He tryin to be an Indian?"

"I don't think so," Willy said. "Beau, you tryin to be a Indian?"

Beau shook his head.

"Why's he have a gun?" Jason Abel asked.

Beau ignored the Yankee, and when no one else took up the question, Sonny took a deep breath, exhaled, and said, "So's anyone comin in here intent on robbin us will be greatly discouraged in doin so. Let's play."

The raises followed, four, up two, another two, call, a see-yours-plus-three. The call was eleven dollars to Willy. His face remained expressionless as he fumbled with one stack of silver dollars, counted out eleven, then capped the stack with a ten-dollar gold piece. "Ain't much, but it's all I can afford."

Sonny matched the twenty-one dollars. Without comment, the cowboy folded, pulling his hat down and sliding the cards to Sonny. Jason Abel scratched at a piece of lint on the felt cover, arched his eyebrows, and asked what the cost was.

"Fifteen," Sonny said.

The Yankee counted out twenty-one and added five. "Cost you eighteen, foreman," he said.

"As wildcatters say, guess I brought in a duster." The foreman folded his hand, grimaced, and swallowed a jigger of whiskey.

"Same to you," Sonny said to the stevedore, who quickly matched the pot. He looked at the sailor. "Fifteen to you."

The sailor, reluctant to part with more money but confident in his hand, pushed out a ten-dollar bill and five silver dollars.

"Five to you, kid."

Willy reached inside his shirt pocket and plucked out a twenty-dollar gold piece. "All I got left. May's well lose it, too."

"Where's a boy get that kind'a money?" the sailor asked.

"Does it matter if you win it?" the stevedore said.

The sailor grunted.

"To me?" Sonny scratched his ear. "Guess I'll just match it." He unfolded a bill that he set atop Willy's gold piece.

Jason Abel looked back and forth from Willy to Sonny. "You two related?"

Willy's eyes narrowed. Abel, obviously surprised by the intensity of the stare, turned to Sonny, who asked the stevedore if he wanted to call the bet.

"Man asked a question," the cowboy said.

Willy took in a deep breath and exhaled. "You're a Yankee, right?"

"New York and proud of it."

"Well, that explains it." Willy scooted his seat back and stood. "Can't tell a Georgia peach from a Texas viper when you see one, can you?"

"What's that mean, boy?"

The stevedore said. "Means the kid here's tellin you it's best to put a cap on your well."

Jason Abel looked at the others for support, but it was obvious they were all against him. He shrugged. "Just a question."

As the stevedore lit up a fresh cigar, Willy returned to his seat. He pointed to Beau, who sat, yawning and stretching, as he leaned into the rifle he held between his open knees.

"That boy there's Beau," Willy said. "I think you woke him."

Beau waved shyly. The stevedore called.

Mumbling, the sailor thumbed his bankroll. "I only got eighteen and change," he said.

"I'll mark you two dollars," Sonny said, tossing two coins to the sailor.

"That's brotherly," the sailor said and dumped his money into the pot.

"Must want his eighteen pretty bad," the Yankee said.

Sonny ignored the jab and said, "Guess ever'one calls." He turned to Willy. "What you so proud of, kid?"

Willy exposed his hand, a full house, eights over kings.

"Beats me," Sonny said, tossing in his hand.

"Boys, I think you been had," Jason Abel said.

Neither the roughneck nor the sailor opened his hand.

"Well?" the Yankee said.

Willy bent forward and rubbed his eyes with his knuckles. When he looked up, he leveled his gaze on the Yankee as if taking aim. "Guess we got us a situation. Someone wanna give this fella a gun?"

No one at the table moved. Willy opened his coat and pulled out a nickel-plated Smith & Wesson .38 with a bone handle he'd won in a game the month before. He set it down on the table where the pot lay and said, "Beau, come're."

Beau rested the rifle in the crook of his arm and approached the table.

"Got your pistol?" Willy asked.

Beau nodded and removed a short-barreled Colt .44 from a shoulder holster.

"Lay it down by mine so's the grip's pointed to big mouth there. So's . . . ," he said, pointing at Jason Abel, "he can grab it."

Beau placed the Colt gingerly on the pot next to Willy's gun and walked back to the platform, where he sat unconcerned.

"Pick it up," Willy said.

The Yankee swallowed and stared at the guns.

Looking at Sonny, Willy said, "Maybe he needs some advantage. Push it closer." Willy's expression seemed painted on, his eyes almost imitations of eyes.

Slowly, everybody but Sonny, Willy, and Jason Abel stood and backed away from the table. Sonny pushed the gun closer to the Yankee, then stood and joined the others out of the line of fire. The stevedore puffed furiously on his cigar.

Jason Abel looked about, appealing his case. "The best you chumps had going for you was playing the better hand between the two of them . . . That's the best. Don't you see?"

Willy stared across the table. "Pick it up."

The Yankee, seeing he'd gained no support, faced Willy. "Hell, you're just a kid."

"Don't need a Yankee to tell me what I am. Pick the gun up."

The Yankee looked back at the others again. "This is crazy. Don't you see? The game . . . It's rigged."

"You ain't doin yourself no favors," the cowboy said. "If I was you, I'd try for that gun or excuse yourself out the door."

Jason Abel shook his head and scooted his chair back, as if to stand away. Willy gazed at him unflinchingly. The Yankee dived for the gun, but before he could cock the handle, Willy had his revolver in hand, cocked and aimed. Jason Abel shook his head and started to set the gun down. As if it had weight and mass, the shot filled the room. Nitrate and sulfur overwhelmed the odor of cigar and whiskey. Besides the ringing sound, the only noise in the room was the sound of urine dripping from Yankee's pant cuff onto the wooden floor.

Jason Abel dropped Beau's weapon and stared down in amazement. He touched his palms to his chest and looked at Willy. "See what you made me do?"

"Best get control'a your bladder if you intend to stay in Texas," Willy said. He reached down, recovered the second pistol, and tossed it to Beau. As he stuffed his revolver in his belt, he looked at the roughneck, then the sailor. "Either of you beat my boat?"

When neither answered, Willy said, "I assume that to mean no." He scooped the pot into his hat and, pointing Beau toward the door, announced the game was over.

When Sonny met them at their room above the Falling Star, he admonished Willy about the law and how guns upset citizens and how it could be called a robbery. "'At no-talkin cousin of yours and your bad judgment are gonna net us time behind bars." He talked as if Beau wasn't present.

Beau lay on a cot beneath the open window. Willy sat on his own bed, dividing money into two even piles. He let Sonny finish before speaking.

"You done?"

"No. Not until I reach your hard head."

"Then near as I can tell, you *are* done."

"Willy, we got us a soft bed here. I don't want it goin bad. You hear me?"

"And I don't want you dealin up no more hands to me. And we already talked about Beau, who ain't deaf, even if he don't talk much."

"You could of kilt him. Or Beau could of, just as easy."

"Could of. I'm thinkin we just make our own problems. Hell, we take fellas what can't wait to be took anyhow without no tricks. What if one'a 'em was smart enough to see you set the hand?"

"The bankroll, Willy. We gotta protect that. Hell, we had a chunk in action there."

Willy shook his head. "I could of took all their money, even that Jason fella's. They weren't no good. I don't feel right workin with a bad deal."

"But . . ."

Willy fixed his eyes on Sonny. "You ever run me up a hand again, I might just shoot you."

"Willy, we agreed."

"No. Was you said it." Willy looked at the ceiling. "Me and Beau's hungry. Let's go over to Nuevo Laredo. Have us a steak."

"Willy, maybe you could visit a lady. Hell, you seem in need, and heaven knows Beau needs someday to be with one, sooner the better. Might normalize him."

"That's what I like about you, Sonny. Mixing hell and heaven and whores in one breath." Willy smiled as he pocketed his share. Going to prostitutes wasn't the same as being with Lisette—prostitutes with their crucifixes nailed to the walls above their beds, ready to pray for forgiveness as soon as a man's pants were pulled up, his belt buckled, and his money handed over.

Willy motioned for Sonny to pick up his split.

The gambler sighed and picked it up. "We okay?"

"Yeah, but me and Beau are thinkin of movin on for a time. Figure I can bank my own game if I have to. Besides, I got me a girl back in Bedloe. Someday I'll find us somethin up in New Mexico and settle down. Heard it's nice there."

"Willy, you ain't ready to go off on your own and make it my way. Maybe we been here too long and should move on to better pastures. Say, inland or up to Galveston."

"Maybe. But me and Beau, we ain't been on saddles for a time, and it might do us both good not to see each other for a day or two. 'Sides, I ain't never seen the ocean, not the way my pa described it, miles of sand and nothin but waves."

"It's just water. Gulf or ocean, that's what it is. I seen plenty of it. Ain't the ocean anyhow. It's the Gulf of Mexico. If you know what it looks like already, what's to see?"

"Don't know until I see it."

21 Midday they reached the edge of some sand dunes and heard the waves roar before the Gulf even came into view. Willy looked at Beau, who smiled back. They goaded their mounts up the dunes, and when they reached the crest, the vast body came into view. Breakers thrashed the shore and dissolved into a white foam that fanned out, then receded. Atop the dunes, they sat their horses and took in the sight. The beach glistened amber and appeared as smooth as carpet. Shorebirds hovered over the water. Here and there one dipped its wing and plunged into a swell.

Willy said as much to himself as to Beau, "She was raised near the sea."

"I wanna go swim."

"I'm thinkin it might be a place for us to settle, some town near here."

"Wuh-what town? Ain't no tuh-town."

"Somewhere's they is. See, we got us a stake goin. Soon enough, we'll be able to bankroll our own spread. You, me, Lisette."

"Puh-Panther Jack ain't gonna luh-like that."

"He ain't gonna have no say in it."

"You can wuh-watch it all duh-day," Beau said. "Me, I'm goin in." He whooped and slapped his hat against the gelding's flank.

Willy followed down to the beach, both shouting as if possessed. The horses' hooves sank into the sand. They dismounted and went on foot, leading their horses, so they could investigate this new world. Willy stood a moment, listening to the plunging surf and feeling the spray blow in on his cheeks. His chest swelled as he imagined bringing Lisette here. They walked the horses up the beach over seaweed tangles that looked like heaps of entwined serpents. A blue-legged crab sprang out of some sediment, then scurried sideways to the water.

"It's somethin, ain't it?" Willy said.

"Ain't nothin buh-but water, Willy. Hell's bells."

There was no way Willy could account for it and didn't bother bringing it to Beau's attention, but in the months they'd been crossroading with Sonny, Beau's stammering problem had diminished and often disappeared entirely. He even talked more often. There had to be an explanation, but Willy was baffled to find one. He speculated that it had to do with Beau's being away from Clay or maybe even Ruth.

"You're talkin like a normal man," Willy said, mentioning it for the first time.

"Uh, ain't nuh-nothin normal about the way a Texan talks."

Willy knocked Beau's hat off. The wind caught it, and it tumbled up the sloping beach. Beau ran after it, but stopped when it settled atop the soft sand. "I'll guh-get it on the way back."

Willy reached over and tussled Beau's hair. "You happy?"

"I ain't complainin, if thu-that's what you muh-mean."

In the marshy inlets the air was rich with odors. They came upon a beached fish, its smell so rank the horses pulled away. Willy picked up a starfish, smelled it, and tossed it in a wave. A few feet away was a small spiny ball. Willy turned it over with the point of his boot, trying to determine if was plant or animal.

"Looks meaner 'an a cactus, Beau."

Beau grabbed his hat from the sand. They mounted and galloped the horses north for another half mile, then slowed the animals, dismounted, and led them by the reins. Beau walked silently beside Willy, who was lost in thoughts of the future. Though the idea of going in the water terrified him, the beach and the potent sound of the waves inspired him. He saw a world full of possibility, filled with good things to share with those he cared about. Gambling seemed a trade for all climates and all times. In three months, they'd amassed a hefty bankroll, nearly three thousand dollars. Sonny had plenty left to teach. Willy and Beau would stay partnered up with him until Willy learned all he'd need to go off on his own, every strategy and move. He'd have money enough to take care of the family and start one of his own with Lisette. They'd have children, maybe live by the sea.

Then he looked at the swells farther out, the white caps rolling in, and saw beyond the beauty of the breaking waves the immensity of the waters, the sea as Panther Jack had described it—a vastness painful for the eye to behold. He recalled the terror of his wild journey under the river's surface and cast aside any thought of settling near something so formidable. No, never, no child of his would live near water like this. He'd be content with a ranch with waves of tall grass on rolling meadows and slow-feeding cattle.

He pictured a ranch house, not one so opulent as the Mexican hacendado's, but inviting and tranquil in its simplicity. "Beau," he said, "I figure to have us one of them tiled patios like that Mexican don."

Beau didn't seem to hear, or it didn't matter to him. Beau, who never asked for a thing and was grateful for whatever came his way, was the happiest person Willy knew. He envied that. He shook his head and went on with his musings. A few steps later, he realized that Beau had stopped and hobbled his horse.

Willy looked back. "What's wrong?"

"Let's guh-go in," Beau said.

"Why?"

"I wuh-want to, Willy. Reason enough, ain't it? Not luh-like we got a guh, goddamn ball tuh-to go to."

Willy looked again at the roiling waters and felt, as he sometimes did in dreams, the grasp of the river pulling him under. "Let's walk a bit more."

"We ain't never suh-swum in no ocean," Beau said.

"I ain't never swum in nothin by choice," Willy said.

"Well, I huh-have, and I-I intend on it ruh-right nuh-now."

Willy kept his saddle and looked down. "Beau, we should be talkin plans. You know, take care'a the family and all. See, the way—"

"It's huh-hot and I'm guh-goin in."

"Stubborn sumbitch," Willy muttered, then said, "It ain't a horse. You can't harness the damn thing."

Beau dropped the reins, unbuckled his belt, and looked at Willy. "Yuh-You handle th-the huh-horses. I'm guh-goin suh-swimmin."

Beau sat and pulled off his boots, then stepped out of his trousers and shed them. He stripped off his shirt and stood in his long johns, a pale, wiry figure between Willy and the dark-blue waters. His long johns went next.

"Whatever you got in mind, Beau, it's crazy. That ain't no cow pond."

Beau's clothes lay in a pile at his feet, and he turned away from and stood facing the beach.

"Fool," Willy said, "get your clothes on."

Beau, his mind seemingly closed to any thought but the ocean, walked down the sand and into the water. He stood at the beach's edge as a retreating wave covered his knees and looked back. "You suh-scared?"

Willy saw it as a challenge, one he didn't want to take up. "What if I am?"

"Old Lopez tuh-tossed muh-my suh-stones and tuh-told me—" Beau laughed without finishing what he'd started to say and rushed out into the high surf, where he cast himself into a dying wave that enveloped him. A few seconds passed before he surfaced and hollered back that the water was fine.

Willy thought he might as well go in, though not too far, and let the water allay the bite of the sun for a time, but not venture beyond where the water rose to his waist. He tethered the horses, undressed, and tossed his clothes over his saddle. It felt fine to be naked in the open air, boots off and free as an animal in the wild.

Waves washed over him as he approached waist-high water. Beau swam back and taunted him by splashing him with water. Willy splashed back. Beau splashed him again and dared him to come farther out. Willy went deeper, deeper than he'd intended, and a wave washed up to his shoulder, the next one to his neck. He felt a compression in his chest, turned, and started back for shore. Then a current grabbed him, and his feet were jerked off the sandy bottom. He felt an instant of panic. He flailed his arms about and tried to gain footing, but the Gulf waters proved more powerful than the Rio Grande.

The current pulled him away from shore and under. Then an instant later the wave that had sucked him under seemed to collapse, and Willy's feet touched down. A back tow pulled at him. He struggled against it and made it to the shallows, then lumbered ashore, chest heaving, limbs limp, grateful to feel warm sand on his bare feet. He sat and caught his breath, pleased to have solid ground under him and thinking, never again.

He looked out over the surface and saw that the current had shifted. Beau bobbed atop a swell that was carrying him seaward. His face joyful, he waved back at Willy. He seemed to be laughing. Willy rarely saw him laugh and smiled at the thought of him out there, free enough to laugh at nothing. The next instant the swell white capped and collapsed.

Beau slid from sight.

Willy hollered at him, but Beau didn't answer. Two more swells rose and broke. Willy watched intently, waiting for his cousin to resurface. He didn't. "I'll put a shameful hurt on you!" Willy shouted.

Panic struck, he sprang to his feet and ran down the beach into the water. A wave rose up and met him. It swept him up and the next instant pushed him downward. Another gathered him up. He found himself afloat on a high wave, his eyes stinging from the salt. How it happened was a mystery, but he was paddling atop the water as if he'd always known how to. When the wave rose even higher, he glimpsed the back of Beau's head at the base of a retreating wave several yards away. He shouted his name and paddled farther out. A swell rose up in front of him and peaked like a pyramid. It broke and washed over him. He lost his bearings and tumbled down its ever-steepening slope. A moment later, it crashed ashore and heaved him down hard on the wet sand.

When the sea around him leveled, he found himself lying facedown, watching bubbling white foam fan out across the sandy shore. He crawled to dry sand, sat, and caught his breath. The sky had clouded and the water turned slate. He looked toward where he'd last seen Beau, took a few deep breaths building courage, and charged into the surf. His eyes and his lungs burned, but he paddled out again, somehow managing to reach the point where he figured Beau had disappeared. Swimming seemed, if unnatural, at least easier this time. He gathered a load of air in his lungs, kicked his feet, and dove beneath the surface.

He opened his eyes, but saw nothing. The salt burned into them. He surfaced, gulped in air, then dived again, this time deeper. He stayed under longer, but saw only schools of tiny fish, flashing like silver knives as they darted around him, and a few round creatures with sharp spines on the sandy bottom. Gasping for air, he surfaced and slowly paddled toward the shallows, where he stood and waded to the shore.

Clouds blocked the sun. Goose pimples rose on his skin. Beyond the reef where the waves thrashed upward, he sighted an object floating on the swells. It was barely discernible, perhaps, he thought, just his eyes betraying him. Still, he called to Beau, but the sound of his voice was swallowed by the crashing waves. He called out until his voice went hoarse. Then he slumped down and drew his knees close.

Cloud after cloud drifted by. In time, the chill air made him stand and move. He dressed, mounted his horse, and rode the beach up and back, again and again, looking for any sign. Beyond the horizon's edge, effluvium from a ship's smokestack trailed into the sky. He crisscrossed the shoreline in both directions until the tangerine sun smoldered in the west and turned the tips of the waves crimson. Finally, the vastness of the sea itself overwhelmed him, and he was sure Beau had been lost to it.

He found Beau's horse wandering the dunes above the shore. He unsaddled the animal and, in removing the saddlebags, was surprised by their heft. He opened them and found more than fifty silver dollars in them along with another sixty-seven in bills, money that apparently mattered little to his cousin. He unsaddled his own mount and before night fell gathered drift-wood together in a pile, set a fire, and waited. For what he was unsure. A miracle, the fall of night, sunrise, or whatever came.

The heat from the flame had little effect on his shivering. He tried to console himself by thinking of Lisette and conjuring up images of the house and patio he planned to have and the meals she'd serve to those who came. None of it gave him comfort. His future had always included Beau. Now the future seemed as obscure as the darkening void beyond the glow of his fire and as endless as the surf slashing the shore.

Throughout the night, in between naps, he fed the fire.

THE SUN ROSE acetylene-white on the horizon. Willy saddled the horses and mounted his. With Beau's animal in tow, he rode to the water's edge, where gulls cawed and pelicans splashed manic-like into the surface. Choppy waves raced to the sand and spread out softly and evenly as a white linen cloth. He rode the shore north a mile, seeing no sign of Beau, no hope of it anywhere, then turned southward and followed the same track. He came upon Beau's boots and hat and clothing and using his bare hands dug a hole in the sand for them and covered the articles. He stood over the buried belongings and tried to muster some appropriate words.

All that came to him was to repeat over and over, "I'm sorry. I should of stopped you. I'm sorry."

Before this moment, the single emotion that had most determined his char-acter had been anger. But now Beau was gone, and Willy realized that he'd be forever bound by the chains of guilt. A never-before-experienced numbness engulfed him. He had no words for what he felt and no anger to somehow counter it, and it chilled his heart.

Heading inland, Willy stopped once to look back and was dismayed to see how tranquil and slight the slate-colored waters seemed from a farther distance.

22 Willy and Sonny traveled a backwater circuit, sleeping on hard cots in shabby hotels or under saddle blankets beside some trail. Willy learned as Sonny plied his craft, finagling seats in Elks Lodges or Rotary Clubs where play was soft or in bars or smoky back rooms where

spotting a gypsy move could result in the brandishing of a knife or gun. They employed a sophisticated con game, heavy-fingered shuffles, deliberately bad decisions, excessive chatter. Wherever they went the pride of the men at the table was invariably greater than the talent, and after they'd anesthetized their suckers with the con, Willy and Sonny went to work.

They lazed about hotel lobbies or cafés until midafternoon when Sonny brought out the cards and made Willy practice. Sonny, shaking his head, scolded Willy. "You need hands, boy. Your fingers are like pig's knuckles. Relax 'em, feel with the tips." To get the touch Sonny insisted he'd need to master the deck, Willy shaved with a straight razor while holding a deck of cards, whenever he buttoned his trousers or shirt and even when he pulled on his boots. Though he had no intention of ever cheating, he drilled himself, dealing deuces until he could pluck the second card from the deck as easily and as silently as he could the first. Hiding a card in his palm proved difficult. His hands were small and still calloused from dirt labor and pushing steers. The process was gradual, but slowly the hands softened, the touch came, and Willy could gypsy a deck with an ease of motion that closely matched Sonny's.

Sonny insisted the game could be beaten only one way, and that was to cheat. But Willy resisted.

"How you gonna know if some fella's doin you, if you can't do 'im?"

"I'll know."

"You keep foldin on good hands."

"Yep. That's the truth of it. I ain't havin no part'a cheatin, 'less somebody takes to cheatin us first."

That hadn't happened. Sometimes players were so bad, they lost even when Willy and Sonny tried to let them win. Players came from all manner of backgrounds—bankers or merchants, cowboys or roughnecks—and Willy had no desire to cheat a working man or a fool. He insisted there was no call to do so, that a fool's perfectly capable of cheating himself out of his own coin. As he'd promised, he folded whenever Sonny ran up a hand.

In dots of civilization scattered from the Brazos south to the Rio Grande and from Del Rio east to the Gulf Coast, Willy played the dumb-luck kid with fumble fingers. As the others drew on their whiskey bottles, he drank amber-colored water from a flask, bet up a pot on two weak pairs, and folded against a bad bluff, all of it designed to put the chumps to sleep. By the time the whiskey had dulled the others' judgment, Willy's dumb luck took over. He was just a kid, and the gruff-voiced gamblers dismissed his luck. Stakes increased, pots grew, and Willy kept getting luckier. The remarks rang out with consistency—"Damnedest luck I ever saw." Then, before the players knew it, the game was over and they were boned out and pocket empty. They gathered up their tired limbs and left the table muttering.

On occasion, the suspicion they were being had came to suckers before they were boned out, and Willy and Sonny had to lose some money back.

Too often, Sonny liked to overstay and take more than a fair bite out of a man's wallet, which bothered Willy when he found himself on a horse at night running for the county line to get away from some angry sucker who might be a sheriff's brother-in-law. On two occasions their exits from town took place in a panic in the middle of the night on horseback, five minutes ahead of an angry pack of roughnecks and cowhands. More often small-town merchants and politicians, friends of the local sheriff who fancied themselves clever at a poker hand, complained to the law. Willy saw it as bad business.

What Willy couldn't flee were his feelings that Beau's death lay on his shoulders, and his dreams of swollen waves and an endless expanse of water reminded him of his cross. Try though he might to avoid the ghosts, when his eyes closed, visions rose up against him—Beau, a grinning face bobbing on a swell, calling to him, or Beau stiff as a sheet of ice washed ashore, a pale body Willy never saw, but could conjure up all the same. He imagined his ma, her tone accusing, asking him if he wasn't supposed to be watching over Beau. Where was Beau now?

When not riding a chair at a card game until dawn, he drank sour mash until the fog dulled his thoughts. He awakened haunted with the feeling that he was like Cain, cast out into the land of the unclean, as the sermon went, cast out because he'd killed a brother, not just from jealousy, but because his pride had been injured.

If only for periods, poker freed him of the dead, as the self-accusation gave over to the tension of peeking at cards or studying every wrinkle on an otherwise empty face. Each night Willy's skill multiplied, the bankroll grew, and as they moved into populated towns, the pride they encountered increased and tempers more often brought games to the edge of violence. Still, Sonny insisted on cheating at the worst possible times.

When Sonny was confident that Willy could handle bigger games, Sonny said it was time to try San Antonio, Port Arthur, or Galveston.

"Fine with me, but no cheatin 'less we's cheated," Willy said.

"Okay. Where to?"

Willy didn't want to see the Gulf again. "San Antone."

"Okay, after that Galveston. It's a wild place. Got itself wiped out by a wave once, but now . . . Well, we'll pick what bones we can in San Antone first."

23

They rode into San Antonio in the night and registered at the Sam Houston Hotel. Willy had seen nothing like it, save for a hacienda or two south of the border. A man in uniform offered to carry their bags to the room. Willy showed him his saddlebags and said that he'd been trucking them across Texas for six months and the stairs didn't appear all that steep that he couldn't manage on his own. Their room was plush, the bed the softest thing Willy had felt since holding Lisette's breast, and they had a balcony that overlooked the town square. Willy stared at the shadows on the wall and listened to Sonny's snoring. Sleep came slowly.

In the morning, Sonny awakened Willy and told him to dress, that a maid would be coming in to clean the room.

"It ain't dirty.

"These people got different views on that."

"A maid? How much that cost us?"

Sonny smiled. 'At's right, a maid, Willy. Comes with the bill. We're livin in the lap of luxury here. And we gotta pay for it. Keep that in mind when we're lookin at our bankroll in the middle of a table. I'm goin down for some breakfast. Then I'm goin to the police station to reacquaint myself and make an impression with the fine men who wear badges here."

"You promised. No cheatin."

"We'll see."

Willy grabbed Sonny by the arm as he turned to leave.

Sonny, his face deadpan, stared at Willy. "These men gonna be serious. Some downright mean, no clodbusters or snake-oil drummers or drovers. This town's the bad side of Texas. Are you ready for it?"

"I got this." Willy pulled back his blanket to expose his revolver.

"Just get you in jail," Sonny said. "They's some water for shavin and a towel in that bowl on the dresser."

They heard a noise that sounded like an automobile, but not the same, a harsh whining sound that rose and fell. Sonny walked to the balcony.

"Come look," he said.

Willy hurried to the balcony and stepped out on it. High in the sky a biplane turned in wide circles above the town. It twisted in the air like a corkscrew toward the clouds, then suddenly pitched groundward, still spiraling. Willy had seen a dozen or so automobiles the night before as he rode into San Antonio. He'd heard of a machine that flew over Corcoran City and had listened to tales about others, but here was the first show of flight he'd witnessed.

"Buzzes like an insect in a field of honeysuckle," he said. "Wish Beau could see it. Boy, would he be wantin to go up in one!" Saying it saddened him. He looked down where people had gathered beside the street and in the town center.

Sonny came up beside him. "Willy, you ain't appropriately dressed."

Willy looked at down at his long underwear. "Guess not." He took a last look at the airplane and retreated into the room.

"When you get through cleanin up, look beside the bureau."

Holding the deck, Willy scraped his jaw with the razor. In the mirror, he saw a lonely man gazing back. Here, then onto Galveston, he thought. He remembered the ride to the beach, his wanting to go to Galveston. He'd thought of it as a place where money fell out of men's pockets, and there was the sea for Lisette to take pleasure in. Then, as if the room had suddenly filled with seawater, the salt smell came to him and he pictured Beau drifting away on slate-colored waves. He looked again at the old eyes on the young man in the mirror.

Behind the dresser in the corner, Willy found a two-and-a-half-foot-long object wrapped in a white cotton cloth and tied with string. He untied the string, unfolded the cloth, and removed the gun. Holding it in his palms, he measure the weight and balance. It was a 16-gauge Savage with a barrel sawed down to ten inches. Willy opened the breach and looked in the chambers, clean but scored. He wondered why Sonny had bought it.

He snapped the breach shut, wrapped it up in the cloth, and went to dress.

SONNY WAS SEATED at a table beside a window when Willy joined him.

Sonny smiled, laid his napkin down, and looked around the room. "Filled with gentlemen and ladies," he said.

"Saw the shotgun, Sonny. Guessin it ain't for shootin bird."

"You still ain't much for casual conversation, are you?"

"Not much."

Sonny pointed in the general direction of south. "River runs through here. It ain't the most impressive river, kind'a slow. It's noted mostly for bodies what float down it on occasion. Shotgun's for those what would take what's ours."

"Thought you said I was ready. I can shoot just fine."

"You can. But they's thugs here. You're a kid, Willy, barely seventeen. Hell, 'at's why these chumps is so eager to get in a game with us." Sonny tapped his fingers on the top of the table. "I seen ten maybe twelve shootins. Shoot one, you may never hafta shoot another."

"I shot men, all right. Don't mean I want to."

"Back a ways, I saw you ready to."

"That Yankee had no fight in him. All mouth. I knew it, you knew it."

"Well, if the time comes, you got a scattergun. I'm goin now." Sonny stood. "Eat somethin and wait for me."

After eating Willy returned to the room and locked the door. He got the shotgun out, wiped it down with the cloth, and laid it atop the dresser. He flopped down on the bed. Fingers entwined behind his head, he lay thinking of Lisette. It'd been six months. Much had happened. American soldiers were fighting Germans in France, alcohol was about to be outlawed, and Beau had drowned. He wondered if Lisette longed for him as he did for her and how she would react if she saw him. He was lying on the bed working through those thoughts when Sonny's key rattled in the lock.

Sonny sat down on his bed. "I got us an invite to a game. Told 'em I met this dumb cowboy kid—that's you—who's got more bankroll than brains."

'At's what we're here for."

"Willy, you been pretty quiet 'bout what happened to Beau," Sonny said.

Willy unlaced his fingers and sat up. "I'm thirsty," he said and walked to the door.

"I'll go with you," Sonny said, reaching for his coat.

Willy cut a look at him, then, seeing his own reflection in the mirror over the dresser, smiled coldly. "We been seein too much'a each other." He opened the door and paused.

Sonny was looking at him, his lips drawn tight.

"I appreciate the present, Sonny." Willy pointed at the shotgun. "And your company for the most part. Don't want you thinkin otherwise, but Beau ain't your bidness."

WILLY WAS STARING down at the San Antonio River when Sonny hollered and waved. With him was a stranger. From the way they leaned toward each other as they talked, the man and Sonny seemed old friends. Willy waited for them.

"This is the kid I was talkin 'bout," Sonny said as they neared.

Willy nodded to the man.

"This here's Willy," Sonny said.

The man offered Willy his hand.

"Ernest Wooling's the name. Proud to meet you. Sonny speaks highly of you."

A pale, thin man, taller even than Panther Jack, he had a narrow face and bushy eyebrows that rose as he spoke. Gambler was evident in the way he dressed and shook hands. Since teaming up with Sonny, Willy had developed the sense to see the difference between gamblers who gambled and gamblers who didn't, and Wooling didn't seem the type to gamble on anything.

"Yes, sir."

"Ernest has a poker room outside of town."

The man waved Sonny off. "Not a room. A big tent. Brought it from a army major. Big enough for two tables, six men at each. And it fills ever weekend. 'Course I rent from a cattle buyer. Not the tent, the spot I put up on."

"He wants us to have it," Sonny said.

"Wants us to have it?" Willy glanced toward the river, thinking, why?

"Might work out for us," Sonny said. "The sheriff don't mind it much. I checked on it."

Willy looked at the stranger. "Where you know Sonny from?"

"Parts and places. You know, we butted up against each other here and there. First was in Mississippi. Down Biloxi, I believe."

'At's right," Sonny said. "I was dealin faro."

"And cheatin," Wooling said.

"Why you want to do this for us?"

Wooling and Sonny exchanged looks. Wooling cleared his throat. "I'm sellin. Can't run two tables by myself. Headin to Dallas. Biggest thing to happen to Texas lately is the farmin bidness. That money happens to be in Dallas. Forget cow towns."

Willy looked at Sonny. "Why don't we go on to Dallas?"

'They's pickins left here. Ain't that right, Ernest?"

"Plenty for one operator. Slowed down some after the boys out at Camp Wilson was sent over to France, but they's still enough men driftin in to find work. I'll take you boys over and introduce you proper like to the sheriff."

Willy smiled and started walking. They followed along.

"What's his percentage?"

Sonny patted Willy on the shoulder. "I told you he's a smart boy. Got a heart good as a loyal hound and fingers like sticks three months ago. Now he can face down a hangman and false cut a deck with one hand."

Willy's cheeks reddened. Wooling winked and said that he knew Sonny was a con and there was no need in being embarrassed.

"How much?" Willy asked.

"The cost of the tent?"

"No, sir. The cost of the sheriff. My experience says sheriffs ain't cheap."

Wooling laughed. "One way to find out is to go ask. This way," he said and changed direction.

"Dallas, you say?" Willy said.

"Biggest city in the state. Gonna be to Texans the same as New York City is to Yankees."

Sonny smiled. "Hope it does Texas better 'an that."

24 The skirt of the tent fluttered in the wind as rain pelted the canvas roof. Hanging on each of the tent posts were two lanterns swaying back and forth. Inside the tent usually smelled of liquor and body odor and cigarette smoke, but this night it smelled of wet manure and animal urine that floated in from the nearby stock pens. Both tables were in action, Sonny at one with four players and Willy at the second with five. The week had been good to them. They'd pulled in seventeen hundred dollars off the two games, a fortune in Willy's mind, enough with what he and Sonny had accumulated to take his share and look for a spread.

Tonight, Sonny was losing. As agreed, they'd kept the games honest, and a string of second-best hands had cost Sonny four hundred dollars, all of it going to a loudmouth wildcatter. Sonny folded his hand, moved tables, sat to the left of Willy, and whispered that skill couldn't beat a man who stays to draw an inside straight against a pair showing.

Tossing in a silver dollar, Sonny said, "Change'a luck. Deal me in."

It was the signal for Willy to switch tables. He gathered up his money and took the seat vacated by Sonny. The wildcatter, a hay bale of a man, stared at him.

"What's this? A boy sent to do a job a man can't?" he said.

Willy smiled at the others, then locked eyes with the wildcatter, who stared back contemptuously. The tent had been a good investment, and the sheriff wasn't too greedy. Most nights they'd won double on what they'd risked at the tables. It was a dry county, but early each evening a man named Pickens came around and sold a bottle or two of what he called whiskey. It was, Willy found out after spitting out a mouthful, a form of rum made from sugar cane that came from the moldering cane fields near Galveston. Sonny had his own sources for whiskey, and late in the night, as the early losers trickled off, he'd produce a bottle and pass it around the table, a gesture of goodwill well received.

Willy set his dollar on the table and offered each of the men a self-conscious smile, a piece of the con he and Sonny ran on players.

"What's your name, boy?" the oilman asked.

Willy grinned. "Why, it's Boy. Why ask if you know it already?"

"Funny little thing, aren't you. Hell, boy, I shit turds bigger 'an you."

"Well, ain't no way I could shit a turd as big as you." Willy held his grin.

"You gotta name?"

"Why?"

'Cause I wouldn't call a fella big as you anything but Mr. Somebody."

'At's fine by me. Mr. Somebody it is." The oilman looked at the men. "Guess a boy's money spends as good as a man's."

Willy drew well and promptly won the next hand, then two more. As he raked in the pot from the third hand, the wildcatter snorted. Willy looked at him and sniffed the air. "If the rain keeps up, this place gonna smell awful rank."

"Never mind the smell," the big man said.

The deal went to Willy, who called for the ante. The wildcatter tossed in his dollar so hard the coin rolled past Willy and went off the table. Willy was dealing. He looked down at the coin, which settled near the tent skirt. The wildcatter sat waiting for Willy to pick it up, but Willy shuffled, passed the cut, and pitched the cards out, bypassing the wildcatter.

"You forgot me," the wildcatter said.

"You wanna see cards, you gotta have an ante on the table. Right, fellas?"

None of the other plays spoke. The play went forward. Willy folded at the first bet. The wildcatter drummed his fingers on the table. Willy held the deck and dealt the hand to the others and called the bets and raises. As the last two players traded raises, the wildcatter and Willy traded looks of mutual scorn. The hand finished, Willy calmly passed the deck to his right and looked at the big man. The wildcatter leaned forward and ran his tongue over his lips. He set his hands shoulder width on the table and knotted his thick-fingered mitts into fists.

"What's your real name, boy?"

The player to Willy's right, a soldier, stopped his shuffle. Others sat nervously watching the big man. At the next table play ceased in the middle of a hand.

Willy gazed back without blinking. "Willy, but it's awright to call me Mr. Bobbins."

The man pounded his palm on the table. "Well, Willy Boy. I'd appreciate like hell you bendin over and pickin up my ante so's I can play this here hand."

"Mr. Somebody, I bet like hell you'd appreciate that." Willy made no effort to move.

One player, a soldier with corporal stripes on his sleeve, said he'd get the coin. Another spoke, saying that it was a friendly game and he'd toss in a dollar for the wildcatter.

The wildcatter said, "Leave it for the boy."

The tent skirt flapped in the wind. The rain drummed steadily on the canvas. No one moved or spoke.

Then a man spread the flaps and asked, "This where the game is?"

The man stood inside the entrance as the flaps snapped behind him. The tent seemed to suck in the wind. No one looked at or answered him. All eyes shifted from the wildcatter to Willy. The corporal broke the silence with a fart. Someone said he could call that bet and farted. Except for Willy and the wildcatter, the players laughed nervously.

"Hell's bells, I'll put up for the big fella, just to see a hand." A wrangler who called himself Pecos tossed two dollars in the kitty. "Come on, boys. We came to play."

The newcomer went to Sonny's game and took a seat. The corporal finished his shuffle, offered the cut to Willy, then dealt the hand. The game went forward, but the tension, now somewhat muted, remained.

Willy won that hand and one more, then folded the next two. The wildcatter passed on his turn to deal. He'd lost a pot or folded on every hand since Willy had sat down. He grumbled as the losses mounted.

The next hand, seven-card stud, showed a possible straight for the corporal, who stayed. The wrangler, holding the deck, folded with a four and nine faceup, as did another player who held a three, queen. The big man drew an ace to a pair of nines showing and raised twenty dollars. Willy caught an ace to his sixes and raised back twenty. A double call followed, and when the pot was even, the cowboy dealt out the final faceup cards—king to the corporal's queen, jack, ten; another ace to the wildcatter; an ace to himself.

The wildcatter led off with twenty dollars. Willy matched and bumped the pot ten.

"Must hate money, boy," the wildcatter said.

"I like yours."

The corporal matched the pot, which told Willy all he needed to know. The wrangler dealt the last cards down. Willy didn't check his.

The wildcatter glanced back and forth at Willy and the soldier. "Don't know where a boy and a soldier get that kind'a money." He spread two twenty-dollar bills in the center.

"Get it from you," Willy said. He matched and raised twenty.

The wildcatter's cheeks darkened. The corporal matched the pot.

Willy looked at the wildcatter. "Don't need to turn it over. Got yourself a pair a aces with them nines, and that's the sad truth," Willy flipped over his hand. "Full boat, sixes over."

When the deck next came to Willy, the wildcatter gunned every move as Willy shuffled. Willy announced the game—Omaha Hold 'Em—and dealt out the hole cards. He buried one card, thumbed off three cards facedown, and turned over the flop, a pair of sixes and a seven. The wildcatter raised forty. A double bump brought the pot to three hundred dollars. Willy matched the bets without looking at his down cards. The wildcatter cut an eye at him and snorted.

The turn card was the eight of clubs. Two players folded, one called, and the wildcatter matched the bets and stared at Willy, who raised it another forty. The remaining player dropped out, except for the wildcatter, who took a swallow on a bottle and went all in. The soldier whistled and lit up a fresh cigar.

'At include that silver dollar?" Willy asked.

The man looked at the coin and nodded. "Your call."

Willy finally looked at his hole cards—an ace of hearts and an eight of diamonds for two pair. He figured the man for a straight. Luck, Willy thought, it comes and goes for some and seems to live with others. He stared across the table at the burly man and said, "Count it down."

The wildcatter spread out the last of his money—one hundred and seven dollars—and pushed it to the center of the table. Willy set the deck down, matched the man's money, and added a dollar to cover the one on the floor. The big man turned his cards over and showed a nine-high straight. He took a swallow off his bottle and stood. Willy turned his hand over. He needed an eight or a six on the river to win.

The wildcatter chuckled. "You got fire under your feet now, boy."

"Well, they was gettin cold anyhow."

Willy set the deck atop the table so there would be no doubt about the deal. He burned the top card and turned the river card up, an eight of spades.

The wildcatter stared at it. "Ain't it somethin how that happened," he said.

Willy calmly passed the deck on and reached out to rake in the pot. As he divided the bills and coins, he remembered the silver dollar. He bent over, plucked the coin up out of the mud, and tossed it across the table, where it landed with a flat-sounding *ting* in front of the wildcatter.

"Your lucky dollar."

The wildcatter pursed his lips and muttered. In a breath, he reached across the table, grabbed Willy's collar, and jerked him over the layout with a violent wrench that spilled the table on its side and dumped the money on the floor. Caught by surprise, Willy could do little to defend himself and took a punch to the gut. Then the man shoved him out through the flaps into the rain and said, "Been cheatin us all day, I'd say." He pointed to Sonny. "Him too."

He kneeled and scooped up bills and gold coins. He was about to stuff his pockets when Willy charged through the flaps. The wildcatter wheeled around, both his hands clutching the money. He dropped the bills in one hand and grabbed for Willy's collar. That was all the edge Willy needed.

Willy rained blow after unanswered blow to the big man's face before he had the good sense to let go of both Willy and the cash. He took another blow and staggered back, fists raised. Willy figured he had little chance inside the tent. He needed room to maneuver. He backpedaled through the flaps and stood his ground two steps outside. When the man emerged, Willy was waiting. He landed three blows and moved to the left before the man could grab him. Weaving back and forth out of arm's reach, Willy again waited. When the man was in range, Willy lashed out with a series of stinging jabs. The blows did more to enrage the man than they did harm. Sneering and confident, he lumbered toward Willy, doing exactly what Willy expected.

The others, except for Sonny, stepped outside and formed a circle. Willy retreated and circled left as the man advanced. The wildcatter lowered his head and charged. He threw a wild swing that Willy ducked. The next blow grazed Willy on the crown of his head. Willy answered with a stinging combination. Two jabs landed on the man's nose, followed by an uppercut to the solar plexus, then another jab and a left hook above the man's eye. The big man's brow began bleeding. He fired off a wild swing, lost his footing, and stumbled forward. Willy laid three chopping shots on the same cut eye. The third sent the wildcatter to his hands and knees in the mud.

Dripping blood from the nose and above his eye, the wildcatter drew himself up on one knee and raised a hand as he caught his breath. The others urged him to get up. Two reached out to help him. He shook them off, looked up, and spat blood at Willy's feet.

"Had enough?" Willy asked.

He shook his head and spat out more blood.

"Suit yourself, fat man." Willy motioned for him to get up.

The man gathered himself and stood. He stepped back, cocked his hands, and waited. Again Willy circled to the left. The man turned in step with him.

"I'm gonna break you in two," the big man said and stepped closer.

Willy grinned and lashed out with a quick left to the man's nose. The blow caught him coming in, and the crunching sound and solid feel of the punch told Willy all he needed to know. The wildcatter bellowed and, despite his broken nose, lowered his head and charged. Willy sidestepped the charge and aimed another blow at the man's eye. The wildcatter flopped to the ground, belly down. He lay gasping for air.

Willy stood over him. "Got me a sister tougher 'an you, big mouth."

The man clawed at the mud until on his knees. Two players helped him to his feet. He cocked his hands and motioned for Willy to come to him. Willy hit him in the mouth twice and stepped back. The wildcatter's eye was closed. He staggered about as he tried to bring Willy into focus with one eye. Willy circled in the direction of the closed eye.

"Gawdamn, boy, hold still!" the wildcatter looked up to the sky and roared.

Willy calmly walked up and thrust the toe of his boot into the man's crotch. The wildcatter shrieked, grabbed his groin, and collapsed in the mud. Willy hovered above him, waiting. But the fight was gone from him.

Willy took in a deep breath and exhaled. "Rain did raise a smell around here," he said and turned and went inside the tent.

The others looked at the fallen wildcatter as he lay groaning. Then, one at a time, they went inside, leaving the troublemaker to deal with his troubles. The money lay scattered around the table. Sonny, his arms folded, stood guard over it. He set the table back on its legs and helped Willy gather up the money. They stacked the bills and separated the coins.

'Bout how much he have when he started?" Willy asked the others.

The wrangler volunteered that it was about a hundred dollars. Willy counted out one hundred and ten, walked outside and stuffed the wad of bills in the wildcatter's shirt pocket.

The wildcatter looked up through his one good eye. "You cheated me, boy."

"Don't make me kill you, mister." He looked at the others. "Someone get his horse."

Willy, the corporal, and the wrangler lifted the man onto his mount. Willy slapped the horse on the rump and shooed it away, and then the three of them returned to the tent.

A few hands later, the corporal and three others said goodnight and drifted off. They left broke, but in good spirits thanks to the fight and the whiskey in their bellies. Soon two more left. The six who remained continued the game on one table. Sonny brought out a bottle of Irish whiskey, took a swallow, and handed it to the nearest man.

Even when the whiskey ran out, the players refused to quit. An hour passed, then two, without Willy or Sonny managing to break the others. The game continued into the dim light at predawn. The men sat droopy-eyed and stared at their hole cards. The wind and rain died off. Crickets chirped. An owl hooted. Some steers lowed in the distance. Willy yawned and stared up. When he looked back at the table, he shook his head and folded with a four and nine in the hole.

A horse rode up. The others seemed not to notice, but Willy sat straight and listened a moment. He excused himself and walked to the corner of the tent, where he lifted the lid of a long wooden box. The players stopped the game and watched as he unwrapped the cloth holding the shotgun, opened the breach, and loaded it. He returned to his seat and positioned himself sideways to the tent flaps. He set the gun on his lap, barrels aimed at the entrance.

They finished the hand, and Sonny asked if Willy was in.

"Believe I'll set this one out." He motioned to the men nearest the entrance. "I'd appreciate you boys givin me some room."

The men opposite Willy moved their stools aside. Willy waited. The footfalls got louder as the intruder sloshed across the mud toward the tent. Then the flap flew open, and the wildcatter, revolver in hand, filled the entrance. His right eye was closed, his nose caked with blood. He breathed through his mouth. Those with their backs to him looked back, but held their seats. He raised the revolver and told them to get clear of his aim.

"I come for the boy. No one else."

Willy held the scattergun under the table. "Fellas, would you move aside a sliver so's Mr. Somebody won't shoot nobody by accident?"

The men stood and spread to opposite walls of the tent.

"Thank you." Willy pulled both triggers at once.

Chips of wood, paper notes, and coins flew into the air where the buckshot blew a hole in the table. The wildcatter staggered back through the opening and fell. He lay faceup. Only his boots remained inside the tent.

Willy walked around the table and looked down at the man. A gurgling came from his throat. His chest rose and fell convulsively. A chipped piece of pine about a half-foot wide in a crescent shape lay at his side. All, except Sonny, stared at the dying man. His eyes were closed, and he was shaking his head.

Willy looked at the chunk of table blown out by the shotgun. "Guess we gonna have to move the game to the other table. Someone might go find the sheriff."

No one moved.

"Well, then, I guess they's no hurry. But if he starts to stink, we'll have to move 'im."

25 The lawman, lanky with a dark muzzle, told Willy to have a seat. He lit a cigar, inhaled in quick spurts, took a deep puff, and blew out a stream of smoke. He held the cigar at arm's length, admiring it. "It and whiskey and women who can't talk." He laid his feet atop the desk and let the silence hang for several seconds as he studied Willy. "You're a mite young to be causin so much ruin, boy. And they ain't too much to you otherwise, from my perspective. What's a boy like you doin fightin a man like Amos Peabody?"

"Been growin into my boots lately, as my ma would say."

"Your ma ain't here, so answer the questions straight."

"Was him fightin me."

The deputy puffed on his cigar and stared. Willy knew resolute silence could win a poker hand, but he had no hand to play here, except the facts. And it seemed the lawman didn't care much for clever answers. Willy leaned back in the chair. Horse hooves clattered on the street right outside. In the background automobile exhaust belched. Willy wasn't yet used to the city, where sounds penetrated even the brick walls of the jailhouse.

It occurred to Willy that Texas was changing even as he sat there. He'd heard of farmers and ranchers walking away from their life's work with their pockets full of paper and their fields turned into groves of oil derricks. Motorcars were getting to be so commonplace that the city made accommodations for them to be parked on the street side.

"If you're through gazin at the wall, we got bidness." The deputy cleared his throat and continued. "Let's start over. Name's Hilbert Aikman. I'm the detective 'round here, and I'm gonna give you some advice, Bobbins. You wanna shoot people, find some other place."

Willy grinned. "Where's a good place to be shootin people?"

"Ain't funny, Bobbins," the deputy said, but his eyes glinted with amusement. "You're too small for that mouth."

"Hell, can't help my size none. All I really got to say is he had a gun and was gonna shoot. I shot first. That's it, just like them fellas say." Willy scratched his nose. "This is still Texas, ain't it? Man here's got to defend hisself. Write it down, and I'll give it my mark."

Aikman's cigar had gone out. He chewed on it as he wrote. When he put his pen down, he read it over silently and laid the completed document before Willy.

"You want me to read your statement before you sign?"

"I trust you to get it right."

Willy wanted to hear what else the detective had to say, and then he could better judge his own situation. The way he saw it, everyone was playing a game of some kind, and everyone wanted to win. Some did. Most didn't. It was poker without cards, and the way to win was knowing what game a man was playing, how he planned on playing it, and if he had the skill to hold up to the pressures of playing. The deputy was a good old boy just doing a job. Cops weren't paid much, so their best chances at winning were to get the upper hand on a crook or take money to look the other way.

"We got enough witnesses who say you shot in self-defense. Me, I'm a skeptic. I see it this'a way. Man thinks he was cheated comes back after his money. Can't say as I blame 'im."

Willy was only half listening to the detective, who was jawing about his theory.

"You hear me, Bobbins?"

"Yes, sir. Don't cheat. Don't hafta. His luck run out was all, Sheriff."

"I ain't no sheriff." The detective dropped his feet, his boot heels banging the wood floor. "His luck run out? Damn right. Shootin a man with a short-barrel shotgun. I figure you was maybe lookin to get a reputation so's you can go on cheatin without some fella takin issue with it. Is 'at how it is?"

Willy figured that the only theory that mattered was the theory that the sheriff himself didn't want to lose his cut of the action. "He come back set on killin me. Believe it says as much in them papers you got."

"You want to read 'em?"

"Can't really cipher words, Sheriff."

"I ain't no sheriff."

"Yes, sir. I see that now. I did meet the sheriff. You ain't him."

The detective set his cigar aside and waved the statements at Willy. "These boys could be friends'a yours. Could be a pack'a lies and a waste'a paper."

"Just met them boys last night, 'cept for Sonny."

"That'd be the other cheat." Aikman set the papers before him. "I'll read what they say."

Willy listened as the detective read the witness statements. They were brief, no two were identical, but all agreed the wildcatter initiated the fight and returned intent on shooting Willy. So easy, Willy thought. Had he been wanting it, as Aikman suggested? Willy was ready to concede that point, but it didn't matter. As he saw it, the wildcatter was dead, and Willy was justified. Nothing would change that. He felt no remorse and nothing could change that either. He wanted the cop to finish his say, so he could leave. There was money to be made, and it couldn't be made sitting at a desk.

After Aikman finished describing the shooting according to eyewitness accounts, he banged his fist on the top of the desk. "That's perdy much it, less you wanna add anythin?"

"Reports don't say I ended up with a couple'a dented coins and a twenty-dollar bill with holes in it. That deserves some thought."

"Not much."

"What happens now?"

"Some fella put up bail. All the witnesses is probably willin to lie and swear to it at a inquest, but you'll go before a judge for runnin a casino."

Willy smiled broadly. He pointed to the flag. "Hell, Mr. Aikman, this is Texas. A tent to keep the rain out and a friendly poker game is a way a life here."

"Bobbins, men don't die in friendly games. And there was whiskey."

"You're right. One unfriendly fella can ruin a game." Willy set his gaze on the cop. "A man can see you're a sportin man, Mr. Aikman. What? Horses? Craps?"

The detective relit his cigar, leaned back, and propped his boots atop the desk. "Bobbins, San Antone's a city now and growin. They ain't no room for you."

"You want me gone?"

"Gamblin's a vice, and alcohol's against the county law. Soon gonna be that ever'where."

"Mr. Aikman, they's a war on, and you got soldiers runnin 'bout lookin for vice. And they and others can put a dollar in a man's pocket faster 'an you can say, 'Willy, you're free to go.'"

"Why would I say that?"

Willy saw that Aikman was a man who liked his cards exposed. "You bet on balls, don't you?"

"What's 'at?"

"Hold 'Em. 'At's your game, Mr. Aikman."

The detective held the cigar away and licked his lips. "Hold 'Em *is* the only card game, Bobbins."

"Well, now, we agree on that. 'Spose, just 'supose, you was to get a invite to a game, would that hit your fancy? And 'spose, Mr. Aikman, you got staked to a game, say, a hunert dollars?"

The lawman's eyes narrowed. "You're mighty young to be so bold with your supposin."

"Yes, sir. But 'spose."

The cop flicked the ash off his cigar and examined the glowing tip. "This is Texas."

Willy glanced back up at the flag. "It shore is. Yep."

"You seem a mite old for seventeen, Bobbins, but a mite young to be killin. Can I have your word on no more killin?"

"You got my word on that. I mean, maybe your presence could stop those unfriendly types? It's somethin to think on."

"Bobbins, you're quick at jumpin into a proposition. Ever hear'a bribery?"

"Bribery? It's, like Sonny says, hypo-thet-ical. Mr. Aikman, if you're some kind'a saint, I apologize. But I figure a man like you sniffin about to flush out gamblin has somethin in mind."

Aikman pushed the statement toward Willy and handed him the pen. "Your mark's required to make it official."

As his mark, Willy scratched down a capital *W* the way Sonny had taught him in jail.

"Nice meetin you, Mr. Aikman. We'll be movin beyond where that rancher Norton keeps his stockyards. Be a few fellas who'll make a lot more noise 'an effect, maybe soldiers lookin for that vice you ain't got in San Antone."

The detective stood and extended his hand. Willy shook it.

"It was a matter of time for Peabody," Aikman said. "Went 'round stirrin trouble all the time, bullied anyone he could. Guess he didn't count on meetin a snip like you. Witnesses say you give ol Peabody a skinnin, fist and cards both. Don't think I'd wanna play Hold 'Em with you, Bobbins."

"Mr. Aikman, I wouldn't wanna play anythin with me." Willy walked to the door. He paused before opening it. "You won't be showin up, will you?"

"No."

Willy had missed something. "Wanna say why?"

"Sheriff's term's comin up. I intend to run. Politics, Bobbins. You lose if you stay."

"If you win, can I come back?"

"Be next year." Detective Aikman pointed to the door with lettering that read "Sheriff." "That poker stake, Bobbins, think it could put a dollar toward a campaign?"

"I'd say maybe yes." Willy nodded. "Call me Willy. I'll see you in a year."

26 The game was Omaha Hold 'Em. Willy held a two and a four in the peek. A three of spades, a queen of clubs, a nine, and a seven of hearts lay in a line in the center of the table, and Willy was going for low when a six of diamonds showed next. The player, a dandy dressed in a white muslin suit, pulled a gold watch out of a vest pocket. He held it momentarily. Caught in the lamplight as it twisted, its chain seemed a living thing. He set it atop the pot. It was a watch the likes of which Willy had never seen. He coveted it, as his ma would say, sinfully.

"I'll call that wager," the man said. "This should be sufficient to cover it."

"If it's real," Sonny said.

"You may test its heft, sir, should you wish to," the player said.

"No need," Willy said.

"Pot's right," Sonny said.

Willy figured an ace, deuce, an ace, three, or a deuce, three would take the pot. Sonny double-checked to the power and signaled to Willy with a raised pinkie knuckle that he held a deuce, three or lower. That informed Willy that he should fold if his hand was higher. Willy looked at the watch. He knew Sonny would sell it when he won the pot, and Willy wanted to win it outright. Instead of folding, he bumped the pot fifty more, which scared off a longshoreman and a sailor.

When the call bet came to the player who'd bet the watch, he said, "I've got this." He removed a diamond stickpin. "Valued at two hundred. I raise that much."

"What you do fer a livin," Willy asked, "mine gold?"

The player said, "No, my father does. Copper as well. He financed some of Mr. William A. Clark's ventures in Nevada and Arizona."

"Never heard of 'im."

The man muttered "Bumpkin" just loud enough to be heard.

The betting continued. Three bumps later, Sonny narrowed his eyes on Willy as if saying he should drop out, but Willy didn't, so Sonny did. In all the pot now consisted of a diamond ring, a gold cigar case sitting atop two thousand dollars in cash, and the watch. Only Willy and the dandy were left vying for it.

Willy examined the cigar case. "Gold-plated. This don't cover no two-hunert-dollar raise." He uncorked the bottle to pour a drink. It was empty. He turned it upside down and looked up its throat. "Dry."

"I can't call again, sir," the player said, "unless as a gentleman, you'll accept my marker or allow this call without raising back. As is apparent, I come from wealth and we honor debts."

Willy looked him up and down. "Would you accept my marker if I decided to raise and couldn't produce cash?"

"Being a gentleman, I would."

"Okay, then, I'll make my mark on the paper. I raise a hunert dollars more."

"You can't raise. I'm still attempting to call, and you can't be sure I'll not raise back."

Willy leaned forward and raised his eyebrows. "Where you from?"

"Baltimore. That's in Maryland."

"I know where it is." Willy handed the cigar case back to the man. "Write out your paper and keep that case."

Willy was rethinking his strategy. He'd thought the dandy would fold, but that proved not the case. More than a thousand of Sonny's and his bankroll was in action. He decided on another kind of bluff.

He held up the bottle. "I'm leavin to get another. I trust you, bein a gentleman."

"I could take offense at that," the man said.

Willy paused at the door. "Take offense, but leave the cards be."

In his room across the hall, Willy sat on the bed and calculated the probabilities. The longer he considered the hands, the more certain he was that the player likely had him beat and couldn't be bluffed. And Sonny had held better cards. Willy knew he'd never hear the end of his losing a pot that big on a bluff. It was the watch and his coveting it that brought him to this point.

"Damn," he muttered.

He had to go turn his hand over or . . . He lifted a laundered shirt. Underneath lay a pistol. He stuffed it in his belt so it would be seen, then walked back into the poker game. Instead of sitting, he remained by the door and stared at Sonny.

"Sumbitch, you set the hand. I saw it." He drew the pistol and aimed it at Sonny. "Two'a you been workin us all night."

"You're crazy, sir," the dandy said, pushing his chair back and rising.

Willy swung the barrel in the man's direction. "Sit, 'less you want it?"

The man shook his head.

Willy addressed the other players. "You fellas all been took by these slicks."

The players looked from face to face. The notion they'd been cheated took hold with the sailor and longshoreman. Assured he had them thinking his way, Willy stepped behind Sonny, placed the gun barrel to his head, and said, "Give these fellas some money."

The dandy said, "This is insane, gentlemen. Don't you see . . ."

"Tell 'em what you did."

The man looked at their faces, then at Willy, and said, "Sir, you are no gentleman."

"And neither're you." But Willy was impressed. He cocked the hammer and laid the barrel against the back of Sonny's head. "I said give these men their money."

Sonny fainted and bumped his head on the table on the way to the floor. Willy figured he'd overplayed his bluff, but now he had to go through with it. He fired once, intentionally missing Sonny while putting a hole in the hardwood floor.

The dandy's lips quivered. "You shot him."

"'At's a fact." Willy reached into the pile and gave the longshoreman and sailor a handful of cash, what he figured to be enough to satisfy them.

"Knew it all along," one said.

"Yep," the other agreed as he took his share.

Calmly, Willy suggested the players take the dandy outside and teach him a lesson. "I'll take care'a the dealer here."

The man offered no resistance as he walked to the door between the sailor and the longshoreman. When the door closed, Willy nudged Sonny with the toe of his boot and said, "You can get up."

Sonny looked up. "You gone loco, boy?" He crawled to his feet. "Damn it. You were shootin at me."

"Nope, the floor."

Sonny saw the hole. "Hope you didn't shoot no one in the room below."

Willy placed the watch in his pocket and pointed. "Think you better get to the livery while I get our clothes. I got a feelin no judge gonna understand why you're alive."

Willy headed for the door. Sonny was shoveling coins into his pockets when he stopped to check the hole cards of the hands. He looked first at Willy's cards—the two and the four. He glared at Willy, then turned over the dandy's hand, a two and a five.

"You had 'im beat straight up. He was just a fool lookin to lose."

"And he did." Willy felt fresh admiration for the stranger who never wavered or showed fear. "We're finished here. I guess you get your way. I'll go on to Galveston with you."

27 The air smelled of salt and ammonia and solvents. A gull rose level with the veranda, hovered for an instant, and drifted back toward the bay. Willy set his pork sandwich aside, leaned back in his chair, and propped his boots atop the balustrade. Black smoke rose from a ship's funnel as it headed seaward. Sitting next to Sonny, Willy was mulling over matters, some having to do with Beau, others with Lisette, most involving Sonny. He couldn't give lip to the problem, but something about their arrangement made him ill at ease. Ready to set out on his own or not, the time had come for him to leave Sonny behind and try his own luck at gambling. See if he was ready.

For weeks now, he'd let himself dream of having a fine piece of land and building a life with Lisette. When he imagined her, too often it was to picture her coupled with Panther Jack. He tried to shed that by building another life in his imagination. Problem with that was, he didn't want to be a dreamer any more than he wanted to be a drifter, but living a drifter's life seemed to demand that he imagine a future with roots and a family, and having money enough was all it took.

The outgoing ship began a slow turn on a northeastern tack, the smoke dissipating over the harbor. Willy watched and wondered if, after what happened to Beau, he could ever travel on a ship. Besides, where would a ship carry him, but someplace where he'd be among strangers? He was homesick, but returning to Bedloe was a tough prospect. He needed sufficient money to fix matters for his family plus enough left to take Lisette to the better place he had in mind for them. There were other hurdles—Bobby Grimes's friends, Clay's betraying him, and having to tell his ma what had happened to Beau. She'd asked him to watch over Beau. He'd failed, and the thought of telling her further reminded him of his failure.

"You don't want it, pass it over," Sonny said.

"Pass what?"

"The sandwich."

"I'm fine with it." Willy touched his upper lip. It was tender from a punch delivered by a drunken longshoreman.

"This is the place, Willy. Hell, we're kings. Why would we even think'a leavin?"

Willy didn't see a kingdom. He saw instead a realm of opportunity, a port booming with war activity and vice. Still partly unfinished from the damage the hurricane that had destroyed it in 1900, it smelled of sea brine and smoke from the burned coal that fueled the steamers. On busy days fifty or more ships lay anchored in the port. Shipping yards stored bales of cotton high as a house. Boxcars of grain, barrels of refined oil, and livestock by the hundreds left from its docks each week. On any given hour and into the early night, city walkways were dense with sailors and others in uniform, or laborers coming from or going to the docks, men who sweated through a twelve-hour shift, then looked for some vice to squander their envelopes on. The Army Corps of Engineers had a battalion of combat engineers camped nearby. Whores brought in from at least five countries, dozens of saloons, and countless floating poker games served their wants.

But Willy was done with it.

"Ever think, Willy, that we're takin money from people what need it?"

"Can't help but think that. Hell, I been one'a those in need of money too long myself. You askin so's to be philosophical again?"

"Just askin. Hell, 'til we teamed up you'd never heard the word. See what you gained? Think about what you'd be givin up."

"I knew what the word meant. I ain't dumb, boy, just can't read's all."

"So, *do* you think about how we get money, and does it maybe bother you?"

"Maybe, but it's plumb hard to care 'bout a man who's foolish with money. My pa, rotten as he is, bein one."

"You just made my argument for me. Man wants to lose it, he will. Ain't our responsibility. Is 'at what's been concernin you?"

"Maybe you're what's concernin me."

The previous night, he'd told Sonny he was planning on leaving and wanted his share of the bankroll. He'd hinted at doing so several times before, but Sonny, who had a way of charming a listener into thinking he was the most important man on earth, had convinced Willy otherwise. Willy knew afterward that he'd been conned, and last night, swearing it wouldn't happen again, he'd stood firm.

Sonny nudged Willy's arm. "Stick around, boy. We'll be rich. You believe that, don't ya?"

"Yep, I *do* believe it."

Sonny was right. There was cash enough floating about for every cross-roader in Texas to turn copper to diamonds. Galveston was also the center of a huge black market for rationed goods. A man named Blackwell ran a bank crap table with loaded dice and one roulette game with a gaffed wheel. Sonny had rented a shack near the docks where he set up the card table.

"Hell, we got the cops who walk the docks lookin away. And 'at town marshal keepin keep watch over our game. You don't need the shotgun. I don't understand you, Willy. What about gratitude?"

What Sonny viewed as ideal, Willy saw as abject. The war might end, with it the war boom and the demand for so much vice. An amendment to prohibit alcohol hadn't yet passed, but the mere speculation that it would pass had driven up the cost of beer and whiskey, and as demand for booze rose, Willy figured prices would go even higher. Whiskey and rum occupied a huge amount of warehouse space at the Galveston docks. Willy suspected that was much the same case in Houston and Port Arthur. He saw a better future in peddling booze than in playing poker.

He and Sonny had begun arguing over whether using their bankroll to stock up on whiskey and rum was a better use of it, Willy seeing it as a sure bet if they priced their booze low enough to beat the competition. Sonny maintained that the price was just a reaction to rumors about the passing of a dumb law. He insisted there was no way to enforce the law anyhow.

"Hell," Willy said, "most'a Texas been a dry for years. Alcohol's ever'where."

"You still thinkin about puttin money in whiskey, boy?"

Willy locked eyes with Sonny. "Never mind what I'm thinkin."

"I met sheriffs that ran roadhouses on the side, food in the main room, gambling and booze in the back room. You think that'll change? Poker, boy. That's our ticket."

Beside butting heads over whether to become bootleggers, they also often argued over what had happened in Port Arthur with the dandy and Willy keeping the watch. Lately, Willy had been going to bed angry and waking up the same. Then, too, he worried about his mother and sisters and hoped that Glen Fellows was looking after the family. He had no way of getting money to them, and Sonny, who squeezed a penny so hard it made Lincoln's head flinch, insisted on holding the bankroll and doling out just enough to keep Willy fed and clothed. Willy picked up his sandwich and took a bite.

Sonny took a slug from a bottle of sour mash and handed it to Willy. The whiskey burned the cut on his lip, but warmed his stomach. He relaxed, took a second jolt, and passed the bottle back. The ship had made some progress across the bay, and another was leaving the dock. Willy watched tugboats guide the ship into deep waters. The smoke trailed off.

"You still set on takin off tomorrow?" Sonny asked.

"Can't pass me a drink and expect me to change my mind." Willy looked at the gold pocket watch, rubbed it in his thumb, then opened the face and read the time. He luxuriated in the sight of the watch and let it lie in his lap so he could admire it awhile. Then as he rubbed its face, his mind turned to home and Lisette's, her bark-colored skin illuminated in moonlight, lips moist as they pressed down on his shoulder.

"Why you always rub that watch?"

Willy extended his hand for the bottle. "Why you so full'a questions today?"

Sonny took a quick drink and gave up the bottle. He looked at Willy with one eye. The other was bruised and nearly closed. "'Cause I can't believe you're takin off when turkeys show up and stick out they necks faster 'an we can kill and pluck 'em. Besides, where you off to?"

"Got me this." He held the watch up. "And some ideas." He'd meant for some time to buy a watch, though he'd never dreamed of one of this magnitude, a Swiss timepiece heavier than a twenty-dollar gold coin and finer than the one Panther Jack pulled out to flash his importance. It served to remind Willy of the danger of coveting.

"You mad 'cause I pulled you off that dockworker?"

"It's done, ain't it?" Willy polished the watch on his sleeve, then placed it in his pocket. After taking a quick drink, he motioned for Sonny to look out at the bay. A freighter was steaming into port, passing over the wake of another that had departed. "How long you figure it'd take to get to New Orleans on one'a them?"

"Don't know. Two days, maybe. Why?"

Willy had thought of New Orleans ever since Sonny had described the clubs on Royal and Baron Streets. "Figured we might go."

"Don't wanna, Willy. It's good right here, but I won't try to stop you."

"Lotta players, I bet. You got some history you can't attend to there?"

Sonny was silent for a long time. He reached for the bottle. He held the rim to his lips, thinking, and said, "Ever'one's got history. Speakin of which, I haven't asked for a time, but, Willy, what happened to Beau?"

"You should of made it longer, Sonny."

Sonny pointed at the bay. "Sure is beautiful. All that water, ain't it beautiful?"

"If you say so."

"You know I almost didn't put up bail for you in San Antone."

"That right?" Willy's eyes were intent on the freighter. That Aikman, he thought, might make me a lotta money.

"You didn't have to shoot 'im. You could of put that scattergun atop the table and scared 'im."

"I could of."

"Ain't you happy with the money we made?"

"Sure am, but I likely won't be here when you come back."

Sonny took a draw off the bottle and extended it to Willy, who shook his head. "You want more 'an half the take?"

"I'm fine with it."

"I invested a lot in you, then you do fool things. You had that dandy beat. I was holdin better 'an you, and you risked the bankroll for a watch. Then that gun goes off . . ." Sonny's words trailed off. He again offered the bottle to Willy.

Willy grabbed the bottle, took a drink, and passed it back. "I might take me a ride on one'a them boats."

Sonny removed his boots and propped his feet beside Willy's on the banister. "You didn't hafta black my eye up."

"Had to, Sonny." The animal blast of the ship's horn shot over the water. Willy stood. "At night 'at's a sad sound to hear, ain't it?" He looked down at Sonny, who remained seated. "You'd like me to give you this watch, wouldn't you? Is 'at what's stickin in your craw? Hell, you kept the pin and the ring and the pot, a hunert in it. That should of been the last said."

"I taught you ever'thing you know." He handed the bottle to Willy.

"And you're a good old boy for it." Without taking a drink, Willy set the bottle in Sonny's hand and closed his finger over it. "I'm set on seein New Orleans. Maybe a fortune's waitin there, so I'll be needin my half, and don't cheat me one penny."

Sonny took a quick swallow and stared off. "You ain't ready, Willy. Got more to learn."

"Guess I'll go learn."

"Your temper'll cause you problems."

"Might. Might not. I'll see my money by this afternoon."

Willy took another look at the bay, its waters smooth, and the horizon. He knew he wouldn't take a ship across those waters to New Orleans. A train could take him there faster. Knowing that made the trip he had to make and had been avoiding easier. His people had to hear about Beau, and he had to see Lisette and tell her his plans. He gazed out over the bay, where the ocean and sky formed a smooth curve, a plume of smoke dissipating on the horizon where the ship had disappeared, the only sign that it had ever existed.

"Since you're so set on knowing," he said, "Beau drowned. Out in all that water. Now you know. You can look at that sea all you want. I can't take the same pleasure in seeing it."

28 Willy listened to the rattle of steel on steel as the train pulled out of Houston, bearing southwest to San Antonio and Laredo. He cracked the window. Home in time for his seventeenth birthday, a thought that brought a smile to his lips. Then he thought of home without Beau, and returning seemed bittersweet. Thoughts of Beau put him in a brooding mood.

The conductor approached and took Willy's ticket.

Willy asked, "This train stop 'bout eighty mile north'a Laredo?"

"Used to. No more. This here train don't need water. One short stop in Corcoran City to let passengers off and pick up one or two. Anythin else, sir?"

Willy figured even a train was a marketplace for a little vice. "Never been on a train before. You think a fella can find a card game to pass time?"

"Kind'a young for cards, ain't you?"

Willy offered a sheepish smile. "My pa says I learn fast." He opened his coat and removed his watch from the inside pocket for the conductor's consideration.

"Fine watch, boy."

"Pa left it to me when he died, along with a little money." Willy slipped the watch in his pocket.

"What kind'a stakes might you want to play?"

Willy shrugged. "Ain't played much. What's fair?"

The conductor punched Willy's ticket and handed it back. "They's usually a couple a fellas on this run strike up a game. Drummers, not real good, I don't guess. Maybe I could swing you an invite. You got funds?"

Willy looked about to see who might be watching, then motioned the conductor closer. Blocking other passengers' view, the conductor turned his back to the aisle and leaned forward. Willy took out his bankroll and held it in a closed hand for an instant, looking side to side, then over his shoulder before opening his fist. Willy was flush. In addition to his share of the bankroll, he'd sold his and Beau's geldings and saddle gear.

"Got a bit, I'd say," the conductor said.

"Yes, sir. Ever'thing Pa left. Near three thousand. Takin half'a it to my sister what's gettin married."

The conductor stood and stepped back. "You wait here, Mr. . . . ?"

"Bobbins. Willy Bobbins."

Willy set the bankroll on his lap where it would be most conspicuous and reached in his other coat pocket for his whiskey flask.

The conductor told Willy drinking wasn't allowed, that it was against the law. "You might wanna go to the dining car and be discreet."

"Here now. What's one swallow?"

"Guess I didn't see it after all."

Willy took a drink and passed the flask to the conductor, who took a quick nip and handed it back.

"Wait here, Mr. Bobbins. I'll see what I can do for you. Anythin else?"

"Just for this train to stop somewheres near Bedloe or Pearsall."

The conductor screwed his face pensively, studying the possibility. "Well, I don't know."

"Might be worth fifty dollar. If it can be arranged somehow."

"We'll see about that, but later."

Willy replaced the flask and peeled off a ten-dollar bill from the wad. "I'll be here."

FOUR MEN AND WILLY sat around a table in the walnut-paneled compartment of a car between the diner and the smoker. Now and then a knock came, the door swung open, and a black waiter in a red jacket entered with a round of drinks. Willy's opponents were a dry-goods merchant named Earl; Grant and Frank, who claimed to be salesmen by trade; and a surveyor, Al, who was destined for Monterey, Mexico, to survey for an oil company. They seemed to be anything but card savvy, soft pickings for Willy, who'd anticipated a backroom game featuring a lot of hard staring and very little talk. The pots rarely exceeded twenty dollars, and the players tended to remain in to the last card. Willy found himself mostly listening to the surveyor who'd traveled throughout Louisiana, Oklahoma, and Texas marking boundaries for drilling companies.

"Been doing it eight years now, surveying leases. Soon as something hits, a town booms just like mining towns fifty or sixty years ago when gold was the driver. Can't run a car or a train on gold. Of course, some strikes are shallow, and the pools aren't very big. Fizzle out in a year. Towns do the same. I'm in at the beginning. I see both the well and the collapse coming, but can't hang around to take advantage."

"Is 'at right?" Willy said. "I'll call the two dollars and raise two." He placed the coins on the white linen.

Grant, the salesman next to Willy, folded. "Who invited this kid?"

Willy smiled. "Hell, I come in here 'cause I heard they was a preacher givin a sermon on the sins of gamblin. Figured it'd do my soul some good."

"I'll see," the surveyor said, tossing in five dollars and raising the pot a dollar. "Yeah, look at Beaumont. When the Spindletop blew in seventeen years ago, it turned the world on its ear. Whoever called it black gold called it right."

The other salesman, Frank, matched the pot. Willy turned his cards over, winning with two pair, kings over threes. "So," Willy said, "what's a fella 'spose to do to take advantage of these opportunities as you see 'em?" He scooped up the pot.

"Don't seem like you miss too many opportunities," Frank, a big man with red splotches on his cheeks, said.

Ignoring the salesman's remark, Willy addressed the surveyor, "What you say your name was?"

"Al, Alan Stanford."

"You a Yankee?"

"From Montana actually. Great state. You ought to visit it someday. World's largest copper mine is there in Butte. Anaconda runs the state."

"Anaconda?"

"William A. Clark owns it, a mining company."

Willy recalled the name. "I heard'a him. You sound a bit like a Yankee."

"Sorry." The surveyor smiled apologetically. "Guess I should sound like a westerner."

"You gonna talk or deal, kid?" Grant said.

Willy flipped a silver dollar into the center of the dining cloth. "Anny up. Seven-card stud. Jacks or better to open."

When everyone had cast down a dollar, Willy dealt out the first three cards. "Ace high, Mr. Stanford. Your bet."

The surveyor peeked at his down cards and offered up two silver dollars that everyone matched. Willy's mind was on what the surveyor had discussed. He played loose and by staying with a pair of threes and ace high lost the hand. That eased the tension. He passed the deck and watched the first salesman shuffle. The man riffled the edges, angled them with his thumbs, and rammed the halves together, then pulled them apart so neatly and quickly the move seemed one motion.

Willy prickled. They were sandbagging. He, the merchant, and the surveyor were marks, and the two drummers weren't drummers. If Willy's suspicions held true, the turn would come now. Grant, a man of forty with thick wrists, called five-card draw and dealt. His meaty hands held the deck awkwardly, but his thumb was smooth as it peeled off cards. It was a sham, the clumsiness just a technique to disguise a gypsy move. Willy folded on a pair of tens. Frank cut an eye at him as if he knew what Willy held.

Willy pretended to sip from his flask as he looked about nonchalantly. It would be easier to catch from the corner of the eye, as Sonny had schooled him in ways to best see a move. Look to the side, instead of straight on. Use the reflection in a mirror or a window to catch it. Your mind will lie to you.

Trust what your eye tells you. As he'd been taught, Willy stared at the darkened window behind Grant as if indifferent to the game.

The surveyor took a card. Grant dealt it from the bottom. Willy saw it clear as a horse crossing his path. After the draw, Grant raised the bet ten dollars. Before the betting stopped, the pot grew another sixty dollars, triple the size of any previous pot. Two-bit cheats, Willy thought. He figured the surveyor for two pairs and Grant for three of a kind or a straight. The pot grew another thirty dollars. Only Grant and the surveyor remained. It fell as Willy had anticipated, the phony salesman winning with three eights and the surveyor losing with jacks over twos.

The deck moved to the second salesman. "Game's a little slow for me," Grant said.

"And I'm stuck," Frank said.

"How 'bout two-and-four?" the merchant said. "I'm down some myself."

Frank winked and held up three fingers. "Let's go three-and-six."

The others agreed. Willy looked at the window to catch the reflection as Frank shuffled.

"What's so interestin out there?" Grant asked. "Ain't nothin but darkness, boy."

"Thinkin," Willy said.

Frank slid his palm over the deck before passing left for the cut. Willy waited until the cut, then laid his revolver before him, touching the grips with his fingertips.

"What's this?" the merchant asked.

"Nothin much," Willy said. "I'd just like to see that deck in the middle of the table."

"You're crazy, kid," Frank said.

Willy set his aluminum eyes on Frank and gripped the revolver. "Maybe."

"What're you sayin?" Grant asked, glancing at Frank.

Frank said, "Hell, boy, you the one been skinnin us."

"Best put that deck down real easy like, or I'll shoot it out of your hand, then put a hole right in the knot of your tie." Willy leveled the barrel on Frank's wrist. "Saw a fella in Corpus Christi take one in the throat. His head wobbled back and forth like a chicken for a time 'fore he spilled hisself to the floor. And don't try nothin like droppin the deck 'cause that may make my finger move."

"Are you robbin us?" the merchant asked.

"Nope, but they want to. Go on now. Set it down."

Gingerly, Frank laid the deck down at the center of the table.

Willy said to the surveyor. "What was those jacks you had?"

"Diamonds and clubs."

"Turn the deck over. See if they's the bottom two cards."

The surveyor spread the deck upside down. The bottom cards were the jack of diamonds and the jack of clubs.

"Spread the rest."

The surveyor complied.

"No fourth jack," Willy said.

The surveyor examined the deck. As Willy had said, the jack of spades was missing.

"Don't move none, Frank. Kinda looks to me like you're a jack off." Willy said. He grinned coldly. "Mr. Stanford, go on and see if they ain't a jack somewhere near this drummer's seat. Knock 'im off his chair if you have to."

Stanford found the fourth jack in between the salesman's knees. Willy pointed with his free hand to the pile in front of the first salesman. "I believe 'at's your money, Mr. Stanford." He turned to Grant and asked, "How much you pay the conductor to let you run this game?"

"You ain't gettin away with this," Grant said.

Willy held his smile. "How much?" He cocked the revolver.

Grant shook his head.

"Don't rile me," Willy said.

"Twenty dollars, plus ten percent," Frank said.

"And I bet you cheat him at that. Mr. Stanford, you wanna teach either of these fellas a lesson 'fore I shoot them?"

"You can't shoot us," Frank said, but his expression indicated there wasn't much conviction behind his words.

"Mr. Stanford?" Willy asked.

The surveyor shook his head. The merchant stood and moved toward the door.

"Where you goin?" Willy said.

"Thought I'd step out, maybe go to the smoker and find me a cigar," the merchant said.

Willy nodded and said, "Enjoy it."

He ordered the two salesmen against the wall, then signaled for the surveyor to leave. He inched his way backward to the door, opened it, and slipped out into the passageway. On the way to the dining car, Willy ran into the waiter carrying a fresh round of drinks. Willy dropped two silver dollars on the tray. The waiter stared at the coins.

"Won't be needin no more drinks." He dropped a twenty-dollar silver certificate next to the coins. "Take that to the conductor. Tell 'im . . . Tell 'im I'll be eatin.'"

The surveyor waited in the dining car.

"Be happy to buy you dinner, Mr. . . ?"

"Willy. Name's Willy. I'd be pleased to join you if you'll tell me about them opportunities."

They ordered porterhouses and baked potatoes. As they ate, the surveyor told Willy how men who move into an oil town want everything at once and that businesses spring up overnight as the law of supply and demand takes hold. The towns, he said, are fairly lawless and violent. Stanford was discussing Dallas as the hub of business in the state when he motioned for Willy to look over his shoulder. Frank and Grant crossed the room and sat at a corner table nearby, glaring as they settled in. Willy nonchalantly cut off a slice of meat.

Stanford glanced at the cardsharps, then at Willy. "What're you going to do?"

"Don't know yet."

"Aren't you worried about them?"

"You say Dallas, huh?" Willy forked the bite into his mouth.

"What?"

Willy finished chewing. "Dallas. You say it's gonna be big."

"Yes. Blocks of warehouse. It's a banking and farming center. There's opportunity there."

Just then the conductor entered and spoke with his accomplices. He nodded several times and looked in the direction of Willy and the surveyor.

"May's well get it done." Willy calmly wiped his mouth on a napkin and stood. "I'll be back. Some water'll do me if the waiter comes by."

As Willy approached their table, the conductor moved to intercept him. "Am I gonna hafta call the police in San Antonio?" he said.

Willy looked first at Frank and Grant, then the conductor. His voice loud enough to draw the attention of everyone in the dining compartment, Willy said, "It's kind of you to ask, but I figure those two thieves there learned their lesson. No need for the police."

The conductor turned so as not to be overheard and whispered, "'At's not what I mean. You pulled a gun on 'em."

Willy whispered back. "I sent you a twenty."

"So?"

"He was there." Willy pointed to his dinner companion. "You see a gun, Mr. Stanford?"

The surveyor shook his head. "Gun? Is there some misunderstanding here?"

"It won't work," the conductor whispered.

Willy looked at the merchant, who sat by himself at a table. "You was there!" Willy hollered across the room. "You see a gun?"

The merchant looked at Frank and Grant. "No. But I sure recall us quittin the game when you pointed out that those men were cheatin me and that man there with you."

The conductor looked around and saw everyone staring at them. Some turned their attention to Frank and Grant and muttered.

Willy looked past the conductor at the two cardsharps. "Mr. Stanford here's a important officer with the oil companies." He motioned the conductor closer and whispered, "You tell those sumbitches I won't be so gentle next time. I just owe my dead pa some kindness, you see."

"We have our own railroad detectives, Mr. Bobbins," the conductor said, glancing in the direction of Frank and Grant. "They could get involved."

Willy figured a man who pandered a crooked card game also had a woman or two working for him as well. He leaned close again. "Wonder what they'd say 'bout you pimpin for a crooked card game. And keepin whores on a train?"

"They's no . . ." The conductor stopped and looked at Willy.

"'At's a good idea," Willy said in a booming voice. "Turn 'em over to your detectives. I don't much care, and neither does my friend here. Now, I got bidness to talk." Willy backed up to the table and sat.

Ignored by Willy and Stanford, who continued their previous conversation, the conductor lingered for an awkward moment as the diners in the car turned their attention on him and the cheaters. He cleared his throat and apologized for the scene, saying that it was a misunderstanding, then walked to the table where the cardsharps sat. He spoke to them briefly and excused himself. When the door closed behind the conductor, Frank and Grant bowed their heads in conference.

Stanford pushed his plate aside. "Are you always this bold, Willy?"

Willy didn't regard of himself as bold or brave. If he let one sharp take him, it would be an invitation for another to try. "Mr. Stanford, it's just bidness."

The surveyor shook his head in amusement. "I'm sure you'll do just fine in a boomtown."

"I'll keep my eyes in that direction, but I'm on my way home. Then I'm lookin to go to New Orleans. Right now I gotta figure out how to stop this train."

"Those cords hanging shoulder high. Pulling on one'll have the effect you seek. I think it's against the law to use it, though."

"You may sound like a Yankee, but you make more sense 'an any I ever met."

Before Willy and Stanford finished their meal, Frank and Grant gave Willy one last look, then walked in opposite directions down the aisle and out the compartment doors. Willy smiled when Sanford said that he was concerned for him. Willy pulled out his bankroll to pay for the meal, but Sanford shook his head.

"It's my pleasure. You've made this trip entertaining."

"Thank you. Next one's on me."

"If we meet again."

Willy stood and shook the surveyor's hand. He needed to get to his bag stored above his seat in the Pullman. He went in the direction that Grant had taken. Assuming Grant and perhaps someone else would be waiting in the next car or the one beyond, Willy planned accordingly. He stepped out on the metal platform that bridged the two cars. The sound of steel wheels on the rail was near deafening. He'd earlier noted the ladder leading to the roof. He mounted the foot of the ladder and pulled himself atop the train.

The sensation of the train's motion was much different outside and atop the car than inside. He crawled a distance before he had a sense for how the car swayed, then he stood and waited tentatively until sure of his balance. He walked slowly to the edge of the train car, where he lay on his belly and scooted forward. Grant waited on the edge of the platform below, his body pressed against the guard rail, in one hand a revolver, in the other a lit cigarette. His eyes were locked on the exit door in anticipation of Willy's appearance.

The rattle of the wheels drowned out all other sound. Willy eased forward until he could get a grip on the top rail of the ladder. He grasped it with his palms up, inched forward until his shoulders were over the end on of the car, and drew himself up on his knees. No different, he thought, than swinging on a tree limb. He lunged forward and down. He landed within two feet of Grant, who turned too late to use the revolver. One shove and Grant plunged backward over the guard rail and off the platform.

When he reached his seat, Willy pull the cord. The train's whistle sounded just before the wheels locked, and the screeching sound of steel grinding on steel announced the emergency stop. The momentum of the train tossed passengers forward. Even though he was prepared for it, the force of the sudden slowing threw Willy down. Seconds later, the train stopped. Willy rose and after gathering his valise from the overhead headed for the door.

Other passengers had been thrown to the floor. Stunned and confused, they looked around as they climbed to their feet. One man who'd apparently seen Willy pulled the cord asked why he'd done it.

Willy pointed out the window. "Saw a man fall from the train."

"Oh." That seemed to satisfy him.

As the others stood and gathered their wits, Willy slipped by and went out the door. The steps down from the platform were raised, so he grabbed the guard rail, swung down, and walked away. He didn't know exactly where he was, but he'd walked a good distance across Texas before. Under much worse circumstances.

29 His face sunburned, Glen Fellows greeted Willy with a warm handshake and smile. Inviting him to sit, the sheriff lit a pipe and puffed vigorously until the smoke circled his head like a wreath. "Guess you heard?"

"Heard?"

"Nell and me's gonna marry up this Saturday. Ain't it what you come for?"

At hearing the news, Willy's expression didn't alter. He had other matters in mind. "I come to take care'a bidness."

"Well, you're stayin for the weddin, I'll guess. Where's Beau?"

"Been meanin to come back for a while. Been busy travelin."

"Beau comin later? Your ma'll sure 'preciate seein the two'a you. Me and Nell got a spread three mile east, sixty-four acres. Drought's lifted. Think maybe I'll plant."

"Glad to hear it. How's Ma?"

"Makin it. Not much money comin her way since you left. With Clay the way he's been . . . well, it's worse 'an ever. Ebbin been carryin her on the books. Flour and sugar and rice and woman's things. She talks a lot about you and Beau comin back. Mostly Beau. Seems she's riled at you."

"Ebbin, how much she owe him?"

"A hunert's a good guess, but he ain't troubled her over it. He's a decent man—if you forget he's into ever'one else's private bidness."

Willy recalled how he and Beau used to wait outside Ebbin's until he took his lunch and afternoon nap in the backroom. They removed their boots, snuck in barefoot, and pilfered some licorice, sometimes jawbreakers or rounds for their .22.

"Who can I trust to hold some money?" Willy asked.

Fellows sucked on the pipe a moment, contemplating an answer. "I keep some in the bank, but ain't got no faith in it. 'Course, they's always Panther Jack."

Willy shook his head. "Rather chance puttin my hand in a sack full'a snakes."

"Ain't that a fact. How much money you talkin?"

"Two thousand."

Fellows whistled and looked at the cell on his left. "You holdin up okay, Junior?"

A gray-bearded man on the other side of the bars smiled, his hollow mouth showing only pink gums. "Yeah. Holdin up fine, Sheriff."

"Gettin yourself a earful?"

"What's 'at mean?"

"It means mind your own bidness. Willy here's about to be my bother-in -law. And he ain't no one to mess with."

The toothless smile vanished, and the prisoner lay back on his cot, face to the wall.

"Hurt 'is feelins, I guess." Fellows puffed on his pipe. "You ain't asked about Clay. Guess you don't know."

Willy didn't hear Fellows's question. He was picturing Lisette the way he'd first seen her as he sat beneath the tree at Panther Jack's. He wondered how she'd greet him, if she thought of him the way he did her, wondered if his brother-in-law-to-be had seen her. He wondered, but he dared not ask.

The sheriff tapped his fingers on the desk. "You okay, Willy?"

"What?" Willy blinked. "Me? Fine."

"Seemed lost there for a time. Anyhow, thought you should know your pa lost 'is leg." Fellows gave this information time to sink in before continuing.

"Not long after you left, doctor come down from Corcoran City and done sawed it off."

Willy looked at the wall. A cockroach emerged between two slats. He watched its slender antennae explore the grain. He pictured his father seated beside the table, as he was the last time they spoke. Being that Clay was a prideful man, Willy wondered how his losing a leg had affected him. "How'd 'at change 'im?"

"He blames you."

For a time, neither seemed to know what else to say. Then Fellows filled in the missing details. "Come down with a fever. Was the leg or him."

Willy watched the cockroach crawl down the wall. He had his own view of blame, and it wasn't the same as Clay's. The roach meandered in Willy's direction. He rose out of his seat and smashed it.

"Drought or otherwise, one thing Texas's got for certain is cockroaches. Come in six legs and two." Fellows opened a drawer, uncapped a bottle, drank from it, and passed it to Willy.

"We still a dry county, Sheriff?"

"Yep. No one would dare violate it either."

Willy saluted his soon-to-be brother-in-law, took a swallow, and set the bottle between them on the desk.

"What about me?" the prisoner said, pointing to the bottle.

"Never you mind," Fellows said. "You can't handle bein sober, and you can't handle whiskey. About the only thing you can handle is your pecker. Now, stay outta our conversation."

"I said my say." The prisoner turned his back to the bars, farted, and promptly collapsed onto the bunk.

"Two thousand." The sheriff whistled again softly and sucked on his pipe, which had gone dead. He lit a match on his trousers. "What you and Beau been up to? Cattle bidness?"

"Cards, Sheriff."

"I told you before to call me Glen. You should, seein as how we're family." Fellows relit his pipe and leaned back. "Must be damn good at cards, Willy."

"They's a lot who ain't. Some's even worse 'an Clay."

Fellows smiled. "If he was a terrible player, it'd be an improvement."

"A fact. How's the rest of the family?"

"Gettin by. Ten months of some rain. Seems the damn drought's over. Least for now. Your sisters worked, and your ma's garden been feedin 'em. I told you about Ebbin already. Your pa's got a still somewheres. 'At's some'a his poison we drank. Sit, we'll have us another."

Willy shook his head and took out his bankroll. "The money, Glen. I mean it for them."

Fellows pointed with his pipe in a general direction and said, "In Corcoran City they's a lawyer, Texas boy what went to one'a them eastern schools. Hear tell he's an honest sort and smart as anyone."

Willy peeled off a hundred-dollar bill and laid it atop the desk.

"You growin green now?" The sheriff picked it up, snapped the edge of it, and sniffed it. "Fresh outta some garden."

"Weddin present." Willy smiled and walked to the door. "You'll make Nell a good husband. Get somethin nice for her with that. I'd 'preciate you not sayin I been 'round." Willy looked at Junior, who was obviously eavesdropping. "And don't you go waggin your tongue neither."

Willy took two silver dollars from his pocket, walked to the cell, and tossed them on the cot where the prisoner lay.

The sheriff stood. "Will we be seein you at the weddin?"

"Can't say."

"How about Beau?"

Willy opened the door and left without answering.

WILLY STEPPED UP to the front window of Ebbin's Livery and Dry Goods. It was the sole store and the hub of information that passed around the community. Gossip mostly. A wagon pulled by a mule team stood ready in the street. Willy peered inside the window and, seeing Mr. Ebbin busy with a customer, waited. Time was nearing high noon, and the street was deserted. When the door opened and the customer stepped out, Willy turned away, so as not to be recognized. Once the mule team drove off, he peeled two hundred-dollar bills off his bankroll and entered.

Mr. Ebbin looked up from behind the counter.

"'Member me, Mr. Ebbin?" Willy said.

"Can't hardly forget you and that cousin'a yours, or brother. Been a blessin lately 'cause I ain't seen neither'a you, not since Beau brought them stable horses back. That's near half a year."

"Yes, sir." Cash in hand, Willy stepped up to the counter. He placed the two bills on the counter in front of the merchant. "You been a decent sort with my ma. I'm ashamed me and Beau used to steal from you. That should 'bout cover it."

Mr. Ebbin scratched behind his ear. "What's this?"

"Can't say for sure how much we took or how much you got on the books feedin Ma, but I wanna make it right."

"'At's a lot a money, son."

"Yes, sir. I figure you'd be right by Ma if she needed something."

The merchant snatched up the bills and pocketed them. The money was as much for Beau as it was for Ruth, a sort of insurance that things might go well for Beau if heaven existed, which Willy doubted. Still, underwriting Beau's soul seemed a good thing. He took out his watch, held it at a conspicuous angle, and opened the face so that Mr. Ebbin would have to admire it. He wanted word of his success to reach *her*.

"Nice timepiece, boy."

"Yes, sir." Willy returned the watch to his pocket.

"I hitched a ride in from Corcoran City on a wagon, Mr. Ebbin. I'll be needin a horse 'til I can buy one. You know who might have a couple for sale?"

"Couple?"

Willy nodded.

"New fellow here, Herb Gosset, got 'im a couple dozen, most for sale. Wouldn't let 'im know how much money you got, though."

"Who says I got money?"

"'At watch says it." Mr. Ebbin patted his pocket. "And what I got tucked away says it."

Willy felt assured that word would reach Lisette. Come dark, he'd go to the church and wait. "I ain't a fool, Mr. Ebbin. Herb Gosset'll find it out soon enough if his price ain't fair. I ain't my pa."

"That's a benefit." The merchant nodded several times to himself. "I'll go out to the livery and drum up a horse. If yer lookin to buy a saddle, I can fix you up."

"How long a ride to the Gosset place?"

Ebbin smiled. "Depends on what horse I saddle for you."

Willy chuckled.

"About a hour, I figure. The old Carpenter spread up west. Carpenter lost it to a tax lien. I ain't been by there. Don't get out much. Most people come to me."

For reasons he didn't understand, Willy wanted the merchant to linger. "Guess Ma been comin in regular."

"Not so often." Ebbin scratched at his throat just beneath the collar of his shirt. "Too bad about your pa's leg."

Willy looked out the window and followed the progress of a horse-drawn wagon. When the team had passed by, he turned to Mr. Ebbin. "Guess that leg keeps 'im home."

"Not your pa, Willy. Hell, he's got hisself a half-dozen roosters mean as a norther in midwinter, and I hear if you got a thirst, he's still the old boy to see. 'Course I don't imbibe."

"None?"

"Once't a year at most, so I'll have somethin to ask forgiveness for."

Willy glanced at the merchandise in the glass display case. A jackknife with a brass handle caught his eye.

"If you buy a horse, I can get you a fine saddle, boy."

Willy glanced at the merchant and raised two fingers. "I may be needin two."

"I'll have the boy to saddle a mount for you. No charge." Ebbin swung about and left through the side door.

Willy walked behind the display case, reached inside, and snatched the jackknife. He opened the blade and felt its edge. He closed the blade and slipped the knife in his pocket. Beau, he thought, would be proud of a little theft. He stepped to where the saddles were displayed and ran his hand over the carved leather. One was an intricate basket weave, the other tooled with scrolls and flowers. That one he would buy for her.

30 Moonlight filtered through the church window. The door opened, and the night breeze seemed to carry her into the threshold. She peered in, called his name, and waited in the door, the contours of her body illuminated, in her hand a carpetbag. He stepped into the light and told her, as he'd told her the night before, that he'd been waiting too long, and if she was ready now, they could set their plans to leave.

She dropped the carpetbag and hurried to him. He held her at arm's length and looked into her eyes, searching them for commitment. Her eyes glistened.

"I'm ready," she said.

"Tonight then," he said.

They kissed and held each other in a long embrace. Willy, feeling her chest rising and falling in rhythm with his, found himself aroused. Months of separation had only heightened his hunger for her. He pulled away and looked at her again. She smiled knowingly and kissed him. He closed his eyes and lay his palm between her breasts and felt her heartbeat.

"What is it?" she asked.

He pressed his lips to her ear. "Just to know."

"Know what? Are you being a mystery?"

"On the road, I thought if I could, I'd reach inside and hold your heart."

"That might hurt." She swatted at him playfully.

He cut an eye toward her belongings. He wanted assurance of her loyalty, needed to know what all was in the carpetbag. Her clothes, yes. But what about the ledgers? "You bring 'is books?"

She shook her head. "I couldn't."

"You couldn't find them?"

"No, Willy, I found them. I couldn't do it."

"Couldn't do it?" He was let down on hearing this. Dealing with him as he had, Willy reasoned that Panther Jack's accounts were probably a sham at best. Taking the books seemed not only justified, but necessary. He couldn't leave and let Panther Jack foreclose on his ma. He figured his former partner would do it now as much out of revenge as greed.

"He was not always bad to me, Willy."

He stepped back. "You said you'd do anything."

"I'll do whatever else you ask. All he has is the books, the money he loaned to others. He lives by that. It's the same as if you asked me to kill him."

"'At's a thought." Willy weighed the options. "Hell's bells, he'll figure out how to skin folks again. It's what he's good at. He holds figures on my pa. Ma could lose ever'thing."

She looked down at the floor. "I'll be gone, and he'll be all right. But if I . . ."

He lifted her chin so that he could stare into her eyes. "We're goin to New Orleans. It's 'sposed to be like where you come from. I told you. No one'll care nothin about us there. I can make money playin poker."

Her eyes widened. She smiled, but it was waxen. "Let's go, Willy. Now."

"I need them books."

"Why?"

"I told you. Didn't you listen?"

"Why would you punish him?"

He let his hand drop to his side. "It ain't punishin."

"He knew about us. He could have, but he didn't beat me." Her eyes pleaded. "You understand."

"You said anything?"

"Not that. He saved me from a terrible life and brought me here. I would not have been with you. You're young, Willy. You don't understand."

"I ain't so young. I've done things grown men ain't done." He shook his head and turned away. He walked up the aisle to the altar and stared straight ahead.

"We'll be all right, won't we?" she asked.

He wheeled about and glared. "You're gonna ruin it." Guilt over Beau rose up inside him. "Between Pa owin Jack and what money I gave for the family . . . He'll put my ma out, her with the girls and a baby. Your ma's dead. If you had family, you'd understand."

He lowered his voice, but continued to cajole her into seeing matters his way. He saw them so clearly. Why couldn't she? She'd betrayed them and their plans. He'd forgive that because she wasn't thinking clearly. He reminded her how he'd thought of her constantly for months and had returned for her. If they intended to be together, she had to prove it by doing as he said. Couldn't she see? His plan was simple. If Panther Jack's books were gone, Clay's mark would be gone too, and claims against him vanished.

"I love you, girl, but I gotta be sure my family's taken care'a. You see?"

She didn't answer him, just held her hands over her breasts and gazed back without blinking. The look on her face was one he'd never seen before.

"We'll do good in New Orleans. I promise." He reached his arms around her.

She dropped her arms to her sides and nodded, but she didn't speak.

Satisfied she understood now, he said, "You go on back and get 'em. We got time. You can take the horse I bought you. It's saddled."

Her lips trembled. She wiped the back of her hand over her eyes and said, "Go back?"

"'Less you got a better idea."

She said nothing more, just turned and went to the door, where she picked up the carpetbag. Willy watched her leave and then sat at the end of a pew. She'd left him flummoxed. He bowed his head. He heard the horse leave. From the sound of the hoof beats, it appeared she was heading toward town. It occurred to him that if she intended to return, she would have left her belongings.

Gone and in the wrong direction. That realization turned quickly into regret. He hurried to the window, hoping to catch sight of her, hoping he was wrong. But he was right. Heat rose up from his neck. His cheeks flushed. His chest sank. His arms seemed leaden. He'd promised her a new life, hadn't he? Wasn't that enough? He turned away from the window and gathered his thoughts.

As he dwelled on it, his emotions shifted from fear of losing her to anger. "Hell with it," he said. "She wants to save a man who cheated, 'at's her decision."

He felt his belly tighten. Panther Jack had given her what Willy couldn't, but she'd chosen to leave that life behind. Let Panther Jack keep his books, his house, his bed. Willy wanted only his woman.

He hurried to the door, threw it open, and hollered her name. Thinking he'd find her and undo his mistake, he ran to his horse, mounted, and rode toward town. Along the way he slowed here and there, peering in shadows along the roadside, calling her name. The road was as empty as the night was dark. He reached the town line and walked the horse through the center. Dead! A single light in a room above the livery was the sole sign that life still existed. He wondered why she would choose to ride here where she was the topic of gossip, envied and hated and unwelcome. He rode through the hamlet in one direction, then another, then another until his horse had trammeled most every loose clod of dirt on every street. But he saw no sign of her or her horse anywhere.

He circled back and covered the route to the church again, from time to time stopping and calling her name. He rode into irrigation channels, anywhere he could. She'd vanished.

He began to doubt his decision about the direction. She'd had time to ride two miles to Panther Jack's. He turned the horse, rode past the church, and pushed the animal to a gallop.

To the right of the road, he saw something dart out of the corner of his eye. He couldn't determine what it was. He spurred the horse and rode into the wooded scrub. He reined the animal back and forth, weaving his way through the trees deeper into the brush. An owl, startled from its perch, flew off a tree limb, its wings snapping as it passed over his shoulder. He called her name. He whispered her name.

Willy could no longer trust his eyes. He halted the horse and listened. The only sound was the breeze combing through the branches. He wondered if in desperation he'd conjured up movement beside the road. Finally, he saw the futility of his quest, turned his mount, and dug his knees into the horse. Still, he sought her out up and down the road for an hour, then another. Three miles south of Bedloe, he surrendered all but one hope.

The house was dark. He looked for the horse, found it nowhere in sight. He dismounted and walked boldly to the door. He knocked, and when he got no immediate response, he pounded on it. A light went on. Willy took a deep breath and exhaled. The door cracked opened, and Panther Jack, his navy Colt pistol in one hand and a lantern in the other, peered out.

"What you want from me, boy? Ain't you got enough?"

"She in there?"

Panther Jack held a lantern up and looked in Willy's eyes. "Left you already? Ha!"

Willy backed away from the door.

"I never should'a got involved with you," Panther Jack said. "She told me about the two of you the day after you left. Never."

The door shut, and the light inside went out. Willy backpedaled from the door that now represented his last hope.

Panther Jack could have shot him. It was certainly warranted and the opportunity was ideal. Willy pondered that as he gathered the will to lift himself atop his saddle. He gazed at the house a last time and wondered why Panther Jack didn't kill him, and if the circumstances were reversed, would he have shot the horse trader? He reined the horse south in the direction of the border.

"New Orleans," he said, and then he repeated it louder, so that it seemed true already that he'd been there and had uncovered something magical in naming it.

When he'd first mentioned the city to her, the sound of it had taken on a musical ring. He said it aloud again and listened for the ring, but it had lost that magic. He tried to summon images of the streets as Sonny had described them, brick paved and lighted at night, the very pictures of the city he himself had painted for Lisette. But he could no longer conjure those visions.

Sonny had told him more than once that mixed relationships were not uncommon and mostly disregarded in New Orleans. Based on that, Willy had assured her that no one would care if a man and woman weren't the same color, a belief he and she would never test.

New Orleans was just a destination, nothing more.

Some miles later he came upon the horse she'd taken, grazing aside the road. He roped and tethered it behind his mount. He didn't look for her.

Part III

||||||||||||||||||||||||||||||||||||||||||||||||||||||||||||||

Don't Play to an Inside Straight

It was an invisible killer beyond the scope of doctors to battle, beyond the ability of the populace to comprehend. It came suddenly and moved swiftly, no place immune, no person beyond its reach, hospitals overwhelmed, neighborhoods quarantined, public gatherings outlawed. It hit the healthiest the hardest and confounded the physicians who treated them. For once the youthful ones didn't survive the clutches of the virus; too often, their lungs filled and they drowned in their beds.

31   For five days Willy meandered south and east, cutting through cedar breaks and walking the horses at a slow pace over the rolling hills of the Edwards Escarpment and down into the flatlands of the eastern range. His troubles rode tail on him and awaited him at the next juncture. Lisette's horse ambled behind him, its only burden an empty saddle, a constant reminder of how dumb he'd been. She'd seen his hand clearly and called his bluff. In his demand for revenge, she'd seen his weakness—an intemperate man who couldn't settle for just having happiness.

He slept beside trails at night and during the day rode from farm to farm or ranch to ranch. The country he traversed, much of it fenced, was sparsely populated, square mile upon square mile of dry grazing land and farm soil gone to dust, yielding up little more than sage and pale clump grass and weed. When he came upon a ranch or farmhouse, he'd stop and ask permission to water his horse. Despite suffering their own troubles with weather and crop failure, the people he met were hospitable. Three families fed him and his mount, and two of them offered him a bed for the night. He had too much on his mind and found it difficult to keep even his own company, much less that of others, so he'd politely thanked them and moved on.

He saw no need to push the horses and little reason to hurry. He figured New Orleans hadn't moved in a couple of centuries and would be there when he got there. Besides, he couldn't outrun his thoughts. Though it would have been wiser to head into San Antonio and take a train from there, he figured instead to drop in on Miles Oberlee and pay another debt that was long overdue. Over a year had passed since Clay killed the Mexican. In the intervening period, Willy, not yet a month past his seventeenth birthday, had killed men, shot another's foot off, rustled well over two hundred head of cattle, bribed a Mexican official, spent three months in jail, and robbed a man of his watch. He felt guilt for none of it, but he'd lost Beau and now Lisette, losses that left him remorseful and feeling desolate. Willy saw no future in loving anyone the way he did Lisette or Beau. Though it pained him terribly, he accepted that the loss of them would haunt his life until a grave claimed him. He was done with it all. Love and guilt and pain fitted together like a three-fingered glove on a five-fingered hand.

Though the drought had lifted, another hot spell had hit South Texas, and by midmorning of his sixth day on the trail, the heat was closing in on unbearable. The sky was the same pale blue in every direction of the compass. A thin breeze swirled up dust. He pulled his bandanna over his mouth, and nose, relaxed in the saddle and watched the horizon. In his grim state, Willy began to dwell again on death and the taking of life. He'd looked inside men as he aimed the barrel of a gun at them and had seen what a man surrenders at that moment—not just his life, but everything he has and is in the world, be it king or kingmaker or crop sharer. Given the course he'd chosen, he might have to kill again. He took no pleasure from the prospect, just accepted it as fact. He'd never kill for money. He wasn't his pa, couldn't kill a man and steal from his victim's body. A good killing, as he saw it, is something a man has to do. It can never be something he wants to do.

Nor could he see any benefit in punishing another. Revenge had been his mistake with Panther Jack. He'd wanted to punish him, in part because of his uncertainty whether Panther Jack or Clay or both had betrayed him and Beau. And because *she'd* been Panther Jack's woman. Willy came to understand another element of being human. Fear. Some fear. Others incite fear. If one man can laugh while serving guests a banquet in the shadow of another man swinging at the end of a rope, he commands respect because the guests know they eat or die at his whim. The idea of owning a spread and having a modest, peaceful life no longer interested him. He wanted power, not the kind reserved for a Mexican don, but just enough to claim his rights in the world. That, he assured himself, would come.

AT DUSK on his sixth day on the trail, he came across an abandoned oil derrick that seemed familiar. He set a campfire and cooked beans, then tossed down for the night. At daybreak he rode south and east to where the land was mostly juniper and white pine. The undergrowth thickened, and as he passed on, travel became more difficult. It took the better part of the day before he heard the river and an hour of skirting the shoreline for him to find the cove. Even after he came upon it, he couldn't be sure it was the same one. No sign of Lucy remained, not a bone. He circled around a salt-cedar thicket until he found a foot trail that he might recognize.

Branches whipped against his legs as he spurred his mount up the narrow trail. Where the undergrowth all but blocked passage, he dismounted and led the horses on foot. He recalled his odd journey up this same trail, children appearing and disappearing, their laughter, the hunger pangs in his belly, and then emerging into a clearing.

Shortly after dismounting, he cleared the thicket and came face-to-face with the daughter. She stood at the edge of the bean field, a hoe in hand. After a daylong ride, he was surprised how quickly he'd arrived from the river, a journey of mere minutes. That day the year before it had seemed so far from the river, and in his exhaustion he'd lost all sense of the world. It appeared as he remembered the place. He smiled at the girl, who stared back as if conjuring up a foggy memory of the man who appeared out of the brush like a vision.

"You remember me?" he asked, then, seeing no reaction, removed his hat.

Her attention turned to his horses for a moment, then back at him. She nodded.

Willy looked toward the house, where smoke rose above the brush. "Your ma home? *Su mamá?*"

She nodded and pointed.

"'At's answer enough."

He walked on. The girl followed. When he arrived beside the adobe house, he tethered his horses under the trees. The mother appeared at the doorway. Her baby stood beside her, holding the hem of her skirt. The woman was big with another pregnancy. The toddler pressed her face into the mother's skirt. The older daughter came up beside Willy. She smiled broadly and called to her mother in Spanish.

Willy angled his face in her direction, "Tell your ma I'm awful hungry."

"*Tiene mucha hambre, él,*" she said.

The mother nodded and walked off with her little girl in hand. She glanced back at Willy, her eyes slanted and suspicious. The two sons appeared from a trail that led to the river. One held up a string of catfish for the mother to see.

"Where's your pa?" he asked the girl.

"*Papá,* he works for a farmer," she said, pointing east.

The mother tossed more wood on the fire and bent over the grill. He squatted under a tree, where the woman, curious but cautious, brought him tortillas and beans. He ate slowly under the watchful eye of the daughter and the sons, both of whom had grown by inches.

"You have two horses and ride alone, *señor?*"

Willy nodded.

"Are you all right?"

He blinked. "What's your name? I never asked before."

"Augapita, *pero me llaman* Pita."

"Well, Pita." He looked at the animal. "I brung that one horse for you and your brothers."

"For us?"

"Guess so."

"But why?"

"Don't matter. Guess you better build a corral for 'im, elsewise he'll eat up that whole field'a bean shoots soon enough."

The daughter explained to her brothers what Willy had said. They ran shouting to their mother. Willy watched their joy and felt terribly alone. When he finished eating, Willy gave the woman four twenty-dollar silver certificates and a gold piece. She looked at the bills as if she didn't trust them.

"Tell 'er that they's real enough," Willy said to the daughter.

The girl explained, and the mother folded them neatly, tucked them away in the waist of her skirt, and examined the single twenty-dollar gold piece from different angles. She spoke to Willy. The daughter translated that the amount was too much for a meal, although it was obvious he'd enjoyed it. Willy said the food was fine and worth even more.

He saddled himself on his horse. "That horse was bought for runnin away. You remember that when you ride it," he said, but the meaning was lost on Pita. He reminded her to keep it away from the bean shoots, reached in his pocket, and gave her five dollars for feed.

"Where you going?" she asked.

Willy looked down at the girl, her eyes dusky, much like Lisette's. She seemed too fragile to survive such a harsh life. He winked. "I'm headin maybe to New Orleans. That's in Louisiana."

"What's it like?"

"Don't know for sure."

"Why are you going?"

"'Cause it's what I got mind to do."

32 Willy never saw Miles Oberlee or turned his horse west, and on an overcast day, four days after his train ride, he stood in the foyer of a house a half mile away from the French Quarter. The house, long and narrow with heavy storm shutters on tall windows, seemed as foreign as the speech of the people of New Orleans with their peculiar way of dropping r's from words. Willy could see from the living room straight to a back door more than fifty feet down an arched hallway. The windows were

raised and shutters opened to allow in a breeze that floated up from the delta. Sunlight glimmered off the polished hardwood floor.

The woman walked Willy to a bedroom. "Have a seat, young man."

Willy sat at a table by the window.

She pulled up a chair. "What brought you to New Ah'lens, Mr. Bobbins?"

He stood, walked to the open closet, and stuck his head inside. "Never had one'a these."

"I said, what brought you?"

"A train, Mrs. Lemeaux."

"Ya like New Ah'lens?" she asked.

"Some. That hotel, well, it's a might uppity for a cowboy."

"You like what you see of the city?"

He looked about the room and said absentmindedly, "Don't yet know, ma'am."

"If you want the room, it'll be twenty dollahs a month. That includes two meals a day. Do you like red beans and rice, Mr. Bobbins?"

Willy discovered his first day in the city that New Orleans-style food was very much to his liking. He loved jambalaya and gumbo but favored the red beans and rice, which came to life with a sprinkle of hot sauce. The food went down easily, even if the local language was a bit hard to adjust to.

"Yes, ma'am. Two meals. I stay out late mostly."

"You'll have your own key. Don't be bangin on the door. If you wake me, you'll hear the walls shiver." She smiled a knowing smile. "What is it keeps you up?"

"I gamble, ma'am. Your house being two blocks from the Quarter suits me fine."

"You're in the right city to get yourself plucked, Mr. Bobbins."

"'At's what I hear."

He spread open his wallet and handed over a twenty-dollar bill for the first month's rent.

"No women, Mr. Bobbins. Ours is a Christian home."

"That go for drinkin?"

"Mr. Bobbins, we're Christians, not saints."

WILLY WASN'T the sole boarder. His room was at the back of the house across the hall from a widow named Mrs. Ducroix, whose husband had been killed in the Civil War. The oldest person Willy had ever seen, she was bent like a question mark and feeble, and her hair, tied back with ivory combs, was a tangle of fine gray wires. A Confederate flag, which she kissed each night, hung like a portiere from the canopy of her bed. She talked constantly of her dead husband and spoke of him as if he lived in the present.

"Charles likes the summer evenings," she might say, or "He prefers morning services to afternoon because the priest's best at wakin people up then." She was nearly deaf and assumed others were equally hard of hearing. She shouted 'most every word. Her grandson had enlisted in the army and was in France in the trenches, but Mrs. Ducroix refused to answer his letters because he joined up with "them shameful Yankees." It seemed clear to her that Charles Ducroix, even though dead almost sixty years, was opposed to the war.

"Good morning, Mr. Bibbins!" she said, as Willy stepped into the hallway. It was past noon, and she sat in her rocking chair that faced the door.

He waved, said good morning, and calmly corrected her, saying his name was Bobbins.

She smiled, nodded her head, and said, "Glad to hear it."

"Willy. Remember?" he shouted. "Willy! Plain Willy?"

"Plain Willy?" she said. "Sorry, Mr. Bibbins!"

It had taken two weeks for him to get her to call him just "Plain Willy." He'd repeated it numerous times, the volume of his voice increasing as his exasperation grew. Eventually, she seemed to grasp what he was telling her and called him Plain Willy thereafter, unless she forgot, and then she still addressed him as Mr. Bibbins. Soon everyone else referred to him as Plain Willy.

The back lawn looked out over a narrow inlet. On Sundays, Mr. Anthony Lemeaux, the landlady's son, cooked gumbo in a big pot in the backyard, which, like the house, was long and narrow. Mr. Lemeaux was burly and nearing forty. He had a black beard that was turning gray at the muzzle. His three boys and daughter attended the cookout after midmorning Mass and afterward came to the house. Mr. Lemeaux was not a widower. His wife had vanished seven years before on the very day a neighbor by the name of Emory Lisper embezzled nine thousand dollars from a freight company. Often Sunday-afternoon conversations revolved around the latest sighting of the couple, who were seen by two witnesses in Vera Cruz, sighted by four in Bogota, and by one in St. Petersburg. Mr. Lemeaux, who'd done well as a fish merchant, kept a private detective on retainer to track the couple's movements. The wife was never mentioned by name.

Mrs. Lemeaux referred to her as "the woman."

The other one who attended the Cajun boils was Mrs. Lemeaux's daughter, Colleen. She was in her early thirties and stood nearly a head shorter than Mrs. Lemeaux. She was the only one among the adults who didn't call him Plain Willy. She was shy and attractive, had wavy hair that hung in wisps over her brow, and light-brown eyes with long dark eyelashes. Twelve years before she'd married Clyde Gaston, a ship's officer who spent long months at sea and short weeks onshore. She had a wistful way of looking off and a soft, hesitant way of talking that aroused more than Willy's curiosity. She lived a half mile away and in the morning often came to her mother's and sat alone in the kitchen, drinking tea. He found himself drawn to her and figured it best to avoid her, which wasn't easy on Sundays when the Lemeaux family gathered after Mass.

This particular afternoon, she sat on a rock looking across the open water. Willy walked to the shore and acknowledged her with a tip of his hat.

"Hello, Willy," she said.

He wondered what occupied her attention. "What're you lookin at?"

Her mouth drew into the shadow of a smile. "The fish."

Willy gazed out to where she looked but saw nothing besides water and a boulder that jutted up about ten feet from shore. Though he'd never witnessed Beau on his outings in Brownsville, he pictured him watching flocks of birds leave the shore and take flight. The next image that flashed before him was Beau bobbing on the waves as the current pulled him away.

"Are you okay, Willy?" she asked.

"Yes, ma'am. Fine." He stood and tipped his hat before leaving. She didn't look up.

Willy crossed the lawn and took a whiff from the pot.

"Near ready, Plain Willy, but try it." Mr. Lemeaux offered a taste off a wooden spoon.

"We got news that Mr. Lisper was sighted in Atlanta, three weeks ago," Mrs. Lemeaux said. "We're getting clos'ah to her."

"Mother, we aren't."

"You need to divorce that woman."

"Willy, have you . . . No, you'd be too young to marry," Mr. Lemeaux said.

Willy thought of Lisette and how they intended to run off as Lemeaux's wife and Mr. Lisper had. Then he looked at Colleen Gaston, who hadn't moved a twitch. Seeing her, her arms wrapped over her knees, hair blowing in the breeze, stirred something in Willy. He wanted to ask about her. The family never volunteered any information. Willy asked Mr. Lemeaux if he was ever suspicious that the detective might be less than honest about the sightings.

"Why would you think that, Willy?"

"Well, sir, I had my share'a dealins with the police, and I ain't found 'em to be so upright as you might of."

Mr. Lemeaux ladled a bowl of gumbo and handed it to Willy. "This boy who works for me's a Pinkerton-trained man. Wants to get 'em bad as I want 'em. Them and the rewah'd."

"Yes, sir, you're probably right. Takes quite a fella to work on somethin seven years with no pay." Willy nodded slowly as he took a mouthful of gumbo. He swallowed it and closed his eyes to express his appreciation.

"Why, I pay him a good sum."

Willy grinned widely. He could have continued the tease, but another matter was on his mind. He'd heard of clubs beyond the fringes of the city, high-stakes limits where wealthy fools lost future cotton inventories, where merchants and bankers spent their bankrolls.

"This is right fine gumbo, Mr. Lemeaux. Say, you buy fish from Cajun men, right? Do you know of any card games? Any good ones?"

"Plenty in New Orleans. Hell, boys around he'ah take up they'ah profession, you know, cards or bettin horses before they'ah twelve."

"Not here. Out in the bayous."

"Willy," Mr. Lemeaux said, "you don't go into bayou country."

He looked up at the sky and mumbled something to the effect that they were a simple people. "We're old French, my family. Them Cajuns are Acadians, Canadian French, clannish in they'ah ways. Ahn't dangerous, or so they claim, but fun-lovin. But I seen a fish peddler." He used his sleeve to wipe the sweat away as he stirred the gumbo. "In the Entagalia Brothers' Market who stood face-to-face with a big Cajun fish'ah man, arguing over a tub of catfish. Next thing we saw was that fishmonger walkin around with his throat slit open so wide you could see the gullet. For a moment he stared at passers-by like he was trying to recognize someone, then the blood spuh'ted out like out of a hose. The Cajun moved on to the next buy'ah like nothing had happened. Got his price, too. That's some ha'ahd negotiatin, I guess. Someone went for the police, but the boy went back to bayou country and vanished. No one's brung him out to my knowledge. Probably still there. Not much law in the swamp, Willy."

"That merchant, was he cheatin the man?"

"That's the notion he got."

"Guess it's safe to say they have a game or two. Maybe it'd go fine if no one cheated no one."

"Don't be a fool, boy. The devil ain't tough enough to take on the likes of them."

Willy thanked Mr. Lemeaux for the advice and added that the devil wasn't a Texan.

They talked and ate until midafternoon when everyone retired for a nap.

IT RAINED that afternoon, and the evening was sultry. Willy caught the mule-drawn streetcar by the canal and rode to L'Nautique in the Quarter. As they neared Bourbon Street, the sound of bands playing Dixieland rumbled onto the streets, as did the fragrance from the kitchens that drew diners from as far away as Memphis and Atlanta. Pedestrians crowded the sidewalks and wandered into the street, ignoring streetcars and automobiles. Horse-drawn carriages rattled up and down the roadway, stopping and dropping off passengers at clubs and restaurants and taking on new ones. One black man played a trumpet, and another picked at a banjo as two young boys danced in the center of a crowd. The music was loud and lively, and a crowd had gathered to watch, some clapping hands to make a beat.

The usual bouncers manned the door at L'Nautique, ready to bar entry to undesirables or overzealous cops who weren't yet aware of the limitations of their office. The doormen, familiar with Willy, knew him as "Texas" or "Cowboy." He removed his hat and raised his arms. One frisked him, and he nodded to the next one, who opened the door and motioned him in. Besides poker, blackjack, and roulette, the house served everything from bad whiskey to fine champagne to prostitutes who awaited the call of one of the dapper bosses. A single clap of the hands from a boss summoned liquor; a double clap called forth a woman. The idea of a law prohibiting alcohol possibly coming seemed to have no effect on the people of New Orleans, determined as they were to make the most of those remaining months.

Willy strolled past a house girl, who lifted her eyebrows and asked if he was as randy as he was young. He smiled and strolled into the brightly lit casino. Everything about it spoke of money. Its walls were decorated with damask wallpaper made in France, Persian carpets lay on the floors, and crystal chandeliers imported from Italy hung from the ceiling. Cigar and cigarette smoke drifted up from a table where two men Willy figured to be poker mavens sat. He watched their play a moment and determined that, at best, he might break even going up against them. He was quickly learning why Sonny had left New Orleans and taken his game on the road. Too much competition for every dollar. Pros nipped away at weak players and bit chunks off the hides of amateurs. Their schooled faces masked the collusion behind every bet. Operating in league, they controlled many of the stud and draw poker games.

Willy was wise enough not to buck up against players acting in concert. That had been his and Sonny's game, and it was for suckers. The two he watched sat with three he'd never seen before. He assumed them to be novices, easy pickings for the pros. One motioned to him. Willy wondered what he wanted, but wasn't curious enough to go to the table and find out. He gestured with a hand, shook his head, and moved on. He felt something telling at work and glanced back to see if the men were watching him. They were. The feeling troubled him as he wove his way through the casino.

He landed at a table where four men, strangers to him, played five-card stud.

"Want a drink?" a suited man asked.

"Sour mash," Willy said.

A hundred-dollar pot, typical on a good night in Galveston or Port Arthur, was rarely seen in the fancy rooms that overlooked the Quarter. In two months Willy never once saw a take exceed two hundred dollars. There had to be bigger games elsewhere. He waited for someone to give him a sure line on where. In the meantime, he was holding back for the right opportunity, one when the stakes were worth the time and risk and he'd be playing against everyone at the table and not two or three sharps bent on bleeding some chump.

He seldom played more than an hour in any casino and never tackled roulette, blackjack, craps, or baccarat—house games, sure to empty a sucker's pockets. He studied the environment—brightly lit ceilings, red carpeted floors, long mirrored walls behind the mahogany bars, the white-gloved doorman, the oversize bouncers, the exaggerated politeness, the brass-barred cage where markers were issued and chips turned into money. Mostly, he directed his attention to action on the green felt, the constant motion of croupiers, the hustle of a stick man calling out propositions before the dice moved. Older men manned the blackjack tables. They dealt as if they were lead-fingered and apologized for their clumsiness, but won hand after hand. Willy considered each turn of their wrists, each unnecessary movement of a thumb, each joining of deck halves, and concluded they were popping deuces, switching hole cards, and rolling the deck and bringing the deadwood to the top—cheating virtually every known way.

Even on the honest side, casinos owned all the odds, but L'Nautique took no risks. It was, as Sonny would say, "flat as an anvil" most every game. Still, people pushed their way through the doors, eager to be cheated by the artful old men who sailed the cards to them with expressionless faces and graceful accuracy. He wondered if the players knew they were being cheated or if they were simply cattle dumb, like some of the cowboys he and Sonny had fleeced. The business was both exciting and problematic. He thought of what it might be like to run his own casino and compete with the flat stores by offering clients something unusual, such as an honest deal and good whiskey.

Tonight, following his routine, Willy sat at a low-stakes game, where he could earn enough to pay his expenses. Occasionally, he had a bad night and had to reach into his bankroll to pay rent or buy a meal. A few times he lost on purpose to hide his skill. A winner's reputation wasn't good to carry into the big games. The man to Willy's left tossed down a dollar. "Not much excitement in this," he said.

"Playin's playin," Willy said.

"This ain't playin, friend. The real games are out in the bayous."

"Never been there." Willy matched the bet and looked away.

The betting went around. The high player showed a pair of jacks. Willy held a queen down and one showing. His next card was a jack.

"Seen a two-thousand dollar pot at Mama Dufois's."

Willy cut an eye his way. "'At's a lotta a money."

The first hand played out. Cautious not to push his bets, Willy played the next three, won sixty dollars, and tossed in his dollar to see the coming cards.

"I can get you into a game," the man said.

"I'm in a game," Willy said.

"No, I mean a *game*."

Willy folded the next two hands, sipped on his whiskey, and watched. He was interested in what the stranger had to say, but even more interested in seeing how he would play his hand with an ace and a king showing against a pair of nines and a pair of tens. The man folded on the second raise and looked at Willy.

"Follow me," the man said and stood.

Willy stood away from the table.

"Mario Anselmo," the man said and offered Willy a handshake.

33

Willy looked up at Mama Dufois. A squat woman in her fifties with shiny black hair and large brown eyes, she wore an apron that covered her corpulent chassis and bore stains from a day's toil at the stove.

"Like de food, boy?" she asked.

Mopping sweat from his forehead, Willy replied it was the finest he'd eaten since arriving in Louisiana. "'At's a passel of fine food, ma'am."

The old woman's mouth, hollow save for a few teeth blackened at the gum, spread open in an uninhibited smile. She told him there was no charge for the *belles callas* that she set before him.

"My food de finest in de bayou," she said. "Maybe de world, though I ain't seen much of it. No need to if it's no better dan dees." She slapped his shoulder and broke out in a hearty laugh that vibrated through her body.

Willy ate rice cakes and watched the entrance, wondering if either the boatman or Baby Jasper would show. He'd hired a boatman in Monroe to take him to Mama Dufois's for two dollars one way and another two to return him after the poker game. The boatman had long since pulled away from the dock. Willy had rushed to the end of the peer and hollered out for the man to stay, but the Cajun merely laughed, dug his pole deep into the still water, and shouted that he'd be back after supper or sometime much later.

Mama Dufois busied herself at the stove. Pots steamed. She stirred one vat and then another. Willy pondered his circumstance. Mario, the Italian in the casino, assured him his passage in and out was guaranteed. Willy had explained that he didn't swim and didn't trust water, other than that he drank or bathed in. Mario claimed no man had ever encountered problems in the bayou, that the people of the bayou were "kind simpletons" and easily taken advantage of.

"What you look at, Willy?" the old woman asked.

"Trees, I guess."

"We are de island in de water," she said. "You see nothing but what de tree let you and what de water bring. People come. Baby Jasper come wit dem."

Beyond the screened porch was a verdant woodland of willow and moss-covered cypress. A mist rose from the still water. The island's shore faded into the late-afternoon shadows of the bayou. A well-worn path led from the porch to a planked dock on stilts, extending some thirty feet into the swamp, providing sufficient landing to accommodate a half-dozen boats at once. As the sun lowered, the humming of the cicadas tailed off and the crickets' song rose, a sound soon joined by a refrain of mosquitoes and a chorus of throaty bullfrogs. Willy felt a longing for the sounds of night on the Black Plains—an isolated bird taking wing, a lone coyote, a scurrying lizard—each distinct.

The canopy became a darkened mass silhouetted by a tangerine light, everything enclosed by vegetation and deep shadow. The shifting light tricked the unaccustomed eye. This wasn't land as Willy knew it, not the land of cattle and horses and rolling range. Like Lisette, it seemed seductive and mysterious. He thought of the day in Mexico beside his pa as they gazed out over the high plateau. That land was canine, snarling fangs and bristling hair. This was feline, sharp claws and stalking shadows.

Darkness engulfed the swamp as if a lid had been placed over it. People streamed out of it, the first signs lanterns that guided their boats across the glossy surface of the water. They came singularly or in families, moored their craft at the dock, and hiked the short path to the house. Some carried canvas bags. Mama Dufois greeted each man and woman warmly, shouting out names and waving her spoon or ladle.

They took stools at pinched tables and chattered in French. Willy was an obvious oddity in their realm. One looked at him and said something that prompted a round of laughter. Mama Dufois scolded them robustly in French. Thereafter, they ignored him and drank and ate and talked and laughed, but none louder than Mama Dufois, who divided time between them and her stove. The room filled with exotic aromas. It was the smell of comfort. Willy felt certain both Mr. Lemeaux and Mario Anselmo had been wrong for thinking in opposite ways. Though clannish, these weren't secretive and distrusting simpletons.

Still, with five hundred dollars folded in a wallet and another two hundred hidden in his boot, he figured it wise to remain unobtrusive and follow Mario's advice, whose directions had been simple enough: "Hire a boat to take you to Mama Dufois's, south of Thibideaux. When you order your meal, tell the old woman you came to see Baby Jasper about hunting gators." He'd insisted the pots would be big and the play soft.

After their bellies were filled, three men carried their stools outside the door and spread open the canvas bags they'd toted inside. They began tuning instruments, a fiddle, guitar, and banjo. A man at the nearest table asked Willy where he came from and what prompted him to come to their world. Nothing in his manner hinted of hostility. Willy answered politely that he was from Texas and had come to see the bayou. He offered nothing more and contented himself to watch.

Couples and children danced on the wide porch. Willy thought about leaving without Lisette. He'd not danced much, but considered now the idea of dancing with her. He pictured the Texas countryside where the sun's full arc could be witnessed, where sunsets were bloodred in summer and silver in spring. If Beau had lived, it would be different. They'd be on a spread, running a herd of beef-heavy heifer and Angus. He felt homesick. Even a poor family was still a family. He wondered about his ma and baby Sean and if Nell's wedding went well.

Boats continued to tie onto the dock. The screen door swung open. One, two, sometimes three at a time new faces entered and greeted Mama Dufois with hearty embraces and a *"Bon soir, Mamá."* The crowd swelled to three dozen; some stood at the elbow tables and drank beer and ate *huitres diables.* Some brought fiddles, banjos, and guitars. Music, fast and twanging, filled the room and drowned out the swamp sounds.

Every so often Mama Dufois came by his table and told Willy to be patient, "Baby Jasper be comin," but as the night stretched out, Willy began to feel uneasy. Voices seemed to grow louder, and people were taking more notice of him. He felt afloat in a swell of people, their high-pitched conversation taking him aloft and suspending him helplessly, just as the ocean had.

He thought again of Lisette, how she'd ruined him for whores. Nothing less than a woman's full passion would ever suit him now. He wondered what she might be doing. Had she run off? Or did she go back to Panther Jack? An unexpected loneliness enveloped him.

Then a solo boat docked, and a huge black-bearded man, his waist equatorial, leaped gracefully onto the dock. He ambled up the path, whistling as he came, and threw open the door. He shouted greetings to those present, then hurried to the stove, where he lifted Mama Dufois from the floor and swung her about. When he set her down, she pointed out Willy. They whispered a few words, and then the man waved and walked over. He snorted a half hello and swung his leg over the chair, the floor creaking beneath him as he settled into the seat.

"I be Jasper, what dey call me Baby." He laughed heartily. "You want gators?"

"'At's right. Been waitin some time to do it," Willy said.

"The food was good, no?"

"Yep."

Baby Jasper looked him up and down. "Look a bit small for da gators we got. Maybe you want to tink it over."

Willy shook his head. "I come for gators, bigger the better." The conversations at the other tables had slowed. He looked about. Some who sat nearby were watching the exchange, their expressions curious but at the same time aloof.

"What's your name?"

"Willy."

"You hain't from Lou'siana."

"Nope. Texas."

"I heard somewhere Texas has gator. But not bayou gator." Nodding slowly, Baby Jasper set his eyes on Willy. "I fix you up. Cost twenty dollar."

Mario Anselmo hadn't mentioned a fee. Although Willy could afford it, he knew it would be seen as a sign of weakness and thus unwise to hand over money without making a fuss. "Fella name'a Mario didn't say nothin about no twenty. Said you'd take me to catch'a gator was all."

"He hain't nothing to say dat. It'll be twenty."

Willy hesitated, as if considering the fee, then shook his head.

His black eyes never leaving Willy, Baby Jasper lifted his bulk from the seat. "Guess you hain't so interested in gator."

Willy stared back. "Seems so."

The big man stood there, waiting.

Willy sensed he'd made his point. Now it was a matter of pride to the Cajun, and some compromise would set matters right. He leaned back. "Okay, ten."

"Twelve." Baby Jasper sat. "First, I eat, den gators. You pay, *hein?*"

"Ten, and I'll pay for your dinner."

The big man rubbed his belly and grinned. "You take a chance, eh?"

The musicians played. Willy watched his companion eat. Baby Jasper's appetite seemed insatiable. He lifted a bowl of *soupe a l'aie* to his lips, swallowed the broth in two gulps, and set the bowl down. Driblets clung to his beard. Barely chewing, he swallowed a dozen crawdads doused in hot sauce, three chicken breasts, a bowl of gumbo and another of *haricots rouge et ris*. Finished, he wiped his fingers on the tablecloth, stroked his beard, and said, "We go."

Baby Jasper untied the rope and motioned for Willy to board. He mounted oars on the gunwale and sat on the center seat, belched twice, and began stroking.

The craft moved smoothly over the lagoon's mirrored blackness. At night, the waters seemed even more intimidating than in daylight. As the boat glided away, the island and lights from Mama Dufois's soon dissolved. For a time, the music carried faintly over the water's surface and Baby Jasper hummed along with it, but the sound faded once they turned into a channel where mangroves thickened on the shore.

Willy had no way of gauging how far they'd traveled in what seemed at least an hour, but they appeared to be nearing their destination when Baby Jasper turned the craft toward land.

As they approached the shoreline, everything suddenly smelled of decay. A cloud of mosquitoes descended on the boat. Willy slapped at them to little effect.

"*Jamais de la vie,* you hab guts coming here by you'self. Don't make you so smart."

"Been awright 'cept for the mosquitoes," Willy said and kept swatting.

"Dos mosquito is bad, *hein?* Eat up a man hain't use to dem." Baby Jasper laughed and rowed on. "Where you meet dat Italian pimp?"

"You mean Mario?"

Baby Jasper grunted. "Pimp."

"In the Quarter. A poker game."

The journey continued following the shoreline. The deeper they went into the murk, the louder the insects and frogs. The sameness of features was disorienting. Willy wondered how Baby Jasper managed to recognize landmarks, day or night. The channel narrowed, and the shadowed banks closed in on them. Willy heard a thunderous splash nearby.

"Gator got him a bird."

Suddenly, the lagoon and the shore both seemed familiar to Willy. For all he knew they were going in circles. The shadows of the dense mangroves stretched out over the water. The darkness was viselike. Besides deep water, Willy now realized a new fear—being trapped in a limited space. He'd been advised. Warned.

"Soon," Baby Jasper said. He directed the boat straight toward the far tree line. Near shore Baby Jasper struck the oars, let the boat glide, and moved forward to the bow. The boat shifted with his weight. His back to Willy, Jasper stoop over and gathered up something from beneath the bow cover.

"This the place?" Willy asked, more wary now of his host than of the water or the strange island environment.

"Must be."

"Should I do somethin?" Willy asked. He moved his hand close to his pistol. "Maybe help in some way?"

"Not yet, *hein*?" Baby Jasper said, fumbling with something to free it.

When Baby Jasper rose up, he displayed a double-barreled shotgun, the barrel end aimed at Willy's midsection. He calmly lowered himself and rested his haunches on the bow. "I saw the rebolber. You gib it up," he said. "Be careful 'bout it. Two fingers, *hein*?"

Willy removed his revolver as told and dangled it between thumb and forefinger.

"Good boy." Baby Jasper's dark eyes were hidden in the shadow of his brow, but his toothy smile glistened in the dim light. "Now, drop it."

The gun hit the hull with a thud. The sound made Willy feel even lonelier than earlier.

"Now your wallet."

Willy held the wallet out as well.

"Drop it next to the rebolber."

Mosquitoes swarmed about Willy's face. He dared not move to fend them off. He released the wallet and sat staring at the bearded man in a silence hard as iron. Sonny's words echoed in Willy's head. Not ready. As the bow touched the bank, Baby Jasper, in a display of agility that belied his bulk, sprang to his feet and jumped to shore without turning his back on Willy. He motioned for him to come forward.

Willy walked carefully to keep his balance. Accepting that he was to blame for this situation, he stepped off the craft and, with an amused smile, faced his antagonist. "What now?"

"Step away. To your left, *hein*." He watched Willy move aside two steps. "No, furder."

Willy kept side-stepping until Baby Jasper said, "Dere." Then the Cajun walked past Willy and boarded his boat. He lowered the shotgun and using his other hand launched the craft from shore with an oar.

He laughed as he took a seat and set the oars. "Tanks for visiting de bayou. You will hab no trouble finding de gator—if de water moccasin don't get you first."

Willy watched the boat labor across the moonlit pool and disappear in the shadows of the far bank. Then he sat and stared at the moon. Above the hum of mosquitoes, he heard a gravely baritone singing, the song interrupted by occasional laughter. When that sound faded, all that remained were the mosquitoes and the night and the body of water that Willy dared not enter.

34

At sunrise Willy followed the shoreline, picking north for no particular reason other than that was the direction in which he first stepped. He kept the sun to his right as he struggled through tangles of cypress and vines so thick that if he moved inland only a few yards, he lost sight of the lagoon. Roots strangled the bank and snaked over each other like steel cable spun into a giant web. There was no way to easily navigate the swamp. Where it appeared smooth, he sank into mud up to his calves. He bumped his shins on iron-like roots. He tore his trousers, bruised his knee, and jabbed his palm on a thorn the size of tenpenny nail, but far sharper. His anger rose in proportion to the temperature and the angle of the sun. He vowed that if given the opportunity, he would put a bullet in the big man's gut.

As he navigated a tall crop of roots, dead leaves stirred beneath his foot. A charcoal-brown snake about two inches wide emerged. Willy stopped midstep as it slithered forward at an unhurried pace. It paused beneath his foot, tasted the air with its tongue, and sat motionless. He'd encountered several snakes that rattled at intruders, then hurried on about their business. The longer the snake lingered, the more he wondered if everything in the swamp traveled at the same speed as Baby Jasper, who'd arrived late, delayed business for pleasure, and took his sweet time to pull off his robbery. Finally, the snake moved on as if unaware of ever being in Willy's presence. Willy moved on as well.

The sun had cleared the treetops, and he could see across the bayou. Tendrils of vapor rose from the water's surface. He saw no identifiable landmark, just acres of water and mangrove-lined shores. Despite having to navigate obstacles, he stuck to the bank, root after root, a punishing passage made more difficult by his riding boots. At a particularly thick outcropping of root, he hugged the trunk as best he could, and as he stepped up onto the massive roots, the world went out from under him and he found himself on his back in the murky shallows, gazing up at the boughs.

He stood, drenched head to toe, clenched his teeth, and shouted, "Sumbitch! I'll kill you!"

He remembered his thoughts about not killing for revenge, but at the moment, nothing seemed more vital than the anger burning inside him. He pulled himself upright and climbed ashore. As he sat between two roots and rested his back, he was reminded of his journey down the Rio Grande. It was barely a year. He should have learned better, learned more, been more cautious. But then, too, he'd survived the river.

Dripping wet, he rose to his feet and set off. He negotiated a fair distance without incident, and then as he transferred his weight from one root to another, he twisted his ankle and fell again, this time bumping his head on a root. He slowly gathered himself upright and set his weight gingerly on his left ankle. He hobbled about, looking for something to use as a walking stick and found a branch adequate enough.

A few minutes later, he entered a canebrake. His boots sank into the soft, damp earth. Razor-like blades of the cane sliced at his face and neck and hands as he pushed the plants aside. Insects, half mouth and half wing, swarmed about, biting him rapaciously. He considered turning back, but that would take him nowhere he hadn't already been. Whatever was ahead might lead him to Mama Dufois's.

Sometime later, his skin bleeding from the fine cuts, he limped out of the canebrake onto solid ground and headed west by southwest for no good reason except to keep moving. As he progressed, sunlight and sweat inflamed the cuts. He reached a clearing that sloped gently down to a bayou, where an eight-foot alligator lay in the sun, its tail extending into the lagoon. The beast paid him no attention. At the far fringe of the clearing stood a bungalow with a corrugated roof. Smoke discharged from its stone chimney.

Willy realized that all along Baby Jasper had simply rowed to the far side of the same island. He limped across the clearing to Mama Dufois's cottage. The screened porch faced the shore and the landing dock. He opened the screen door and knocked. The floor creaked under the weight of footfalls, and then the door swung open and Mama Dufois stood in the threshold. She studied him head to foot, taking note of his mosquito-bitten face, his still-damp clothing.

"I was here last night, 'member?"

"*Oui. Cré tonnerre!* You early," she said.

"Come lookin for Baby Jasper," he said.

"'E's not 'ere," she said.

"I'll wait."

"Don't serve 'til da sun's way over dere." She pointed to the west. "But from de look of you, some egg and bread might fix you up, *hein?*"

Willy followed her to the kitchen, where she told him to sit. She gave him a damp cloth and a salve, instructing him to use them on his bites, then she turned away and set a pan on the stove. "I hab bacon left over." She pointed at a plate on the table where he sat.

He fingered a strip of crisp bacon. "I left last night with Baby Jasper."

She held two eggs in one hand and adjusted the handle of the pan.

"Ah, Baby Jasper, a good man, yes."

She broke the shells with one hand.

"No," Willy said.

She seemed not to hear him. The eggs sizzled. She grabbed a pot holder, gripped the handle, and leaned away from the popping grease. "Egg in da mornin hain't much wit'out *café noir.*"

"Coffee, yes, ma'am. He put a shotgun to me and took my money."

"I feex coffee, no?"

"Yes'm. Way I see it, ma'am, Baby Jasper's a good man if it's good to steal from a stranger." He studied her face, looking for a reaction, but her expression was indecipherable.

"'E don't steal from friends," she said.

He was too exhausted and hungry to feel anger at the moment. The smell of the bacon and eggs reminded him of mornings before he, Beau, and often Nell headed off to a neighbor's to work the fields. Don't steal from friends, he thought and smiled to himself. "Guess 'at's a virtue."

She turned the eggs, scooped them onto a plate, and set it in front of him. "I get you *café.*"

He forked a bite of egg into his mouth, then some bacon, and chewed voraciously. "Thing is," he said between bites, "Baby Jasper forgot to search me and plum missed this."

He reached into his boot top and extracted the two hundred-dollar bills. The money sat atop the table, inviting comment. Mama Dufois pretended not to see it as she poured him a mug.

"Set me ashore without a search. Cost 'im two hunert dollars, silver certificates."

She kept at her task.

"Took my gun," Willy said.

She wiped her hands on her apron.

"I'd like to think you got nothin to do with it."

Smiling, she took a seat at the table. "Man business don't interest me. Boat come in from Thibideaux 'bout noon, bring sugar and coffee. He take you back. No fare." She smiled and, using only her fingertips, pushed the mug closer to Willy. "Wouldn't tell anyone on de boat 'bout no two hundred dollar. Dey's good men, but money . . . we keep it a secret, *hein?*"

He chewed on a bite of bacon as he considered the message he wanted passed on. He swallowed the bacon, took a drink of coffee, and said, "You tell Baby Jasper Willy'll be back for 'is money. Just tell him that."

The old woman shook her head. "I got my business here. You wanna come back for food, fine. But dey's bayou folk and den dey's others."

Willy finished breakfast and offered her money. She refused, saying she had no change for such large bills. He thanked her and said that if he returned, he'd be pleased to pay her what he owed her.

He sat on the porch on a rope couch drying off and admiring lilies that grew wild around the sides of the cottage. He considered how he'd deal with the matter of Baby Jasper. Not soon, but someday. He dozed for a time, and when he awoke, the bayou seemed not so much foreign as it did magical. He figured Beau might've been at home here. At the lagoon's edge, he noticed what at first he thought was a log, but then realized it was an alligator, about five feet long, basking in the sun a body length from the water's edge. He saw movement in the undergrowth not far from where he'd emerged less shortly before. Even though he was looking directly at the moving brush, he was nonetheless stunned when a hairy yellowish boar stepped out, head to the ground as he sniffed and snorted.

It was the tallest pig he'd ever seen, and it wasn't rotund like those penned and fattened by farmers in Bedloe. The boar looked up from its foraging and, seeing the alligator, grunted, hunched its massive neck, and charged. The alligator swiveled its long body and tail around with amazing speed and grace and opened its jaws. The boar stopped, lowered its head, and stood stiffly some four feet away, sniffing the air as it took in the waiting rows of jagged teeth. The animals faced each other in that manner for a time, until the reptile turned around, like a trolley at the end of its route, and crawled to the edge of the lagoon. It quickly sank below the surface. The boar grunted and paced back and forth above the shore where the alligator had submerged. It inched cautiously toward the water. As it neared the bank, the water erupted suddenly in a silver spray. The alligator's head emerged, its jaws open wide as it lunged for the boar's head. Somehow the pig managed to escape the jaws and trotted back into the woods. The alligator crawled up the bank and resumed sunning itself.

"You lucky that pig don't eat you," Mama Dufois said to Willy.

Willy looked over his shoulder. The old woman stood wiping her hands on her apron.

Willy thought how strange this place was and that Mr. Lemeaux was probably half right in warning him about it. He'd seen enough to realize that all a stranger coming in here could ever conclude about the bayou and its folks would be no more than half right.

Noon came and went, but the boat didn't arrive. He waited in the sun and as his cuts scabbed, they began to itch. Mama Dufois brought him more coffee and apologized, explaining that schedules worked better in towns. A little after one o'clock, the boat landed at the dock. Besides the supplier, the boat was manned by two large black men who unloaded crates of food and four kegs of beer. As a favor to Mama Dufois, the supplier, a tiny white man with a shiny bald head, took Willy aboard without question or charge.

Willy stepped gingerly into the boat and seated himself beside the supplier, who leaned against the tiller. After the boat was untied and moving over the calm waters, one of oarsman signaled the supplier up front for a conference. They whispered a few seconds, and then the man, his head shining with sweat, returned aft and sat beside Willy. "You want go to Thibideaux?"

Willy nodded. "Left my horse there."

"Boys dere figure you should take a turn at da oar. Dey hain't up to rowin de whole way and watchin you sit here like a lord."

Willy looked into the impassive eyes of one of the men. His forearms bulged and rippled as he put his back into the stroke.

"What'd you say 'bout it?" Willy asked.

"I told de boy hit's up to you."

"Never rowed before."

The boatman knitted his brow. "Dey be angry."

Willy, in pain from his swollen ankle, shrugged and limped to the bench. He said nothing to the oarsman, just took the oar handle and planted the blade in the black water. He looked at the thick cypress guarding the shores. He would return, he figured, when healed and when ready, when the matter of revenge diminished and he could determine if he was being rowed in circles. In the meantime, he was learning how to row himself in a straight line, a skill a man in swampland should know. Maybe elsewhere as well.

35 At O'Banion's by the levee in Jefferson Parish Willy saw the potential for achieving the way to the life he'd imagined for himself. Joe O'Banion, a third-generation Irishman whose family had started a restaurant that featured the first lottery in the parish, owned and ran the operation by himself. Soft-spoken and confident, he was a slight man with ebony eyes, and when he spoke, his voice was warm, his language

precise. He walked up behind players at a game, rested his arm over their shoulders, and told a story or took the place of a dealer behind a game and dealt a hand or two. No one in his establishment was a stranger for long.

His manner created a strong sense of trust between his patrons and him. "How's the family, Michael?" he might ask. No one was ever just Mike or John or Pete; they were Michael or Jonathan or Peter. Joe figured anyone willing to give him money merited respect. To everyone who came to his place, Joseph Patrick O'Banion was simply Joe. He knew when a man was celebrating a wedding anniversary and invited him to bring his wife in for a free dinner. Champagne waited at the table for the couple, and though he had waiters and bartenders working for him, he was just as likely to bring a round of drinks himself and set them before his customers. He took their money, but it was money they willingly risked. He never resented a winner, often telling the gambler to take the profits home to the wife and put it to good use. He knew the names of men's wives as well, and often the names of their children, remembered what a man liked to drink, and knew when one had consumed his limit. On occasion Joe was known to take a drunken loser to his own home to sleep it off and in the morning, before sending the fellow off, stuff some bills in his pocket, cautioning him not to tell anyone because it might harm the reputation of a gambling hall. If a man's wife doubted where her husband had spent the night, Joe sent word that the man had been with him, and sometimes flowers to soothe any bad feelings.

If he had favorites among his employees, it never showed. He was quick with a tongue-lashing and equally quick with praise, and he was a fair pay-master who gave out turkeys for Thanksgiving and bonuses at Christmas and was the first to lay down a twenty-dollar bill for a sick dealer's family, keeping him on wages until the illness passed. Willy heard that a dealer named Brunson Gomez, so crippled with arthritis he could no longer hold a deck, limped in once a week with the aid of a cane and picked up an envelope at the casino cage. For twenty-two years he'd been an O'Banion dealer, until he could no longer complete a shift. He thought the bills in the envelope were a half share of a night's tips the dealers set aside for him. Then after picking up his envelope, he walked to each table where his former workmates still dealt and silently mouth "thank you." Willy was impressed when he heard it was Joe that Brunson should have thanked. The workers kept the secret of the money's source because Joe O'Banion wouldn't allow word of it.

O'Banion's was less garish than the New Orleans clubs. It had both a restaurant and a bar. Parish aldermen and the sheriff were, like everyone else, friends of Joe's and paid regular visits. Any cop was welcome to come in for a free meal. Willy learned that Joe was not a crook, just a business-man, and none of his dealers cheated him or the customers. One thing only seemed to raise Joe's blood pressure—to be cheated by someone. He never called the law on those who stole from him. His policy was to break a hand or a finger or, if the infraction was truly egregious, an arm or leg. He employed large men to ensure honesty among his customers and employ-ees. The bouncers weren't encouraged to be ruthless, just efficient.

Mr. Lemeaux told the story about a dealer who had a track habit and had gotten in debt to some young Italians who were running a loan-shark busi-ness. Joe caught his dealer passing off chips to a player on a roulette game and asked, "Why didn't you come to me? You could have owed me at no interest and no hurry to pay."

According to the story, the dealer said he was too ashamed to ask, and Joe said, "So you steal from me instead." He stuffed two hundred dollars in the man's pocket and added, "Maybe this'll keep those Italians from killing you, but I wouldn't bet on it." Then Joe turned to his bouncers and told them to break the man's left hand before taking him home.

On occasion, Willy noticed Joe watching him. Joe raised an open palm and half nodded, but didn't approach the table. He rarely entered the poker area. The house took a two percent rake off the winning pot, so unlike rou-lette, blackjack, or craps, Joe had little direct interest in the action, unless the pots got too big. He provided cards, table, and dealer, nothing more.

This was the third night in a row Willy played at O'Banion's. Willy, the two previous nights, had fattened his bankroll, but tonight he was chewing up the green felt. Joe approached him at the end of a tense poker hand. The dealer had called Joe to the game because Willy and another player asked that the table stakes be raised.

"I'd like to buy you dinner, young man," Joe said.

There was Joe in a black silk suit, black shirt with a starched white collar, and a red rose bud in his jacket lapel, his hand open and outstretched. Willy, like anyone who'd ever met Joe, instantly felt he'd found a friend.

"I got a game goin, but thanks," Willy said.

"Name's Joe. I look after things here." He released Willy's hand.

"Nice to meet you, Joe. Could you bump the table stakes?"

"Your name? I didn't quite catch it."

"I didn't throw it." Willy started to place a bet, but the cards were already in the air.

"When you're young," Joe said, "there's a lot of hands ahead . . . Mister?"

"Bobbins. Willy Bobbins. Everyone calls me Willy or Cowboy."

"Willy, huh? Would that be short for William or Wilbur?"

Willy had never before been asked. "No, sir. It's plain Willy. Fact, they's an old woman calls me Plain Willy. Do you have hot chili here, Joe? I'm from Texas, and I shore miss it."

"Well, Mr. Bobbins. Join me in my restaurant. Mrs. Powell, who runs the kitchen, is a fine cook. We'll see if she can come close."

Joe waited and watched how the hand played out, then walked Willy to the restaurant. They seated themselves at Joe's table. Joe signaled over a waiter. Mt. Lemeaux had said that Joe felt casinos were too rough for a woman. Those who worked for him were cooks or kitchen help. He apologized for having no chili, but insisted Willy would enjoy a meal of redfish *courtbouillon,* the specialty of the house.

"Helluva place you got, Joe," Willy said.

"Ah, it's a gambling joint, and I'm proud of it. It's got my name out there lit up for the world to see. Why, His Eminence Archbishop Blenk, bless his dead soul, came here for a meal or two when he was still living. Ate what you're about to. He said it was a fine place, so long as I kept it a moderate place. I was then, and am now, a staunch parishioner at Matre Dolorosa, seats in the first pew being reserved for me and my family. How old are you, Mr. Bobbins?"

"Call me Willy."

"I'll work on doing that."

Willy decided to add some years to his age. "If you gotta know, I'm near 'bout twenty."

"How near about? The truth now."

Willy saw in Joe's expression that he wouldn't accept a lie. "Near eighteen."

Joe coughed to hold back a laugh. "Well, young Mr. Bobbins, I see you're quite a poker player." He looked Willy over. "So, you'd like our table stakes raised."

Willy pushed the brim of his hat up and leaned back. "Way I see it, sir . . ."

"Joe, everyone calls me Joe. That and honesty are all I ever insist on."

"Way I see it, Joe, is you got nothin to lose no matter how high the table stakes. You get two percent of more's all."

Joe took a sip of water and set it down. "A fair assumption. Look around, Mr. Bobbins."

Willy looked down into the busy pit and admired the graceful artistry of a white-haired blackjack dealer so old that he was bent like a fishhook.

Cards left his fingertips and hung for an instant in midair before gliding to a smooth landing behind each bet.

"Mine's a nice place. Not rough like the Quarter or the One-One-Eight-and-A-Half on Barrone. No women here, except those who come with husbands and play roulette or the slot machines, and, of course, the cooks, and they're as moral as my own grandmother, a saint of a woman at that. Look around again, Mr. Bobbins."

Willy did as asked. Next to the blackjack games were three roulette wheels, each with heads precisely balanced, Willy had heard, and rotating in endless counterclockwise revolutions. A dealer sent a ball spinning in a clockwise blur. At crap tables, stick men barked out proposition bets.

"When the sheriff says, 'Joe, it's time to shut down for a while,' I do. I keep the restaurant open to feed the help, and I keep them on the payroll. When the sheriff says it's time to open up again, I do. I have forty dealers, ten waiters, and five cooks and dishwashers, and some, I guess you could say, gentlemen, who work for me. This place feeds families, a fact I never lose sight of."

As he spoke, Joe stared at Willy, but not in a threatening way. "Nothing's more important than being honest. No matter what you do. Never hurt someone if you don't have to. Mr. Bobbins, you could hurt my customers. Tell me, is one of my dealers helping you?"

Willy stared back. "Joe, you seem like a decent man, but don't ever ask me no question like that. I play fair. 'At's all." Willy stood to leave.

"Fine. Keep your seat, Mr. Bobbins. Please, have a meal on me."

Willy looked around the casino again and sat back down. "I'd shore like to work in a place like this, for a fella like you, Joe." He merely meant it as a compliment.

Joe went on as if he hadn't heard Willy. "This is a family business. I have two sons and a nephew I've raised who'll someday work here. They'll feed their families."

"I can see that," Willy said.

"You see, Mr. Bobbins, my clientele are also my friends. I won't allow them to get too drunk or lose more than they can safely afford. I don't allow fighting and, Mr. Bobbins, no high-stakes poker. People get mean over that kind of money, and I'm not a mean man. The games I prefer are roulette and craps, games of luck and not skill. You, friend, are a skilled player, especially for one so young."

"I see. You aim for me to leave."

"I'm going to feed you and ask you politely not to return. Not because you're skilled or want the stakes raised, but because you're young, and it doesn't look good to the cops who come in here."

"Can I come back when I'm older? Maybe work for you?"

"I start workers as waiters. No one walks in here and just gets behind a gambling table."

The waiter announced Willy's *sope mais avec chevrettes* and placed it before him. He snapped a serviette and laid it across Willy's lap.

"You know, Joe, what I been thinkin is that I wouldn't mind learnin 'bout this bidness from a man like you. Maybe not now, I guess, but sometime."

"We'll see in time, Mr. Bobbins, if you don't get yourself killed first."

Willy took a taste of the soup. "Mighty good."

O'Banion stood. "Enjoy it."

Willy looked up. "'Bout gettin myself kilt, I don't plan on that, Joe. See, you're lookin at a lucky feller. Got no education, no looks to speak of, no hope so's the world sees it. What I got is luck."

"I believe that, Mr. Bobbins, but even a cat has only nine chances. How many do you have?"

Willy looked down at the napkin, at his soup, and, finally, at Joe. "Joe, I'm gonna tell you the truth 'bout myself. I'm just a ordinary Texas cowboy."

Joe offered a friendly and knowing smile. "Mr. Bobbins, I don't think so."

36 Willy swung his foot onto the runner and readied himself to step down from the carriage. He looked up at the two-story house and noted the darkened windows. Like most belonging to the once wealthy in the parishes around New Orleans, it was a Victorian-style house with cupolas and spires and had fallen into disrepair. It was squeezed between two other houses that, like it, needed paint. Light from a single window on one side stretched out onto the wall of the adjacent house. He swung down from the carriage and stood under the gas streetlight.

He sized up the situation, looking for signs of activity. He didn't like what he saw and asked the driver if he was sure this was the right house.

The black man nodded. "Yessa, it's the place."

Though he was tempted to tell the driver to drive on, Willy hesitated to do so. Since his episode in the bayou, he'd been on a streak, and the promise of another lucrative night proved too alluring to resist. He'd take a chance.

Wasn't that gambling? He swung down from the carriage, paid the fare, and added a half-dollar tip, then told the driver to return in five hours. As the horse carriage clattered up the street, Willy stood encircled in the glow of gaslight.

Willy's bankroll had grown to more than four thousand dollars, a sum he could have only imagined a year before. But it wasn't enough, mostly because he didn't know what enough was and didn't have anything in mind to do with the money. The way he saw it now, a bankroll was just money meant to make more money.

He mounted the porch and faced the door. He didn't knock, as he'd been instructed. He turned the knob, pushed open the door, and stood in the foyer looking about. Above a door leading to a hallway hung the head of a brown bear, its teeth exposed as if ready to bite. Light from an open door spilled out into the hallway. He called out and waited for an answer.

"That you, Cowboy?"

Willy recognized D'Longo's voice. "It's me."

"We're down here! Come on in," D'Longo called back.

Willy followed the hallway to the open door and stood in the threshold, surveying the room. The lighting was a bit too dim for a card game. Seats that were supposed to be filled by flush bankers were empty. D'Longo and two others, strangers to Willy, sat at a card table, their smiles too big for his liking.

"'Sposed to be a party," Willy said.

"Canceled," D'Longo said.

The two strangers nodded in agreement. They, like D'Longo, were dark-complected men with dark eyes that looked to him like those of fish buyers measuring a day's catch.

"Where's the rest'a the players?"

"Be along, Willy," D'Longo said. "Something came up. Businesses kept them. Come in. That's yours." He pointed to a seat between the door and window.

Empty seats and a lame explanation. Despite his impulse to do so, Willy didn't turn and leave. He wasn't familiar with this part of Jefferson Parish and didn't want to risk walking the streets with a thousand dollars, a quarter of his bankroll, in his pockets. The heft of the gun in his waistband gave him courage enough to see how the game played out. The men stood as he crossed the room. He stood at the seat D'Longo had pointed out and shook hands as the others, Athenos and Jeepy, were introduced.

Once the others sat, Willy settled in his chair. "Not much light. Makes it hard to see the blind."

Jeepy mumbled. D'Longo eyed him. "Well, we're all handicapped the same," he said.

"Guess so."

D'Longo sat across from Willy, telling him that these games usually start late, but they could get warmed up with a few hands before the suckers arrived. Willy eyed the room, lit by three lanterns. The single door was to his right, with a window on his left, and a poster promoting a boxing match hung on the wall behind and above D'Longo's head.

"Who's them fellas in the picture?"

D'Longo broke the seal on a box of Bicycle Cards. "Them?" He didn't look up. "That's Dupree and Batterham, middleweights. Fight was fixed. Fucking Cajun won."

Willy pretended lack of interest. Out of the corner of his eye he saw D'Longo open the deck of cards. The Italian fumbled with the lid. It was obvious from the way he handled the deck that he was unaccustomed to handling one. Willy began measuring the space surrounding him, the window one step, the door at least four, Jeepy blocking that path. The room, bare except for the poster, a boar's head, table, and chairs, was so poorly lit it distorted the features of the men.

Willy cut an eye in the direction of Jeepy, then Athenos. Neither took notice, or at least pretended not to.

"Well, Texas. I heard you beat John Fingers and Pug Newman outta four big in a stud game," D'Longo said. "Hell, you must be flush."

On the night in question Willy had taken the last pot, which wasn't four thousand, but closer to fifteen hundred. A rumor of wins circulated among the poker-playing community, the winning pots growing in size as each mouth passed on the story. Willy knew better than to admit to any number.

"Lost most'a it back," he said. "I'm just a dumb cowboy who can't hold on to money. Ain't got much better luck with women."

Willy waited until the others showed their stakes money. The money came out, the others laying stacks of five-, ten-, and twenty-dollar bills in front of them.

Athenos said, "You need money to play, Cowboy."

"I got money."

Jeepy's eyes searched Willy's coat. His hand slid from the tabletop. Willy caught a last glimpse of the fingertips as the hand moved beneath the level of the table. Willy pressed his elbow against the bulge in his waistband, feeling its hardness for security.

"Where I come from," Willy said calmly, "men keep their hands showin in a card game."

Jeepy looked at D'Longo and Athenos.

"Where's your stake, Willy?" D'Longo asked.

"In here." Willy patted his coat pocket.

Willy reached in his coat pocket and pulled out some bills. He laid them on the table and spread them with one hand.

D'Longo called the game, seven-card stud, a five-dollar ante, ten-dollar raise. Willy tossed in a bill and stared at Jeepy, who wouldn't meet his gaze as he matched the ante. The others laid their fives on top.

D'Longo set the deck before Willy. "Willy, you can have the honor of shuffling."

He was certain now that they wanted his hands occupied when they made their move. He needed one free to use the revolver. He didn't pick up the deck. The others sat waiting, not speaking, as if each was uncertain as to who should act first. The silence swelled like a boil as the men looked at one another without truly looking.

Willy broke the silence. "Where I come from, we cut high card to see who shuffles."

"Just being friendly," D'Longo said, "but we can do it your way."

That eased some of the tension.

"You cut first, Willy."

"Nah, I'm superstitious."

"Easy enough," D'Longo said. "We're all friends." He leaned forward and touched his sausage fingers to the deck. "Tell us about you, Willy."

"Not much to say."

D'Longo laid the deck in the middle of the table. Jeepy cut a card from the deck and turned a seven of diamonds faceup. The third man pulled off a jack of clubs. D'Longo cut a queen of spades. Willy cut with his left hand and smiled as he turned over a three of clubs.

"Can't always be lucky," he said, inching his foot slowly to the right and locking his right boot heel into the base of the table leg.

"Seven stud," D'Longo said. "Nothing wild."

When the cards came, Willy used one hand to pretend to peek at his blinds as he kept his attention on the others. Out of the corner of his eye he saw Jeepy slide something out of his waist and hold it below the table. A third card came to each.

"You didn't tell us anything about yourself," D'Longo said.

Willy looked from face to face. "Had me this notion once to buy a ranch, but now it appears like I'm just a dumb Texas cowboy who come out here to get robbed."

D'Longo smiled. "Willy, we—"

Willy thrust his legs sideways, sprang to his feet, and dumped the table over. The distraction threw off Jeepy's timing. Willy drew his revolver and fired off one wild shot as he charged the window. He covered his head with an elbow and crashed through the pane. The fall was short, some four feet, but he landed on a cobbled walkway that led to the back, and his gun clattered across the stones as it slid out of reach. He quickly rolled to his hands and knees and scrambled toward the gun. As he got a grip on the stocks, he felt a pain in his side from a long shard of glass lodged just under his ribs.

D'Longo peered down from the window ledge and said, "You're fucked now, Cowboy."

Willy rolled on his back, took aim, and fired a single round. D'Longo's head disappeared inside the window frame. Willy took advantage of the moment to look up and down the walkway for the best path to escape. At one end, the walkway opened onto the street where Jeepy and Athenos were certain to head. In the other, it turned right and dead-ended into a wooden fence. He didn't know what was on the other side of the fence, but it seemed the better choice. Willy rose to his feet and began running.

His heels pounding on the stones compromised him. A single round whined past him. A short distance ahead stood the wooden fence, a six-foot barrier he could put between him and his pursuers if he could get to the other side. He glanced back at the silhouette of a head leaning out the window and saw a muzzle flash. Another lucky miss. He figured to vault the fence on the run, a quick grab and over. A third bullet passed over his shoulder. He planted his left foot to pivot left and was jolted by a pain that shot up his leg. Another bullet whizzed above him as he fell face forward.

Despite the pain, he managed to gain his footing. Clutching the gun, he limped to the fence.

One pursuer fired four shots in quick succession. Willy saw two things in his favor. His pursuers were bad shots, and in knowing that he was armed, none would be hurrying to come after him. He stuffed the gun in his waist, gripped the top of the fence, and pulled himself up and safely over. When he tumbled to the ground on the far side, he felt another lancing pain in his leg. Gritting his teeth, he rose to his feet. He found himself in the back yard of a darkened house. He tested the leg and found he could walk on it.

Footsteps sounded on the far side of the fence. Willy heard D'Longo directing his accomplices from his position at the window. To his left a huge willow with low-hanging branches cast a broad shadow. Willy limped over and slipped into the cover of the branches. He looked back at the fence and wondered why his pursuers hadn't yet climbed it and if they would. In the opposite direction, he saw what appeared to be a gate that led out to an alley or perhaps another street. He couldn't be sure where it led, but it seemed more promising than staying where he was and risking a shoot-out.

Halfway to the gate, he stumbled and fell forward onto the damp lawn, losing his pistol. He cussed under his breath, rolled over, and lay listening. He heard nothing other than crickets and mosquitoes, but then the gate and the hinges creaked.

Willy inched silently toward to the gun. The grips were still beyond his reach when two Italians slipped inside the gate and spread apart, their footsteps whispering across the soft grass. Willy had no choice but to lie still and hope they'd be content in robbing him. He wondered if this was what Joe O'Banion had hinted at, tapping the last of his nine lives. Even if it was just superstition, here it might get him killed. Then he recalled how he'd resigned himself to drowning in the river, but its waters had coughed him up. And luck had served him at the tables. He only hoped he had some left.

They stood over him, their breathing heavy. He opened his eyes wide as if in a death stare and held his breath. One of the men rolled Willy onto his back.

"He alive?"

"Ah, stupid," Jeepy answered, "can't you see?"

"Look at him. Nothin but a kid."

The toe of a boot crashed into his side. Willy didn't flinch or utter a sound, just kept his eyes open wide and fixed on nothing.

"That oughta tell you. See his side? He's bleeding bad."

Jeepy reached down and pulled Willy's coat back. Straight ahead, Willy thought, look straight ahead. He willed himself not to breathe, show no indication of life. He was thankful that they were an efficient team of thieves. As Jeepy searched the coat, Athenos kneeled down and tore at Willy's trouser pockets, taking whatever was inside and turning them inside out. They found his wallet and stripped him of his watch. Athenos waved the money in Jeepy's face.

"Try him again," Jeepy said. "In case."

Willy took another sharp kick to his ribs. Though his lungs ached for air and his eyes burned, he didn't breathe and he didn't blink. D'Longo arriving distracted them enough that Willy managed two quick breaths. D'Longo asked, "He dead?"

"Be stinking by morning," Jeepy said. "Wanna make sure?"

It began sprinkling. They turned their backs to Willy and debated briefly whether to shoot him for insurance. A strange sense of self-awareness took hold of Willy as he listened to them decide his fate. He became curious in a fresh way about death and wondered how the bullet would feel tearing through his flesh and how long the pain would last. Would his bladder let loose? Did that always follow death? He hadn't noticed much of anything about the *vaquero,* the rustlers, or the wildcatter he'd killed. Why hadn't he noticed something more about their dying acts?

The discussion shifted to whether to hide the body. One noted that a few lights had come on in nearby houses. D'Longo said, "Let the police deal with it."

Jeepy said, "Ain't no reason for us to hang around and get wet. We got what we were after." He held the watch out for D'Longo to admire, then stuffed it in a pocket.

As they turned away, the third man said, "Some tough Texan, huh?"

D'Longo laughed and said, "Should've kept his boots in cow shit where they belonged."

Willy remained motionless until certain he was accompanied by only the sounds of the night and the smell of damp grass. He let air into his lungs and rolled to his side, both painful. He saw a faint reflection of light off metal. His revolver lay an arm's stretch away. They'd somehow overlooked it.

He rolled himself into a ball and lay trembling and gulping in air. It seemed that there was not enough air in the atmosphere to fill his lungs, and because his ribs were injured, every breath hurt.

The air wasn't particularly cold, but the rain brought a chill to it. Drops beaded on his cheeks. The lights in houses nearby went out. No one would care if he lay there and died. It occurred to him how alone he was in the world, and a fierce determination rose up in him. He felt neither grateful nor relieved to be alive, just lucky. Robbed and left for dead, he'd been stupid. All over a thousand dollars. Taking his money and watch was business, but kicking him was an insult to a dead man, even one who was actually alive.

The irony of stealing his watch wasn't lost on him. He considered another irony, that of the body hanging from a rope and swaying back and forth as a Mexican don feasted. He understood the horror of what he'd not fully comprehended before. A man must be as cautious or violent as a wild animal, and if another man needs hanging, you hang him and you don't let it ruin your meal.

He had to move before any police arrived. His trembling subsided, and he mustered strength enough to crawl to the gun. He stuffed it carefully in his waist and slowly rose to his feet. He didn't realize the extent of his injuries until he stood. His right leg barely supported his weight. His ribs made it difficult to breathe without halting in midbreath. And he bled badly from his side.

A mist filled the air. He could barely distinguish form from shadow as he crossed the wet grass. He took several shallow breaths and hopped to the fence, where he felt around until he found a loose plank. Grimacing, he pulled and twisted at the board until it ripped loose. He located a rock large enough to drive the nails out of the wood. Then he battered one end of the plank with the rock, again and again. When the pain became too much to bear or took his breath away, he paused. Finally, the board split down the center. He pulled it apart and tested both pieces to see which would better serve him. No more anxious to meet up with the cops than the Italians had been, he planted the makeshift crutch and swung his good leg forward.

Half dazed, he trekked instinctively westward. The injured leg grew numb. Both the bullet wound and the cut in his side steadily bled. What hurt most were his ribs. The more Willy thought about D'Longo and his accomplices, the angrier he got. He needed that anger, it and constant motion. He fell into a rhythm—crutch, foot, crutch, as he reminded himself over and over of Sonny's prophesy that he wasn't ready for New Orleans. This was what Sonny had in mind. This wasn't Texas.

Later, the sky broke open. Willy's mind drifted into what seemed a dream. Dogs barked at his passing. He paid them no mind, just labored on under a seemingly endless tunnel of shadows. Images appeared in front of him, visitations—his ma holding baby Sean and waving to him, Beau cutting off a piece of jerky and handing it to him, Lisette slipping out of her smock, the barn that held the hay loft where he and Beau hid to avoid chores. He asked

Beau what he'd done with the knife they'd stolen. Beau shook his head and faded into the mist. The road appeared as the slow turn into the main street of Bedloe. Now he passed the Methodist church. Lifting his leg to mount the steps, he stumbled and fell to his knees in a puddle.

A man rode by on a wagon, slowed the team, and asked if he needed help. Willy gazed up with dull eyes and didn't answer.

"It's raining, you damned fool," the man said.

Willy shivered and looked off into the mist. "Can't stop," he said. "Gotta find Lucy."

"Well, good luck," the man muttered, snapped the traces, and drove on.

Willy surveyed his surroundings. He vaguely remembered talking to someone, or had he imagined it? He felt pain in his ribs and lower in his side. He touched his side and grimaced. Blood stained his fingertips. He rubbed his face and looked up at a halo surrounding a streetlamp, soft droplets of rain falling through it. He stood staring up at the light, confused as to how he'd gotten here, wherever here was.

From behind a mongrel charged up, its teeth exposed. The hair on its back looked like a spray of needles as it stopped a length away. Its wide-set eyes studied him. Willy blinked and looked down. He felt an urgent need to urinate. He placed his weight on his good leg and held the board in both hands.

"Go on!" he shouted and swung the board at the animal. The dog sniffed the air, then offered up a low growl as it slunk away.

Willy unbuttoned his trousers and began relieving himself. The dog returned and circled him. Willy addressed it in low soothing tones, but emboldened now, it came close and snarled. Willy aimed his stream at its face. The mongrel retreated, shaking its head as it did. Willy didn't bother buttoning his trousers. He clutched the board under his armpit and started in the direction of the next streetlight, a block away.

That was the last sight he was aware of.

How he reached the house, he had no idea, but as the sky lifted, he climbed the three steps of the stoop, opened the door, and stepped inside. Mrs. Ducroix, who often couldn't sleep and prowled the house during the predawn hours, somehow heard a clatter on the wooden floor. She found him lying facedown inside the threshold, trousers unbuttoned, boots extended onto the porch.

"It's Plain Willy!" she shouted loud enough to rouse the neighbors. "The damned Yankees have shot 'im!"

37

Willy lay on his back in the Catholic hospital, squinting up at the detectives and shaking his head. Though his leg was in some pain, four days after his encounter with D'Longo, Willy's wounds were on a quick mend. The ribs were another matter. Sitting upright was difficult, standing almost unbearable. The doctor had assured him that ribs took time to heal and nothing could be done to speed the process. Willy was sleepy and tired of fielding questions, and he had no intention of helping the police solve any crime, even if he was the victim. Adding to Willy's distrust of the police, corruption in the Big Easy and surrounding parishes was commonly accepted. Give up a name to the wrong cop, and who knew what might follow? Willy wouldn't risk it. Besides, he had his own plan in mind.

The taller officer nudged his partner. "We're wastin time with him."

The shorter cop said, "That right, Bobbins? We wastin time with you?"

"Can't give you names if I don't know 'em."

"Bobbins," the tall detective said, "I wouldn't develop a fondness for Louisiana. You might do better back in Texas. That's your home, right?"

"Texas, yep. I'd do better there, huh?"

"Yes."

"I ain't in a hurry, though. Found me a new friend over there. 'At's him." He pointed to the old man in the next bed. Mr. Alderez, who'd been a riverboat pilot, was in the final stages of colon cancer. For three days now, Willy had witnessed the old man refusing morphine and enduring pain far beyond what Willy was in. Mr. Alderez simply explained that he wanted to be aware of every moment 'til his last.

"Him and me plan on doin the town when we get better. Ain't that right, Mr. Alderez?"

The old man, his face pale and drawn, looked over and winked.

Willy felt privileged to meet Mr. Alderez's family, a son, a daughter, and five grandchildren. The daughter and her three children visited the old man in the morning. The son and his two, a boy fifteen and a daughter nine, came in the evening. The young ones sat beside the old man, held his hand or wiped his brow with a damp cloth, or lifted a glass of water to his lips. Seeing them interact with Mr. Alderez in such a loving manner stoked a feeling of longing in Willy, a longing for his own family and the kind of father he'd never had. Willy vowed if he was ever a father, he'd be a loving one, one who on his deathbed would receive the kind of caring and respect that Mr. Alderez had earned.

The tall cop nodded. "Did an Italian shoot you?"

"Don't know who shot me."

"Okay. How much was it you actually lost?"

"Like I said, twenty, maybe twenty-five, dollars. 'At's 'bout all I ever carry."

"So you never heard of Apollo D'Longo?"

The previous day the same cops had questioned him. Leaving out names, Willy had given them a sketch of what happened—three men had lured him into a card game and robbed him of twenty dollars. He insisted he'd never seen them before. He hadn't heard, so he didn't know their names. Unsatisfied, the officers said they'd return, that maybe he needed another day or two to remember.

"I'd remember a funny name like that."

The cop nodded. "How about Jepson, goes by Jeeps or Jeepy?"

"Same there."

"Well," the shorter cop said, "you're lookin a lot better than when we first came. Seems your memory would improve."

"Doctor says I'm a lucky man."

The doctor summoned to the house determined that Willy had lost a dangerous amount of blood, but his wounds weren't serious. He'd been rushed to the hospital for surgery to close the holes the bullet had made passing through his calf.

"Luck won't stop them from trying again. You might think about that," the tall cop said.

"I sure will. Thank you."

"Let's try Thimios Athenapopulus. Also known as Tim Athenos."

"Name like that, I'd be known by somethin else too. I 'preciate you boys askin. Say, these fellas have dark hair? And was one of them short and kind'a fat?"

"That describes them pretty well."

"Can't be the fellas that robbed me. They was all redheads, freckled kind'a like."

The tall cop leaned over the bed. "You're puttin yourself in a bad way, Bobbins. These men are still out there, and if they think you're talkin to us, well . . . a dead man can't testify."

"Dead man can't do much of anything, so's I hear. Got no actual experience with it."

"Well, you might soon."

"I thank you for your kind words."

The tall one turned to the shorter one. "Saves us paperwork. Let's go."

Mr. Alderez turned his head to Willy. "Sure wish I could have me a shot a brandy." He closed his eyes and gritted his teeth as he took several short breaths. The cops pretended not to notice, but Willy couldn't look away. Though nurses tried to keep Alderez comfortable, sometimes the pain sent him into fits of moaning. Other times, he bore it without a sound as he was now doing.

Willy motioned to the taller cop. "Could you have the nurse to come and see about Mr. Alderez here? He's got bad pain."

"Bobbins, how is it you know his name, but not the men who robbed you?"

"Guess 'cause he offered it to me."

Mr. Alderez moaned and raised a limp hand, as if signaling something to Willy.

"He's hurtin. Please. He's an old man."

The old patient moaned again.

The shorter cop said, "We'll tell someone. You think about those names, Bobbins."

"I'll give it some attention."

When the cops left, Willy turned to Mr. Alderez. "Soon as I get out, I'll bring a bottle of fine brandy."

The old man mustered a toothless half smile and said in breathy voice, "I was fakin a bit, Willy. So's they'd take their business elsewhere."

"I know it."

Mr. Alderez winced. "Cognac, Willy. vsop. You're a good boy." He held up a trembling hand and clenched his jaw so as to hold back a moan.

By the time the nurse arrived, Mr. Alderez's pain was gone. He lay silent, his head resting on the white pillow, his eyes fixed on Willy, his jaw slack, mouth open, exposing the toothless pink cavity. The short cop entered behind the nurse. The nurse pulled the sheet over Mr. Alderez's face.

"He was an old man," the cop said.

"A perdy brave one, if you knew him."

"Bobbins, you don't know this place. Those men might kill you next time."

"Yes, sir."

The officers left, the nurse at their heels. A few minutes later, two order-lies arrived with a stretcher and wrapped Mr. Alderez in the sheet he lay on. They lifted him from the bed by his feet, and shoulders and as they lowered him to the stretcher, a burst of gas escaped him.

"Done shit himself," one said.

They dropped him roughly onto the stretcher.

"Ain't no way to treat 'im," Willy said.

"Don't make no difference to him," the orderly at Mr. Alderez's head said.

"No. But it does to me. And it would to his family."

Without speaking, the orderlies gripped the handles of the stretcher and lifted it.

"Deserves respect." Willy sat up and spat the words at them as they left. He grimaced and lay back in pain. Ribs take time, he thought. But he had time, something Mr. Alderez no longer had. He'd use it more wisely now.

38

When Willy returned to the house from his stay at Charity Hospital, Mrs. Ducroix nursed him as she would have her husband had he been wounded somewhere closer to home than Shiloh. She'd said of her late spouse that she'd forgiven him all his faults, but could never pardon his dying so far away from her. She fed Willy oatmeal for breakfast, bullion for lunch, and greens and split-pea soup for dinner. When Willy said it was his leg and not his stomach that got shot, she smiled in a motherly way and said, "You're a nice boy, Plain Willy, but thankless. At least you didn't go off and join up with the Union."

As soon as Mr. Lemeaux arrived each evening from gathering rent and feeding pigeons in the park, Mrs. Ducroix cornered him and dragged him to Willy's room, where the three of them played Pitch until ten, with one break to eat Mrs. Ducroix's greens and split-pea soup. Mr. Lemeaux, who hated playing cards, said, "Sure'll be happy to see you get better, Willy, so's you can entertain yourself."

On the Sunday Willy's ribs were sufficiently healed for him to walk around without pain, Mr. Lemeaux held a Cajun boil.

Sitting in a chair half-turned in her direction, Willy noticed Colleen devoted less time to gazing out over the water and more to listening to the stories he told the children. Occasionally, though she never looked at him, he saw her smiling at the punch line. He enjoyed the way the family tended to one another and fed off their small joys. As was the case with Mr. Alderez's family, Willy admired and envied the Lemeauxes' deep caring for one another, in particular Mr. Lemeaux, who prided himself in encouraging his grandsons' ceaseless curiosity and anarchic ways. Abel and Nicholas, especially in their independent spirit, reminded Willy of Beau and himself.

When not hanging over Willy and asking him what it was like to get robbed and shot, the boys tossed a baseball to each other and sang songs with familiar tunes but with lyrics Willy never heard before. Colleen, upon seeing Willy's confusion, told him that the boys made up their own lyrics and what he heard today might not be what he'd hear tomorrow. His experience with Mr. Alderez's family and the Lemeauxes resurrected thoughts of Willy's having a family and of owning a spread with a fine house.

He recalled, as his mother got older and gave birth, how melancholy she was when two babies, both sons, had died in childbirth. She had three daughters, but only one boy, Willy. Though she did treat Beau as if he were her own child, she'd wanted another son. Then Sean lived, and Ruth had seemed content just looking at the baby's face. She sat patiently rocking him back and forth, her arms never tiring, her gaze never straying. There was something deep and mysterious in the relationship between mother and newborn that a father couldn't duplicate and Willy couldn't imagine.

As the gumbo steamed, the boys talked about the coming World Series that would pit Ernie Shore and the powerful Red Sox against Jimmy Vaughn and the Chicago Cubs.

"Which team you think'll win, Willy?" Nicholas asked Willy.

"Yeah, Willy, who?" Abel pressed.

Willy, who'd never seen a game and knew nothing about baseball, thought it over, then snapped his fingers and said, "Probably the team with the most players."

This brought a surge of laughter from the boys.

"What's so funny?" Willy asked.

The boys laughed again and charged away to throw the ball.

"Willy," Colleen said, "baseball teams got the same number'a players."

"Oh."

"It's who scores the most runs in nine innings."

After the gumbo, the boys went wading in the river and found the ball. Willy watched tensely until both returned to shore.

"It's ready," Mr. Lemeaux said. "Willy, how 'bout a hand with the pot?"

Willy took a towel and held one handle as Mr. Lemeaux held the other. They poured the meal out on the tabletop, and the family gathered around, standing up. Colleen positioned herself to Willy's immediate left as Mr. Lemeaux bowed his head and said grace. The family reached in and began feasting. Willy felt Colleen's hip brush against his. He didn't put much into it—it was natural they would be close, standing as they were—but he felt a fire light in his belly and he blushed.

Willy's stories had brought him celebrity among the neighborhood children, and the grandsons sometimes brought a friend to meet Willy Bobbins, cattle rustler. They'd sit in a circle at his feet, listening, open mouthed and wide eyed. Willy had learned to shape the narratives, embellish this point, understate the next, find the right image, use asides not only to explain, but as seasoning. He noted when the children laughed and when their attention strayed.

Adults, too, began to gather around Willy and seemed equally charmed by Willy's accounts, especially Mrs. Ducroix, who'd sit smiling and nodding as if she heard every word. But neither the children nor the adults were who Willy directed his stories to. He wanted Colleen to hear them. And whenever Clyde Gaston's bride failed to show, the stories weren't as clever, the descriptions weren't as vibrant.

After the meal, the grandsons again asked Willy who was going to win the World Series.

Undaunted this time, Willy looked at Colleen and said, "I think the team that scores the most runs will."

His second answer baffled the boys as much as his first response had amused them. They sat at his feet and asked him to tell again about stealing cattle in Mexico. A few feet away Colleen sat with her back to them. He described the tall, mean longhorns that ran only because a horse was bigger. He told of being taken hostage to the hacienda and watching as the don and his guests ate on the patio, music playing in the background. He didn't mention the hanged man or the young *chollo* whose job it was to swing the dead man to and fro.

Abel said, "Bet you could of shot your way out."

Willy grinned and said, "I wouldn't be here ifin I had."

"Tell another, Willy," Abel pleaded.

"Okay, see me and Beau used go to Ebbin . . ."

When Willy finished his story about Beau stealing a pocket knife, Ms. Ducroix, nearly shouting, said, "How about that Plain Willy? What a rogue! Got shot by the Yankees, though he denies it!"

Willy looked at Colleen, who glanced at him over her shoulder. Smiling, she whispered, "She didn't hear a word, Willy."

"I heard that," Mrs. Ducroix said.

Willy and Colleen turned away simultaneously so that the old woman wouldn't see them laughing.

39

Weeks passed, and Willy, though still on crutches, was anxious to get out of the house. He limped about, sometimes morose, sometimes lighthearted, but almost always bored. Finally, he gave up his crutches and, with his diminished bankroll, headed back to the Quarter to recover his losses. His leaving in the evening disappointed Mrs. Ducroix. By then she was addicted to playing Pitch and so enjoyed Willy's company that she told him, "Don't go, Plain Willy. I'll play for money." She said it with such sincerity that he hesitated, but then told her that he owed her enough already for her kindness and couldn't go deeper in debt to her. Besides all that, she was too good a player for him, and he needed his money.

On the fourth night at the tables, Willy looked up from his game at L'Petit Tulare and saw D'Longo enter with a man he didn't recognize. They found seats at the table next to Willy's. D'Longo, pretending not to see Willy, counted out a stack of bills and laid them on the felt. His companion sat to his right. D'Longo whispered something to him, and the man looked at Willy, then whispered something back at D'Longo.

Keeping his seat, Willy played his next three hands, glancing on occasion at the next table. D'Longo still avoided any eye contact with him. The seat to his left was open. His companion seemed less interested in cards than he was in Willy. For a few more hands, Willy and D'Longo's companion exchanged looks, while D'Longo, smiling scornfully, looked around the room when not looking at his cards or the pot.

Willy decided the game of cat and mouse was over. He told the dealer to deal him out, gathered his winnings, limped to the table, and stood behind the empty seat next to D'Longo. "I see this here game's got some action." He took the empty seat and looked at all the players, except D'Longo.

"Seven card, ten and twenty," the dealer announced.

D'Longo tossed in his ante. "It's a closed game."

Willy laid money on the table. "I got funds."

A man in a white gabardine suit seated across the table said, "You heard what Apollo said."

D'Longo's companion stood and moved toward Willy. Willy kept his eyes on the one in white, a heavily jawed man, dapperly dressed. His wavy black hair shined dark blue in the light of the chandelier. "I apologize. I'm just a friendly sort, come to play poker."

The man considered Willy for a moment, then looked at the men seated at his side.

As Willy stood to leave, he leaned in D'Longo's direction and spoke, low at first, but louder as he progressed. "Been meanin to come 'round for my property. Was stove up a while, but I figure to be healthy enough now. I 'preciate you takin care of it for me."

"I have a friend you might have to talk to." D'Longo spread his coat so Willy would see the stocks of a revolver.

"Always happy to make a new acquaintance," Willy said.

The others at the table exchanged glances. As the dapper man laid down his ante, he eyed both Willy and D'Longo. He had dark brown eyes and thick eyebrows. From the look on the man's face as he gazed at D'Longo, Willy sensed that something hard sat between them.

The dapper man said, "The cowboy's my guest." He looked at Willy. "Have a seat."

Again Willy took the empty seat and tossed in two silver dollars. The dealer dealt the three cards. The man in white looked at his cards, surrendered them, and folded his hands in front of him. "You," he said smiling at Willy, "what's your name?"

"Willy. Willy Bobbins. Yours?"

"Okay, Bobbins." The man nodded without offering his name. "Open your coat so we'll know you're unarmed."

"Beg pardon?"

"Open your coat."

The men on either side of the speaker stood and moved toward Willy, who held his coat open and turned side to side so all could see he had no weapon.

"Okay. Let's see how you play."

Lacking in the game was the usual banter. The man to D'Longo's right seemed merely to go through the motions. Those obviously in the camp of the dapper man played more seriously, but it was clear the other game, the one between D'Longo and the man in white, had nothing to do with cards. By the fifth hand, Willy knew who was bluffing, who wasn't, who to fold against, and when to press a bet. He won three of those five hands. The man in white stayed on two pair and lost, folded the next hand, then holding three fours stayed through the end of the next hand. He was calm and competent, but no pro.

Those few hands put Willy up over two hundred for the play, a good night's win. He lost the next hand, and after the dealer collected the house's percentage, Willy said, "Fellas, it's been right fine playin with gents like you." He scooped up his earnings and pushed his chair back.

"Cowboy, you invited yourself into a private game." The dapper man placed his elbows on the table and touched his index fingers together as he studied Willy. "By asking yourself in, you forfeit any privilege of leaving with our money when it suits you. Stay and amuse us."

"Didn't know I was so well thought of." Willy scooted the chair close to the table and placed his money on the layout in front of him.

As the next hand came around, Willy began the story of how he and Beau stole a Model T from the wildcatters. By the time he reached the part about three bare-footed roughnecks chasing the car around as Beau ground the gears, the men were smiling.

"He didn't know nothin 'bout that pedal on the left, but he had the other one pressed down flat as a tortilla. One old boy was a holdin onto the door, and Beau just calm as nothin turns the car right and opens up the door. I raise ten," Willy said and tossed a bill on the pot.

Only the man across from him saw the bet. "Then what?" he asked.

"Then this fella 'bout eight feet tall with no shoes on was hangin like laundry in the wind and tellin Beau to stop. But Beau ain't had an idear what to do, so he just kept that contraption goin in a tight circle to the right. Could of gone on all night and might of if . . ." Willy turned over his down cards. He showed a full house.

The dapper player tossed his cards in. Willy scooped the pot into his pile of money.

"Finish the story," the man said.

"Well, Beau decides to try another pedal. Next thing I know, my head felt like a horse had kicked it, and that giant fella hit the ground so hard it started a earthquake and near toppled the derrick. You boys probably felt it here in Louisiana."

Willy watched the start of the shuffle, then separated the money from the pot into the appropriate stacks.

"You ever lose?" D'Longo said.

"Depends mostly on if it's an honest game. This one's honest. Or if someone's got a trap set." He looked D'Longo in the eye.

The man across from Willy coughed for attention. "What happened then, Bobbins?"

"Willy. Call me Willy. 'At's what my friends do." He smiled and looked innocently from face to face. "My bet?"

D'Longo grunted, "Yeah."

Willy tossed in a five-dollar ante. "'At's pretty much the story."

The cards came around. Willy had two eights in the peek and another showing. The player to his left bet twenty, the next one folded, the man across from Willy matched the bet, as did the next. D'Longo followed suit. Willy matched it and raised eighty.

"Hey, that's four times the limit," D'Longo said. "Pull it back."

The man in white raised a hand. "We'll play Willy's game."

Those who stayed matched Willy's bet.

"I think there's more to that story, Willy," the man said.

Willy caught a jack. "Well, me and Beau got away. 'Course, we took down their tent along the way. Damnedest thing, lookin back at a half-dozen grown men heavin rocks at a car what was near outta sight. We headed over to Pearsall. Never been there, but heard about it. So we take off in that general direction . . ."

The bets went around. Two players folded, leaving only the dapper man, D'Longo, and Willy. The bet was forty to Willy. He stayed in.

"Then?"

"We drive for the better part'a the night." Willy drew a king, no help. "We was tearin down fences where necessary 'til we'd find us a road. By then Beau's got the hang'a drivin that contraption." The bet was sixty to him. He had to play coy to build the pot. He looked at his stacks, at the exposed hands of the others, and last at his down cards. He counted off sixty. "I'll see it." He tossed the bills in.

"How long is this story?" D'Longo asked.

The dapper man gave D'Longo a leaden stare.

"I'm here to play," D'Longo said.

"No," the man said, his expression unchanged, "you came here because I wanted to talk."

D'Longo clenched his fists and cut an eye at Willy, who tipped his hat. The cards came. The man opposite Willy had two kings showing. D'Longo caught a jack of spades and had three spades up.

The dapper man bet forty. D'Longo matched it. Willy went through his previous ritual of looking at everyone's up cards and then his own before he called.

"Go on with the story, Willy. I think it's bringing me luck," the man said.

"Not much more. Just about the time Beau's got that contraption mastered, the damn thing up and dies. Stranded us in the middle a nowhere." Willy stopped to watch the last up cards dealt.

The dapper man caught a ten, D'Longo a king of spades, and Willy a king of hearts. The dapper man looked at D'Longo's hand and bet sixty. D'Longo saw it and raised it twenty. Willy called. He knew D'Longo had the flush. The dapper man was probably pat with a full house. He decided to fire up the last bet. He saw the bets.

"That's all?" D'Longo asked.

"Hell, boy, you got dandered up when all this started over eighty dollars."

"I meant, was that the end of the story? And don't call me boy."

"In Texas, it don't mean nothin." Willy paused as if thinking it over. "Hell, thinking on it, I guess it may mean the same here."

"What's that mean?"

"It means *boy* means nothin."

The dapper man smiled. "Apollo, he got you. Finish the story, cowboy."

"We come across some farmer. Sold him the car. Told 'im up front it was broke. That didn't seem to bother him none. He give us twenty dollars and a free meal for it. When he come back with food, he brung a jug. Poured a little in the engine and some down this hole by the window in front. Then he bent down to crank it alive.

"Hell, we were laughin by then. He got a few sputters. Shot some more corn whiskey in the engine and cranked again."

"This is a story with no end," D'Longo said and looked at the dealer. "Deal them."

The down cards came. The dapper man checked to D'Longo, who bet forty. Willy stared through him and calmly raised him eighty.

"You're all bluff."

"'At's right."

The dapper man matched the bets. D'Longo raised eighty more. Willy counted his money. He had only sixty-six dollars left.

"All I got," he said.

"Too bad," D'Longo said.

The man opposite Willy counted out fourteen dollars and passed it across the table.

"You can't do that," D'Longo said.

"Just did."

They stared at each other as Willy placed eighty dollars on the pot and called the hand.

The dapper man folded his hand without looking at D'Longo. "He's got you. Finish the story, Willy."

"I want to see what he's holding," D'Longo said.

"He's holding your nuts, Apollo," the dapper man said. "Go on, cowboy."

"Well, that farmer's got his hands on the handle ready to pull when I ask if he's tryin to get it drunk, which causes Beau to laugh harder. But the farmer, he turns that crank, and don't you know that thing jumps to life like it just woke up. He pulls the crank out and walks over and says, 'Ain't you dumb sumbitches ever heard'a gasoline?'"

The dapper man laughed. So did the others, except for D'Longo and his companion.

"What did you say then?"

"I said, 'Never heard of it, then I ask 'im if he ever heard'a stolen property.'" Willy turned over his peek cards. "Show your flush," he said to D'Longo, who merely shook his head and mucked in his cards.

Willy looked at D'Longo. "If Beau had been alive that night, you wouldn't be here."

"Well, he wasn't." D'Longo looked about as if soliciting aid, then, receiving no response, turned back to Willy. He slipped his hand inside his coat to let Willy see again that he was armed. Willy snorted, looked down as he fingered his money, then back at D'Longo. "Ever hear'a stolen property?" Willy said, but his tone didn't court laughter.

D'Longo drew his pistol. The dapper man's henchmen brandished theirs. At nearby tables, players pushed back their chairs and looked for a safe exit. One crawled under the table. The toughs beside the man in white circled the table and headed toward D'Longo. The dapper man halted them with a raised hand.

"The cowboy's my guest now, same as you, Apollo," he said. "Put it away."

D'Longo eased the pistol into his holster. "It was supposed to be a private game, Angelo."

Others in the room seemed to breathe as one. With a casual wave of the hand, Angelo motioned to henchmen to holster their weapons and return to their stations. A man burst through the door and looked around. Angelo addressed him in French. The man nodded and backed out through the door.

"So, cowboy, what's the problem here?"

Willy stared at D'Longo. "Apollo there took my watch, one Pa give me before he died."

The dapper man looked at D'Longo. "Is that a fact?"

D'Longo offered up an open palm. "I came for a peaceful game. Now I'll leave."

The man accompanying D'Longo stood. They said their good-byes to Angelo and, hands raised, palms exposed, backed out of the door.

"Guess that's it," Angelo said. "Willy, huh? Name's Angelo. I own a tobacco shop across the street. Come see me. Oh, and if you're smart, you'll carry. Apollo won't forget tonight."

Angelo offered his hand to Willy to shake and announced that the game had ended, and then he and his compatriots stood.

40 The late September night was cool, and a fog had swept in from the coast. Much of New Orleans was covered in it, even the Quarter. Willy had walked Bourbon Street for a time, taking in the fog. Another kind of fog hung over the city as well, although most of what Willy knew about it came from Mr. Lemeaux's accounts that repeated from other sources. In his latest report, Mr. Lemeaux relayed that the mayor or some other official was going to proclaim an order forbidding public gatherings. What Willy noticed in his walk was that the streets at seven in the evening were largely empty of people, no musicians, no boys on the street offering a boot shine.

As he stepped up and let the bouncer at L' Petite Tulare search him, Willy only hoped there would be some poker action. Business had been thin lately. A stout man in a suit identified himself as Guy and greeted Willy as he entered. Willy recognized him as one of Angelo's henchmen. He gently nudged Willy aside.

"Angelo wants you to go to the tobacco store."

"What for?"

"He didn't say. I gotta search you."

Guy nodded and Willy raised his arms. The man took Willy's revolver and said politely, "You'll get it back later. Follow me."

They walked out a white side door with gold-leaf trim that opened to an alley. Guy led Willy across the street to stairs that led to a second-floor door. He knocked three times on the door and waited. A voice told him to enter. He opened the door and stepped aside for Willy.

Angelo sat at a six-sided table, beside him one of his associates, whom Willy recognized. The three others seated seemed out of their league in a card room. Angelo nodded to Guy, who, without speaking, turned and vanished through the door. Willy stood embarrassed that all those in the room were staring at him.

"Here's the young player I mentioned." Angelo motioned Willy to sit opposite him.

Willy did so and looked sheepishly at each of the others in turn.

"As I said, he'll bring flavor to the game."

A silver-haired man stretched his arm across the table, palm open. "I'm Baxter Blaney."

"Judge Blaney," Angelo clarified.

"Yes," the judge said. "We hear you're a rogue and a cattle rustler, Mr. Bobbins."

"Willy, sir. Not no more. Not since I learnt to rustle wallets with a deck'a cards. Does 'at make me a rogue?"

The men laughed.

"Mr. Bobbins," the judge said, "do you like our New Ah'lens food?"

"Second only to your New Orleans money."

"Fine then, let's play then. We'll have food brought in later and see if that sharp Texas tongue can handle some real spice."

Willy was introduced to a banker and an exporter who dealt in weaponry, after which the judge asked, "Do you have plans if the war ends, Mr. Bobbins?"

"If it ends, yes, sir. Same plans I had before, but maybe bigger."

"And what would those be?"

The conversation had revived his dream of having a ranch, but now it saddened him. Without Beau and Lisette to share in it, the dream seemed hollow. "Well, Judge, I'm superstitious and talkin about somethin don't get it done."

Willy won most of the next seven pots, and then the conversation abruptly shifted to a looming vote on something the players called a constitutional amendment. Willy was familiar with the temperance movement. More than half the counties in Texas were dry, and he knew there was a movement afoot to make the country go dry, but these men had insight into the pending change.

The banker said. "It's women up north and Baptists down south."

Another of Angelo's associates cleared his throat. "What's it going to stop? The day it's passed, twenty boats'll steam out of Havana filled with rum."

"It could shut down the Quarter," the judge said, "and ruin business, Angelo."

Another player said, "Hear some health official's intent on doin just that."

"Three hospital's full already, I hear," the judge said.

Angelo took a draw on his cigar and exhaled the smoke. "Let's don't talk about that. My wife's gone crazy keeping up with the housework since Leona's been down with it. Anyhow, if liquor's outlawed, I'll prosper."

"How's that?" the banker asked.

"Men want what they want. It's simple. And everyone in here will do fine."

The talk turned to the possible end of the war, which the men at the table agreed was only weeks away. Willy knew of boys from Bedloe who'd gone to the trenches, and he'd talked with others who sons were serving. He decided not to discuss it, especially once the talk shifted to President Wilson. He listened, taking in the wisdom of the men at the table, who were far better informed, it seemed, than most who talked about such weighty matters.

Willy, too, had opinions about the war, but his were more personal, figuring as he had that the end of the war would mean a slippage in cattle demand. The cost of breeder cattle might likely go down. Some ranchers taking a setback might look to sell off. For him it came down to economics. He saw a bright future for someone with gumption and luck and a bankroll in hand.

Ending the conversation, the judge said, "Let's get food and some liquor up here before the war's over and everything a man enjoys is against some law. Besides, I'm tired of losing to this damn Texan. Angelo, I thought you said he'd come to amuse us with a story or two. Can you do that, Mr. Bobbins?"

"Sir, been kind'a hard to get a word in so far."

The men chuckled.

As they waited for food to come, Angelo passed out a round of fresh cigars. The men lit up, and talk began anew, this time about an illnesses sweeping New Orleans. One said it was an epidemic that started with troops in the trenches. Another said that was true, and doughboys were dying from it. There was no cure. Another said it was started by Kaiser Wilhelm, who was a megalomaniac. The judge said it was no rumor; it was in the country now, and accounts in the newspapers were accurate.

"William Randall Hearst never gave an accurate account of anything," the banker said.

"That's William Randolph Hearst," the judge said.

"Doesn't matter, Your Honor. He's still a fabricator."

A waiter entered carrying a tray of long pink shells with white meat inside and plates for the guests.

"Ah," the judge said, "crab legs came just in time to save Mr. Hearst's reputation from further slander."

When play resumed, Willy told a story about his rustling cattle in Mexico. The men lost graciously. Willy pressed his bets gradually, never enough to stir ill feelings. He tripled, then quadrupled, his pile. By midnight, he'd won more than seven hundred dollars. When the game came to a close, each player thanked him for the pleasure of his company and the poker lesson. They exchanged well wishes and filtered out. Angelo asked Willy to take a seat at the poker table and stay a while. "Did you have a good time?"

Willy patted his coat pocket. "Shore did."

"Good. We hold a game every two weeks or so. First we discuss . . . well, business of some mutual interest. I'd like for you to join us, but not until the business conversation is out of the way. What do you say?"

"Be pleased to."

"That's settled. I liked how you handled D'Longo. They left you for dead, didn't they?"

"They did. But they were wrong. And I 'preciate you doin me this way." Willy took his winnings out of his pocket and divided the money and laid half in front of Angelo.

"What's this?"

"Commission."

"Willy, I didn't invite you here so we could fleece them. You saw me throw in hands just so they'd win. That's all yours. I don't care how much you win, but it wouldn't hurt to lose a hand or two. They're not good players, and they can afford to lose. More than you can imagine. Their profession is making money. They hate losing to each other, but not to a professional. If one beats you now and then, it'll make him feel good."

"That don't make sense."

"Let's say it makes sense, because it suits my purpose."

"Makes some sense when you put it 'atta way. Even though I don't know your purpose."

"Never mind. I brought something for you." Angelo reached in his pocket and produced a watch. "Does this look like your father's?"

"'At's it."

He walked around the table and set the watch in front of Willy. "We're friends now, Willy. My last name's Cabresi. You need something, come to me." He waited for Willy's response, then patted him on the shoulder. "Guy will give you your gun and drive you home. I'll see you in two weeks. Don't come in the meantime."

"Why?"

"Why what?"

"Why you doin this?"

"Took guts to do what you did. I heard the rest. You got a look, Willy. D'Longo's too dumb to see it, but others do. I do. Maybe, in time, you might be useful in another way."

"How's 'at?" Willy looked in the mirror and checked his hat.

"We'll see."

Willy looked at Cabresi's reflection in the mirror. The dapper man was grinning.

"Look forward to seeing you in two weeks."

Willy agreed to return, but he didn't make it back.

41

On the Sunday following his good fortune at the cigar store, Willy was telling a story to the children when Mr. Lemeaux called to Colleen and said, "You finish with the gumbo."

No one paid attention as Mr. Lemeaux handed the spoon to his sister, who followed him into the kitchen. Right as Willy was describing how the deputy in Laredo had stepped out on the street at the very moment Bobby Grimes was about to pull the trigger, Colleen shouted from the other room, "No."

Everyone turned to look in her direction as she returned to the living room. She motioned to Willy and sat down by the fireplace, her hands shaking. He joined her and waited as she gathered herself enough to say, "He's got it."

Just then, his head, wet with perspiration, Mr. Lemeaux staggered into the room and collapsed to the floor, where he lay shivering. A dark silence fell over the family. So far they'd been spared, but tales circulating told horrific accounts of the epidemic—hundreds dying from it, hospitals overflowing with more waiting to die.

"I'll send the children to my home with Mother and stay here," Colleen said.

Willy helped Mr. Lemeaux up the back steps. Mrs. Ducroix, a tray of fresh bread in hand, passed them as they entered.

"Mr. Lemeaux's got the flu," Willy informed her. She laid down the tray, then followed as he propped up Mr. Lemeaux and helped him down the long hallway to the man's room. Mrs. Ducroix stood in the threshold while Willy pulled the bedcovers back, sat Mr. Lemeaux down on the bed, and lifted his legs gently. The man trembled and complained of being cold. Willy undressed him to his long underwear and pulled the covers up.

Colleen brushed past Mrs. Ducroix, crossed the room, and touched the back of her fingers to her brother's forehead.

"They say it kills mostly the young and healthy!" Mrs. Ducroix thundered. "You think the Yankees brought it?"

"Guess they's no point in tryin the hospital," Willy said to Colleen. He looked past her to the old woman leaning against the doorjamb, her hand gripping her collar.

"Right."

Mr. Lemeaux groaned. Colleen told Willy to get blankets. He found one in the hall closet and tore another from his own bed. Mr. Lemeaux lay feverish, calling for his wife.

Mrs. Ducroix grabbed Willy's sleeve as he walked by. "I have brandy, Plain Willy. In a drawer. Mrs. Lacy two doors up says there's a pill that helps—asper—or something seems the only thing helps. Go see her and find out. I'll be here."

The old woman's voice seemed a normal pitch for the first time to Willy's recollection. Willy told Colleen that he'd return as soon as possible.

Mrs. Lacy proved reluctant to open her door. She stood away from the screen and said the pills were called aspirin and came in a powder as well. She said the apothecaries were sold out. Willy said he could get some, but needed to call first. She had one of the two telephones on the block. She let him in and explained how to use the phone. After numerous rings, a man answered the call. Willy recognized Guy's voice.

"I need to talk to Angelo . . . 'bout somethin called aspirin."

"He's sick. Took 'eem to de 'ospital," Guy said. "Who's you?"

Willy identified himself.

"Willy. What Willy?"

"Plain Willy, the poker player. You drove me home. The cowboy, remember?"

"'Ome?"

Willy had experienced enough Cajun humor to recognize that Guy was playing him. He took a different strategy. "For your help Angelo'd want me to give you a hunert dollars."

"I teenk," Guy said, "maybe he'd want two hundred for me."

"Yep, two hunert's what he'd say. You come pick me up."

THEY DROVE THE STREETS on a seemingly endless quest, went all the way to Jefferson Parish, visiting drugstores, hospitals, doctors. They found no aspirin, but one doctor said that aspirin was going for ten dollars per hundred on the black market. They returned to New Orleans and scoured the city for black marketeers at an address off Canal Street, but had no luck until a black woman who claimed she could cure anyone with voodoo directed them to find Jean Paul, a yellow-eyed mulatto who worked on the docks.

They never found Jean Paul, but an arduous search landed them on the waterfront docks talking to an Italian stevedore, who drove the price up to fifteen dollars per hundred. Knowing nothing about the pills, what they were or how to administer them, Willy handed the man a hundred dollars and was led to a warehouse.

As Guy stood watch at the entrance, the Italian pried open a crate, which was part of a shipment waiting delivery to a distributor. The dockworker tossed the pry bar to the floor. Willy, unable to read the labeling, had to trust the stevedore. He watched him pull out a canister and hold it up. He told Willy it contained ten thousand dosages, which seemed a huge number, but Willy wasn't going to argue the matter.

"I ain't countin the gawdamn things, just open it and I'll take what's fair."

The stevedore broke the seal and opened the canister. Willy reached in with both hands and stuffed tablets in his pockets until they bulged. He called to Guy and had him do the same. Willy said to the dockworker, "Pleasure dealing with an honest man, 'stead'a them doctors."

On the way to the Lemeaux house, Guy began to sweat. Willy told him to swallow some aspirin. The Cajun took too many, and they lodged in his throat. He gagged and choked until they came up. Complaining of intestinal cramps, he stopped the car near an alley and ran into it, dropping his pants along the way. After evacuating his bowels, he vomited.

Willy helped the Cajun back to the Model T and slid in behind the steering column. Receiving half-lucid instructions from Guy, Willy drove. He stalled the Model T a few times, got out and cranked it to life, and then twice headed in the wrong direction. Late that night, he pulled it to a stop in front of the Lemeaux house. Leaned against the door, Guy was lost in delirium. Willy managed to hoist the Cajun onto his shoulder and carry him to the house.

He stored Guy on a couch by the bay window, dumped the pills on the table, and called for Colleen. When she emerged from the hall, he handed her tablets too fast. Some spilled onto the floor. "Take one," she said.

He placed one on his tongue, which he promptly spat across the room. "Terrible."

Colleen touched her tongue to one. "I'll be back."

She returned with two glasses and a pitcher of water. She poured them water and demonstrated how to take the pill. "I'm afraid, Willy, that Mrs. Ducroix has it too."

THEY WORKED together getting their patients to swallow the aspirin. Mr. Lemeaux vomited his up three times before one stayed down. The two of them went from room to room administering to the sick, wiping foreheads with towels they rinsed in basins. Through the night they helped each other. Twice Colleen brought Willy aspirin and made him swallow two. When the grandfather clock struck two, she came into Mrs. Ducroix's room and sat beside Willy on the bed.

"How is she?"

"Don't know. Sick. Guess the others are the same."

"Pretty much. The pills may help."

"I ain't seen much evidence of it."

"Willy, I'm going to sleep. You better do the same."

He stood and walked to the window, where he opened the shutters. "The neighbors."

"What?" Her eyelids drooped as she looked up.

"Got me an idea. I'll be back."

He found Guy's clothes hanging on the back of the couch. He emptied Guy's pockets of the pills, and as he did, he came upon the two one-hundred dollar bills he'd given him. Willy stuffed the money in his pocket, then mixed the pills with the others on the table. He turned to go to the kitchen, and as he did, he looked at Guy, lying in a fetal position, shivering, unconscious. Willy pulled the bills out of his pocket and returned them to the Cajun's trousers. In a kitchen drawer, he found a paper sack, filled it with pills, and left.

He started with the nearest neighbor, knocking until he got an answer.

"Go away!"

"It's Plain Willy," he said. "I got pills for you. Pills 'at'll make you better."

"Nothing wrong with us."

"All the same, you'll need 'em."

When the door opened, Willy scooped a few tablets out of the bag and handed them to the scared man. From there he walked east and pounded on the next door. At each door, the faces hid behind screens. Some said the flu was already in their house. Some were angry, others scared, but all were grateful as they received the offering. Willy worked his way up the street. Some doors wouldn't open to him, no matter how he much pleaded his case. The house that ended his mission was Clyde Gaston's. Willy had never seen the place before, but knew from the way it was kept that it was the house she slept in. It pained him to think of it as Colleen's, as the house she shared with another man who was never around. He knocked on the door, and when it opened, he gave Mrs. Lemeaux a handful of pills, along with instructions to take them with water.

"How's my son?"

Willy didn't know. He pacified her with a lie. "He'll be fine. Mrs. Ducroix's got it."

THE SACK WAS nearly empty when Willy returned to the house. Colleen was asleep in his bed. He sat and gazed at her sleep-softened face. Her eyes flickered open, and she reached out for his neck. "Lie with me."

She pulled him to her, closed her eyes, and nestled close to him. Her breasts rested softly against his chest. He felt the rise and fall of her ribs and her breath on his throat. He'd been with Lisette and a string of prostitutes. That was what Willy knew of women. He wondered how it would be with one like Colleen, who seemed too delicate to touch. He brushed a sweat-curled lock away from her forehead with the backs of his fingers. He studied the closed eyelids, pictured how her eyes glistened as she tilted her head and listened to his tales. He remembered at first that he'd paid her little attention. She was married, and he'd seen her as one kind of woman. Now, they'd been through something together, and he saw her as another kind entirely.

Though near and warm, she still seemed ethereal. She was temptation. He wanted her. And he couldn't have her. He gently rolled away from her onto his back.

She murmured, "No," and curled up. Soon she was breathing lightly. He took a pillow and lay on the floor.

IN THE MORNING Colleen said she had to go home, that she'd return. At the door, she asked if Willy would drive her, saying she'd like that. "We've never talked."

He thought about the possibility of him and her if they rode off together. "Hell, ma'am, I was lucky to get to the house without killing off the entire population."

She rose up on her toes and kissed him on the cheek. "Thank you for the pills and . . ."

He stationed himself at the open door and watched her walk until she vanished up the street. With three patients to watch over, he would need his strength. Willy returned to the house and boiled water for soup.

42

His fever hit two days later, chills at first, followed by sweats, then vomiting and diarrhea. It felt like a hundred dull needles driven into his joints. With no one around to nurse him, he took to his room, carrying a pitcher of water and a handful of aspirin. Too weak to hold the pitcher, he dropped it to the floor, and it shattered.

The next morning, he rose out of bed half-conscious and cut the soles of both feet without realizing it. He lay for three more days. When the fever broke, Willy opened his eyes to sunlight and the neighbor lady, Mrs. Lacy, standing at the foot of the bed.

"Mr. Bobbins, I bandaged your feet. And I took some clean clothes out of your dr'ahs and laid them at the foot of the bed. If you'll go and change, please, I'll clean up your bedding."

Willy blinked until she was fully in focus.

"Do you think you can manage?"

"Don't know, ma'am." He moved his right arm. His hand felt incredibly heavy, his legs even more so. He inched his way to the edge of the bed and slowly sat up.

"Not too much at once, Mr. Bobbins."

"Couldn't if I had to."

She reached for him and let his weight rest on her shoulder as he stood.

His legs seem liquid. "How long I been out?"

"Five, six days. I found you two days ago. Kept water and pills in you. Lucky you're young and strong. Mr. Lemeaux is still too weak to move. Seems I'm been one of the ra'ah people spa'hed the worst effects of the virus."

"Mrs. Ducroix?"

"You're lucky" was Mrs. Lacy's answer. She helped him to the screen and brought the fresh clothes. As she changed the sheets, she relayed what had transpired while he suffered the fever. She said that the people in the neighborhood were grateful he'd brought the aspirin.

"Only Mr. Anders, who'd been a bugle boy in the War with the Union, and Mrs. Ducroix, whose husband fought for the South. That's irony, Mr. Bobbins."

He started to tell her to call him Willy when his knees buckled. He took the screen with him as he collapsed. He tried to get up, but slid back down. Mrs. Lacy helped him to sit. Except for the shirt twisted around his neck, he was naked. He tried to cover himself. She straightened the shirt and buttoned it, then helped him into his trousers.

"Just sit on the floor for now. Some soup'll get you going," she said.

"Split pea?"

"If that's what you want. Or black-eyed?"

He nodded, meaning either or anything at all.

She told him that the day before, some men had come for the Cajun and the car. They'd given her money for food and helped move Mr. Lemeaux out of the bed while she'd changed the linen.

"It's his washed linen I'm puttin on your bed. It hung out in the air and sun. Smells fresh. It'll help kill the sickness."

TWO DAYS LATER, Willy regained much of his strength, though he'd lost several pounds. He made arrangements with Angelo, who'd also recovered, to have Mr. Lemeaux moved to Colleen's while he continued to recover. She too had come down with the flu, but through it all, she'd cared for her nephews and niece and mother, but Abel had come down with pneumonia and on the fourth day of his fever he died. As Willy rode the trolley down Canal Street, now almost deserted, he knew what he had to do next. Still, he walked the streets of the French Quarter for hours, thinking it through. Most everything was closed because of an order from the government to prevent public gatherings.

The next day, certain Mr. Lemeaux and the rest of the family had pulled through, Willy gave a good portion of his money to Colleen, handing it to her in a sealed envelope and telling her not to open it for three days. Money mattered less to him than it ever had, and he hoped they would use it well. At the same time, he knew no amount would compensate their losses, especially the boy.

With two changes of clothing packed in a bag, he mounted the trolley and sat by himself. The conductor told him that a man named Dr. Rollen had instated a rule, "that only one passenger was allowed standing for every two seated." The rule hardly seemed necessary. The flu had so reduced the number of fares that everyone was seated.

An elderly man said as Willy passed, "Did you hear?"

"Hear what?"

"War's over. Germans surrendered. Read it in the *Bee*. Headline's 'November Eleven.'"

"Well, that's somethin."

"Won't be no celebratin," the man said. "Not here. Over two thousand dead from the influenza. Yep."

"Yes, sir, I 'spose 'at's the case."

Willy moved on and took a seat in the rear. Several passengers were, like him, pale and gaunt and tired, their eyes disaffected. The sight disheartened him. So much death had descended so quickly that existence itself seemed mere illusion and survival no more than a magician's trick. One couple, young and ripe with each other, snuggled together in a seat, their fingers entwined, their happiness a sort of obscenity in the face of so much adversity, but Willy saw in them some assurance that luck still existed in the world, that the cards could and would be reshuffled.

That evening, he purchased a train ticket to Brownsville, then went to the French Quarter and ate until he couldn't stand another bite. He went to the cigar store and up the side stairs. Angelo Cabresi opened the door. He seemed fully recovered from his illness.

"I come to say I'm leavin, but I 'preciate your . . ."

Angelo raised a finger to his lips. "Nothing to appreciate. This was bad, this sickness."

"I'm goin home to Texas, see my family."

"I'd invite you in, Willy, but I have a wake to go to this evening and a funeral in the morning. It's good you came. The pills helped many. Maybe we'll be of some use to each other in the future."

"Well, maybe."

Afterward, Willy bought a bottle of sour mash, found himself two Bourbon Street prostitutes, and wound up in a hotel suite. He closed his eyes as he rolled on the bed with the women, first one, then the next, imagined the first to be Colleen, the second Lisette. Then late in the night he sent them away and counted losses, each loss different. First Beau, he thought, then Lisette, Colleen, women who'd garnered his deep feeling, and old Mrs. Ducroix dead and the boy Abel, named after the first slain in the Bible, a name that seemed doomed to him now. His days were going fast, and he saw little good in them. In the morning he sat on the edge of the bed, his head throbbing. When finally he stood up and took some steps, he walked like a man who'd climbed out of his own grave.

He spent four more days in the Quarter and one hundred and twelve dollars because money seemed not to matter. He had only four hundred left of his once fat bankroll when he sat down in the train. He was headed home and with just enough money left to fill his pockets. What he needed was something good to fill his mind.

43

The wagon team clattered to a stop in the town center. Willy extricated himself from the straw, hopped over the tailgate, and grabbed his valise. "I thank you kindly," Willy said. "Here, take this." He offered up a half-dollar.

The farmer looked at his wife. She shook her head.

"Wouldn't be hospitable to. Wish you the best." He flicked the traces twice.

Willy stepped to the side of the road and watched the wheels churn up dust as the wagon went on its way. He pushed the brim of his hat back and looked up and down the deserted street, not even a horse hitched to a rail. Only a motorcar, a black Oldsmobile parked in front of the livery.

"I'll be," he said and crossed the street.

Willy opened the door to the sheriff's office and peered in. Dumbfounded, he stood in the doorway, looking at Tom Plummer, who leaned back in a chair behind the sheriff's desk, hands folded in his lap. Plummer stood, his lanky form unfolding into the shape of a cornstalk.

"Where's Sheriff Fellows?" Willy asked, taking note of the five-pointed silver star on Plummer's shirt.

"You mean your bother-in-law? Took sick. 'At damn flu come through here two weeks ago and laid up the whole countryside. Don't know yet who all it ain't kilt. They's a bunch 'at died. Say, what you doin back, Willy?"

Willy set his valise on the bench by the door. "What you doin in here, being a horse thief and all? Still holdin on to Bobby Grimes's pecker?"

"'At ain't funny."

"Well, what ain't funny to one is a laugh for another. How'd you get that star?"

"I asked first."

"So you did. I don't know what I'm doin back as yet. Just come is all. That badge?"

"I been special deputy for near three months, and when the flu come along, Mr. Fellows put me in charge'a the office. 'Sides, I don't steal horses and cows no more. See, me and Lena Sorenson's gettin hitched. Her old man says he wouldn't abide his daughter marryin up with no criminal. Says it don't bode well for a Christian family. 'At's why I become a special deputy. His wife up and died. She went to San Antone to see someone called Fatty Arbuckle. Never heard the name 'fore that."

Willy digested this. Mrs. Sorenson was his ma's closest friend. That would be tough on his ma. "Too bad. She was a stern one."

"She was against Lena and me marrying up too. Now it mean nothin 'cause Lena said yes."

"Guess Lena ain't heard about your peculiar fondness for donkeys."

"Willy, that ain't nothin but town gossip."

Willy nodded. "Well, town's full'a gossip, ain't it?"

"I hear about you now and then, Willy. Bein's I'm 'round your sister and all. Hell, heard you was rich, then heard you was dead. Didn't know what to believe."

"Well, I guess you could say I'm alive."

"Looks that way. Where you been?"

"The truth of it is, Tom, I been to college. Got me one'a those sheep-skins what give me the right to know nothin and admit to it without embar-rassment."

"Really?"

"Tom, you're a likable sumbitch, but kind'a gullible."

"Well, shore nice to see you. 'Course, I gotta inform you the law's dif-fer'nt now that the sheriff's married and gone to the Methodists after your sister left the pope and all, which may be worse 'an goin to hell. Don't mat-ter it was Nell he married. Hell, he arrested your pa twice for fightin, though they ain't so much fight as fuss in him these days. Sheriff locked him up mostly so's he wouldn't get hisself hurt. Sheriff told Panther Jack to keep his questionable stock outta sight of the citizens of Bedloe."

"'At a fact?"

"A fact. Yep. And Panther Jack, he's all alone now. His nigger girl up and left some months back. Hear she hit 'im over the head when he was sleepin. Stole his books, she did. Damnedest thing. Didn't take nothin else, but that and some clothes."

"Stole his books?"

Willy stared at the star on Plummer's shirt. She'd returned for the books as he'd asked. It took a moment for the knowledge to fully sink in, then it moved through his chest like thorns and settled in his gut. How had he missed her on the road? Why didn't he wait? Had she cut across the fields and arrived after he left? All along, he'd expected her to be here, with Panther Jack. Nearby where he could find her. Had he known of this, he might not have returned.

"Stole his books?" he mumbled.

"What's 'at?" Plummer asked.

"Nothin." Willy cut a hard eye at Plummer. "Don't be callin her a nigger."

"Willy, it ain't gonna bother her none. 'Sides, what else would I call her?"

"Lisette."

Plummer said, "Well, she was a pretty one for a . . ."

The look on Willy's face told him not to finish. Willy wanted to strike out at someone, but he had no one to blame but himself.

"Don't mean nothin, Willy. Was she your gal or somethin?"

Willy looked out the window. He knew Plummer was horse dumb and intended no harm. Besides, no one knew her as Willy did, her passion, her sadness, her tenderness. How could anyone understand those the way he did? It was his fault. She was blameless. His anger subsided.

"You awright?" Plummer asked.

"Yep. Guess it don't matter what you call her. Don't say it to me, just the same."

Plummer bowed his head, then took his seat. "Guess you'll be headin out to your place?"

Willy detected something in the way Plummer asked. "Why not?"

"Oh, just askin."

"I ain't in no hurry to see Pa, but I been missin Ma and the others. Need me a horse. Left mine in Louisiana."

"'At where you went to college?"

"Tom, I can't read a lick to speak of. Can't do much more 'an make my mark. Nice seein you." Willy picked up his valise.

"Willy?"

Willy paused. Plummer studied his fingernails as if he'd never seen them before. "'At fever didn't much care . . ."

Willy reached for the latch, but hesitated. "Somethin you didn't tell me?"

"Well." Plummer avoided Willy's gaze. "Like I said, that fever didn't care . . . Your ma and that baby brother. And he was sick anyhow, from what no one knew ... I don't ... Your ma was the one come to Sorenson's to care for Lena's ma."

Willy turned to the door and stared as if seeing through it. He watched as his hand closed on the latch, saw the door open and his fingers slip away from the handle. He stepped out in the shade of the overhang, gripped the valise tightly, and looked up. He seemed to be floating above the roofline looking down at himself, earthbound and powerless and numb. He thought to blame God for all the misfortune, but changed his mind. His mother's prayers had floated up to a deaf heaven. In the end, God had nothing to do with this. There was no one to blame, nothing to rage at.

He'd been away too long and had come home too soon. He rubbed his eyes, looked in the direction of the livery, and stepped down from the walkway.

44

Willy pushed though the door, warmed his hands over the stove, and walked into the open bedroom. Nell sat at the bedside watching over Clay. Willy stood in the doorway. Clay saw him, and his eyes filled with hostility. He mumbled something incoherent.

"How is he?"

"Heard you ridin up." Nell stroked Clay's forearm. "Doin fine now."

Willy looked over his shoulder. A pot rested on the stove.

"Coffee?"

Nell nodded. She looked his way for the first time, seemed to be constructing a question, but she didn't ask it.

Willy walked to the stove and called from the kitchen. "Where's Anne and Hazel?"

"Married and gone, both of 'em. One a few weeks back. The other four months ago."

"Anyone I know?"

Nell emerged from the bedroom and stood in the threshold. "He blames you for the leg. Says you could of taken him to a doctor."

"Just would of lost it sooner." Willy poured a cup and sat at the table facing her.

The coffee was bitter. He set it aside. "How long's this been a sittin?"

"'At's all you got to say?"

He didn't answer.

She stared at him a moment, then said, "Ma's dead, and the baby. Guess you know."

"I heard from Tom Plummer."

"You're a cold man. Go away for near a year, no word 'cept you come by once and flash a gold watch to impress someone, then gone."

"Yep. Cold, 'at's me."

"Didn't care nothin about your ma."

Willy glared at her. "Give money to a Corcoran City lawyer for her."

"Don't come to my weddin, neither'a you. And where's Beau?"

Willy pointed toward the bedroom. "Make sense to you, her dyin and him alive?"

"He's your pa."

"He's *your* pa."

"You're a stranger."

Willy splayed his legs out and looked down at his boots. "I know what I am. I come back thinkin I'd do right, sort'a eat my pride and . . . Well, this is what I come to." He saw the losses increasing. In the span of his short life he could list from his family his ma, Beau, Sean, grandparents, and uncles. There were the two rustlers whose names he never knew, and the one who'd said his name but that Willy couldn't remember, and the wildcatter. To those deaths he added those he might perhaps have to kill and those that life itself took. That was how it was.

"Don't you feel nothin, Willy?"

He looked at his sister. "Way I see it, feelin somethin's about the hardest thing to do."

She stood tall, her hands on her hips. "Where's Beau, Willy?"

"Got hisself drowned in the ocean near Brownsville. Some nine months past."

"Him too?" She grabbed the doorjamb for support.

Willy came to her and led her to a chair. She sat, her expression lusterless, disbelieving. She placed her arms on the table, buried her head between them, and cried.

He took her wrist and held it gently.

She glanced up, her eyes wet but accusing. "Don't you care?"

"I cared and I care. What's there to do but care?"

Willy released her wrist. She buried her head again in her arms. Her chest heaved violently. He scooted his chair back and paced the floor. He glanced into the bedroom once and saw that Clay was resting. When Nell seemed to have exhausted her tears, Willy kneeled beside her, laid his arm over her shoulder, and pulled her close. "Was it bad for Ma?"

"Sean went first. I didn't tell her. Then she went. She caught it from Mrs. Sorenson. Died blamin herself."

"Weren't just here. I tell you, Nell, seems half the world died or near died. New Orleans. On the train people talked about the fever hittin and the war. Ever'body knew someone who died."

"How'd it happen, Willy?"

"What? Beau?"

She nodded.

"We was ridin on the beach and stopped, and he went in. I was right behind him. Last I saw, it was like him hangin from that barn, way he did just before he jumped. His face all puckered up, like he'd do somethin no matter what, or hold his breath 'til he passed out? He was there, then he wasn't."

She took his hand. "I prayed over the baby, and Glen went for the priest. Father David came in time for Ma. She died blessed."

"But she died."

Nell pulled her hand away. "I thought you'd want to know."

He stood and paced again. "I seen men die. You look in their eyes, it's like they're chasin somethin far off. Somethin no one can catch."

"You couldn't do nothin for Beau?"

"I ain't no swimmer, but I tried."

She shook her head. "My husband come down with it, but he's better."

"Tom Plummer said as much." Her husband, Willy thought. Nell, a woman. A strange and terrible homecoming.

"Glen and Tom Plummer buried Ma and Sean, beside the others."

Willy nodded.

"They're just north of Grandma Betty and Grandpa George. I put flowers there. Glen took sick right after he buried 'em. You okay, Willy?"

"Yeah, fine as can be, considerin."

"I been wonderin, did you leave 'cause of that woman? Panther Jack's. Glen says that's what it was."

"Heard you and he's both gone Methodist. Guess that gives people the right to speculate on gossip."

"'At's not nice." She wiped her eyes on her sleeve.

"Any liquor in the house?"

"No."

Willy rubbed his eyes. "Was my fault. I couldn't admit it for a time, but he did what I said. I mean Beau. I could'a said don't and stood between him and the water. He loved that sea. Like to think he died happy, poor boy that he was with a lame foot and all." Willy stepped over to the bedroom door. Clay lay under a rumpled blanket.

"He asleep?" Nell asked.

"Like the world's all fine." He leaned against the jamb and gazed off. "Somethin happened to Beau, a miracle. He started losin his stutter. 'At day on the beach, he was talkin clear as you and me. Sounds crazy now, but it's true."

She wiped her eyes with the hem of her skirt and stood. "Put some fresh coals in the stove, and I'll fix up some supper. I want you to know, I ain't happy with you."

"Tell the truth, I ain't happy with me neither. Got any coffee what ain't got horse shit in it?"

"Little manure won't hurt no Bobbins." She smiled.

"Guess not, seein as how we come by it naturally from him."

She walked toward the bedroom, but hesitated. "Anne took off to New Mexico with a traveling preacher. 'Caused a stir." Saying this seemed to shore up Nell. "And Hazel married up with a horse trader from Fort Stockton. He's wild. Not so wild as you, but wild. Tell you about 'em later. It's gettin cold."

She left the bedroom door open.

"Are you happy, Nell?" he called out.

She didn't answer.

His boot heels thumped as he walked to the stove. A board squeaked. He saw the head of a nail protruding. He lifted the coal bucket and poured a dozen chunks on the coals, then stoked the fire. He turned his attention to the fireplace, vented the flue and spread kindling on the hearth, then laid two split logs on top and lit the fire.

When he was young, the fire had been his duty in the cold months—stoke the coals at night, and first thing in the morning place the logs on the hearth and breathe the fire to life. The stove was next. Beau, even with his lame foot soundless as a snake, followed him in the dark, the floor so cold their toes went numb. And his ma would emerge from the bedroom and slip into her apron. Then Beau would wake up the girls and tell them Willy and he were ready to eat. When left to their own devices, the boys would fry eggs and top them with chilies so hot it burned their throats.

"Nell!" he called out. "I got us a fire goin!"

Willy stared as the fire in the stove cast flickering shadows. He wasn't certain what he would do next. He was hungry and tired, but warm. And alive. And home. He felt a draft rise up. He noticed another nail head sticking up and examined the floor more closely. Several boards needed attention. Maybe he'd look after them, fix up the place.

Nell, her brow knitted and her eyes downcast, stepped out of the bedroom and stood just inside the kitchen. "Willy?"

"What?"

"You couldn't of—" She turned as if to go back into the bedroom.

"Couldn't of what, Nell?"

She drew her shoulders back and faced him. "Been with her. Not like with Glen and me being together."

"Never said I was."

"Panther Jack said so."

They stared at each other, neither speaking for a time, Clay's labored breathing in the bedroom and the stove fire crackling in the background the only noise.

"Get what's on your mind done with," Willy said.

"It's against the law even to be with a black, and marrying one could never happen. It was against it for Panther Jack, just as well. And her. I didn't know it 'til Glen told me. He said it was a fool law and he wasn't gonna arrest no one for it, but someone else might."

"Not in Louisiana," Willy said.

"There too. Ever'where in the South laws are made to keep people with their own kind."

Willy walked over to her and stood an arm's length away. "Laws to make me . . . Nell, what's my kind? How's the law to know?"

"I don't know." She reached out both her arms and took him in an embrace.

"Her name's Lisette," he whispered.

"I heard. It's a perdy name."

45 Willy stayed by his pa's sickbed for a week after Nell had returned to her home. He cooked a pot of menudo or chili every morning and brought a bowl to Clay twice a day. For a time, he spoon-fed him, Clay glaring all the while and taking each bite reluctantly. After Clay was able to eat on his own, he took to waving Willy off or asking if Willy

was trying to poison him. He refused to eat until Willy left. Despite Clay's comments, when Willy returned for the bowl, he found it emptied. Without comment, he'd gather up the dirty bowl and spoon and wash them.

During his weeks of recovery, Clay had spoken only to complain about the food or to tell Willy he was unwelcome in the house. The final words from Clay the day he stood on his own were "Don't want you near me."

"Could of poisoned you," Willy said. "Be thankful I didn't."

Willy patched the roof of the barn and moved to the loft, which he converted to a room by walling in the face and two sides with boards taken from the old fence. It made for drafty but livable quarters. He kept to himself, pounding nails, repairing planks, and doing other odd jobs on the spread and picked up work elsewhere, hauling hay or loading stock for Mr. Ebbin. Though the county was recovering from the prolonged effects of the drought, there still was scant work to be had. His thoughts often strayed to going back on the road and playing poker, or perhaps, despite painful memories of the epidemic, returning to New Orleans, maybe go to work for Joe O'Banion or Angelo.

Fact was he resented his pa as much as Clay resented him. Still, out of a sense of obligation, Willy stayed, though in what seemed, since his conversation with Nell, a gloomy day-to-day present. He was indecisive about any future and clung obsessively to the past. Despite the unlikelihood of its happening, he waited for some word to come of Lisette, perhaps her returning to Panther Jack, but not a whisper came of her, not from Mr. Ebbin or any of the men and women he traded with. Gradually, Lisette became a specter in Willy's thoughts, a woman who'd vanished in the shadows of boughs on a moonlit night, one who existed now only in a pew in a darkened church or in a field at the side of a dirt road. She'd vanished everywhere else, even on the tongues of the town gossips.

Willy's brief words with Clay consisted mostly of deciding who'd cook a meal on a particular evening or water and feed the horse, the only one being a nag that Glen had hustled up for Clay some months before. Come dark Willy retired to the drafty barn, crawled under his bedroll, and slept the sleep of the haunted, tossing and turning much of night. In the morning he awoke, stiff and weary, and trudged to the house, where he sat at a silent breakfast table as Clay glared. Finished, he went out to labor on the place or rode in to see if Mr. Ebbin had any work for him.

Nell came to visit, but she mostly visited with their pa while Willy busied himself with one small task or another.

In late December news came via the merchant that a law making the production, transportation, and possession of alcoholic beverages illegal had passed Congress and was sent to the states for ratification. Willy relayed the news he'd gotten from Mr. Ebbin to Clay, who sat half asleep at the table with a blanket over his shoulders. He blinked Willy into focus and said, "You still here?"

"Want me to leave, say it."

But Clay didn't.

ONE COLD EVENING, as Christmas drew near, Willy, intent on leaving forever, packed his bedroll to sleep on and a sack of beans to keep him alive. He left those in the barn and went outside. He had money left, enough to find a poker game somewhere and build up his bankroll. He walked to the turn in the road where he studied the horizon in every direction, wondering which horizon might be the right one to head into.

He remembered his boyhood before the drought hit Texas, times when his uncle ran the spread and cotton grew in the field and cattle grazed in the pasture, and he and Beau, knee-high to his own pa then, worked the land. He thought about things he'd lost or left behind—money, horses, people. Burdened by guilt, he speculated on what better course he might have taken and what his ma might have expected from him. He was certain she'd loved his pa. Why else would she endure the life he'd given her?

For the first time since arriving, he walked to his ma's and Sean's graves. That morning he'd seen his pa at the graves, talking in a rambling way, his words drifting back to the house. He wondered what his pa had said here. He placed a hand on the wooden cross with her name crudely etched on it. "Guess he talks to you 'cause no one else in the world wants to hear what he has to say. Probably still tells you about them Spaniards makin him deef in 'at ear'a his. Wished you'd of had it better. Don't know what else to say."

He stood a while, his hand and eyes on the grave marker, as if waiting for her to speak to him. Then he nodded to the grave and said, "I'll try." He let his hand drop to his side and returned to the barn.

AS WINTER DAYS drew shorter, Willy decided it was useless to nail boards and clean lofts. The place seemed beyond repair, and he had no desire and saw no end purpose in repairing it. Clay seemed unmoved by his efforts and continued avoiding him. Fine, Willy thought, he'd just leave it and return to New Orleans, where he could make money at poker and learn the casino business, earn money enough to return to Texas, and buy himself his own spread, run cattle. That, he saw as the answer, taking money from those willing to offer it up in the hopes of winning more. He knew casino odds, knew farming odds, both stacked against a man. Farming, it seemed, was even tougher. What middlemen didn't take, the government was ready to take, fingers and thumbs everywhere, finding their way into a man's pocket.

Though he felt no obligation to tell Clay, he decided to all the same make a final effort to mend matters. He found his pa sitting in front of the unlit stove, staring at the door. Clay didn't look up.

"I'm goin, Pa. Maybe tomorrow."

"Go on then. Ain't like you been around all that much anyhow."

"Nothin here. You may's well leave too. You can come with me if you want. Don't know how a one-legged ol man can make this place earn him anything. Hell, don't see how a healthy young man could."

"With you. Ain't likely I'd go anywheres with you."

Willy shook his head. "What you gonna do? Cockfights? Make liquor?"

"What I do don't matter."

"Maybe. Maybe not. You ain't likely to keep this place, not from runnin cockfights and sellin rotgut."

"Whatta you know, Willy? I mean, about this place."

"I know it's a curse."

"Curse? It's where your ma's buried and our baby boy. Your uncle, my brother, and his wife. And my pa. And his pa. Sam Houston hisself give it to my granddaddy. Your great-granddad fought at San Jacinto. He married my grandma here, built this house on the very spot of their wedding. Leave it? You can't leave what won't leave you."

"Ain't nothin I didn't know."

Clay looked at Willy for a time, then folded his hands in his lap and stared at them. Willy asked if he wanted him to heat some coffee. Clay shook his head and rubbed his stump. Willy looked at the leg, cut off just below the knee, and the single-staff crutch propped on Clay's lap.

"Fine. I'm getting some sleep. Maybe be in the barn for the night or gone."

"Suit yourself."

"Okay. Hope you enjoy being a cripple and waitin here to go in the ground with the rest." Willy turned toward the door.

"I still have dreams, boy."

Willy turned back. "Of what? Gettin rich?"

"No. I dream I'm walkin on both legs. Just that. Then I wake up from it and feel it in me, like that leg's ready to walk, then I touch it and I know it's a damned dream."

"My fault, I guess. I mean, your leg."

Clay shook his head. "No one to blame but me."

"Glad you finally see it."

Clay cleared his throat and stared at the floor. "I ain't been a good man, not since the war with Spain. Changed me, it did. I come back in uniform and married your ma, hopin to be good. I loved her. Still do. I was a sad case as a husband. Sad case as a pa."

"Sayin it don't make no difference."

Clay smiled a wan smile and clasped his hands to the arm of the chair. "See, 'at's what happens to a boy when a man ain't a good pa. Hell, I worked this place and provided fine 'til the drought, but that ain't the same as doin what a man's 'spose to do for his kin. Drank too much. Now go on. Don't need you here to tell me what I am ever'day."

"I never said nothin 'less you brought it up."

"Is in your eyes, boy. I see you taken measure ever'time you look at me."

"You would'a let me drown."

"I shot a man would'a kilt you. Shot 'im and sent you into the river hopin you'd live. Hell, you were her favorite, though I don't much understand that. No, sure don't. But I blamed you for the leg, and I was wrong. I could'a found a doctor. But I let it go."

"This is more talk than I wanted. It ain't just that. What about when Beau was shot and them cows was stole? That was you told those boys."

Clay shook his head. "I'll be damned if that's the case. Why, you were both my boys. Him too. Hard as I was on you, I'd never betray you. Never. No sir."

"You weren't just hard on us. You were hard on ever'one. Ol Lopez and his kind, especially."

Clay looked up. "A man gets into the habit of thinkin one way. Ain't easy to change. Go ahead and go. I wish you . . . well, better 'an you got from me."

Willy opened the door and left.

HE STOPPED atop a hill and wrapped himself in his blanket. He was restless and for a time lay looking at the cold moonlit sky marred by a few wispy clouds. Then he looked back at the gentle flats and realized that all of it, before the Civil War, before carpetbaggers came to Texas, before the long drought sucked it dry, had been Bobbins land. The fact of his own roots and a new awareness of the past that held spirit over the ranch struck him in a way that even recent events, the war, the coming Prohibition, the epidemic, and what little history he knew never had.

What he saw was land his grandfather had been forced to sell off, four hundred and twenty acres to pay "Yankee" taxes. And more lost since to foreclosure when the crops failed and the cattle fed off dust. Willy thought about the bitter history of his people. Those who'd taken from them. They who'd lost. His great-grandfather Patrick, charged with robbery, had fled Wixford to Dublin, where he'd labored first as a dockworker, then as a sailor. He'd deserted ship in Newport, Virginia, but found nothing of interest there, so he drifted west through Kentucky, Tennessee, and Arkansas, and at age twenty-three landed in Texas, where he'd fought under Houston and distinguished himself at the Battle of San Jacinto by shooting six Mexicans who'd straggled out of a patch of brush waving white handkerchiefs. For service to the Republic of Texas, he was rewarded with citizenship, fifty head of cattle, and two sections of grazing land east of the central plateau, land confiscated from a Mexican don loyal to Santa Anna. Patrick had married Leila Morse and over the next fifteen years mastered drunkenness the way any true artist masters his craft.

One night as his horse slaked its thirst at a pond, Patrick Bobbins fell off and drowned in two feet of murky water, the first of the American Bobbins lost to drowning. Leila was forced to sell a hundred and sixty acres to keep a roof overhead and food on the table.

More of the spread was lost in parcels to taxes after the Civil War, when Willy's grandfather George Samuel Bobbins, a veteran of the losing side, reclaimed four horses from Yankees who'd stolen them from him. A military court sentenced him to a year's hard labor.

Willy had never considered the history of the Bobbins land in this way. The land and those who peopled it were inseparable parts of the same history, and now their remains rested there. He wondered if the bitterness that consumed his father began with his own father's incarceration, with seeing slices of their land amputated multiple acres at a time.

As the moon settled in the western sky, Willy surrendered to the fact that he couldn't sleep, because he couldn't run from who he was and who he should be. After him, there were no more male Bobbins, and maybe his obligation lay here with the land and with his pa. Maybe, he thought, this is the spread he'd been dreaming of having. He rolled up the blanket and hiked back to the barn, where he climbed the ladder to the loft and slept intermittently.

When he awakened, the air was dry, and the sun outlined the bare trees. He looked at the ocher fields blanketed with weeds and winter dew. What he saw beneath the fallow was the promise of black earth. He decided to turn the fields green again as they'd been when his grandfather was alive and farming and ranching. Twenty acres of alfalfa. Thirty of cotton. It was here all along. He'd make his father's father's father's spread his own.

He arose before dawn and went to his mother's grave. Over the years he'd paid little attention to the family cemetery, but as the sun rose behind him, he looked at the dates on the gravestones. He remembered his uncle Emit, Beau's father, the last Bobbins to really work the soil, and he vaguely remembered his grandfather and grandmother. And there was the third Bobbins brother. He pictured Uncle Rubin, whose wife had run off with another man, and he was determined to hunt them down. He'd tracked them to San Angelo, and, crashing through a bedroom door to exact revenge, he'd caught a .45 round in the chest.

His great-grandfather had died at age thirty-seven, his grandfather at forty-one, his uncle at age thirty. Young, all, Willy thought, and now interred in Texas earth. He'd known the names the way he knew the Bible stories that came from the priest's lips to his ears. They'd seemed little more than inventions of the imagination—Grandpa George, Grandma Betty, Uncle Rubin, Uncle Emit, and now no grave for Beau. Death all around. In seeing and knowing death as it is and was, Willy no longer viewed them as stories, but as men. Men like him. Can't, he wondered, a man live long and be a Bobbins? Can't one live without rage? Work this land and find peace? This, it seemed—the present, future, and past—was in the stones that Old Lopez had cast at the time of Willy's birth.

He tipped his hat to his mother's grave and started toward the road.

He walked to Nell's, borrowed a horse from Glen Fellows, and rode into Corcoran City. He found the lawyer in his office. He'd honored Willy's request and distributed the funds in increments. There was enough left with what money Willy had brought with him to purchase a horse, two mules, and seed to plant corn and cotton and alfalfa. He returned that afternoon and walked into the house where Clay sat at the table playing solitaire.

"I intend on workin the place," he announced. "You can stay if you want. I won't expect no more outta you 'an Ma did."

"'At's a disappointment." Clay smiled for the first time since Willy had returned.

46 Willy kept an eye on the earth that he and Beau had called Clay's rock field. Other than some bramble and spiny plants of wild berries, it was rested and ready. He recalled his last efforts in that field, his and Beau's. They'd plowed and planted sixteen acres of alfalfa with seed given them by Mr. Gallagher, their intention to earn enough to buy two horses. Clay had asked what they were up to and, after hearing their plan, had insisted the soil wasn't fertile enough to produce even two cuttings. From then on he'd watched their progress with detachment. In the late spring a fortunate rain came, a soft drizzle that lasted two days. It turned the field emerald and left the crop ready for an early harvest. They'd cut it and then borrowed Mr. Gallagher's mule team to haul the hay to market. When they arrived on the buckboard that afternoon, four men were in the field, the alfalfa was already cut, and they were loading it onto a bailer. Clay had sold the crop out from under them to Cyrus Moss. A week after the last cutting he rode up mounted on his roan, reached down, and told Willy to climb up behind him because they were going to get a pony named Lucy.

"Wished you was here," he muttered, meaning Beau. "Could use the help, boy."

For Beau and for a dozen other reasons, Willy intended to turn that field into more than a memory.

HE SLEPT in the barn loft and waited out the cold months. In March, at a time when dew still coated the ground in the early morning, he awoke before the sun rose and began tilling the field, plowing the dark earth behind two mules he'd named Ruby and Emerald. For reasons he couldn't say aloud, he felt he had to blister his hands and strain, almost to the point of tearing them, the muscles in his back and shoulders. He was willing to endure anything to restore the farm and, at the same time, himself. The labor was difficult, the mules stubborn, and dark became light and then dark again before he finally surrendered to exhaustion and ate a dinner of bacon and beans. He told himself as he suffered through the chill of cold mornings and the sting of the afternoon sun that none of it should come easy.

Willy fought hard for every inch of baccate earth he gained. Twice a week he awoke before dawn and mucked stalls and corrals of neighboring ranches for manure that he loaded into a wagon and spread on the fields. Sunup to sundown, after feeding chickens and the mules and horse, he settled in behind the team. The field was rough and filled with stones, berry bushes, and a few small boulders, but the topsoil was rich and it ran deep. The plowshare cut through the hard-crusted earth like a flat-bottom boat through choppy waters. Willy liked the smell of the dark earth, especially when it was moist. For years the land had been neglected, but it sat ready to produce. He saw it as bequeathed him to work by his ancestors. It was land he could pass on if Lisette ever returned and bore him a family. He clung to such romantic notions to drive his ambition, especially when he gazed at the unplowed land where he could graze cattle. The place needed livestock—bring in a good crop and buy seed cows and pay Sorenson for the use of his bull.

By the end of four weeks behind the plow, he'd gained some control over both apparatus and animals, but only after suffering a bruised chin, a blackened eye, and sore ribs when a forceful pull on the reins caused the mules to back up, driving a guide into his chest. Once he found himself lying on his back. He lay looking up at the sky and laughing, then crawled to his feet and scolded the animals.

"Damn mules ain't girls!" Clay cackled from where he'd perched himself on a log. One of the rare occasions he'd left the shade of the porch.

Willy shouted back, "They ain't boys neither!"

Clay's normal habit was to sit on the porch and puff on his hand-carved pipe as he watched Willy's labor progress. When Willy went out of sight of the porch, Clay repositioned himself in the shade of the nearest tree in the yard to better observe. He never spoke, just sat, puffed on his pipe, and kneaded his stump. Whenever Willy encountered boulders or stump roots and had to dig them up, Clay chuckled and punctuated his enjoyment with a flurry of pipe smoke.

When Willy saw his father grinning, he shouted, "Hope you're entertained, Clay Bobbins!" Or, "Only thing funnier is a one-legged fool with no prayer'a holdin a woman again."

As the labor hardened Willy's muscles, the silence hardened his heart, and he grew more and more taciturn. He found pleasure only in work. Routine guided his days and nights. He entered the house only to cook breakfast and dinner, and sometimes missed doing one or the other. Work and sleep took priority over food. When he had time, he went to the barn and worked on a new crutch for his pa.

On the nights he cooked, Willy did so under Clay's often obdurate gaze, preparing the meal and never looking up from his task or in any way acknowledging Clay's presence. Willy filled a plate and set it on the table within arm's reach of Clay, then took his meal outside to eat under the stars or on the porch if it was raining. He enjoyed the calm at dusk, the countryside abuzz with insects, and the sight of barn swallows and bats darting about. A mosquito bite now and then didn't trouble him. When he ate, he did so slowly and stared at the acres he put under plow, pleased now with his effort and hopeful of good results.

His meal finished, he entered the house and gathered up his pa's dishes and utensils whether he was through eating or not. He washed the dishes outside at the pump. Clay was usually in bed by the time Willy returned the cleaned plates to the cupboard, then completed the day by climbing up to the loft and wrapping himself in a blanket.

Once or twice a week Nell visited, bringing loaves of bread, a jug of moonshine for Clay, and gossip from the town and outlying areas. In January the Prohibition Act was ratified as an amendment, but wouldn't become law for another year. Ever since the passing, a struggle ensued between the Bible thumpers and those who carried on as before, a struggle all the more apparent in the central plateau and Bedloe, where Calvinist roots ran deep. The debate even touched the Bobbins clan. Glen Fellows, now a devout Methodist, disapproved of Nell's bringing whiskey to Clay. But he looked the other way, just as he'd always done with those who trafficked in liquor. Business was business, and scoundrels and drunkards were voters.

After relating whose child had broken what window, which woman was expecting and how soon, who had a new tractor, and whose still the revenuers had smashed, Nell worked on Willy and Clay. She tried to mediate their differences, talking first with Clay and then Willy, but her considerable efforts as peacemaker continually failed.

"Willy, you gotta understand about his leg."

"I'm thinking in fall, when the crops're in, I'll get some lumber and make a corral."

"He can't help himself."

"Ain't that the damned truth."

Before she left, she berated each for his stubbornness, saying that they were like two winds blowing at each other without stirring a breeze or two goats butting heads over which could stand on a rock. One night she brought news that she was pregnant and would be coming around less often. She gave one last desperate effort to reconcile the two, but when that failed as miserably as her previous efforts, she said, "You two can shoot each other for all I care."

"That'd take too much work for him," Willy said and stood.

"You won't try?" she asked.

"What? Shooting 'im? Anyhow, I'm happy for you, Nell," Willy said as he walked toward the door. "Hope it's a boy."

"Hope it ain't one like him," Clay said.

Willy fired a look at his father and opened the door. Desperate for rest, he left the two of them and climbed into the loft. He was asleep long before Nell rode off.

WORK SUBDUED Willy's other concerns. His money was all but gone. Nell was pregnant, and Glen Fellows, his health diminished from a protracted bout with pneumonia that followed his episode with the flu, still had difficulty keeping food down. Panther Jack had made noise about getting even with Willy, but so far had stayed clear of him, "out of fear," according to Nell. An old rumor still floated around the town that Willy had killed three rustlers single-handedly and was wanted elsewhere, but was protected from prosecution by Glen Fellows. Few, if anyone, doubted the information. After all, Willy had shot Bobby Grimes's foot off, as promised. Willy was thought dangerous. With that came an odd respect.

What people thought or whatever rumors spread meant little to Willy. He lived now for growing and harvesting.

BY LATE APRIL, Willy could look out over forty acres of well-furrowed black Texas earth, most of it fertilized and half of which he'd seeded by hand. He hitched the mules to a wagon he'd bought on credit from Mr. Ebbin and rode into Bedloe to buy more seed. Nell had mentioned that telephones were coming to Bedloe, and on the ride in Willy witnessed evidence of this, surveyor stakes that marked the route and naked poles that lay beside the roadway.

A snake sunned itself in the middle of the road. As the mules neared, it coiled and rattled. Willy stopped the team, thinking the snake would slink off, but it held its ground like an obstinate squatter. He set the brake and climbed down to chase the snake away, but it merely hissed and took a wild strike at him. He left to find a stick to use on it. Before he could find a branch appropriate to the task, the snake struck at one of the mules. Willy watched the mule rise up and slash its hooves until it ground the reptile into pulp in the road's surface.

"Ain't that somethin." He rubbed each animal's neck and checked the harness. "Snake killers deserve some oats."

He mounted the wagon, released the brake, and snapped the reins. The mules weren't Lucy, and farming wasn't as stimulating as moving twenty or thirty longhorns thirty miles in day, but Willy felt good just the same.

Mr. Ebbin listened patiently as Willy explained that he'd prepared more acres than he'd started to and now needed more seed—cottonseed for ten acres, alfalfa for five, and corn for five. Mr. Ebbin's eyes never seemed to look away from Willy's lips, and when the last word was out and an echo in the ear, Mr. Ebbin shook his head. "Can't let you have that much on credit, Willy."

"I'll pay when the crops is sold. Hell, I done work for you, and you known me all my life."

Ebbin smiled. "I ain't gonna hold that against you."

"Well, hell, I put what I could under plow. Now I hear this. Why didn't you tell me when I bought that wagon on credit?"

"Your farm ain't got much history for producin."

"Nobody's worked it since my grandpa and my dead uncle. I got it furrowed, and you ain't seen better topsoil. It ain't worn out like some other places 'round here."

Mr. Ebbin again shook his head. "War's over and that affects farmers, Willy. Crops ain't gonna be in such high demand."

"Corn and cotton and alfalfa, they's always in demand. I plan to build a corral in the winter. Buy a breedin stock. If the crops produce enough, a fine bull. Maybe a dozen cows."

"Willy, you need collateral. I'm a bidnessman, not a gambler."

"We get any kind a rain, those fields'll be plump by September. That land was good to my great-grandfather, who was no kind of farmer, and my grandfather, who was. Hell, we owned a mile of it every direction 'til the Yankees stole it. It was ours before they was a Bedloe."

"You worked for others, but you never farmed, boy." Mr. Ebbin pleaded with his eyes.

"Me and Beau brought in enough alfalfa once to buy a filly."

Ebbin seemed to see his reasoning had no effect on Willy. He took a different approach. "Maybe you can get Glen to sign."

"No. It's gotta be my doin."

Mr. Ebbin shook his head again.

Willy couldn't hold back his frustration. "You're shakin your head at me once too often."

"You're bein stubborn, Willy. Bidness is bidness, and you don't own that spread. It's your pa's, and he's got tax liens on the farm right now. 'Nother six months, it's likely to go up on the auction block."

The news stunned Willy. He'd always figured the attorney had taken care of any taxes. He considered this a moment, turned and stomped to the door, and went outside until he regained his composure. When he reentered, he narrowed his eyes on Mr. Ebbin. "I ain't done this all for nothin. If I can bring in a crop, I'll fix them taxes. How much you need?"

Mr. Ebbin stroked some figures down on a paper, added the columns, and recalculated. Finished, he showed the itemized list to Willy, who only read the total figure—one hundred and seventy-two dollars. Willy had less than two dollars and change in his pocket. He looked out the window as a Ford passed by. Willy did what he'd seen Panther Jack do on many occasions when negotiating a business venture. He removed his watch and examined the face. It was 10:40 a.m. He considered using the money he had on him to buy a pint and get drunk by noon and give some thought to walking over the next horizon, as he'd thought to do in the winter. When he looked back, Mr. Ebbin's gaze was fixed on the watch.

"How much you want for that, Willy?"

Willy looked at the watch. He flared his nostrils, closed the cover, and rubbed it softly on his shirtsleeve. "Hell, this thing's Swiss made. Them numbers is diamonds. It's worth over three hunert easy."

"How much?"

Willy looked at the watch and the sacks of seed against the wall. "This cost me a partner. I got shot in New Orleans, so's some fella could rob me of it, then it come back my way again. It belongs to me like a horse belongs to a fella."

"How much?"

"Two hunert and the seeds."

"A hunert and the seeds, and you give me ten percent'a the crop."

"Two hunert, the seeds, and I give up eight percent."

Ebbin nodded. "Hand me the watch."

Willy looked at the seed as he stretched out his hand and passed the watch to Mr. Ebbin. He felt the watch leave his hand, felt it deep under his skin.

47

The fields planted, Willy turned to other labor, built a new henhouse, replaced slats in the barn, and searched the county for two seed cows and a bull. No matter how he occupied himself, his eyes strayed skyward, where his hopes lay in the clouds flowing westward from the Gulf. Time seemed measurable only by the mood of the sky and by daylight extending into darkness and darkness into daylight, repeated until a week passed, then a month, then two and three. The seasons existed not as spring or summer, but work and hope.

As the days became longer and warmer, waiting for rain grew more difficult. Early May brought two showers, but through the second week of June, vagrant cloud chased vagrant cloud over the western horizon without leaving so much as a sprinkle. All the while, Clay's words kept running through his mind, as if they were the pronouncements of a prophet: "I ain't the kind of man to hang over a fence and watch for clouds, and neither are you." Still, he watched. Then two days of continuous but soft rain produced sprouts and renewed Willy's hopes. He walked carefully among the growing plants, reaching down here and there to pull a weed or touch a tendril as he might a newborn. His hand had produced this. Daily, he measured the plants' progress. The corn grew fast, nearly a foot a week. Cotton stalks inched up as if growing were painful. He watched with the awe of one witnessing a divine act.

Then off and on in late June it rained for two weeks. The crops matured, and he strutted into the fields, admiring his handiwork, but the infrequent rains brought an onslaught of weeds. He hoed in the morning when it was cool and left barn chores for the afternoon. Hoeing proved harder blister-raising labor than even plowing. At night, sore and tired, he stooped over the stove.

Clay, still stubbornly reticent, had taken to snorting if he didn't like what Willy cooked.

On one occasion, while preparing black-eyed peas, Willy reeled about and shouted, "You ain't got nothin to bark about, old man. You don't like what's cookin, fix it your own damn self. And I ain't puttin up with no more snortin. I'll take that damn crutch away and break it in two."

Clay looked away and began whistling. Willy set the metal ladle aside on the stove, took the clutch as promised, and broke it over his knee.

"Damn you, boy," Clay said and spat at Willy.

"'At's right. Damn me."

Willy stomped off to the barn, climbed to the loft, and pulled out his bag from under the bed. He rifled through it until he found what he was looking for—an unopened deck. When he came down from the loft, he grabbed the crutch he'd finished more than month before. On the way out of the barn, he kicked a chicken out of his path.

He threw open the door, walked over to where Clay sat at the table, and laid the crutch on his lap.

Clay looked at the crutch, then ran his hand over the smooth surface of the wood and the padded armrest. But he didn't speak.

For the first time since his return, Willy sat at the table with Clay. He opened the deck, separated the jokers, and shuffled the cards three times, then stripped the deck once, reshuffled, and slammed the pile down in front of Clay.

"High card cooks dinner tomorrow."

Clay shook his head.

"Then you ain't eatin, old man, 'cause I'll take care'a me, and to hell with you."

Clay stared at the cards.

"Have it your way." Willy walked to the stove and grabbed the iron ladle off the top. Heat shot through his fingertips. He shouted, "Sumbitch!" and he sent the ladle across the room.

It rebounded off the wall and clattered to the floor beside the table. Clay, stunned for an instant, chortled and slapped his thigh over the sight of Willy skipping about and fanning his fingers in the air. When the pain subsided, Willy blew on his fingers and muttered curses. Arms folded over his chest, Clay leaned back in his chair and watched.

Willy was about to scoop up the ladle when he cut an eye at his pa. "Think it's funny?"

Clay nodded.

"Glad you think so." Willy returned Clay's grin, then calmly kicked the chair out from beneath him. His pa landed on the floor beside the ladle.

Willy bent down to pick up the utensil. "Too bad you can't talk. Shore bet you'd like to say somethin now," he said and scooped up the iron ladle.

OTHER THAN FEED CHICKENS and watch the sky, Willy did little for three days except sit on the porch, play solitaire, and worry about the weather. In the evening he brought the deck inside and set it on the table in front of Clay. But Clay didn't budge. On the fourth day, Willy served Clay a plate of ham hocks and lima beans. Clay looked at the plate of yellow beans and pig fat, then up at Willy. "This all you gonna feed me, beans?"

"Ain't rustlin no steer for someone got no teeth. You want somethin different, you make it."

Willy brought his own plate to the table and took a seat. Halfway through the meal Clay snorted, reached over, and cut a stack of cards from the deck. He turned over a nine and held it faceup. Willy pulled off a stack and exposed a king.

Clay slammed his fist down beside the deck, "Guess it's about the only way to get a decent meal 'round here."

WILLY RETURNED to the fields, and the pattern of life continued as before, weeding, watching, and waiting. The weeds were unrelenting. A furrow at a time he hacked at them and pulled them up. Two or three days later they returned. The blisters he raised on his palms in March had long since turned to shiny callouses. Those thickened. His hands and arms and back grew stronger. It was stoop labor. He bent and rose and bent down again. Each day he carried a few boulders he'd unearthed in February and March to the edge of the cornfield, and by the first of July a knee-high wall of loose rock separated the corn from the cotton. He tried not to think about either the future or the past. The corn cockle and thistle beneath his feet, the hoe that cut the tough stems, and the cloudless horizon required thought enough.

Each night he and Clay cut cards to see who would cook the next day. Clay lost five nights in row, every time complaining it was supposed to be an even proposition and Willy had probably marked the deck. On the sixth night Willy lost. Then Clay went on another losing streak, a practice that continued throughout the summer.

The same week that Clay opened his mouth and spoke, Willy moved himself into the house.

Clay took over feeding the chickens. Afterward, he parked himself on a barrel near the fields. Willy's weather vigil became Clay's, and at night over beans and pork rinds or chili and squash, the conversation centered on rain. Clay maintained that he'd never seen such a dry spring, and June wasn't much better. Willy reminded him of the long drought. Then a day of rain lifted their spirits and caused a shift in the conversation. As it drizzled, Willy and Clay sat on the porch, shared a few snorts of moonshine, played double solitaire, then went to bed. The rain lasted three days, followed by a week of sunshine. Weeds sprouted everywhere, but Willy got a first cutting of alfalfa.

It was time now to watch the horizon and hope for clear skies

That day Glen Fellows rode Nell over in the wagon. He was healthy again, but now a farmer as well as sheriff and expecting father, he had little time for visiting. Willy noted that his brother-in-law seemed to have regained his old form. He jumped down from the wagon and came to the other side to help Nell down.

"What brung you?" Clay asked.

"Well, some bidness and this," Fellows said, lifting a basket and jug from the wagon bed. He held the jug up teasingly in front of Clay's face. "It's a sin, you know."

"Hell's bells, it's a damn crime too," Clay said as he snatched the jug from the clutches of his son-in-law.

Nell kissed her father on the cheek and stepped back. She greeted Willy, and when he asked how the baby business was going, she pulled her skirt tight, turned sideways, and patted herself. Fellows, almost twice her age, said he'd be pleased to have it over with, so Nell could drive herself around. He was too old for all the socializing that went with a child coming.

"Been from one end of the county to the other, listenin to how to cure whooping cough and diaper rash. Bet you didn't know cornstarch and berry juice will heal a cold sore."

Nell slapped him on the shoulder. "Glen, they mean well."

"Don't visit this many people durin an election year," he said.

Willy walked them through the fields. They then went to the house to eat. The basket was filled with biscuits and preserves and fried chicken. Once the food was devoured, Clay and Willy passed the bottle.

"So, what's this bidness, Glen?" Clay asked.

The sheriff looked at Nell, who nodded. He cleared his throat and produced a folded piece of paper. It came slowly out of his coat pocket, and he was very deliberate in every movement as he unfolded it. "It ain't good. It's for you," Fellows said. "I ain't takin no pleasure in it."

"It's a paper."

"A court order."

"Can't read," Clay said. "You do it."

"Right." Glasses on the brim of his nose, Fellows centered all his concentration on reading the paper aloud. He read slowly, clearing his throat from time to time and looking at Clay. Finished, he folded the paper and handed it to his father-in-law.

"You're served."

"But this is my place and you're family, Glen. Don't seem proper you puttin a paper in my hand. Even though you did arrest me twice."

"Three times," Fellows corrected. "Ain't my doin, Clay. It's bidness come down from the court. You ain't paid the taxes. It's a wonder this didn't happen sooner."

"I lost my leg. What the hell am I to do?"

"How long?" Willy asked.

"Forty-five days."

"I'm a veteran of the war with Spain. Fought with Teddy Roosevelt," Clay said. "Ain't right. Hell, damn Yankee government stole all our ranch, but what little's left from my daddy."

Willy walked to the fireplace and leaned against it. "Would a touch'a money get this tax fella to shift direction?"

"Too late, Willy. Gotta be paid in full in forty-five days, like it says." Fellows's expression was somber, absolute.

"Two hundred seven dollars?" Willy said. He felt a twinge of remorse for having left so much money behind with Colleen.

"We got ninety if that'll help," Fellows said. He looked at Nell.

"Can't take your money, Glen," Willy said.

"What you mean we can't?" Clay said.

"Just what I said."

"We can take it. Place ain't yours, Willy. I just let you sleep here's all."

Willy ran his tongue on his cheek and stared at Clay. The house seemed to fill with the smell of stale smoke-charred wood left half-burned. Willy's throat went dry. The air was stifling. He excused himself and left the house.

The late-afternoon sky was cloudless and as dry as Willy's throat. He looked at the fields—half-grown cotton, tall cornstalks topped with feathers of silk, his labor. Anger boiled inside him as he waded into the knee-high cotton plants with their wiry branches and tiny waxen leaves lying flat like open hands. A few seemed ready to open, but most were days away from picking. He couldn't do it by himself. He'd need all of the money he had, some thirty dollars, to hire help. He thought about the easy money he'd squandered and money stolen from him. He'd been unwise, had no one to blame but himself. It struck him that he could get up a card game somewhere, but not too far away, maybe Corcoran City. A streak could turn thirty dollars into two hundred or more.

A raven broke the air overhead and cawed as it flew to a distant oak. Willy thought of that long-ago day when Old Lopez tossed the stones and the crow passed overhead, its shadow crossing the proceedings. Was this his prediction? Was this what the old man had seen of Willy's life when he read the stones? Willy kneeled and ran his fingers up a wooden stalk, plucked a leaf, and examined it. He smelled it before crushing it between his fingers. A hot gust broke across the field and combed through the plants. The stems shivered. He'd performed some wizardry here, but he needed more. A month of good weather was all, he thought; bring me that magic.

Willy sniffed the air. He smelled another rain coming. It would come before the bolls spread open. A light rain wouldn't hurt, but once they opened he wanted none. If he could bring in a cotton crop at a favorable price, he could easily pay the debt. When Fellows and Nell stepped out on the porch, Willy stood and crossed the field.

"I didn't want to do that," Fellows said. "Had to, though. Wouldn't be right sendin Tom out here."

"No. I 'preciate that, even if Pa don't."

Fellows lifted Nell up to her seat on the buckboard and walked around to his side.

"You keep your money. I'll bring in that cotton crop."

"You'll need money for a crew. Mexicans'll be comin up in no time."

"Got enough for a boy or two, but if it comes to it, I can pick enough on my own to pay them taxes."

"Looks good from here. Hope you do."

Willy shook the sheriff's hand.

"I'll tell you somethin, but don't get riled," Fellows said.

"What's 'at?"

"Panther Jack's willin to buy the place, but he don't want to bid it, if it goes to county auction."

"Rather burn the damn crops before I'd see him take it." Willy stepped back, said good-bye to his sister, and stood waving as the buckboard pulled away. He remembered the day in Corcoran City when Beau had the barrel of the rifle trained on Panther Jack's neck. He regretted not having him pull the trigger, though he knew it would've been foolish and futile to do so. The past, he was learning, isn't a thing that can be fixed. All that's left is to revisit its mistakes. At least that was how it seemed. He watched the buckboard disappear around a bend and then reappear on a rise, then he looked at the fields. A week, he figured. The future was all in that.

48 Willy picked with both hands, cleaving ball after ball from a plant until it was stripped. The plants produced, as Willy had hoped, the weevils had spared him, and the fibers were long and silky. The sun had beat on his neck most of the morning, and when the first cloud drifted over and shaded him from the sun, he was grateful. He also noticed that the sky on the eastern horizon had darkened and found that disheartening.

He turned his attention to the next plant, then felt a spasm in his back and stood upright. He caught his breath, adjusted the sack that hung from his neck and across his chest, and looked out over a field of white tops.

Three gunnysacks, filled with cotton, and a dozen empty ones lay at the edge of the field. He hoped before nightfall to fill all of them. He bent over and plucked the balls off the stems of the next plant as quickly as he could. His fingers weren't as nimble as those of the Mexicans he'd worked with years before, but as the morning had worn on, he'd gotten more efficient. He thought of Sorenson's daughter marrying Tom Plummer and shook his head. He couldn't imagine the pairing. She was smart, and Tom was dull as a rusted knife.

A breeze kicked up. It cooled him, but brought dust. He paused to wipe sweat off his forehead. He dropped the bag and stooped down to drink from the jug of water. He emptied it in two swallows.

"Pa!" he shouted and held up the jug. "Need me some water."

Clay waved from his perch on the stoop. He aimed a finger toward the east. Willy didn't have to look in that direction to know that a bank of black clouds sat on the horizon.

"Damn fool," Willy muttered, "you think I'm blind?"

Willy swallowed, regarded his field for a moment, then watched his pa struggling across the field in his direction. Willy pulled the sack along and moved to the next plant. By the time he plucked the cotton off those stems, Clay was at his heels.

"It's a bad sky, boy."

Willy stepped to the next plant. "I know." He pulled at the top bolls with both hands. "Get me some water and leave me be."

"Shore. Whatever you say, Willy. But it's bad." Clay set his crutch aside and, bending over to get the jug, fell.

Willy looked up from his labor. "Damn."

He helped Clay to his feet and propped the crutch under his arm. "Go on. I'll get my own water."

"Don't be that way, Willy."

"Don't be that way? You kilt Ernesto and put Bobby Grimes on me and Beau."

Clay looked at him, puzzled and hurt. "Ain't true, boy. None'a it."

"Ain't true? Bullshit, Pa. You—you done bad to people who never done nothin to you."

Clay looked off at the looming sky, his eyes vacant at first, then watering. When he spoke, his voice rasped. "Ernesto, him and me, we lost some steers, maybe ten on the Mexican side. But he went back for 'em. I told 'im leave 'em be. We had enough, but he had family. Like me. We had to feed you and your ma and your sisters, and he had his. So he went back. Never saw 'im again. He was a good ol boy. I felt bad. I lied because I felt bad. You ever feel bad, Willy?"

"'At accounts for one, if I'm to believe you."

Clay swallowed and looked at him. "Well, he didn't wanna push them few cattle to Bedloe. I give 'im a five-dollar gold piece, and don't know what he did with it. Brought those steers in myself."

"Sounds half true, but I got my doubts. 'At leaves Bobby Grimes."

Clay studied his hands and looked again at the sky. "You got me there. I didn't intend nothin. When you and Beau cut me out, I told 'im where to cross and find beeves and promised that I'd help get 'im to . . . Hell, Willy, I never thought he'd bushwhack you. Never mind. You ain't never thought much a me. But I'm . . . I'm wantin you to win here. Now, I'll get you that water."

Willy didn't know what to say. He didn't know what to believe. He'd lived believing one way, and shifting a belief was a hard prospect, as hard as loving someone you resented for years. He looked Clay up and down and said, "Thank you."

THE SUN WAS GONE, and a stiff wind howled over the croplands. Dust swirled up from the crop bed. The corn tops whipped back and forth. Willy drank from the jug and looked to the east. Lightning shot out of the black-bellied clouds and skipped across the horizon. He licked his lips and picked up where he'd left off. The fat bolls swayed about in a circular motion as if to dodge his fingers. He held the stem with one hand and plucked with the other. It was slow going.

He heard Clay hollering at him, but the wind swallowed the words. When the first raindrops came, the driblets whistled groundward and popped on the soft soil, dotting the earth with black marks. He hoisted the sack from his neck and walked out of the field. Clay stood at the edge of the field tugging on a gunnysack full of cotton while trying to balance himself with the crutch. "What the hell you doin?" Willy said.

"Let's move 'em."

"Leave 'em."

When the sky broke, the rain plunged down, strafing the ground with cold, rocklike pellets. The horizons vanished behind silvery sheets of water. It reminded Willy of the storm that fell the night the Rio Grande nearly claimed him. He watched from the porch as the storm's fierce winds bent trees and twisted plants. Within the hour the downpour eased enough that Willy could see the results. His field lay immersed in an inky pool, leaving only the caps of the cotton plants as visible proof that he wasn't looking at a lake.

The wind subsided, but rain continued. When he could no longer bear to watch it, he went inside. It was cool enough to start a fire, but instead, he stripped off his shirt, opened the windows, and spread his arms wide.

"Come on, rain, come on!" he shouted. "Take what you don't want the tax man to have!" He flung open the door and let the cool air rush in. He hopped about on a single leg as he pulled off his boots one at a time, then his trousers. Naked, he ran outside. He spun around in circles and screamed profanities at the sky that were drowned out by the rain.

When Willy opened the door, Clay was seated at the fireplace, pumping the bellows. Willy stood shivering in the threshold, his hair plastered down on his forehead.

He aimed a fierce look at Clay and shouted, "You could of took care'a bidness."

Clay stared at the licking flames.

"You hear what I said, Clay? I said you didn't pay, and now it's all for nothin."

Clay shouted back, "Just don't blame the damn rain on me!"

"If Ma hadn't died, she'd been out along with you."

"I ain't much. That what you wanna hear, boy? That I'm no good? Want me to admit it again?"

Willy turned away and faced the rain. He remained that way for several minutes, watching water spout off the edge of the roof and form a pool beside the porch. He took a deep breath, then stepped back and shut the door.

"I want somethin that makes sense," he said.

Clay held up a quilt in his lap. "You ain't no perdy picture all shriveled up. I'd 'preciate you puttin this over your scrawny ass."

Willy wrapped the quilt over his shoulders and took a seat by the fireplace. Clay handed him the poker, then looked at him for the longest time that Willy could ever recall. It seemed to Willy that all his life, Clay had wanted to see him lose. Now that he had, it seemed as if his pa were seeing himself and all of his own disappointments. There was more in his eyes, a look that both accepted and defied fate.

Clay finally looked away. "You near tore up your ma nursin you. She told me that you'd be a fierce one. Told me I shouldn't be hard on you."

"You miss her?"

"Miss her? I'd rather'a lost another leg." Clay pointed to the fire. "Stoke it up a bit. I'll fix us some soup with peppers." When Willy didn't move, he said, "I was wrong. You ain't like me. You may be better, may be worse. But you ain't like me. Take 'at as a blessin."

After soup, Clay brought out the jug. Snug in his quilt, Willy sat across the table from his pa and they played double solitaire until the jug was emptied.

"Willy, she was a good woman, and I wasn't right by her. You know that."

"I know. Hell, who have you been right by?"

"Ain't many. I was beside her, though, when she passed. Lost the little one first. Barely knee high, but walkin. Broke 'er heart too. I was holdin her hand and tellin her how she had to live, that I needed her. She up and said, 'Dyin is a better place.' 'At's been with me ever since. Dyin was better for her 'an bein with me. 'At don't sit easy on me."

Willy thought a moment. Then he stood. "Could'a been the fever she was talkin about."

"You think?"

"Somethin to consider."

"You made a fine crutch. Did I thank you?"

"Not as I recall."

"Well, hell. Okay, thank you."

The rotgut gone, they went to their respective rooms. By morning the storm had passed, and the fields were submerged.

49

Most of the plants hung limp or lay on the ground, like casualties of a violent battle. Few were salvageable. Willy left alone the plants that had survived; others he tore out by the roots. The loss amounted to half the crop. He spent the next four days, from the first rooster crow to the last blush of sun, on the western side in the fields. He had forty days, and by day ten of it, he knew the crop wouldn't make it.

As the days mounted, Clay became increasingly morose, said he hated leaving Ruth behind, and he spent more time at her grave. Willy wondered why Clay was so taken with caring now. Why after death?

Clay talked about Willy's mother in tender terms, citing times they'd shared when young. He claimed she was as dirty a fighter as any man in a scrape, had once whipped a woman by biting her nose until it bled.

Willy was less nostalgic about Ruth's toughness than Clay was. He remembered how his ma's temper had flared up like a dry bush under a torch. Whenever they could, he and Beau ran off and hid at the first indication of one of her fits. A few times, they were a step slow, and Ruth rained blows on them as a man might, with a closed fist and clenched teeth.

One day in August, Willy stumbled upon Clay as he sat beside the grave, talking nonsense about her coming back and him straightening up. Willy didn't have the heart to interrupt.

The day before the notice of auction was posted, Willy rounded up their stock of chickens and hauled them in the wagon to the Sorenson farm, where he sold them for a handful of silver dollars.

When he returned to the Bobbins spread, he checked the wind, then went to the barn and loaded the wagon with hay. He gauged the wind to be strong enough, and as the mules pulled the wagon over the cotton patch, he forked straw into the breeze in long sweeping motion. Clay stumbled out onto the porch and hollered to Willy, asking him what he was doing.

"It's nearin time to leave, Pa!"

"What you doin, boy?"

"You'll see! So will the whole damned county!"

After the barn was emptied of all but enough hay to feed the mules and horse, Willy marched into the fields with a can of lamp oil in each hand. He emptied the cans methodically, walking while sprinkling oil on the straw. When he was finished, he struck a match and set fire to a pile of oil-soaked straw.

The green plants burned a dark orange and black and sent smoke streaming high. As the fire spread, Willy hooted and shouted. He pranced around at the edge of the field, pointed toward the fire, and told his father to come join him.

Clay limped to his side. "You're crazy, boy."

"They ain't gettin all this, Pa."

"They ain't at that. Hoo-eee!"

Heat from flames drove them back a few yards. They watched the fire spread from the cotton field to the corn field. Red cinders blew upward and black soot rained down. Son and father hopped about, Willy on two legs, Clay awkwardly on one. They joined hands and danced in a circle. They exhausted themselves before the flames did. And when the first of the neighbors arrived to help extinguish the smoldering fire, they found Willy and Clay sitting on the porch cussing at each other as they played double solitaire under the light of a lantern.

WILLY HAD PACKED the wagon and hitched the team by the time the tax collector arrived the day after Glen Fellows served the eviction notice. The official looked dismayed as he surveyed the scorched crops. He threatened Willy and Clay with jail. Willy laughed and said the sheriff was his brother-in-law and not likely to arrest anyone.

Horse tied behind the wagon, Clay beside him on the seat, Willy whipped the reins, and the mules casually stepped out. The tax man blocked the roadway, palm up, trying to bar passage. He shouted that in the name of the law he was claiming all livestock along with the farm.

"I'd be gettin outta the way!" Willy shouted back. "We ain't much amused lately."

"You gotta go through me." The man folded his arms over his chest.

Willy snapped the reins and steered the team down the middle of the road. The man held his ground. Willy flicked the reins again and cropped a little more life into the mules. As the team picked up momentum, the tax man realized he'd misjudged matters and started for the side of the road, but too late and too slow. He yelled as he fell. The front wheel rolled over him and jolted the wagon to the left. Willy flicked the reins. The team pulled forward lazily. Clay uncorked what was left of a jug and handed it to his son.

"Where're the hell you takin me, boy?"

"I made some friends in New Orleans. Nice people. They's a fellow name'a O'Banion owns hisself a casino might teach me the bidness. I suspect they's a future for me in it. Meanwhile, I can slap down some money and poker my way through. Figure I can even put up with you if I got nice people around."

"That's unkind."

"You'd know about that."

Clay smiled, reached over, and patted Willy on the shoulder. "You came out awright. I take no credit for it. Your ma did good by you."

"Sun don't shine at night," Willy said, repeating Sonny's words, words that he'd once dismissed, but that now seemed wise.

"What the hell's 'at mean?"

Willy couldn't explain it exactly. It was an expression that had stayed with him. For a time, he figured it meant a person had to understand the darkness of life to appreciate all of what life is. It also had something to do with accepting the darkness for what it was in all its black clothing. He wondered how much he'd get for the team and the wagon in Louisiana. He hoped enough to put a small stake together. Fifty or sixty dollars was all he needed, that and a friendly game with a few men who wanted to hear a story or two as they laid their coin on the table. He had a few more to tell now.

"Well, tell me."

"Tell you what?"

"The sun, boy, what about it?"

Willy pressed his lips into a smile and snapped the traces. The team came to life. He bent forward on the bench, thinking that someday he'd return to Texas, some future day when he was flush and Texas was ready for a fellow like him.

"Well, boy?"

"Well what, ol man?"

"That sun thing you said."

"It means don't expect somethin that ain't." While that wasn't the most Willy could get out of the expression, it was the most he could hope to pass on.

"'At's plain dumb."

"Yep. Dumb."